THE GIRL
WHO SAVED THE
KING OF SWEDEN

THE GIRL WHO SAVED THE KING OF SWEDEN

JONAS JONASSON

ISIS
LARGE PRINT
Oxford

First published in Great Britain 2014
by
Fourth Estate
an imprint of HarperCollins*Publishers*

Originally published in Sweden as
Analfabeten som kunde räkna by Piratförlaget, 2013

Published in Large Print 2015 by ISIS Publishing Ltd.,
7 Centremead, Osney Mead, Oxford OX2 0ES
by arrangement with
HarperCollins*Publishers*

CIP data is available for this title from the British Library

ISBN 978–1–4450–9984–2 (hb)
ISBN 978–1–4450–9985–9 (pb)

Printed and bound in Great Britain by
T. J. International Ltd., Padstow, Cornwall

The statistical probability that an illiterate in 1970s Soweto will grow up and one day find herself confined in a potato truck with the Swedish king and prime minister is 1 in 45,766,212,810.

According to the calculations of the aforementioned illiterate herself.

PART ONE

The difference between stupidity and
genius is that genius has its limits.

— *Unknown*

CHAPTER ONE

On a girl in a shack and the man who posthumously helped her escape it

In some ways they were lucky, the latrine emptiers in South Africa's largest shantytown. After all, they had both a job and a roof over their heads.

On the other hand, from a statistical perspective they had no future. Most of them would die young of tuberculosis, pneumonia, diarrhoea, pills, alcohol or a combination of these. One or two of them might get to experience his fiftieth birthday. The manager of one of the latrine offices in Soweto was one example. But he was both sickly and worn-out. He'd started washing down far too many painkillers with far too many beers, far too early in the day. As a result, he happened to lash out at a representative of the City of Johannesburg Sanitation Department who had been dispatched to the office. A Kaffir who didn't know his place. The incident was reported all the way up to the unit director in Johannesburg, who announced the next day, during the morning coffee break with his colleagues, that it was time to replace the illiterate in Sector B.

3

Incidentally it was an unusually pleasant morning coffee break. Cake was served to welcome a new sanitation assistant. His name was Piet du Toit, he was twenty-three years old, and this was his first job out of college.

The new employee would be the one to take on the Soweto problem, because this was how things were in the City of Johannesburg. He was given the illiterates, as if to be toughened up for the job.

No one knew whether all of the latrine emptiers in Soweto really were illiterate, but that's what they were called anyway. In any case, none of them had gone to school. And they all lived in shacks. And had a terribly difficult time understanding what one told them.

◆ ◆ ◆

Piet du Toit felt ill at ease. This was his first visit to the savages. His father, the art dealer, had sent a bodyguard along to be on the safe side.

The twenty-three-year-old stepped into the latrine office and couldn't help immediately complaining about the smell. There, on the other side of the desk, sat the latrine manager, the one who was about to be dismissed. And next to him was a little girl who, to the assistant's surprise, opened her mouth and replied that this was indeed an unfortunate quality of shit — it smelled.

Piet du Toit wondered for a moment if the girl was making fun of him, but that couldn't be the case.

4

He let it go. Instead he told the latrine manager that he could no longer keep his job because of a decision higher up, but that he could expect three months of pay if, in return, he picked out the same number of candidates for the position that had just become vacant.

"Can I go back to my job as a permanent latrine emptier and earn a little money that way?" the just-dismissed manager wondered.

"No," said Piet du Toit. "You can't."

One week later, Assistant du Toit and his bodyguard were back. The dismissed manager was sitting behind his desk, for what one might presume was the last time. Next to him stood the same girl as before.

"Where are your three candidates?" said the assistant.

The dismissed apologized: two of them could not be present. One had had his throat slit in a knife fight the previous evening. Where number two was, he couldn't say. It was possible he'd had a relapse.

Piet du Toit didn't want to know what kind of relapse it might be. But he did want to leave.

"So who is your third candidate, then?" he said angrily.

"Why, it's the girl here beside me, of course. She's been helping me with all kinds of things for a few years now. I must say, she's a clever one."

"For God's sake, I can't very well have a twelve-year-old latrine manager, can I?" said Piet du Toit.

"Fourteen," said the girl. "And I have nine years' experience."

5

The stench was oppressive. Piet du Toit was afraid it would cling to his suit.

"Have you started using drugs yet?" he said.

"No," said the girl.

"Are you pregnant?"

"No," said the girl.

The assistant didn't say anything for a few seconds. He really didn't want to come back here more often than was necessary.

"What is your name?" he said.

"Nombeko," said the girl.

"Nombeko what?"

"Mayeki, I think."

Good Lord, they didn't even know their own names.

"Then I suppose you've got the job, if you can stay sober," said the assistant.

"I can," said the girl.

"Good."

Then the assistant turned to the dismissed manager.

"We said three months' pay for three candidates. So, one month for one candidate. Minus one month because you couldn't manage to find anything other than a twelve-year-old."

"Fourteen," said the girl.

Piet du Toit didn't say goodbye when he left. With his bodyguard two steps behind him.

The girl who had just become her own boss's boss thanked him for his help and said that he was immediately reinstated as her right-hand man.

"But what about Piet du Toit?" said her former boss.

"We'll just change your name — I'm sure the assistant can't tell one black from the next."

Said the fourteen-year-old who looked twelve.

♦ ♦ ♦

The newly appointed manager of latrine emptying in Soweto's Sector B had never had the chance to go to school. This was because her mother had had other priorities, but also because the girl had been born in South Africa, of all countries; furthermore, she was born in the early 1960s, when the political leaders were of the opinion that children like Nombeko didn't count. The prime minister at the time made a name for himself by asking rhetorically why the blacks should go to school when they weren't good for anything but carrying wood and water.

In principle he was wrong, because Nombeko carried shit, not wood or water. Yet there was no reason to believe that the tiny girl would grow up to socialize with kings and presidents. Or to strike fear into nations. Or to influence the development of the world in general.

If, that is, she hadn't been the person she was.

But, of course, she was.

Among many other things, she was a hardworking child. Even as a five-year-old she carried latrine barrels as big as she was. By emptying the latrine barrels, she earned exactly the amount of money her mother needed in order to ask her daughter to buy a bottle of thinner each day. Her mother took the bottle with a "Thank you, dear girl," unscrewed the lid, and began to dull the never-ending pain that came with the inability to give oneself or one's child a future. Nombeko's dad hadn't been in the vicinity of his daughter since twenty minutes after the fertilization.

As Nombeko got older, she was able to empty more latrine barrels each day, and the money was enough to buy more than just thinner. Thus her mum could supplement the solvent with pills and booze. But the girl, who realized that things couldn't go on like this, told her mother that she had to choose between giving up or dying.

Her mum nodded in understanding.

The funeral was well attended. At the time, there were plenty of people in Soweto who devoted themselves primarily to two things: slowly killing themselves and saying a final farewell to those who had just succeeded in that endeavour. Nombeko's mum died when the girl was ten years old, and, as mentioned earlier, there was no dad available. The girl considered taking over where her mum had left off: chemically building herself a permanent shield against reality. But when she received her first pay cheque after her mother's death, she decided to buy something to eat instead. And when her hunger was alleviated, she looked around and said, "What am I doing here?"

At the same time, she realized that she didn't have any immediate alternatives. Ten-year-old illiterates were not the prime candidates on the South African job market. Or the secondary ones, either. And in this part of Soweto there was no job market at all, or all that many employable people, for that matter.

But defecation generally happens even for the most wretched people on our Earth, so Nombeko had one way to earn a little money. And once her mother was dead and buried, she could keep her salary for her own use.

To kill time while she was lugging barrels, she had started counting them when she was five: "One, two, three, four, five . . ."

As she grew older, she made these exercises harder so they would continue to be challenging: "Fifteen barrels times three trips times seven people carrying, with another one who sits there doing nothing because he's too drunk . . . is . . . three hundred and fifteen."

Nombeko's mother hadn't noticed much around her besides her bottle of thinner, but she did discover that her daughter could add and subtract. So during her last year of life she had started calling upon her each time a delivery of tablets of various colours and strengths was to be divided among the shacks. A bottle of thinner is just a bottle of thinner. But when pills of 50, 100, 250 and 500 milligrams must be distributed according to desire and financial ability, it's important to be able to tell the difference between the four kinds of arithmetic. And the ten-year-old could. Very much so.

She might happen, for example, to be in the vicinity of her immediate boss while he was struggling to compile the monthly weight and amount report.

"So, ninety-five times ninety-two," her boss mumbled. "Where's the calculator?"

"Eight thousand seven hundred and forty," Nombeko said.

"Help me look for it instead, little girl."

"Eight thousand seven hundred and forty," Nombeko said again.

"What's that you're saying?"

"Ninety-five times ninety-two is eight thousand seven hund —"

"And how do you know that?"

"Well, I think about how ninety-five is one hundred minus five, ninety-two is one hundred minus eight. If you turn it round and subtract, it's eighty-seven together. And five times eight is forty. Eighty-seven forty. Eight thousand seven hundred and forty."

"Why do you think like that?" said the astonished manager.

"I don't know," said Nombeko. "Can we get back to work now?"

From that day on, she was promoted to manager's assistant.

But in time, the illiterate who could count felt more and more frustrated because she couldn't understand what the supreme powers in Johannesburg wrote in all the decrees that landed on the manager's desk. The manager himself had a hard time with the words. He stumbled his way through every Afrikaans text, simultaneously flipping through an English dictionary so that the unintelligible letters were at least presented to him in a language he could understand.

"What do they want this time?" Nombeko might ask.

"For us to fill the sacks better," said the manager. "I think. Or that they're planning to shut down one of the sanitation stations. It's a bit unclear."

The manager sighed. His assistant couldn't help him. So she sighed, too.

But then a lucky thing happened: thirteen-year-old Nombeko was accosted by a smarmy man in the showers of the latrine emptiers' changing room. The smarmy man hadn't got very far before the girl got him to change his mind by planting a pair of scissors in his thigh.

The next day she tracked down the man on the other side of the row of latrines in Sector B. He was sitting in a camping chair with a bandage round his thigh, outside his green-painted shack. In his lap he had . . . books?

"What do you want?" he said.

"I believe I left my scissors in your thigh yesterday, Uncle, and now I'd like them back."

"I threw them away," the man said.

"Then you owe me some scissors," said the girl. "How come you can read?"

The smarmy man's name was Thabo, and he was half toothless. His thigh hurt an awful lot, and he didn't feel like having a conversation with the ill-tempered girl. On the other hand, this was the first time since he'd come to Soweto that someone seemed interested in his books. His shack was full of them, and for this reason his

11

neighbours called him Crazy Thabo. But the girl in front of him sounded more jealous than scornful. Maybe he could use this to his advantage.

"If you were a bit more cooperative instead of violent beyond all measure, perhaps Uncle Thabo might consider telling you. Maybe he would even teach you how to interpret letters and words. If you were a bit more cooperative, that is."

Nombeko had no intention of being more cooperative towards the smarmy man than she had been in the shower the day before. So she replied that, as luck would have it, she had another pair of scissors in her possession, and that she would very much like to keep them rather than use them on Uncle Thabo's other thigh. But as long as Uncle kept himself under control — and taught her to read — thigh number two would remain in good health.

Thabo didn't quite understand. Had the girl just threatened him?

◆ ◆ ◆

One couldn't tell by looking at him, but Thabo was rich. He had been born under a tarpaulin in the harbour of Port Elizabeth in Eastern Cape Province. When he was six years old, the police had taken his mother and never given her back. The boy's father thought the boy was old enough to take care of himself, even though the father had problems doing that very thing.

12

"Take care of yourself" was the sum of his father's advice for life before he clapped his son on the shoulder and went to Durban to be shot to death in a poorly planned bank robbery.

The six-year-old lived on what he could steal in the harbour, and in the best case one could expect that he would grow up, be arrested and eventually either be locked up or shot to death like his parents.

But another long-term resident of the slums was a Spanish sailor, cook and poet who had once been thrown overboard by twelve hungry seamen who were of the opinion that they needed food, not sonnets, for lunch.

The Spaniard swam to shore and found a shack to crawl into, and since that day he had lived for poetry, his own and others'. As time went by and his eyesight grew worse and worse, he hurried to snare young Thabo, then forced him to learn the art of reading in exchange for bread. Subsequently, and for a little more bread, the boy devoted himself to reading to the old man, who had not only gone completely blind but also half senile and fed on nothing more than Pablo Neruda for breakfast, lunch and dinner.

The seamen had been right that it is not possible to live on poetry alone. For the old man starved to death and Thabo decided to inherit all his books. No one else cared, anyway.

The fact that he was literate meant that the boy could get by in the harbour with various odd jobs. At night he would read poetry or fiction — and, above all, travelogues. At the age of sixteen, he discovered the opposite sex, which discovered him in return two years later. So it wasn't until he was eighteen that Thabo found a formula that worked. It consisted of one-third irresistible smile; one-third made-up stories about all the things he had done on his journeys across the continent, which he had thus far not undertaken other than in his imagination; and one-third flat-out lies about how eternal their love would be.

He did not achieve true success, however, until he added literature to the smiling, storytelling and lying. Among the things he inherited, he found a translation the sailor had done of Pablo Neruda's *Twenty Love Poems and a Song of Despair*. Thabo tore out the song of despair, but he practised the twenty love poems on twenty different women in the harbour district and was able to experience temporary love nineteen times over. There would probably have been a twentieth time, too, if only that idiot Neruda hadn't stuck in a line about "I no longer love her, that's certain" towards the end of a poem; Thabo didn't discover this until it was too late.

A few years later, most of the neighbourhood knew what sort of person Thabo was; the possibilities for further literary experiences were slim. It didn't help that he started telling lies about everything he had done in life that were worse than those King Leopold II had told in his day, when he had said that the natives of the Belgian Congo were doing fine even as he had the hands and feet chopped off anyone who refused to work for free.

Oh well, Thabo would get what was coming to him (as did the Belgian king, incidentally — first he lost his colony, then he wasted all his money on his favourite French-Romanian prostitute, and then he died). But first Thabo made his way out of Port Elizabeth: he went directly north and ended up in Basutoland where the women with the roundest figures were said to be.

There he found reason to stay for several years; he switched villages when the circumstances called for it, always found a job thanks to his ability to read and write, and eventually went so far as to become the chief negotiator for all the European missionaries who wanted access to the country and its uninformed citizens.

The chief of the Basotho people, His Excellence Seeiso, didn't see the value in letting his people be Christianized, but he realized that the country needed to free itself from all the Boers in the area. When the missionaries — on Thabo's urging — offered weapons in exchange for the right to hand out Bibles, the chief jumped at the opportunity.

And so pastors and lay missionaries streamed in to save the Basotho people from evil. They brought with them Bibles, automatic weapons and the occasional land mine.

The weapons kept the enemy at bay while the Bibles were burned by frozen mountain-dwellers. After all, they couldn't read. When the missionaries realized this, they changed tactics and built a great number of Christian temples in a short amount of time.

Thabo took odd jobs as a pastor's assistant and developed his own form of the laying on of hands, which he practised selectively and in secret.

Things on the romance front only went badly once. This occurred when a mountain village discovered that the only male member of the church choir had promised everlasting fidelity to at least five of the nine young girls in the choir. The English pastor there had always suspected what Thabo was up to. Because he certainly couldn't sing.

The pastor contacted the five girls' fathers, who decided that the suspect should be interrogated in the traditional manner. This is what would happen: Thabo would be stuck with spears from five different directions during a full moon, while sitting with his bare bottom in an anthill. While waiting for the moon to reach the correct phase, Thabo was locked in a hut over which the pastor kept constant watch, until he got sunstroke and instead went down to the river to save a hippopotamus. The pastor cautiously laid a hand on the animal's nose and said that Jesus was prepared to —

This was as far as he got before the hippopotamus opened its mouth and bit him in half.

With the pastor-cum-jailer gone, and with the help of Pablo Neruda, Thabo managed to get the female guard to unlock the door so he could escape.

"What about you and me?" the prison guard called after him as he ran as fast as he could out onto the savannah.

"I no longer love you, that's certain," Thabo called back.

If one didn't know better, one might think that Thabo was protected by God, because he encountered no lions, leopards, rhinoceroses or anything else during his twelve-mile night-time walk to the capital city, Maseru. Once there, he applied for a job as adviser to Chief Seeiso, who remembered him from before and welcomed him back. The chief was negotiating with the high-and-mighty Brits for independence, but he didn't make any headway until Thabo joined in and said that if the gentlemen intended to keep being this stubborn, Basutoland would have to think about asking for help from Joseph Mobutu in Congo.

The Brits went stiff. Joseph Mobutu? The man who had just informed the world that he was thinking about changing his name to the All-Powerful Warrior Who, Thanks to His Endurance and Inflexible Will to Win, Goes from Victory to Victory, Leaving Fire in His Wake?

"That's him," said Thabo. "One of my closest friends, in fact. To save time, I call him Joe."

The British delegation requested deliberation *in camera*, during which it was agreed that what the region needed was peace and quiet, not some almighty warrior who wanted to be called what he had decided he was. The Brits returned to the negotiating table and said:

"Take the country, then."

Basutoland became Lesotho; Chief Seeiso became King Moshoeshoe II, and Thabo became the new king's absolute favourite person. He was treated like a member of the family and was given a bag of rough diamonds from the most important mine in the country; they were worth a fortune.

But one day he was gone. And he had an unbeatable twenty-four-hour head start before it dawned on the king that his little sister and the apple of his eye, the delicate princess Maseeiso, was pregnant.

A person who was black, filthy and by that point half toothless in 1960s South Africa could not blend into the white world by any stretch of the imagination. Therefore, after the unfortunate incident in the former Basutoland, Thabo hurried on to Soweto as soon as he had exchanged the most trifling of his diamonds at the closest jeweller's.

There he found an unoccupied shack in Sector B. He moved in, stuffed his shoes full of money, and buried about half the diamonds in the trampled dirt floor. The other half he put in the various cavities in his mouth.

Before he began to make too many promises to as many women as possible, he painted his shack a lovely green; ladies were impressed by such things. And he bought linoleum with which to cover the floor.

The seductions were carried out in every one of Soweto's sectors, but after a while Thabo eliminated his own sector so that between times he could sit and read outside his shack without being bothered more than was necessary.

Besides reading and seduction, he devoted himself to travelling. Here and there, all over Africa, twice a year. This brought him both life experience and new books.

But he always came back to his shack, no matter how financially independent he was. Not least because half of his fortune was one foot below the linoleum; Thabo's lower row of teeth was still in far too good condition for all of it to fit in his mouth.

It took a few years before mutterings were heard among the shacks in Soweto. Where did that crazy man with the books get all his money from?

In order to keep the gossip from taking too firm a hold, Thabo decided to get a job. The easiest thing to do was become a latrine emptier for a few hours a week.

Almost all of his colleagues were young, alcoholic men with no futures. But there was also the occasional child. Among them was a thirteen-year-old girl who had planted scissors in Thabo's thigh just because he had happened to choose the wrong door into the showers. Or the right door, really. The girl was what was wrong. Far too young. No curves. Nothing for Thabo, except in a pinch.

The scissors had hurt. And now she was standing there outside his shack, and she wanted him to teach her to read.

"I would be more than happy to help you, if only I weren't leaving on a journey tomorrow," said Thabo, thinking that perhaps things would go most smoothly for him if he did what he'd just claimed he was going to do.

"Journey?" said Nombeko, who had never been outside Soweto in all her thirteen years. "Where are you going?"

"North," said Thabo. "Then we'll see."

♦ ♦ ♦

While Thabo was gone, Nombeko got one year older and promoted. And she quickly made the best of her managerial position. By way of an ingenious system in which she divided her sector into zones based on demography rather than geographical size or reputation, making the deployment of outhouses more effective.

"An improvement of thirty per cent," her predecessor said in praise.

"Thirty point two," said Nombeko.

Supply matched demand and vice versa, and there was enough money left over in the budget for four new washing and sanitation stations.

The fourteen-year-old was fantastically verbal, considering the language used by the men in her daily life (anyone who has ever had a conversation with a latrine emptier in Soweto knows that half the words aren't fit to print and the other half aren't even fit to think). Her ability to formulate words and sentences was partially innate. But there was also a radio in one corner of the latrine office, and ever since she was little, Nombeko had made sure to turn it on as soon as she was in the vicinity. She always tuned in to the talk station and listened with interest, not only to what was said but also to how it was said.

The weekly show *View on Africa* was what first gave her the insight that there was a world outside Soweto. It wasn't necessarily more beautiful or more promising. But it was outside Soweto.

Such as when Angola had recently received independence. The independence party PLUA had joined forces with the independence party PCA to form the independence party MPLA, which, along with the independence parties FNLA and UNITA, caused the Portuguese government to regret ever having discovered that part of the continent. A government that, incidentally, had not managed to build a single university during its four hundred years of rule.

The illiterate Nombeko couldn't quite follow which combination of letters had done what, but in any case the result seemed to have been *change*, which, along with *food*, was Nombeko's favourite word.

Once she happened to opine, in the presence of her colleagues, that this *change* thing might be something for all of them. But then they complained that their manager was talking politics. Wasn't it enough that they had to *carry* shit all day? Did they have to listen to it, too?

As the manager of latrine emptying, Nombeko was forced to handle not only all of her hopeless latrine colleagues, but also Assistant Piet du Toit from the sanitation department of the City of Johannesburg. During his first visit after having appointed her, he informed her that there would under no circumstances be four new sanitation stations — there would be only one, because of serious budgetary problems. Nombeko took revenge in her own little way:

"From one thing to the next: what do you think of the developments in Tanzania, Mr Assistant? Julius

Nyerere's socialist experiment is about to collapse, don't you think?"

"Tanzania?"

"Yes, the grain shortage is probably close to a million tons by now. The question is, what would Nyerere have done if it weren't for the International Monetary Fund? Or perhaps you consider the IMF to be a problem in and of itself, Mr Assistant?"

Said the girl who had never gone to school or been outside Soweto. To the assistant who was one of the authorities. Who had gone to a university. And who had no knowledge of the political situation in Tanzania. The assistant had been white to start with. The girl's argument turned him as white as a ghost.

Piet du Toit felt demeaned by a fourteen-year-old illiterate. Who was now rejecting his document on the sanitation funds.

"By the way, how did you calculate this, Mr Assistant?" said Nombeko, who had taught herself how to read numbers. "Why have you multiplied the target values together?"

An illiterate who could count.

He hated her.

He hated them all.

◆ ◆ ◆

A few months later, Thabo was back. The first thing he discovered was that the girl with the scissors had become his boss. And that she wasn't much of a girl any more. She had started to develop curves.

22

This sparked an internal struggle in the half-toothless man. On the one hand, his instinct told him to trust his by now gap-ridden smile, his storytelling techniques and Pablo Neruda. On the other hand, there was the part where she was his boss. Plus his memory of the scissors.

Thabo decided to act with caution, but to get himself into position.

"I suppose by now it's high time I teach you to read," he said.

"Great!" said Nombeko. "Let's start right after work today. We'll come to your shack, me and the scissors."

Thabo was quite a capable teacher. And Nombeko was a quick learner. By day three she could write the alphabet using a stick in the mud outside Thabo's shack. From day five on she spelled her way to whole words and sentences. At first she was wrong more often than right. After two months, she was more right than wrong.

In their breaks from studying, Thabo told her about the things he had experienced on his journeys. Nombeko soon realized that in doing so he was mixing two parts fiction with at the most one part reality, but she thought that was just as well. Her own reality was miserable enough as it was. She could do without much more of the same.

Most recently he had been in Ethiopia to depose His Imperial Majesty, the Lion of Judah, Elect of God, the King of Kings.

"Haile Selassie," said Nombeko.

Thabo didn't answer; he preferred speaking to listening.

The story of the emperor who had started out as Ras Tafari, which became rastafari, which became a whole religion, not least in the West Indies, was so juicy that Thabo had saved it for the day it was time to make a move.

Anyway, by now the founder had been chased off his imperial throne, and all over the world confused disciples were sitting around smoking while they wondered how it could be possible that the promised Messiah, God incarnate, had suddenly been deposed. Depose God?

Nombeko was careful not to ask about the political background of this drama. Because she was pretty sure that Thabo had no idea, and too many questions might disrupt the entertainment.

"Tell me more!" she encouraged him instead.

Thabo thought that things were shaping up very nicely (it's amazing how wrong a person can be). He moved a step closer to the girl and continued his story by saying that on his way home he had swung by Kinshasa to help Muhammad Ali before the "Rumble in the Jungle" — the heavyweight match with the invincible George Foreman.

"Oh wow, that's so exciting," said Nombeko, thinking that, as a story, it actually was.

Thabo gave such a broad smile that she could see things glittering among the teeth he still had left. "Well, it was really the invincible Foreman who wanted my help, but I felt that . . ." Thabo began, and he didn't

24

stop until Foreman was knocked out in the eighth round and Ali thanked his dear friend Thabo for his invaluable support.

And Ali's wife had been delightful, by the way.

"Ali's wife?" said Nombeko. "Surely you don't mean that . . ."

Thabo laughed until his jaws jingled; then he grew serious again and moved even closer.

"You are very beautiful, Nombeko," he said. "Much more beautiful than Ali's wife. What if you and I were to get together? Move somewhere together."

And then he put his arm round her shoulders.

Nombeko thought that "moving somewhere" sounded lovely. Anywhere, actually. But not with this smarmy man. The day's lesson seemed to be over. Nombeko planted a pair of scissors in Thabo's other thigh and left.

The next day, she returned to Thabo's shack and said that he had failed to come to work and hadn't sent word, either.

Thabo replied that both of his thighs hurt too much, one in particular, and that Miss Nombeko probably knew why this was.

Yes, and it could be even worse, because next time she was planning to plant her scissors not in one thigh or the other, but somewhere in between, if Uncle Thabo didn't start to behave himself.

"What's more, I saw *and* heard what you have in your ugly mouth yesterday. If you don't shape up, starting now, I promise to tell as many people as possible."

Thabo became quite upset. He knew all too well that he wouldn't survive for many minutes after such time as his fortune in diamonds became general knowledge.

"What do you want from me?" he said in a pitiful voice.

"I want to be able to come here and spell my way through books without the need to bring a new pair of scissors each day. Scissors are expensive for those of us who have mouths full of teeth instead of other things."

"Can't you just go away?" said Thabo. "You can have one of the diamonds if you leave me alone."

He had bribed his way out of things before, but not this time. Nombeko said that she wasn't going to demand any diamonds. Things that didn't belong to her didn't belong to her.

Much later, in another part of the world, it would turn out that life was more complicated than that.

♦ ♦ ♦

Ironically enough, it was two women who ended Thabo's life. They had grown up in Portuguese East Africa and supported themselves by killing white farmers in order to steal their money. This enterprise went well as long as the civil war was going on.

But when independence came and the country's name changed to Mozambique, the farmers who were still left had forty-eight hours to leave. The women then had no other choice than to kill well-to-do blacks instead. As a business idea it was a much worse one, because nearly all the blacks with anything worth stealing belonged to the Marxist-Leninist Party, which was now in power. So it wasn't long before the women were wanted by the state and hunted by the new country's dreaded police force.

This was why they went south. And made it all the way to the excellent hideout of Soweto, outside Johannesburg.

If the advantage to South Africa's largest shantytown was that one could get lost in the crowds (as long as one was black), the disadvantage was that each individual white farmer in Portuguese East Africa probably had greater resources than all the 800,000 inhabitants of Soweto combined (with the exception of Thabo). But still, the women each swallowed a few pills of various colours and set out on a killing spree. After a while they made their way to Sector B, and there, behind the row of latrines, they caught sight of a green shack among all the rusty brown and grey ones. A person who paints his shack green (or any other colour) surely has too much money for his own good, the women thought, and they broke in during the middle of the night, planted a knife in Thabo's chest and twisted it. The man who had broken so many hearts found his own cut to pieces.

Once he was dead, the women searched for his money among all the damn books that were piled everywhere. What kind of fool had they killed this time?

But finally they found a wad of banknotes in one of the victim's shoes, and another in the other one. And, imprudently enough, they sat down outside the shack to divide them up. The particular mixture of pills they had swallowed along with half a glass of rum caused the women to lose their sense of time and place. Thus they were still sitting there, each with a grin on her face, when the police, for once, showed up.

The women were seized and transformed into a thirty-year cost item in the South African correctional system. The banknotes they had tried to count disappeared early on in the chain of custody. Thabo's corpse ended up lying where it was until the next day. In the South African police corps, it was a sport to make the next shift take care of each dead darky whenever possible.

Nombeko had been woken up in the night by the ruckus on the other side of the row of latrines. She got dressed, walked over, and realized more or less what had happened.

Once the police had departed with the murderers and all of Thabo's money, Nombeko went into the shack.

"You were a horrible person, but your lies were entertaining. I will miss you. Or at least your books."

Upon which she opened Thabo's mouth and picked out fourteen rough diamonds, just the number that fitted in the gaps left by all the teeth he'd lost.

"Fourteen holes, fourteen diamonds," said Nombeko. "A little too perfect, isn't it?"

Thabo didn't answer. But Nombeko pulled up the linoleum and started digging.

28

"Thought so," she said when she found what she was looking for.

Then she fetched water and a rag and washed Thabo, dragged him out of the shack, and sacrificed her only white sheet to cover the body. He deserved a little dignity, after all. Not much. But a little.

Nombeko immediately sewed all of Thabo's diamonds into the seam of her only jacket, and then she went back to bed.

The latrine manager let herself sleep in the next day. She had a lot to process. When she stepped into the office at last, all of the latrine emptiers were there. In their boss's absence they were on their third morning beer, and they had been underprioritizing work since the second beer, preferring instead to sit around judging Indians to be an inferior race. The cockiest of the men was in the middle of telling the story of the man who had tried to fix the leaky ceiling of his shack with cardboard.

Nombeko interrupted the goings-on, gathered up all the beer bottles that hadn't yet been emptied, and said that she suspected her colleagues had nothing in their heads besides the very contents of the latrine barrels they were meant to be emptying. Were they really so stupid that they didn't understand that stupidity was race-neutral?

The cocky man said that apparently the boss couldn't understand that a person might want to have a beer in peace and quiet after the first seventy-five barrels of the morning, without also being forced to listen to nonsense about how we're all so goddamn alike and equal.

Nombeko considered throwing a roll of toilet paper at his head in reply, but she decided that the roll didn't deserve it. Instead she ordered them to get back to work.

Then she went home to her shack. And said to herself once again: What am I doing here?

She would turn fifteen the next day.

♦ ♦ ♦

On her fifteenth birthday, Nombeko had a meeting with Piet du Toit of the sanitation department of the City of Johannesburg; it had been scheduled long ago. This time he was better prepared. He had gone through the accounting in detail. Take that, twelve-year-old.

"Sector B has gone eleven per cent over budget," said Piet du Toit, and he looked at Nombeko over the reading glasses he really didn't need, but which made him look older than he was.

"Sector B has done no such thing," said Nombeko.

"If I say that Sector B has gone eleven per cent over budget, then it has," said Piet du Toit.

"And if I say that the assistant can only calculate according to his own lights, then he does. Give me a few seconds," said Nombeko, and she yanked Piet du Toit's calculations from his hand, quickly looked through his numbers, pointed at row twenty, and said, "We received the discount I negotiated here in the form of excess delivery. If you assess that at the discounted *de facto* price instead of an imaginary list price, you will find that your eleven mystery percentage points no longer exist. In addition, you have confused plus and minus. If we were to calculate the way you want to do it, we would have been *under* budget by eleven per cent. Which would be just as incorrect, incidentally."

Piet du Toit's face turned red. Didn't the girl know her place? What would things be like if just anyone could define right and wrong? He hated her more than ever, but he couldn't think of anything to say. So he said, "We have been talking about you quite a bit at the office."

"Is that so," said Nombeko.

"We feel that you are uncooperative."

Nombeko realized that she was about to be fired, just like her predecessor.

"Is that so," she said.

"I'm afraid we must transfer you. Back to the permanent workforce."

This was, in fact, more than her predecessor had been offered. Nombeko suspected that the assistant must have been in a good mood on this particular day.

"Is that so," she said.

"Is 'is that so' all you have to say?" Piet du Toit said angrily.

"Well I could have told Mr du Toit what an idiot Mr du Toit is, of course, but getting him to understand this would be verging on the hopeless. Years among the latrine emptiers has taught me that. You should know that there are idiots here as well, Mr du Toit. Best just to leave so I never have to see you again," said Nombeko, and did just that.

She said what she said at such speed that Piet du Toit didn't have time to react before the girl had slipped out of his hands. And going in among the shacks to search for her was out of the question. As far as he was concerned, she could keep herself hidden in all that rubbish until tuberculosis, drugs or one of the other illiterates killed her.

"Ugh," said Piet du Toit, nodding at the bodyguard his father paid for.

Time to return to civilization.

Of course, Nombeko's managerial position wasn't the only thing to go up in smoke after that conversation with the assistant — so did her job, such as it was. And her last pay cheque, for that matter.

Her backpack was filled with her meagre possessions. It contained a change of clothes, three of Thabo's books, and the twenty sticks of dried antelope meat she had just bought with her last few coins.

She had already read the books, and she knew them by heart. But there was something pleasant about books, about their very existence. It was sort of the same with her latrine-emptying colleagues, except the exact opposite.

It was evening, and there was a chill in the air. Nombeko put on her only jacket. She lay down on her only mattress and pulled her only blanket over her (her only sheet had just been used as a shroud). She would leave the next morning.

And she suddenly knew where she would go.

She had read about it in the paper the day before. She was going to 75 Andries Street in Pretoria.

The National Library.

As far as she knew, it wasn't an area that was forbidden for blacks, so with a little luck she could get in. What she could do beyond that, aside from breathing and enjoying the view, she didn't know. But it was a start. And she felt that literature would lead her onward.

With that certainty, she fell asleep for the last time in the shack she had inherited from her mother five years previously. And she did so with a smile.

That had never happened before.

When morning came, she took off. The road before her was not a short one. Her first-ever walk beyond Soweto would be fifty-five miles long.

After just over six hours, and after sixteen of the fifty-five miles, Nombeko had arrived in central Johannesburg. It was another world! Just take the fact that most of the people around her were white and strikingly similar to Piet du Toit, every last one. Nombeko looked around with great interest. There were neon signs, traffic lights and general chaos. And shiny new cars, models she had never seen before. As she turned round to discover more, she saw that one of them was headed straight for her, speeding along the pavement.

Nombeko had time to think that it was a nice car.

But she didn't have time to move out of the way.

◆ ◆ ◆

Engineer Engelbrecht van der Westhuizen had spent the afternoon in the bar of the Hilton Plaza Hotel on Quartz Street. Then he got into his new Opel Admiral and set off, heading north.

But it is not and never has been easy to drive a car with a litre of brandy in one's body. The engineer didn't make it farther than the next intersection before he and the Opel drifted onto the pavement and — shit! — wasn't he running over a Kaffir?

The girl under the engineer's car was named Nombeko and was a former latrine emptier. Fifteen years and one day earlier she had come into the world in a tin shack in South Africa's largest shantytown. Surrounded by liquor, thinner and pills, she was expected to live for a while and then die in the mud among the latrines in Soweto's Sector B.

Out of all of them, Nombeko was the one to break loose. She left her shack for the first and last time.

And then she didn't make it any farther than central Johannesburg before she was lying under an Opel Admiral, ruined.

Was that all? she thought before she faded into unconsciousness.

But it wasn't.

CHAPTER
TWO

On how everything went topsy-turvy in another part of the world

Nombeko was run over on the day after her fifteenth birthday. But she survived. Things would get better. And worse. Above all, they would get strange.

Of all the men she would be subjected to in the years to come, Ingmar Qvist from Södertälje, Sweden, six thousand miles away, was not one of them. But all the same, his fate would hit her with full force.

It's hard to say exactly when Ingmar lost his mind, because it sneaked up on him. But it is clear that by the autumn of 1947 it was well on its way. It is also clear that neither he nor his wife realized what was going on.

Ingmar and Henrietta got married while almost all of the world was still at war and moved to a plot of land in the forest outside Södertälje, almost twenty miles southwest of Stockholm.

He was a low-level civil servant; she was an industrious seamstress who took in work at home.

They met for the first time outside Room 2 of Södertälje District Court, where a dispute between Ingmar and Henrietta's father was being handled: the former had happened, one night, to paint LONG LIVE THE KING! in three-foot-high letters along one wall of the meeting hall of Sweden's Communist Party. Communism and the royal family don't generally go hand in hand, of course, so naturally there was quite an uproar at dawn the next day when the Communists' main man in Södertälje — Henrietta's father — discovered what had happened.

Ingmar was quickly seized — extra quickly, since after his prank he had lain down to sleep on a park bench not far from the police station, with paint and brush in hand.

In the courtroom, sparks had flown between the defending Ingmar and the spectating Henrietta. This was probably partly because she was tempted by the forbidden fruit, but above all it was because Ingmar was so . . . full of life . . . unlike her father, who just went around waiting for everything to go to hell so that he and Communism could take over, at least in Södertälje. Her father had always been a revolutionary, but after 7 April 1937, when he signed what turned out to be the country's 999,999th radio licence, he also became bitter and full of dark thoughts. A tailor in Hudiksvall, two hundred miles away, was celebrated the very next day for having signed the millionth licence. The tailor received not only fame (he got to be on the radio!) but also a commemorative silver trophy worth six hundred kronor. All while Henrietta's dad got nothing more than a long face.

He never got over this event; he lost his (already limited) ability to see the humour in anything, not least the prank of paying tribute to King Gustaf V on the wall of the Communist Party's meeting place. He argued the party's case in court himself and demanded eighteen years of prison for Ingmar Qvist, who was instead sentenced to a fine of fifteen kronor.

Henrietta's father's misfortune knew no bounds. First the radio licences. And the relative disappointment in Södertälje District Court. And his daughter, who subsequently fell into the arms of the Royalist. And, of course, the cursed capitalism, which always seemed to land on its feet.

When Henrietta went on to decide that she and Ingmar would marry *in the church*, Södertälje's Communist leader broke off contact with his daughter once and for all, upon which Henrietta's mother broke off contact with Henrietta's father, met a new man — a German military attaché — at Södertälje Station, moved to Berlin with him just before the war ended, and was never heard from again.

Henrietta wanted to have children, preferably as many as possible. Ingmar thought this was basically a good idea, not least because he appreciated the method of production. Just think of that very first time, in the back of Henrietta's father's car, two days after the trial. That had been something, all right, although Ingmar had had to pay for it — he hid in his aunt's cellar while his father-in-law-to-be searched all over Södertälje for him. Ingmar shouldn't have left that used condom in the car.

Oh well, what's done is done. And anyway, it was a blessing that he'd happened across that box of condoms for American soldiers, because things had to be done in the proper order so that nothing would go wrong.

But by this Ingmar did not mean making himself a career so he could support a family. He worked at the post office in Södertälje, or the "Royal Mail Service", as he liked to say. His salary was average, and there was every chance that it would stay that way.

Henrietta earned nearly double what her husband did, because she was clever and quick with both needle and thread. She had a large and regular clientele; the family would have lived very comfortably if it weren't for Ingmar and his evergrowing talent for squandering everything Henrietta managed to save.

Again, children would be great, but first Ingmar had to fulfil his life's mission, and that took focus. Until his mission was completed, there mustn't be any extraneous side projects.

Henrietta protested her husband's choice of words. Children were life itself and the future — not a side project.

"If that's how you feel, then you can take your box of American soldiers' condoms and sleep on the kitchen sofa," she said.

Ingmar squirmed. Of course he didn't mean that children were extraneous, it was just that . . . well, Henrietta already knew what. It was, of course, this matter of His Majesty the King. He just *had* to get that out of the way first. It wouldn't take for ever.

"Dear, sweet Henrietta. Can't we sleep together again tonight? And maybe do a little practising for the future?"

Henrietta's heart melted, of course. As it had so many times before and as it would many times yet to come.

What Ingmar called his life's mission was to shake the hand of the King of Sweden. It had started as a wish, but had developed into a goal. The precise moment at which it became a true obsession was, as previously mentioned, not easy to say. It was easier to explain where and when the whole thing started.

On Saturday, 16 June 1928, His Majesty King Gustaf V celebrated his seventieth birthday. Ingmar Qvist, who was fourteen at the time, went with his mother and father to Stockholm to wave the Swedish flag outside the palace and then go to Skansen Museum and Zoo — where they had bears and wolves!

But their plans changed a bit. It turned out to be far too crowded at the palace; instead the family stood along the procession route a few hundred yards away, where the king and his Victoria were expected to pass by in an open carriage.

And so they did. At which point everything turned out better than Ingmar's mother and father could ever have imagined. Because just next to the Qvist family were twenty students from Lundsbergs Boarding School; they were there to give a bouquet of flowers to His Majesty as thanks for the support the school received, not least because of the involvement of Crown

Prince Gustaf Adolf. It had been decided that the carriage would stop briefly so that His Majesty could step down, receive the flowers and thank the children.

Everything went as planned and the king received his flowers, but when he turned to step up into the carriage again he caught sight of Ingmar. And stopped short.

"What a beautiful lad," he said, and he took two steps up to the boy and tousled his hair. "Just a second — here you go," he went on, and from his inner pocket he took a sheet of commemorative stamps that had just been released for the king's special day.

He handed the stamps to young Ingmar, smiled, and said, "I could eat you right up." Then he tousled the boy's hair once more before he climbed up to the furiously glaring queen.

"Did you say 'thank you', Ingmar?" asked his mother once she'd recovered from the fact that the king had touched her son — and given him a present.

"No-o," Ingmar stammered as he stood there with stamps in hand. "No, I didn't say anything. It was like he was . . . too grand to talk to."

The stamps became Ingmar's most cherished possession, of course. And two years later he started working at the post office in Södertälje. He started out as a clerk of the lowest rank possible in the accounting department; sixteen years later he had climbed absolutely nowhere.

Ingmar was infinitely proud of the tall, stately monarch. Every day, Gustaf V stared majestically past him from all the stamps the subject had reason to handle at work. Ingmar gazed humbly and lovingly back as he sat there in the Royal Mail Service's royal uniform, even though it was not at all necessary to wear it in the accounting department.

But there was just this one issue: the king was looking *past* Ingmar. It was as if he didn't see his subject and therefore couldn't receive the subject's love. Ingmar so terribly wanted to be able to look the king in the eye. To apologize for not saying "thank you" that time when he was fourteen. To proclaim his eternal loyalty.

"So terribly" was right. It became more and more important . . . the desire to look him in the eye, speak with him, shake his hand.

More and more important.

And even more important.

His Majesty, of course, was only getting older. Soon it would be too late. Ingmar Qvist could no longer just wait for the king to march into the Södertälje Post Office one day. That had been his dream all these years, but now he was about to wake up from it.

The king wasn't going to seek out Ingmar.

Ingmar had no choice but to seek out the king.

Then he and Henrietta would make a baby, he promised.

◆ ◆ ◆

The Qvist family's already poor existence kept getting poorer and poorer. The money kept disappearing, thanks to Ingmar's attempts to meet the king. He wrote veritable love letters (with an unnecessarily large number of stamps on them); he called (without getting further than some poor royal secretary, of course); he sent presents in the form of Swedish silversmith products, which were the king's favourite things (and in this way he supported the not entirely honest father of five who had the task of registering all incoming royal gifts). Beyond this, he went to tennis matches and nearly all of the functions one could imagine the king might attend. This meant many expensive trips and admission tickets, yet Ingmar never came very close to meeting his king.

Nor were the family finances fortified when Henrietta, as a result of all her worrying, started doing what almost everyone else did at the time — that is, smoking one or more packets of John Silvers per day.

Ingmar's boss at the accounting department of the post office was very tired of all the talk about the damn monarch and his merits. So whenever junior clerk Qvist asked for time off, he granted it even before Ingmar had managed to finish formulating his request.

"Um, boss, do you think it might be possible for me to have two weeks off work, right away? I'm going to —"

"Granted."

People had started calling Ingmar by his initials instead of his name. He was "IQ" among his superiors and colleagues.

"I wish you good luck in whatever kind of idiocy you're planning to get up to this time, IQ," said the head clerk.

42

Ingmar didn't care that he was being made fun of. Unlike the other workers at postal headquarters in Södertälje, his life had meaning and purpose.

It took another three considerable undertakings on Ingmar's part before absolutely everything went topsy-turvy.

First he made his way to Drottningholm Palace, stood up straight in his postal uniform, and rang the bell.

"Good day. My name is Ingmar Qvist. I am from the Royal Mail Service, and it so happens that I need to see His Majesty himself. Could you be so kind as to notify him? I will wait here," said Ingmar to the guard at the gate.

"Do you have a screw loose or something?" the guard said in return.

A fruitless dialogue ensued, and in the end Ingmar was asked to leave immediately; otherwise the guard would make sure that Mr Postal Clerk was packaged up and delivered right back to the post office whence he came.

Ingmar was offended and in his haste happened to mention the size he would estimate the guard's genitalia to be, whereupon he had to run away with the guard on his tail.

He got away, partly because he was a bit faster than the guard, but most of all because the latter had orders never to leave the gate and so had to turn back.

After that, Ingmar spent two whole days sneaking around outside the ten-foot fence, out of sight of the oaf at the gate, who refused to understand what was best for the king, before he gave up and went back to the hotel that served as his base for the entire operation.

"Should I prepare your bill?" asked the receptionist, who had long since suspected that this particular guest was not planning to do the right thing and pay.

"Yes, please," said Ingmar, and he went to his room, packed his suitcase, and checked out via the window.

The second considerable undertaking before everything went topsy-turvy began when Ingmar read a news item in *Dagens Nyheter* while hiding from work by sitting on the toilet. The news item said that the king was in Tullgarn for a few days of relaxing moose hunting. Ingmar rhetorically asked himself where there were moose if not out in God's green nature, and who had access to God's green nature if not . . . everyone! From kings to simple clerks at the Royal Mail Service.

Ingmar flushed the toilet for the sake of appearances and went to ask for another leave of absence. The head clerk granted his request with the frank comment that he hadn't even noticed that Mr Qvist was already back from the last one.

It had been a long time since Ingmar had been entrusted to rent a car in Södertälje, so first he had to take the bus all the way to Nyköping, where his honest looks were enough to get him a decent second-hand Fiat 518. He subsequently departed for Tullgarn at the speed allowed by the power of forty-eight horses.

44

But he didn't get more than halfway there before he met a black 1939 Cadillac V8 coming from the other direction. The king, of course. Finished hunting. About to slip out of Ingmar's hands yet again.

Ingmar turned his borrowed Fiat round in the blink of an eye, was helped along by several downhill stretches in a row, and caught up with the hundred-horsepower-stronger royal car. The next step would be to try to pass the car and maybe pretend to break down in the middle of the road.

But the anxious royal chauffeur speeded up so he wouldn't have to endure the wrath he expected the king to exhibit should they be passed by a Fiat. Unfortunately, he was looking at the rear-view mirror more than he was looking ahead, and at a curve in the road, the chauffeur, along with Cadillac, king, and companions, kept going straight, down into a waterlogged ditch.

Neither Gustaf V nor anyone else was harmed, but Ingmar had no way of knowing this from behind his steering wheel. His first thought was to jump out and help, and also shake the king's hand. But his second thought was: what if he had killed the old man? And his third thought: thirty years of hard labour — that might be too high a price for a handshake. Especially if the hand in question belonged to a corpse. Ingmar didn't think he would be very popular in the country, either. Murderers of kings seldom were.

So he turned round.

He left the hire car outside the Communists' meeting hall in Södertälje, in the hope that his father-in-law would get the blame. From there he walked all the way home to Henrietta and told her that he might have just killed the king he loved so dearly.

Henrietta consoled him by saying that everything was probably fine down there at the king's curve, and in any case it would be a good thing for the family finances if she were wrong.

The next day, the press reported that King Gustaf V had ended up in the ditch after his car had been driven at high speeds, but that he was unharmed. Henrietta had mixed feelings upon hearing this, but she thought that perhaps her husband had learned an important lesson. And so she asked, full of hope, if Ingmar was done chasing the king.

He was not.

The third considerable undertaking before everything went topsy-turvy involved a journey to the French Riviera for Ingmar; he was going to Nice, where Gustaf V, age eighty-eight, always spent the late autumn to get relief from his chronic bronchitis. In a rare interview, the king had said that when he wasn't taking his daily constitutional at a leisurely pace along the Promenade des Anglais, he spent the days sitting on the terrace of his state apartment at the Hôtel d'Angleterre.

This was enough information for Ingmar. He would travel there, run across the king while he was on his walk and introduce himself.

It was impossible to know what would happen next. Perhaps the two men would stand there for a while and have a chat, and if they hit it off perhaps Ingmar could buy the king a drink at the hotel that evening. And why not a game of tennis the next day?

"Nothing can go wrong this time," Ingmar said to Henrietta.

"That's nice," said his wife. "Have you seen my cigarettes?"

Ingmar hitchhiked his way through Europe. It took a whole week, but once he was in Nice it took only two hours of sitting on a bench on the Promenade des Anglais before he caught sight of the tall, stately gentleman with the silver cane and the monocle. God, he was so grand! He was approaching slowly. And he was alone.

What happened next was something Henrietta could describe in great detail many years later, because Ingmar would dwell on it for the rest of her life.

Ingmar stood up from his bench, walked up to His Majesty, introduced himself as the loyal subject from the Royal Mail Service that he was, broached the possibility of a drink together and maybe a game of tennis — and concluded by suggesting that the two men shake hands.

The king's reaction, however, had not been what Ingmar expected. For one thing, he refused to take this unknown man's hand. For another, he didn't condescend to look at him. Instead he looked past Ingmar into the distance, just as he had already done on all the tens of thousands of stamps Ingmar had had reason to handle in the course of his work. And then he said that he had no intention, under any circumstances, of socializing with a messenger boy from the post office.

Strictly speaking, the king was too stately to say what he thought of his subjects. He had been drilled since childhood in the art of showing his people the respect they generally didn't deserve. But he said what he thought now, partly because he hurt all over and partly because keeping it to himself all his life had taken its toll.

"But Your Majesty, you don't understand," Ingmar tried.

"If I were not alone I would have asked my companions to explain to the scoundrel before me that I certainly do understand," said the king, and in this way even managed to avoid speaking directly to the unfortunate subject.

"But," Ingmar said — and that was all he managed to say before the king hit him on the forehead with his silver cane and said, "Come, come!"

Ingmar landed on his bottom, thus enabling the king to pass safely. The subject remained on the ground as the king walked away.

Ingmar was crushed.

For twenty-five seconds.

Then he cautiously stood up and stared after his king for a long time. And he stared a little longer.

"*Messenger boy? Scoundrel?* I'll show you messenger boy and scoundrel."

And thus everything had gone topsy-turvy.

CHAPTER
THREE

On a strict sentence, a misunderstood country and three multifaceted girls from China

According to Engelbrecht van der Westhuizen's lawyer, the black girl had walked right out into the street, and the lawyer's client had had no choice but to swerve. Thus the accident was the girl's fault, not his. Engineer van der Westhuizen was a victim, nothing more. Besides, she had been walking on a pavement meant for whites.

The girl's assigned lawyer offered no defence because he had forgotten to show up in court. And the girl herself preferred not to say anything, largely because she had a jaw fracture that was not conducive to conversation.

Instead, the judge was the one to defend Nombeko. He informed Mr van der Westhuizen that he'd had at least five times the legal limit of alcohol in his bloodstream, and that blacks were certainly allowed to use that pavement, even if it wasn't considered proper. But if the girl had wandered into the street — and there was no reason to doubt that she had, since Mr van der

49

Westhuizen had said under oath that this was the case — then the blame rested largely on her.

Mr van der Westhuizen was awarded five thousand rand for bodily injury as well as another two thousand rand for the dents the girl had caused to appear on his car.

Nombeko had enough money to pay the fine and the cost of any number of dents. She could also have bought him a new car, for that matter. Or ten new cars. The fact was, she was extremely wealthy, but no one in the courtroom or anywhere else would have had reason to assume this. Back in the hospital she had used her one functioning arm to make sure that the diamonds were still in the seam of her jacket.

But her main reason for keeping this quiet was not her fractured jaw. In some sense, after all, the diamonds were stolen. From a dead man, but still. And as yet they were diamonds, not cash. If she were to remove one of them, all of them would be taken from her. At best, she would be locked up for theft; at worst, for conspiracy to robbery and murder. In short, the situation she found herself in was not simple.

The judge studied Nombeko and read something else in her expression of concern. He stated that the girl didn't appear to have any assets to speak of and that he could sentence her to pay off her debt in the service of Mr van der Westhuizen, if the engineer found this to be a suitable arrangement. The judge and the engineer had made a similar arrangement once before, and that was working out satisfactorily, wasn't it?

50

Engelbrecht van der Westhuizen shuddered at the memory of what had happened when he ended up with three Chinks in his employ, but these days they were useful to a certain extent — and by all means, perhaps throwing a darky into the mix would liven things up. Even if this particular one, with a broken leg, broken arm and her jaw in pieces might mostly be in the way.

"At half salary, in that case," he said. "Just look at her, Your Honour." Engineer Engelbrecht van der Westhuizen suggested a salary of five hundred rand per month minus four hundred and twenty rand for room and board. The judge nodded his assent.

Nombeko almost burst out laughing. But only almost, because she hurt all over. What that fat-arse of a judge and liar of an engineer had just suggested was that she work for free for the engineer for more than seven years. This, instead of paying a fine that would hardly add up to a measurable fraction of her collected wealth, no matter how absurdly large and unreasonable it was.

But perhaps this arrangement was the solution to Nombeko's dilemma. She could move in with the engineer, let her wounds heal and run away on the day she felt that the National Library in Pretoria could no longer wait. After all, she was about to be sentenced to domestic service, not prison.

She was considering accepting the judge's suggestion, but she bought herself a few extra seconds to think by arguing a little bit, despite her aching jaw: "That would mean eighty rand per month net pay. I would have to work for the engineer for seven years,

51

three months and twenty days in order to pay it all back. Your Honour, don't you think that's a rather harsh sentence for a person who happened to get run over on a pavement by someone who shouldn't even have been driving on the street, given his alcohol intake?"

The judge was completely taken aback. It wasn't just that the girl had expressed herself. And expressed herself *well*. And called the engineer's sworn description of events into question. She had also calculated the extent of the sentence before anyone else in the room had been close to doing so. He ought to chastise the girl, but . . . he was too curious to know whether her calculations were correct. So he turned to the court aide, who confirmed, after a few minutes, that "Indeed, it looks like we're talking about — as we heard — seven years, three months, and . . . yes . . . about twenty days or so."

Engelbrecht van der Westhuizen took a gulp from the small brown bottle of cough medicine he always had with him in situations where one couldn't simply drink brandy. He explained this gulp by saying that the shock of the horrible accident must have exacerbated his asthma.

But the medicine did him good: "I think we'll round down," he said. "Exactly seven years will do. And anyway, the dents on the car can be hammered out."

Nombeko decided that a few weeks or so with this Westhuizen was better than thirty years in prison. Yes, it was too bad that the library would have to wait, but it was a very long walk there, and most people would prefer not to undertake such a journey with a broken leg. Not to mention all the rest. Including the blister that had formed as a result of the first sixteen miles.

In other words, a little break couldn't hurt, assuming the engineer didn't run her over a second time.

"Thanks, that's generous of you, Engineer van der Westhuizen," she said, thereby accepting the judge's decision.

"Engineer van der Westhuizen" would have to do. She had no intention of calling him "*baas*."

◆ ◆ ◆

Immediately following the trial, Nombeko ended up in the passenger seat beside Engineer van der Westhuizen, who headed north, driving with one hand while swigging a bottle of Klipdrift brandy with the other. The brandy was identical in odour and colour to the cough medicine Nombeko had seen him drain during the trial.

This took place on 16 June 1976.

On the same day, a bunch of school-aged adolescents in Soweto got tired of the government's latest idea: that their already inferior education should henceforth be conducted in Afrikaans. So the students went out into the streets to air their disapproval. They were of the opinion that it was easier to learn something when one understood what one's instructor was saying. And that a text was more accessible to the reader if one could interpret the text in question. Therefore — said the students — their education should continue to be conducted in English.

The surrounding police listened with interest to the youths' reasoning, and then they argued the government's point in that special manner of the South African authorities.

By opening fire.

Straight into the crowd of demonstrators.

Twenty-three demonstrators died more or less instantly. The next day, the police advanced their argument with helicopters and tanks. Before the dust had settled, another hundred human lives had been extinguished. The City of Johannesburg's department of education was therefore able to adjust Soweto's budgetary allocations downward, citing lack of students.

Nombeko avoided experiencing any of this. She had been enslaved by the state and was in a car on the way to her new master's house.

"Is it much farther, Mr Engineer?" she asked, mostly to have something to say.

"No, not really," said Engineer van der Westhuizen. "But you shouldn't speak out of turn. Speaking when you are spoken to will be sufficient."

Engineer Westhuizen was a lot of things. The fact that he was a liar had become clear to Nombeko back in the courtroom. That he was an alcoholic became clear in the car after leaving the courtroom. In addition, he was a fraud when it came to his profession. He didn't understand his own work, but he kept himself at the top by telling lies and exploiting people who did understand it.

This might have been an aside to the whole story if only the engineer hadn't had one of the most secret and dramatic tasks in the world. He was the man who would make South Africa a nuclear weapons nation. It was all being orchestrated from the research facility of Pelindaba, about an hour north of Johannesburg.

Nombeko, of course, knew nothing of this, but her first inkling that things were a bit more complicated than she had originally thought came as they approached the engineer's office.

Just as the Klipdrift ran out, she and the engineer arrived at the facility's outer perimeter. After showing identification they were allowed to enter the gates, passing a ten-foot, twelve-thousand-volt fence. Next there was a fifty-foot stretch that was controlled by double guards with dogs before it was time for the inner perimeter and the next ten-foot fence with the same number of volts. In addition, someone had thought to place a minefield around the entire facility, in the space between the ten-foot fences.

"This is where you will atone for your crime," said the engineer. "And this is where you will live, so you don't take off."

Electric fences, guards with dogs and minefields were variables Nombeko hadn't taken into account in the courtroom a few hours earlier.

"Looks cosy," she said.

"You're talking out of turn again," said the engineer.

◆ ◆ ◆

The South African nuclear weapons programme was begun in 1975, the year before a drunk Engineer van der Westhuizen happened to run over a black girl. There were two reasons he had been sitting at the Hilton Hotel and tossing back brandies until he was gently asked to leave. One was that part about being an alcoholic. The engineer needed at least a full bottle of Klipdrift per day to keep the works going. The other was his bad mood. And his frustration. The engineer had just been pressured by Prime Minister Vorster, who complained that no progress had been made yet even though a year had gone by.

The engineer tried to maintain otherwise. On the business front, they had begun the work exchange with Israel. Sure, this had been initiated by the prime minister himself, but in any case uranium was heading in the direction of Jerusalem, while they had received tritium in return. There were even two Israeli agents permanently stationed at Pelindaba for the sake of the project.

No, the prime minister had no complaints about their collaboration with Israel, Taiwan and others. It was the work itself that was limping along. Or, as the prime minister put it:

"Don't give us a bunch of excuses for one thing and the next. Don't give us any more teamwork right and left. Give us an atomic bomb, for fuck's sake, Mr van der Westhuizen. And then give us five more."

◆ ◆ ◆

While Nombeko settled in behind Pelindaba's double fence, Prime Minister Balthazar Johannes Vorster was sitting in his palace and sighing. He was very busy from early in the morning to late at night. The most pressing matter on his desk right now was that of the six atomic bombs. What if that obsequious Westhuizen wasn't the right man for the job? He talked and talked, but he never delivered.

Vorster muttered to himself about the damn UN, the Communists in Angola, the Soviets and Cuba sending hordes of revolutionaries to southern Africa, and the Marxists who had already taken over in Mozambique. Plus those CIA bastards who always managed to figure out what was going on, and then couldn't shut up about what they knew.

Oh, fuck it, thought B. J. Vorster about the world in general.

The nation was under threat *now*, not once the engineer chose to take his thumb out of his arse.

The prime minister had taken the scenic route to his position. In the late 1930s, as a young man, he had become interested in Nazism. Vorster thought that the German Nazis had interesting methods when it came to separating one sort of people from the next. He also liked to pass this on to anyone who would listen.

Then a world war broke out. Unfortunately for Vorster, South Africa took the side of the Allies (it being part of the British Empire), and Nazis like Vorster were locked up for a few years until the war had been won. Once he was free again, he was more cautious; neither before nor since have Nazi ideals gained ground by being called what they actually are.

By the 1950s, Vorster was considered to be housebroken. In 1961, the same year that Nombeko was born in a shack in Soweto, he was promoted to the position of minister of justice. One year later, he and his police managed to reel in the biggest fish of all — the African National Congress terrorist Nelson Rolihlahla Mandela.

Mandela received a life sentence, of course, and was sent to an island prison outside Cape Town, where he could sit until he rotted away. Vorster thought it might go rather quickly.

While Mandela commenced his anticipated rotting-away, Vorster himself continued to climb the ladder of his career. He had some help with the last crucial step when an African with a very specific problem finally cracked. The man had been classed as white by the system of apartheid, but it was possible they had been wrong, because he looked more black — and therefore he didn't fit in anywhere. The solution to the man's inner torment turned out to be finding B. J. Vorster's predecessor and stabbing him in the stomach with a knife — fifteen times.

The man who was both white and something else was locked up in a psychiatric clinic, where he sat for thirty-three years without ever finding out which race he belonged to.

Only then did he die. Unlike the prime minister with fifteen stab wounds, who, on the one hand, was absolutely certain he was white but, on the other hand, died immediately.

So the country needed a new prime minister. Preferably someone tough. And soon enough, there sat former Nazi Vorster.

When it came to domestic politics, he was content with what he and the nation had achieved. With the new anti-terrorism laws, the government could call anyone a terrorist and lock him or her up for as long as they liked, for any reason they liked. Or for no reason at all.

Another successful project was to create homelands for the various ethnic groups — one country for each sort, except the Xhosa, because there were so many of them that they got two. All they had to do was gather up a certain type of darky, bus them all to a designated homeland, strip them of their South African citizenship, and give them a new one in the name of the homeland. A person who is no longer South African can't claim to have the rights of a South African. Simple mathematics.

When it came to foreign politics, things were a bit trickier. The world outside continually misunderstood the country's ambitions. For example, there was an appalling number of complaints because South Africa was operating on the simple truth that a person who is not white will remain that way once and for all.

Former Nazi Vorster got a certain amount of satisfaction from the collaboration with Israel, though.

They were Jews, of course, but in many ways they were just as misunderstood as Vorster himself.

Oh, fuck it, B. J. Vorster thought for the second time.

What was that bungler Westhuizen up to?

◆ ◆ ◆

Engelbrecht van der Westhuizen was pleased with the new servant Providence had given him. She had managed to get some things done even while limping around with her leg in a brace and her right arm in a sling. Whatever her name was.

At first he had called her "Kaffir Two" to distinguish her from the other black woman at the facility, the one who cleaned in the outer perimeter. But when the bishop of the local Reformed Church learned of this name, the engineer was reprimanded. Blacks deserved more respect than that.

The Church had first allowed blacks to attend the same communion services as whites more than one hundred years ago, even if the former had to wait their turn at the very back until there were so many of them that they might as well have their own churches. The bishop felt that it wasn't the Church's fault that the blacks bred like rabbits.

"Respect," he repeated. "Think about it, Mr Engineer."

The bishop did make an impression on Engelbrecht van der Westhuizen, but that didn't make Nombeko's name any easier to remember. So when spoken to directly she was called "whatsyourname," and indirectly

. . . there was essentially no reason to discuss her as an individual.

Prime Minister Vorster had come to visit twice already, always with a friendly smile, but the implied message was that if there weren't six bombs at the facility soon, then Engineer Westhuizen might not be there, either.

Before his first meeting with the prime minister, the engineer had been planning to lock up whatshername in the broom cupboard. Certainly it was not against the rules to have black and coloured help at the facility, as long as they were never granted leave, but the engineer thought it looked dirty.

The drawback to having her in a cupboard, however, was that then she couldn't be in the vicinity of the engineer, and he had realized early on that it wasn't such a bad idea to have her nearby. For reasons that were impossible to understand, things were always happening in that girl's brain. Whatshername was far more impudent than was really permissible, and she broke as many rules as she could. Among the cheekiest things she'd done was to be in the research facility's library without permission, going so far as to take books with her when she left. The engineer's first instinct was to put a stop to this and get the security division involved for a closer investigation. What would an illiterate from Soweto want with books?

But then he noticed that she was actually *reading* what she had brought with her. This made the whole thing even more remarkable — literacy was, of course, not a trait one often found among the country's illiterate. Then the engineer saw *what* she was reading, and it was *everything*, including advanced mathematics, chemistry, electronic engineering and metallurgy (that is, everything the engineer himself should have been brushing up on). On one occasion, when he took her by surprise with her nose in a book instead of scrubbing the floor, he could see that she was smiling at a number of mathematical formulas.

Looking, nodding and *smiling*.

Truly outrageous. The engineer had never seen the point in studying mathematics. Or anything else. Luckily enough, he had still received top grades at the university to which his father was the foremost donor.

The engineer knew that a person didn't need to know everything about everything. It was easy to get to the top with good grades and the right father, and by taking serious advantage of other people's competence. But in order to keep his job this time, the engineer would have to deliver. Well, not *literally* him, but the researchers and technicians he had made sure to hire and who were currently toiling day and night in his name.

And the team was really moving things forward. The engineer was sure that in the not-too-distant future they would solve the few technical conflicts that remained before the nuclear weapons tests could begin. The research director was no dummy. He was, however, a pain — he insisted on reporting each development that occurred, no matter how small, and he expected a reaction from the engineer each time.

That's where whatshername came in. By letting her page freely through the books in the library, the engineer had left the mathematical door wide open, and she absorbed everything she could on algebraic, transcendental, imaginary and complex numbers, on Euler's constant, on differential and Diophantine equations, and on an infinite (∞) number of other complex things, all more or less incomprehensible to the engineer himself.

In time, Nombeko would have come to be called her boss's right hand, if only she hadn't been a she and above all hadn't had the wrong colour skin. Instead she got to keep the vague title "help", but she was the one who (alongside her cleaning) read the research director's many brick-size tomes describing problems, test results and analyses. That is, what the engineer couldn't manage to do on his own.

"What is this crap about?" Engineer Westhuizen said one day, pressing another pile of papers into his cleaning woman's hands.

Nombeko read it and returned with the answer.

"It's an analysis of the consequences of the static and dynamic overpressure of bombs with different numbers of kilotons."

"Tell me in plain language," said the engineer.

"The stronger the bomb is, the more buildings blow up," Nombeko clarified.

"Come on, the average mountain gorilla would know *that*. Am I completely surrounded by idiots?" said the engineer, who poured himself a brandy and told his cleaning woman to go away.

Nombeko thought that Pelindaba, as a prison, was just short of exceptional. She had her own bed, access to a bathroom instead of being responsible for four thousand outhouses, two meals a day and fruit for lunch. And her own library. Or . . . it wasn't actually her own, but no one besides Nombeko was interested in it. And it wasn't particularly extensive; it was far from the class she imagined the one in Pretoria to be in. And some of the books on the shelves were old or irrelevant or both. But still.

For these reasons she continued rather cheerfully to serve her time for her poor judgement in allowing herself to be run over on a pavement by a plastered man that winter day in Johannesburg in 1976. What she was experiencing now was in every way better than emptying latrines in the world's largest human garbage dump.

When enough months had gone by, it was time to start counting years instead. Of course, she gave a thought or two to how she might be able to spirit herself out of Pelindaba prematurely. It would be a challenge as good as any to force her way through the fences, the minefield, the guard dogs and the alarm.

Dig a tunnel?

No, that was such a stupid thought that she dropped it immediately.

Hitchhike?

No, any hitchhiker would be discovered by the guards' German shepherds, and then all one could do was hope that they went for the throat first so that the rest wasn't too bad.

Bribery?

Well, maybe . . . but she would have only one chance, and whomever she tried this on would probably take the diamonds and report her, in South African fashion.

Steal someone else's identity, then?

Yes, that might work. But the hard part would be stealing someone else's skin colour.

Nombeko decided to take a break from her thoughts of escape. Anyway, it was possible that her only chance would be to make herself invisible and equip herself with wings. Wings alone wouldn't suffice: she would be shot down by the eight guards in the four towers.

She was just over fifteen when she was locked up within the double fences and the minefield, and she was well on her way to seventeen when the engineer very solemnly informed her that he had arranged a valid South African passport for her, even though she was black. The fact was, without one she could no longer have access to all the corridors that the indolent engineer felt she ought to have access to. The rules had been issued by the South African intelligence agency, and Engineer Westhuizen knew how to pick his battles.

He kept the passport in his desk drawer and, thanks to his incessant need to be domineering, he made lots of noise about how he was forced to keep it locked up.

"That's so you won't get it into your head to run away, whatsyourname. Without a passport you can't leave the country, and we can always find you, sooner or later," said the engineer, giving an ugly grin.

Nombeko replied that it said in the passport whathernamewas, in case the engineer was curious, and she added that he had long since given her the responsibility for his key cabinet. Which included the key to his desk drawer.

"And I haven't run away because of it," said Nombeko, thinking that it was more the guards, the dogs, the alarm, the minefields and the twelve thousand volts in the fence that kept her there.

The engineer glared at his cleaning woman. She was being impudent again. It was enough to make a person crazy. Especially since she was always right.

That damned creature.

Two hundred and fifty people were working, at various levels, on the most secret of all secret projects. Nombeko could state with certainty early on that the man at the very top lacked talent in every area except feathering his own nest. And he was lucky (up until the day he wasn't any more).

During one phase of the project development, one of the most difficult problems that needed to be solved was the constant leakage in experiments with uranium hexafluoride. The engineer had a blackboard on the wall of his office upon which he drew lines and made arrows, fumbling his way through formulas and other things to make it appear as if he were thinking. The engineer sat in his easy chair mumbling "hydrogen-bearing gas", "uranium hexafluoride" and "leakage" interspersed with curses in both English and Afrikaans. Perhaps Nombeko should have let him mumble away:

she was there to clean. But at last she said, "Now, I don't know much about what a 'hydrogen-bearing gas' is, and I've hardly even heard of uranium hexafluoride. But I *can* see from the slightly hard-to-interpret attempts on the wall that you are having an auto catalytic problem."

The engineer said nothing, but he looked past whatshername at the door into the hallway in order to make sure that no one was standing there and listening, since he was about to be befuddled by this strange being for the umpteenth time in a row.

"Should I take your silence to mean that I have permission to continue? After all, you usually wish me to answer when I'm spoken to and only then."

"Yes, get on with it then!" said the engineer.

Nombeko gave a friendly smile and said that as far as she was concerned, it didn't really matter what the different variables were called, it was still possible to do mathematics with them.

"We'll call hydrogen-bearing gas A, and uranium hexafluoride can be B," Nombeko said.

And she walked over to the blackboard on the wall, erased the engineer's nonsense, and wrote the rate equation for an autocatalytic reaction of the first order.

When the engineer just stared blankly at the blackboard, she explained her reasoning by drawing a sigmoid curve.

When she had done that, she realized that Engineer van der Westhuizen understood no more of what she had written than any latrine emptier would have in the same situation. Or, for that matter, an assistant from the City of Johannesburg's department of sanitation.

"Please, Engineer," she said. "Try to understand. I have floors to scrub. The gas and the fluoride don't get along and their unhappiness runs away with itself."

"What's the solution?" said the engineer.

"I don't know," said Nombeko. "I haven't had time to think about it. Like I said, I'm the cleaning woman here."

In that instant, one of Engineer van der Westhuizen's many qualified colleagues came through the door. He had been sent by the research director to share some good news: the team had discovered that the problem was autocatalytic in nature; this resulted in chemical impurities in the filter of the processing machine, and they would soon be able to present a solution.

There was no reason for the colleague to say any of this, because just behind the Kaffir with the mop he saw what the engineer had written on his blackboard.

"Oh, I see that you have already figured out what I came to tell you, boss. I won't disturb you, then," said the colleague, and he turned round in the doorway.

Engineer van der Westhuizen sat behind his desk in silence and poured another tumbler full of Klipdrift.

Nombeko said that this certainly was lucky, wasn't it? She would leave him alone in just a minute, but first she had a few questions. The first was whether the engineer thought it would be appropriate for her to deliver a mathematical explanation for how the team could increase the capacity from twelve thousand

SWUs per year to twenty thousand, with a tail assay of 0.46 per cent.

The engineer did.

The other question was whether the engineer might be so kind as to order a new scrubbing brush for the office, since his dog had chewed the old one to pieces.

The engineer replied that he wasn't making any promises, but he would see what he could do.Nombeko thought she might as well appreciate the bright spots in her existence, as long as she was locked up with no possibility for escape. It would, for example, be exciting to see how long that sham of an engineer Westhuizen would last.

And all told, she did have it pretty good. She read her books, preferably while no one was looking; she mopped a few hallways and emptied a few ashtrays; and she read the research team's analyses and explained them to the engineer as plainly as she could.

She spent her free time with the other help. They belonged to a minority that the regime of apartheid found more difficult to categorize; according to the rules they were "miscellaneous Asians". More precisely, they were Chinese.

Chinese people as a race had ended up in South Africa almost a hundred years earlier, at a time when the country needed cheap labour (that also didn't complain too bloody much) in the gold mines outside Johannesburg. That was history now, but Chinese colonies remained, and the language flourished.

The three Chinese girls (little sister, middle sister and big sister) were locked in with Nombeko at night. At first they were standoffish, but since mah-jongg is so much better with four than with three, it was worth a try, especially when the girl from Soweto didn't seem to be as stupid as they had reason to believe, given that she wasn't yellow.

Nombeko was happy to play, and she had soon learned almost everything about pong, kong and chow, as well as all possible winds in every imaginable direction. She had the advantage of being able to memorize all 144 of the tiles, so she won three out of four hands and let one of the girls win the fourth.

The Chinese girls and Nombeko also spent some time each week with the latter telling them all that had happened in the world since the last time, according to what she had been able to pick up here and there in the hallways and through the walls. On the one hand, it was not a comprehensive news report; on the other, the audience's standards weren't all that high. For example, when Nombeko reported that China had just decided that Aristotle and Shakespeare would no longer be forbidden in the country, the girls replied that this was sure to make both of them happy.

The sisters in misfortune became friends by way of the news reports and the game. And thanks to the characters and symbols on all of the tiles, the girls were inspired to teach Nombeko their Chinese dialect, upon which everyone had a good laugh at how quickly she learned and at the sisters' less-successful attempts at the Xhosa Nombeko had learned from her mother.

From a historical perspective, the three Chinese girls'
morals were more dubious than Nombeko's. They had
ended up in the engineer's possession in approximately
the same way, but for fifteen years instead of seven.
They had happened to meet the engineer at a bar in
Johannesburg; he had made a pass at all three of them
at the same time but was told that they needed money
for a sick relative and wanted to sell ... not their
bodies, but rather a valuable family heirloom.

The engineer's first priority was his horniness, but
his second priority was the suspicion that he could
make a killing, so he followed the girls home. There
they showed him a patterned pottery goose from the
Han dynasty, from approximately one hundred years
before Christ. The girls wanted twenty thousand rand
for the goose; the engineer realized that it must be
worth at least ten times more, maybe a hundred! But
the girls weren't just girls — they were also Chinese, so
he offered them fifteen thousand in cash outside the
bank the next morning ("Five thousand each, or
nothing!") and the idiots agreed to it.

The unique goose was given a place of honor on a
pedestal in the engineer's office until a year later when
an Israeli Mossad agent, also a participant in the
nuclear weapons project, took a closer look at the piece
and declared it to be junk within ten seconds. The
investigation that followed, led by an engineer with
murder in his eyes, found that the goose had in fact
been produced not by craftsmen in the province of
Zhejiang during the Han dynasty approximately one

hundred years before Christ, but rather by three young Chinese girls in a suburb of Johannesburg, during no dynasty at all, approximately one thousand, nine hundred and seventy five years *after* Christ.

But the girls had been careless enough to show him the goose in their own home. So the engineer and the legal system got hold of all three of them. Only two rand were left of the fifteen thousand, which was why the girls were now locked up at Pelindaba for at least ten more years. "Among ourselves, we call the engineer '鵝'," said one of the girls.

"The goose," Nombeko translated.

What the Chinese girls wanted most of all was to return to the Chinese quarter of Johannesburg and continue producing geese from the time before Christ, but just do it a bit more elegantly than last time.

In the meantime, they had as little to complain about as Nombeko. Their work responsibilities were, among other things, to serve food to the engineer and the guards, as well as handle incoming and outgoing post. Especially the outgoing post. Everything, large and small, that could be stolen without being missed too much was quite simply addressed to the girls' mother and placed in the out-box. Their mother received it all gratefully and sold it on, pleased with herself for once having made the investment of letting her girls learn to read and write in English.

Now and then they made a mess of things, though, because their methods were sloppy and risky. Like the time one of them mixed up the address labels and the prime minister himself called Engineer Westhuizen to ask why he had received eight candles, two hole-punches and four empty binders in his package — just as the Chinese girls' mother received and immediately burned a four-hundred-page technical report on the disadvantages of using neptunium as a base for a fission charge.

◆ ◆ ◆

Nombeko was irritated that it had taken her so long to realize what a fix she was in. In practice, given the way things had unfolded, she hadn't been sentenced to seven years in the engineer's service at all. She was there for life. Unlike the three Chinese girls, she had full insight into what was the world's most top secret project. As long as there were twelve-thousand-volt fences between her and anyone else she could tattle to, it was no problem. But what if she were released? She was a combination of worthless black woman and security risk. So how long would she be allowed to live? Ten seconds. Or twenty. If she was lucky.

Her situation could be described as a mathematical equation with no solution. Because if she helped the engineer to succeed in his task, he would be praised, retire and receive a gilt-edged pension from the state, while she — who knew everything she shouldn't know — received a shot to the back of the head.

If, however, she did her best to make him fail, the engineer would be disgraced, get fired and receive a much more modest pension, while she herself would still receive a shot to the back of the head.

In short: this was the equation she could not solve. All she could do was try to walk a tightrope — that is, do her best to make sure the engineer wasn't revealed as the sham he was while at the same time trying to prolong the project as much as possible. That in itself wouldn't protect her from that shot to the back of the head, but the longer she could put it off, the greater chance there was that something would happen in the meantime. Like a revolution or a staff mutiny or something else impossible to believe in.

Assuming she couldn't find a way out after all.

In the absence of other ideas, she sat at the window in the library as often as she could, in order to study the activity at the gates. She hung around there at various times of day and made note of the guards' routines.

What she quickly discovered, among other things, was that every vehicle that came in or went out was searched by both guards and dog — except when the engineer was in it. Or the research director. Or one of the two Mossad agents. Apparently these four were above suspicion. Unfortunately, they also had better parking spots than the others. Nombeko could make her way to the big garage, crawl into a boot — and be discovered by both guard and dog on duty. The latter was under instructions to bite first and ask master later. But the small garage, where the important people parked, where there were boots one might survive in — she didn't have access to that. The garage key was one of the few that the engineer did not keep in the cupboard Nombeko was responsible for. He needed it every day, so he carried it with him.

74

Another thing Nombeko observed was that the black cleaning woman in the outer perimeter actually did set foot within the boundaries of Pelindaba each time she emptied the green rubbish bin just beside the inner of the two twelve-thousand-volt fences. This took place every other day, and it fascinated Nombeko, because she was pretty sure that the cleaning woman didn't have clearance to go there but that the guards let it go in order to avoid emptying their own crap.

This gave rise to a bold thought. Nombeko could make her way unseen to the rubbish bin via the big garage, crawl into it, and hitch a ride with the black woman past the gates and out to the skips on the free side. The woman emptied the bin according to a strict schedule at 4.05p.m. every other day, and she survived the manoeuvre only because the guard dogs had learned not to tear this particular darky apart without asking first. On the other hand, they did nose suspiciously at the bin each time.

So she would have to put the dogs out of commission for an afternoon or so. Then, and only then, would the stowaway have a chance of surviving her escape. A tiny bit of food poisoning — might that work?

Nombeko involved the three Chinese girls because they were responsible for feeding the entire staff of guards and all of Sector G, both people and animals.

"Of course!" said the big sister when Nombeko brought it up. "We happen to be experts in dog poisoning, all three of us. Or at least two of us."

By now, Nombeko had ceased being surprised by whatever the Chinese girls did or said, but this was still exceptional. She asked the big sister for details about what she'd just said so that Nombeko wouldn't have to wonder for the rest of her life. However long that might be.

Well, before the Chinese girls and their mother started working in the lucrative counterfeiting industry, their mother had run a dog cemetery right next to the white neighbourhood of Parktown West outside Johannesburg. Business was bad; dogs ate as well and as nutritiously as people generally did in that area, so they lived far too long. But then their mother realized that the big sister and the middle sister could increase their turnover by putting out poisoned dog food here and there in the surrounding parks, where the whites' poodles and Pekinese ran free. At the time, the little sister was too young and might easily have got it into her head to taste the dog food if she got hold of it.

In a short time the owner of the dog cemetery had twice as much to do. And the family would probably still be making a good living today, if only they hadn't become, to tell the truth, a bit too greedy. Because when there were more dead dogs in the park than living ones, those white racists had pointed straight at the only Chink in the area and her daughters.

"Yes, that was certainly prejudiced of them," said Nombeko.

Their mother had had to pack her bags quickly, and she hid herself and her children in central Johannesburg and changed careers.

76

That was a few years ago now, but the girls could probably remember the various ways of dosing dog food.

"Well, now we're talking about eight dogs — and about poisoning them just enough," said Nombeko. "So they get a little bit sick for a day or two. No more than that."

"Sounds like a typical case of antifreeze poisoning," said the middle sister.

"I was just thinking the same thing," said the big sister.

And then they argued about the appropriate dose. The middle sister thought that a cup and a half should do, but the big sister pointed out that they were dealing with large German shepherds here, not some little Chihuahua.

In the end, the girls agreed that two cups was the right amount to put the dogs in a dreadful condition until the next day.

The girls approached the problem in such a carefree manner that Nombeko already regretted asking for their help. Didn't they realize how much trouble they would be in when the poisoned dog food was traced back to them?

"Nah," said the little sister. "It will all work out. We'll have to start by ordering a bottle of antifreeze, otherwise we can't poison anything."

Now Nombeko was twice as regretful. Didn't they realize that the security personnel would figure out it was them in just a few minutes, once they discovered what had been added to their usual shopping list?

And then Nombeko thought of something.

"Wait a minute," she said. "Don't do anything until I get back. Nothing!"

The girls watched Nombeko go in surprise. What was she up to?

The fact was that Nombeko had thought of something she'd read in one of the research director's countless reports to the engineer. It wasn't about antifreeze, but ethylene glycol. It said in the report that the researchers were experimenting with liquids that had a boiling point of over one hundred degrees Celsius in order to gain a few tenths of a second by raising the temperature at which critical mass would be reached. That was where the ethylene glycol came in. Didn't antifreeze and ethylene glycol have similar properties?

If the research facility's library was at its worst when it came to the latest news, it was at its best when it came to more general information. Such as confirmation that ethylene glycol and antifreeze were more than almost the same thing. They *were* the same thing.

Nombeko borrowed two of the keys in the engineer's cupboard and sneaked down to the big garage and into the chemicals cupboard next to the electrical station. There she found a nearly full seven-gallon barrel of ethylene glycol. She poured a gallon into the bucket she'd brought along and returned to the girls.

"Here you go — this is plenty, with some to spare," she said.

Nombeko and the girls decided that they would start by mixing a very mild dose into the dog food to see what would happen, and then they would increase the dose until all eight dogs were off sick without causing the guards to become suspicious.

Therefore the Chinese girls lowered the dose from two cups to one and three-quarters, upon Nombeko's recommendation, but they made the mistake of letting the little sister take care of the dosing itself — that is, the one sister of the three who had been too little in the good old days. Thus she mixed in one and three-quarters cups of ethylene glycol *per dog* in the first, conservative round. Twelve hours later, all eight dogs were as dead as those in Parktown West a few years earlier. Furthermore, the guard commander's food-sneaking cat was in a critical condition.

One characteristic of ethylene glycol is that it rapidly enters the bloodstream via the intestines. Then the liver turns it into glycolaldehyde, glycolic acid and oxalate. If there is enough of these, they take out the kidneys before affecting the lungs and heart. The direct cause of death in the eight dogs was cardiac arrest.

The immediate results of the youngest Chinese girl's miscalculation were that the alarm was sounded, that the guards went on high alert, and that it was, of course, impossible for Nombeko to smuggle herself out in a rubbish bin.

It was only day two before the girls were called in for interrogation, but while they were sitting there and flatly denying involvement, the security personnel found a nearly empty bucket of ethylene glycol in the boot of one of the 250 workers' cars. Nombeko had access to the garage, thanks to the engineer's key cupboard, of course; the boot in question was the only one that happened to be unlocked, and she had to put the bucket somewhere. The owner of the car was a half-ethical sort of guy — on the one hand, he would never betray his country; on the other hand, as luck would have it, he had chosen that very day to swipe his department director's briefcase and the money and chequebook it contained. This was found alongside the bucket, and when all was said and done, the man had been seized, interrogated, fired . . . and sentenced to six months in prison for theft, plus thirty-two years for an act of terror.

"That was close," said the little sister once the three sisters were no longer suspects.

"Shall we try again?" the middle sister wondered.

"But then we'd have to wait for them to get new dogs," said the big sister. "The old ones are all gone."

Nombeko didn't say anything. But she thought that her prospects for the future weren't much brighter than those of the director's cat, who had started having convulsions.

CHAPTER
FOUR

On a Good Samaritan, a bicycle thief and a wife who smoked more and more

Since Henrietta's money was gone, Ingmar had to do most of his hitchhiking from Nice back to Södertälje without eating. But in Malmö, the dirty, hungry junior post office clerk happened to meet a soldier of the Salvation Army who was on his way home after a long day in the service of the Lord. Ingmar asked if the soldier could spare a piece of bread.

The Salvationist immediately allowed himself to be governed by the spirit of love and compassion, so much so that Ingmar was allowed to come home with him.

Once there, he served mashed turnips with pork and then settled Ingmar in his bed; he himself would sleep on the floor before the stove. Ingmar yawned and said that he was impressed by the soldier's friendliness. To this the soldier replied that the explanation for his actions was in the Bible, not least in the Gospel of Luke, where one could read about the Good Samaritan. The Salvationist asked Ingmar if he would mind if he read a few lines from the Holy Book.

"Not at all," said Ingmar, "but read quietly because I need to sleep."

And then he dozed off. He woke the next morning to the scent of something baking.

After breakfast he thanked the charitable soldier, said farewell, and then stole the soldier's bicycle. As he pedalled away, he wondered whether it was the Bible that said something about necessity knowing no law. Ingmar wasn't sure.

In any case, he sold the stolen goods in Lund and used the money to buy a train ticket all the way home.

Henrietta met him as he stepped through the door. Before she could open her mouth to welcome him home, he informed her that it was now time to make a child.

Henrietta did have a number of questions, not the least of which was why Ingmar suddenly wanted to get into bed without his damned box of American soldiers' condoms in hand, but she wasn't so stupid as to deny him. All she asked was that her husband shower first, because he smelled almost as bad as he looked.

The couple's very first condom-free adventure lasted for four minutes. Then Ingmar was finished. But Henrietta was still pleased. Her beloved fool was home again and he had actually thrown the condoms into the bin before they went to bed. Could this mean that they were done with all the foolishness? And that they might be blessed with a little baby?

Fifteen hours later, Ingmar woke up again. He started by telling her that he had in fact made contact with the king down in Nice. Or the other way round, really. The king had made contact with him. Well, with his forehead. Using his cane.

"Good heavens," said Henrietta.

Yes, you could say that again. But actually, Ingmar was thankful. The king had made him see clearly again. Made him realize that the monarchy was of the devil and must be eradicated.

"Of the devil?" said his startled wife.

"And must be eradicated."

But such a thing demanded both cunning and patience. And also that Ingmar and Henrietta had a child as part of the plan. His name would be Holger, incidentally.

"Who?" said Henrietta.

"Our son, of course."

Henrietta, who had spent her entire adult life silently longing for an Elsa, said that it could just as easily be a daughter, if they had a child at all. But then she was informed that she should stop being so negative. If she would instead serve Ingmar a little food, he promised to tell her how everything would be from now on.

So Henrietta did. She served *pytt i panna* with beetroot and eggs.

Between bites, Ingmar told her about his encounter with Gustaf V in greater detail. For the first but by no means last time he told her about "messenger boy" and "scoundrel". For the second but by no means last time he described the silver cane to the forehead.

"And that's why the monarchy must be eradicated?" said Henrietta. "With cunning and patience? How do you mean to use the cunning and patience?"

What she thought — but didn't say — was that neither patience nor cunning had historically been salient traits of her husband's.

Well, when it came to patience, Ingmar realized that even if he and Henrietta had created a child as recently as the day before, it would take several months before the kid arrived and, thereafter, years before Holger was old enough to take over from his father.

"Take over what?" Henrietta wondered.

"The battle, my dear Henrietta. The battle."

Ingmar had had plenty of time to think while he hitchhiked through Europe. It wouldn't be easy to eradicate the monarchy. It was something of a lifelong project. Or even more than that. That was where Holger came in. Because if Ingmar died before the battle was won, his son would step in.

"Why Holger in particular?" Henrietta wondered, among all the other things she was still wondering.

Well, the boy could be called whatever he wanted, really; the battle was more important than the name. But it would be impractical not to call him *something*. At first Ingmar had considered Wilhelm after the famous author and republican Vilhelm Moberg, but then he had realized that one of the king's sons had the same name, with the addition of "Prince and Duke of Södermanland".

Instead he had gone through other names, from *A* onwards, and when he got to *H*, while biking from

Malmö to Lund, he happened to think of that Salvationist he had got to know just the day before. The soldier's name was Holger, and he certainly did have a good heart, even if he was careless with the amount of air in his tyres. The honesty and decency Holger had shown him was really something, and Ingmar couldn't think of a single nobleman on Earth with that name. Holger was precisely as far from the book of nobility as the situation demanded.

With that, Henrietta got just about the whole picture: Sweden's leading monarchist would from now on devote his life to bringing the royal family crashing down. He intended to follow this vocation to the grave, and before then he would make sure that his descendants were ready when the time came. All in all, this made him both cunning and patient.

"Not descendants," said Ingmar. "Descendant. His name will be Holger."

♦ ♦ ♦

As it turned out, however, Holger was nowhere near as eager as his father. During the next fourteen years, Ingmar ended up spending his time on essentially two things:

1. Reading everything he could get his hands on about infertility, and
2. Comprehensive and unconventional defamation of the king as a phenomenon and as a person.

In addition to this, he did not neglect his work as a clerk of the lowest possible rank at the Södertälje Post Office any more than to the extent that his boss could put up with; thus he avoided being fired.

Once he had gone through the entire city library in Södertälje, Ingmar regularly took the train back and forth to Stockholm, to the Royal Library. A hell of a name, but they had books to spare there.

Ingmar learned all that was worth knowing about ovulation problems, chromosomal abnormalities and dysfunctional sperm. As he dug deeper into the archive, he also took in information of more dubious scientific merit.

So, for example, on certain days he would walk around the house naked from the waist down between the time he got home from work (usually fifteen minutes before his shift was over) until it was time to go to bed. This way he kept his scrotum cool and, according to what Ingmar had read, this was good for the motility of his sperm.

"Can you stir the soup while I hang up the laundry, Ingmar?" Henrietta might say.

"No, my scrotum would be too close to the stove," Ingmar answered.

Henrietta still loved her husband because he was so full of life, but she needed to balance things out with an extra John Silver now and then. And one more. And, incidentally, yet another one that time Ingmar was trying to be nice by going to the grocery store to buy cream — naked down below out of sheer forgetfulness.

Otherwise he was more crazy than he was forgetful. For example, he had learned when to expect Henrietta's periods. This way he could take off during those futile days in order to make life miserable for his head of state. Which he did indeed, in big ways and small.

Among other things, he managed to honour His Majesty on the king's ninetieth birthday on 16 June 1948, by unfurling a thirty-yard-wide banner that read DIE, YOU OLD GOAT, DIE! over Kungsgatan and the king's motorcade at just the right moment. By this point, Gustaf V's sight was very poor, but a blind person practically could have seen what the banner said. According to the next day's *Dagens Nyheter*, the king had said that "The guilty party shall be arrested and brought to me!"

So *now* he wanted to see Ingmar.

After his success on Kungsgatan, Ingmar lay relatively low until October 1950, when he hired a young and unsuspecting tenor from the Stockholm Opera to sing "Bye, Bye, Baby" outside the window of Drottningholm Palace, where Gustaf V lay on his deathbed. The tenor took a licking from the group of people keeping vigil outside, while Ingmar, who was familiar with the surrounding shrubbery, managed to get away. The battered tenor wrote him an angry letter in which he demanded not only the fee of two hundred kronor as previously agreed, but also five hundred kronor for pain and suffering. But because Ingmar had hired the tenor under a fake name and an even faker address, the demand went nowhere except to the Lövsta rubbish dump, where the site manager read it, crumpled it up, and threw it into Incinerator Number Two.

In 1955, Ingmar followed the new king's royal tour around the country without managing to cause any problems at all. He was near despair, and he decided that he had to be bolder and not settle for just opinion building. For the king's fat arse was more secure on the throne than ever.

"Can't you let it go now?" said Henrietta.

"You're being negative again, my darling. I've heard that it takes positive thinking to become pregnant. By the way, I also read that you shouldn't drink mercury — it's harmful to an early pregnancy."

"Mercury?" said Henrietta. "Why on earth would I drink mercury?"

"That's what I'm saying! And you can't have soy in your food."

"Soy? What's that?"

"I don't know. But don't put it in your food."

In August 1960, Ingmar had a new pregnancy idea; once again it was something he'd read. It was just that it was a bit embarrassing to bring up with Henrietta.

"Um, if you stand on your head while we . . . do it . . . then it's easier for the sperm to . . ."

"On my head?"

Henrietta asked her husband if he was nuts, and she realized that the thought had actually occurred to her.

But by all means. Nothing would come of it anyway. She had become resigned.

What was even more surprising was that the bizarre position made the whole thing more pleasant than it had been in a long time. The adventure was full of delighted cries from both parties. Once she discovered that Ingmar hadn't fallen asleep right away, Henrietta went so far as to make a suggestion:

"That wasn't half bad, darling. Should we try once more?"

Ingmar surprised himself by still being awake. He considered what Henrietta had just said, and replied, "Yes, what the heck."

Whether it was the first time that night or the next time was impossible to know, but after thirteen infertile years, Henrietta was finally pregnant.

"Holger, my Holger, you're on your way!" Ingmar hollered at her belly when she told him.

Henrietta, who knew enough about both birds and bees not to rule out an Elsa, went to the kitchen to have a cigarette.

◆ ◆ ◆

In the months that followed, Ingmar ramped things up. Each evening, sitting before Henrietta's growing belly, he read aloud from Vilhelm Moberg's *Why I Am a Republican*. At breakfast each morning, he made small talk with Holger through his wife's navel, discussing whichever republican thoughts filled him at the moment. More often than not, Martin Luther was made a scapegoat for having thought that "We must fear and love God, so that we will neither look down on our parents or superiors nor irritate them."

There were at least two faults in Luther's reasoning. The first was that part about God — he wasn't chosen by the people. And he couldn't be deposed. Sure, a person could convert if he wished, but gods all seemed to be cut from the same cloth.

The other was that we shouldn't "irritate our superiors". Who were the superiors in question, and why shouldn't we irritate them?

Henrietta seldom interfered with Ingmar's monologues to her stomach, but now and then she had to interrupt the activity because otherwise the food would burn on the stove.

"Wait, I'm not finished," Ingmar would say.

"But it's the porridge," Henrietta replied. "You and my navel will have to continue your talk tomorrow if you don't want the house to burn down."

And then it was time. A whole month early. Luckily, Ingmar had just returned home when Henrietta's waters broke; he had been at the far-too-goddamned-Royal Mail Service where he had finally agreed — upon threat of reprisals — to stop drawing horns on the forehead of Gustaf VI Adolf on all the stamps he could get his hands on. And then things progressed rapidly. Henrietta crawled into bed while Ingmar made such a mess of things when he went to call the midwife that he pulled the telephone out of the wall, cord and all. He was still standing in the kitchen doorway and swearing when Henrietta gave birth to their child in the next room.

"When you're finished swearing, you're welcome to come in," she panted. "But bring scissors. You have an umbilical cord to cut."

Ingmar couldn't find any scissors (he didn't really know his way around the kitchen), but he did find wire cutters in the toolbox.

"Boy or girl?" the mother wondered.

For the sake of formality, Ingmar glanced at where the answer to that question lay, and then he said, "Sure enough, it's Holger."

And then, just as he was about to kiss his wife on the lips, she said:

"Ow! I think another one is on the way."

The new father was confused. First he nearly got to experience the birth of his son — if only he hadn't got caught in the telephone cord in the hall. And then, within the next few minutes, came . . . *another* son!

Ingmar didn't have time to process this fact straightaway, because Henrietta's weak but clear voice gave him a number of instructions concerning the things he had to do so as not to risk the lives of mother and children.

But then things calmed down; everything had gone well, except that Ingmar was sitting there with two sons on his lap when he'd been so clear that there should be only one. They shouldn't have done it twice in one night, because look how complicated everything was now.

But Henrietta told her husband to stop talking nonsense, and she looked at her two sons: first one and then the other. And then she said, "I think it seems like the one on the left is Holger."

"Yes," mumbled Ingmar. "Or the one on the right."

This could have been solved by deciding that it was reasonable to say the firstborn was the real one, but in the general chaos with the placenta and everything, Ingmar had mixed up who was first and who second, and now he couldn't tell up from down.

"Damn it!" he said, and was immediately reprimanded by his wife.

Just because there happened to be too many of them didn't mean that the first words their sons heard should be curses.

Ingmar stopped talking. He thought through their situation again. And he made a decision.

"That one is Holger," he said, pointing to the child on the right.

"All right, absolutely," said Henrietta. "And who is the other one?"

"That one is Holger, too."

"Holger and Holger?" said Henrietta, becoming acutely in need of a cigarette. "Are you really sure, Ingmar?"

He said that he was.

PART TWO

The more I see of men,
the more I like my dog.

Madame de Staël

CHAPTER
FIVE

On an anonymous letter, peace on earth and a hungry scorpion

Engineer Westhuizen's servant relapsed into the distant hope that a general societal change would come to her rescue. But it wasn't easy for her to predict the chances of anything that might give her a future at all, whatever the quality of that future might be.

The books in the library of the research facility gave her some context, of course, but most of what was on the shelves was ten or more years old. Among other things, Nombeko had skimmed through a two-hundred-page document from 1924 in which a London professor considered himself to have proved that there would never be another war, thanks to a combination of the League of Nations and the spread of the increasingly popular jazz.

It was easier to keep track of what was going on within the fences and walls of the facility. Unfortunately the latest reports said that the engineer's clever colleagues had solved the autocatalytic issue and others besides, and they were now ready for a test detonation. A successful test would bring the whole project far too close to completion for Nombeko's comfort, because she wanted to keep living for a while longer.

The only thing she could do there and then was try to slow their progress down a bit. Preferably in such a way that the government in Pretoria would not start to suspect that Westhuizen was as useless as he was. Perhaps it would be enough to put a temporary stop to the drilling that had just begun in the Kalahari Desert.

Even though things had gone as they had with the antifreeze, Nombeko once again turned to the Chinese girls for help. She asked if she could send a letter through them, via the girls' mother. How did that all work, by the way? Wasn't outgoing post checked at all?

Yes, of course it was. There was a white on the guard staff who did nothing but go through everything that wasn't being sent to an addressee who already had security clearance. At the least suspicion he would open the outgoing post. And he would interrogate the sender, no exceptions.

This would, of course, have been an insurmountable problem if the director of security hadn't held a briefing a few years ago with those responsible for the post. Once he had told the Chinese girls in great detail about the security measures in place, adding that such measures were necessary because not a single person could be trusted, he excused himself to go to the bathroom. Whereupon the Chinese girls proved him right: as soon as they were alone in the room, they skipped around his desk, fed the correct paper into the typewriter, and added another addressee with security clearance to the 114 that already existed.

"Your mother," said Nombeko.

The girls smiled and nodded. To be on the safe side, they had given their mother a nice title before her name. Cheng Lian looked suspicious. *Professor* Cheng Lian inspired confidence. The logic of racism was no more complicated than that.

Nombeko thought that a Chinese name ought to have caused someone to react, even with the title of professor, but taking risks and getting away with them seemed once and for all to be part of the girls' nature — aside from the reason they were as locked up as she was. And the name had already been working for several years, so it ought to work for one more day. So did this mean that Nombeko could send a letter in a letter to Professor Cheng Lian, and the girls' mother would forward it?

"Absolutely," said the girls, showing no curiosity about whom Nombeko wanted to send a message to.

To:
President James Earl Carter Jr
The White House, Washington
Hello, Mr President. You might be interested to know that South Africa, under leadership of a regularly intoxicated ass, is planning to detonate one atomic bomb of approximately three megatons within the next three months. This will take place in early 1978 in the Kalahari Desert, more specifically, at these exact coordinates: 26°44'26"S, 22°11'32" E. Afterwards, the plan is

for South Africa to equip itself with five more of the same type, to use as it sees fit.
Sincerely,
A Friend

Wearing rubber gloves, Nombeko closed the envelope, addressed it and added "Death to America!" in one corner. Then she put it all in another envelope that was expedited the very next day to a professor in Johannesburg who had security clearance and a Chinese-sounding name.

◆ ◆ ◆

The White House in Washington was constructed by black slaves imported from Nombeko's Africa. It was a majestic building from the start, and it was even more impressive 177 years later. The building contained 132 rooms, 35 bathrooms, 6 levels, a bowling alley and a cinema. And an awful lot of staff, who between them received more than thirty-three thousand pieces of post per month.

Each one was X-rayed, subjected to the sensitive noses of specially trained dogs, and visually inspected before they went to each individual recipient.

Nombeko's letter made it through both X-ray and dogs, but when a sleepy yet observant inspector saw "Death to America" on an envelope addressed to the president himself, the alarm was sounded. Twelve hours later, the letter had been flown to Langley, Virginia, where it was shown to CIA director Stansfield M.

Turner. The debriefing agent described the envelope and informed him that the fingerprints on it were limited in extent and placed in such a way that they were unlikely to lead to anything more than various postal workers; that the letter had not caused the radiation sensors to react; that the postmark appeared to be authentic; that it had been sent from postal zone nine in Johannesburg, South Africa, eight days earlier; and that a computer analysis indicated that the text had been formed from words cut out of the book *Peace on Earth*, which had been written by a British professor who first argued that the combination of the League of Nations and jazz would bring good fortune to the world and then, in 1939, took his own life.

"Jazz is supposed to bring peace on earth?" was the CIA director's first comment.

"Like I said, sir, he took his own life," the agent answered.

The CIA director thanked the agent and was left alone with the letter. Three phone calls and twenty minutes later, it was clear that the contents of the letter were in complete agreement with the information he had, embarrassingly enough, received from the Soviets three weeks earlier but had not believed at the time. The only difference was the exact coordinates in the anonymous letter. All in all, the information appeared to be extremely credible. Now there were two main thoughts in the CIA director's head:

1. Who the hell had sent the letter?

2. Time to contact the president. The letter had been addressed to him, after all.

Stansfield M. Turner was not popular at the agency because he was trying to exchange as many of his colleagues as possible for computers. And it was one of them — not a person — that had been able to trace the cut-out words to the book *Peace on Earth*.

"Jazz is supposed to bring peace on earth?" said President Carter to his old schoolmate Turner when they met the next day in the Oval Office.

"He took his own life a few years later, Mr President," said the director of the CIA.

President Carter — who loved jazz — still couldn't let the thought go. What if the poor professor had been right? And then the Beatles and the Rolling Stones showed up and ruined everything?

The director of the CIA said that the Beatles could be blamed for a lot of things, but not for starting the Vietnam War. And then he said that he was sceptical of the theory, because if the Beatles and Rolling Stones hadn't already destroyed peace on earth, there was always the Sex Pistols.

"The Sex Pistols?" the president wondered.

"'God Save the Queen', you remember?" the CIA director quoted.

"Oh, I see," said the president.

Now to the question at hand. Were the idiots in South Africa about to detonate an atomic bomb? And was this work being led by an ass?

100

"I don't know about the ass part, sir. We have indications that the work is being supervised by an Engineer Westhuizen, who graduated with top grades from one of South Africa's best universities. He must have been handpicked."

But there were many indications that the rest of the information was correct. The KGB had, of course, already been so kind as to tip them off about what was going on. And now this letter, formulated in such a way that the CIA director was prepared to bet his life that the KGB wasn't behind it this time. Plus, the CIA's own satellite images showed activity in the desert exactly where the mystery sender said it would be.

"But why this 'Death to America' on the envelope?" said President Carter.

"It meant that the letter landed on my desk immediately, and I think that was the point. The letter writer seems to have great insight into how security around the president works. That makes us even more curious about who he is. Cleverly executed, in any case."

The president hemmed and hawed. He had trouble seeing what was so clever about "Death to America". Or, for that matter, the assertion that Elizabeth II was of any race other than the human one.

But he thanked his old friend and asked his secretary to call up Prime Minister Vorster in Pretoria. President Carter was directly responsible for 32,000 nuclear missiles that pointed in a number of directions. Brezhnev in Moscow was in a similar situation. The world did not need another six weapons of the same magnitude. Someone was going to get a talking-to!

◆　◆　◆

Vorster was furious. The president of the United States, that peanut farmer and Baptist, had had the nerve to call and claim that preparations were under way for a weapons test in the Kalahari Desert. Furthermore, he had recited the coordinates of the exact location of the test site. The accusation was completely baseless and incredibly, terribly insulting! In a rage, Vorster slammed down the phone in Jimmy Carter's ear, but he had enough sense not to go any further. Instead he called Pelindaba right away to order Engineer Westhuizen to test his weapons somewhere else.

"But where?" said Engineer Westhuizen while his cleaning woman swabbed the floor around his feet.

"Anywhere but the Kalahari," said Prime Minister Vorster.

"That will delay us by several months, maybe a year or more," said the engineer.

"Just do as I say, dammit."

◆　◆　◆

The engineer's servant let him spend two whole years thinking about where the weapons test could be done, now that the Kalahari Desert was no longer available. The best idea Westhuizen had was to shoot the thing off

102

in one of the many homelands, but not even he thought this sounded good enough.

Nombeko sensed that the engineer's share value was on its way to a new low, and that it would soon be time to drive his price up again. But then something lucky happened — an external factor that gave the engineer, and by extension his cleaning woman, another six months of respite.

It turned out that Prime Minister B. J. Vorster was tired of being met with complaints and ingratitude in nearly every context in his own country. So with a little help, he magically made seventy-five million rand disappear from the country's coffers, and he started the newspaper *The Citizen*. Unlike most citizens, this one had a uniquely, completely positive attitude towards the South African government and its ability to keep a tight rein on the natives and the rest of the world.

Unfortunately enough, an extra-treacherous citizen happened to let this come to the attention of the general public. Around the same time, the goddamn world conscience referred to a successful military operation in Angola as the slaughter of six hundred civilians — and thus it was time for Vorster to go.

Oh, fuck it, he thought one last time, and left the world of politics in 1979. All that was left to do was to go home to Cape Town and sit on the terrace of his luxury home with a whisky in his hand and a view of Robben Island where that terrorist Mandela was sitting.

Mandela was supposed to be the one who rotted away, not me, Vorster thought as he rotted away.

His successor as prime minister, P. W. Botha, was called *Die Groot Krokodil* — the big crocodile — and he had scared the engineer out of his wits in their very first phone call. Nombeko realized that the weapons test couldn't wait any longer. So she brought it up one late afternoon when the engineer was still able to speak.

"Um, Engineer . . ." she said as she reached for the ashtray on his desk.

"What is it now?" said the engineer.

"Well, I was just thinking . . ." Nombeko began, without being interrupted. "I was just thinking that if all of South Africa is too crowded, except for the Kalahari Desert, why couldn't the bomb be detonated at sea?"

South Africa was surrounded by practically endless amounts of sea in three directions. Nombeko had long been of the opinion that the best choice for a test site should have been obvious to a child, now that the desert was no longer an option. Sure enough, the childlike Westhuizen lit up. For one second. Then he realized that the intelligence service had warned him not to collaborate with the navy under any circumstances. There had been a detailed investigation after President Carter in the United States had obviously been informed of the planned test in the Kalahari, and it had singled out Vice Admiral Johan Charl Walters as the prime suspect. Admiral Walters had visited Pelindaba just three weeks before Carter's phone call, and he had gained a clear picture of the project. He had also been alone in Engineer Westhuizen's office for at least seven minutes while the engineer was stuck in heavy traffic one morning (the engineer had edited this last bit during the interrogation, because he had spent a little too much time at the bar where he always drank breakfast). The leading theory was that Walters had become pouty and tattled to the United States once it became clear to him that he would not be allowed to arm his submarines with nuclear warheads.

"I don't trust the navy," the engineer mumbled to his cleaning woman.

"So get the Israelis to help," said Nombeko.

At that moment, the phone rang.

"Yes, Mr Prime Minister . . . Of course I'm aware of the importance of . . . Yes, Mr Prime Minister . . . No, Mr Prime Minister . . . I don't quite agree with that, if you'll excuse me, Mr Prime Minister. Here on my desk is a detailed plan to carry out a test in the Indian Ocean, along with the Israelis. Within three months, Mr Prime Minister. Thank you, Mr Prime Minister, you are far too kind. Thanks again. Well, goodbye then."

Engineer Westhuizen hung up and tossed back the whole glass of brandy he had just poured. And then he said to Nombeko:

"Don't just stand there. Get me the two Israelis."

Sure enough, the test was carried out with the help of Israel. Engineer Westhuizen aimed a kind thought in the direction of former Prime Minister-slash-former-Nazi Vorster for his genius in establishing cooperation with Jerusalem. Israel's on-site representatives were two pompous Mossad agents. Unfortunately, the engineer would come to meet with them more often than was necessary, and he never learned to tolerate that superior smile, the one that said, "How could you be so fucking stupid as to buy a clay goose that was hardly dry and believe it to be two thousand years old?"

When suspected traitor Vice Admiral Walters was kept out of the loop, America couldn't keep up. Ha! Sure, the detonation was registered by an American Vela satellite, but it was a bit too late by then.

New Prime Minister P. W. Botha was so delighted by the results of the weapons test that he came to visit the research facility and brought three bottles of sparkling wine from Constantia. Then he threw a cheers-and-thanks party in Engineer Westhuizen's office, along with the engineer, two Israeli Mossad agents, and a local darky to do the actual serving. Prime Minister Botha would never allow himself to *call* the darky a darky; his position demanded otherwise. But there was no rule against thinking what one thought.

In any case, she served what she was supposed to and otherwise made sure to blend into the white wallpaper as best she could.

"Here's to you, Engineer," Prime Minister Botha said, raising his glass. "Here's to you!"

Engineer Westhuizen looked fittingly embarrassed about being a hero, and he discreetly asked for a refill from whatshername while the prime minister had a friendly conversation with the Mossad agents.

But then, in an instant, the relatively pleasant situation became rather the opposite. The prime minister turned to Westhuizen again and said, "By the way, what is your opinion on the tritium problem?"

◆ ◆ ◆

Prime Minister P. W. Botha's background was not entirely different from that of his predecessor. It was possible that the country's new leader was a bit cleverer, because he had given up Nazism once he saw the direction it was heading, and started referring to his convictions as "Christian Nationalism" instead. So he had avoided internment when the Allies got a foothold in the war, and he was able to start a political career without a waiting period.

Botha and his Reform Church knew that the Truth could be read in the Bible, if one only read very carefully. After all, the Tower of Babel — man's attempt to build his way to Heaven — came up in Genesis. God found this attempt presumptuous; he became indignant and scattered the people all over the world and created language confusion as punishment.

Different people, different languages. It was God's intention to keep people separate. It was a green light from on high to divide people up according to colour.

The big crocodile also felt that it was God's help that let him climb in his career. Soon he was the minister of defence in his predecessor Vorster's cabinet. From this position, he commanded air raids on the terrorists who were hiding in Angola, the incident that the stupid rest of the world called a slaughter of innocents. "We have photographic evidence!" said the world. "It's what you *can't* see that's important," said the crocodile, but the only person he convinced with this was his mother.

Anyway, Engineer Westhuizen's current problem was that P. W. Botha's father had been the commanding officer in the Second Boer War and that Botha himself had military strategies and issues in his blood. Therefore he also had some knowledge of all that technical stuff for which Engineer Westhuizen was the nuclear weapons programme's top representative. Botha had no reason to suspect that the engineer was the fraud he was. He had asked his question out of conversational curiosity.

◆　◆　◆

Engineer Westhuizen hadn't spoken for ten seconds, and the situation was about to become awkward for him — and downright dangerous for Nombeko, who thought that if the idiot didn't answer the world's simplest question soon, he would be toast. She was tired of having to save him time and again, but all the same she fished the plain brown spare bottle of Klipdrift from her pocket, stepped up to the engineer, and said she had noticed that Mr Westhuizen was having trouble with his asthma again.

"Here, take a big gulp and you'll soon regain the ability to talk so that you can tell Mr Prime Minister that the short half-life of tritium isn't a problem because it is unrelated to the bomb's explosive effect."

The engineer drained the entire medicine bottle and immediately felt better. Meanwhile, Prime Minister Botha looked wide-eyed at the servant.

108

"*You* know about the tritium problem?"

"Goodness, no." Nombeko laughed. "You see, I clean this room every day and the engineer spends almost all his time rattling off formulas and other strange things to himself. And apparently some of it got stuck even in my little brain. Would you like a refill, Mr Prime Minister?"

Prime Minister Botha accepted more sparkling wine and gave Nombeko a long look as she returned to her wallpaper. Meanwhile the engineer cleared his throat and apologized for the asthma attack and for the servant's impudence in opening her mouth.

"The fact is, the half-life of tritium is not relevant to the bomb's explosive effect," said the engineer.

"Yes, I just heard that from the waitress," the prime minister said acidly.

Botha didn't ask any difficult follow-up questions; he was soon in a good mood again thanks to Nombeko's eager refills of bubbly. Engineer Westhuizen had made it through another crisis. And so had his cleaning woman.

When the first bomb was ready, the next phase of production went as follows: two independent, high-quality work teams each built a bomb, using the first one as a model. The teams were instructed to be extremely accurate when it came to accounting for the steps they took. In this way, the production of bombs two and three could be compared in detail — first compared to each other and then compared to number one. It was the engineer himself, and no one else (except a certain woman who didn't count), who was in charge of the comparison.

If the bombs were identical, then they would also be correct. It was highly unlikely that two independent teams could make identical mistakes at that high level. According to whatshername, the statistical likelihood of that was .0054 per cent.

♦ ♦ ♦

Nombeko continued to search for something that would give her hope. The three Chinese girls knew some things, like that the Egyptian pyramids were in Egypt, how to poison dogs, and what to watch out for when stealing a wallet from the inner pocket of a jacket. Things like that.

The engineer frequently mumbled about progress in South Africa and the world, but the information from that source had to be filtered and interpreted, since for the most part all the politicians on earth were idiots or Communists, and all of their decisions were either idiotic or Communistic. And when they were Communistic, they were also idiotic.

When the people chose a former Hollywood actor to be the new American president, the engineer condemned not only the president elect but also all of his people. However, Ronald Reagan avoided being labelled a Communist. Instead the engineer focused on the president's presumed sexual orientation, based on the hypothesis that all men who stood for anything different from what the engineer stood for were homosexuals.

All due deference to the Chinese girls and the engineer, but as sources of news they couldn't compete with the TV in the waiting room outside the engineer's office. On the sly Nombeko would often turn it on and follow the news and debate programmes while she pretended to scrub the floor. That corridor was by far the cleanest in the research facility.

"Are you here scrubbing again?" the irritated engineer once said as he came strolling in to work at ten thirty in the morning, fifteen minutes earlier than Nombeko had counted on. "And who turned on the TV?"

This could have ended poorly from an information-gathering perspective, but Nombeko knew her engineer. Instead of answering the question, she changed the subject.

"I saw a half-empty bottle of Klipdrift on your desk when I was in there cleaning, Engineer. I thought it might be old and I should pour it out. But I wasn't sure; I wanted to check with you first, Engineer."

"Poured out? Are you nuts?" said the engineer, rushing into his office to make sure that those life-giving drops were still there. To make sure that whatshername wouldn't get any other dumb ideas, he immediately transferred them from the bottle to his bloodstream. And he soon forgot the TV, the floor and the servant.

◆ ◆ ◆

Then one day it finally showed up.

The opportunity.

If Nombeko played all her cards right, and also got to borrow a little of the engineer's luck, she would soon be a free woman. Free and wanted, but still. The opportunity — unbeknown to Nombeko — had its origins on the other side of the globe.

The *de facto* leader of China, Deng Xiaoping, had early on displayed a talent for outmanoeuvring his competition — before the senile Mao Tse-tung even had time to die, in fact. Perhaps the most spectacular rumour was that he hadn't let Mao's right-hand man, Zhou Enlai, be treated when he got cancer. Being a cancer patient with no cancer treatment seldom leads to a positive outcome. Depending on how you look at it, of course. In any case, Zhou Enlai died twenty years after the CIA failed to blow him to smithereens.

After that, the Gang of Four were about to intervene, with Mao's last wife at the forefront. But as soon as the old man finally drew his last breath, the four were arrested and locked up, whereupon Deng purposely forgot where he'd put the key.

On the foreign-affairs front, he was deeply irritated by that dullard Brezhnev in Moscow. Who was succeeded by that dullard Andropov. Who was succeeded by Chernenko, the biggest dullard of them all. But luckily, Chernenko didn't have time to do more than take office before he stepped down permanently. The rumour was that Ronald Reagan had scared him to death with his Star Wars. Now some fellow called Gorbachev had taken over, and . . . well, from dullards to whippersnappers. The new man certainly had a lot to prove.

Among many other things, China's position in Africa was a constant concern. For several decades, the Soviets had been poking around in various African liberation movements. The Russians' current engagement in Angola was a prime example. The MPLA received Soviet weapons in exchange for getting results in the right ideological direction. The *Soviet* direction, of course. Blast!

The Soviets were moving Angola and other countries in southern Africa in a direction that was the opposite of what the United States and South Africa wanted. So what was China's position in all this mess? To back up the renegade Communists in the Kremlin? Or walk hand in hand with the American imperialists and the apartheid regime in Pretoria?

Blast, once more.

It might have been possible not to take any side at all, to leave a walkover, as the damn Americans liked to say. If it weren't for the contacts South Africa was presumed to have with Taiwan.

It was an open secret that the United States had stopped a nuclear weapons test in the Kalahari Desert. So everyone knew what South Africa was up to. In this case, "everyone" meant all intelligence organizations worth their name.

The crucial problem there was that, in addition to the Kalahari information on Deng's desk, there was an intelligence briefing noting that South Africa had communicated about the weapon with Taipei. It would be completely unacceptable for the Taiwanese to procure missiles to aim at mainland China. If this happened, it would lead to an escalation in the South China Sea, and it was impossible to predict how that might end. And the US Pacific Fleet was right around the corner.

So somehow or another, Deng had to manage the loathsome apartheid regime. His chief intelligence officer had suggested they do nothing and let the South African government die on its own. Thanks to that piece of advice, his chief intelligence officer was no longer a chief intelligence officer — would China really be more secure if Taiwan was doing business with a nuclear nation in freefall? The former chief intelligence officer could ponder this as he worked at his new job as a substitute station attendant in the Beijing subway.

"Manage" was the name of the game. Somehow or another.

Deng couldn't possibly travel there himself and let himself be photographed alongside that old Nazi Botha (even if the idea was a bit tempting: the decadent West did have its charm, in small doses). And he couldn't send any of his closest men. It must absolutely not appear that Beijing and Pretoria were on friendly terms.

On the other hand, there was no point in sending a pencil-pushing lower official with neither the ability nor the sense to make observations. Of course, it was also important that the Chinese representative was important enough to be granted an audience with Botha.

So: someone who could get things done — but at the same time was not close to the Politburo Standing Committee and who couldn't be considered an obvious representative of Beijing. Deng Xiaoping found the solution in the young party secretary of the province of Guizhou, which had practically more ethnic groups than people. The young man had just proven that it was possible to bring together peevish minorities like the Yao, Miao, Yi, Qiang, Dong, Zhuang, Bouyei, Bai, Tujia, Gelao and Sui.

Anyone who could keep eleven balls in the air like that also ought to be able to handle the ex-Nazi Botha, Deng thought, and he made sure to send the young man in question to Pretoria.

His task: to get the message to South Africa, between the lines, that collaborating on nuclear weapons with Taiwan was unacceptable, and to get the South Africans to understand who they were picking a fight with, should they choose to pick a fight.

◆ ◆ ◆

P. W. Botha was not at all excited to receive the leader of a Chinese province; that was below his station. Furthermore, Botha's station had just become even higher — the title of prime minister had been replaced by president. What would people think if he — the president! — were to welcome just any old Chinese like that? If he were to receive all of them, for a few seconds each, it would take him more than thirteen thousand years. Botha didn't think he would live that long. In fact, despite his new title, he felt rather worn-out.

At the same time, he understood why China had chosen the tactic of sending over a minion. Beijing didn't want to be accused of embracing the government in Pretoria. And vice versa, for that matter.

The question remained: what were they up to? Did it have something to do with Taiwan? That would be funny, because their collaboration with the Taiwanese had been over before it had led anywhere at all.

Oh well, perhaps Botha would go and meet that errand boy after all.

Why, I'm as curious as a child, he said to himself, smiling even though he really didn't have anything to smile about.

To lessen this great breach of etiquette, a president meeting with a gofer, Botha got the idea of rigging a meeting and a dinner on the Chinese man's level — and Botha himself would happen to stumble across it. Oh, are you here? May I sit down? Something like that.

So Botha called the director of the top secret nuclear weapons programme and ordered him to receive a Chinese guest who had requested a meeting with the president. He said that the engineer and the guest would go on safari together and then have a fancy, delicious meal in the evening. During the dinner, the engineer must make the Chinese man understand that one oughtn't underestimate South African military engineering, without actually telling the nuclear truth straight out.

116

It was important for this message to make it through. They had to show strength without saying anything. It would just so happen that President Botha was in the vicinity, and a person has to eat, so he would be happy to keep the engineer and the Chinese man company.

"If you don't mind, of course, Engineer Westhuizen." The engineer's head was spinning. So he was supposed to receive a guest the president didn't want to meet. He would tell the guest the truth of the matter without saying anything, and in the middle of all this the president, who didn't want to meet the guest, would show up to meet the guest.

The engineer realized he was getting into a situation in which one might make a fool of oneself. Other than that, he didn't understand anything beyond that he must immediately invite the president to the dinner the president himself had just decided should take place.

"Of course you're welcome to come to the dinner, Mr President!" said Engineer Westhuizen. "You really must be there! When is it, by the way? And where?"

This is how what started out as Deng Xiaoping's concern in Beijing became a problem for Engineer Westhuizen in Pelindaba. The fact was, of course, that he knew absolutely nothing about the project he was directing. It isn't easy to sit and chat and seem gifted when you're rather the opposite. The solution would be to bring along whatshername as a servant and briefcase-carrier. Then she could discreetly feed the engineer clever facts about the project, carefully considered so that he didn't say too much. Or too little.

That sort of consideration was something whatshername would manage splendidly. Just like everything else that cursed person set out to do.

◆　◆　◆

The engineer's cleaning woman received strict instructions before the Chinese safari and the following dinner, at which they would be joined by the president himself. To be on the safe side, Nombeko helped the engineer with the instructions so that they would turn out correctly.

She was to remain an arm's length away from the engineer. Each time an opportunity presented itself, she would whisper conversationally appropriate wisdom in his ear. The rest of the time, she would keep quiet and act like the nonentity that she basically was.

Nombeko had been sentenced to seven years in service to the engineer nine years ago. When her sentence came to an end, she didn't bother to remind him, since she'd decided it was better to be alive and imprisoned than dead and free.

But soon she would be outside the fences and the minefield; she would be miles from the guards and their new German shepherds. If she managed to break away from her chaperon, she would turn into one of South Africa's most wanted. Police, intelligence agents, and the military would look for her everywhere. Except maybe in the National Library in Pretoria. And that was where she would go first of all.

If she managed to break away, that is.

The engineer had been kind enough to inform her that the chauffeur-slash-safari guide was carrying a rifle and he was instructed to shoot not only attacking lions but also fleeing cleaning ladies, should any appear. And as an extra precaution, the engineer made sure to carry a pistol in a holster. A Glock 17, nine by nineteen millimetres with seventeen bullets in the magazine. Not something you can take down an elephant or a rhinoceros with, but it would do for a 120-pound servant.

"One hundred and fifteen, if you please," said Nombeko.

She considered waiting for a convenient moment to unlock the safe in the engineer's office where he kept his pistol and empty it of the seventeen bullets, but she didn't. She would be blamed if the drunk happened to discover it in time, and then her escape would be over before it had even begun.

Instead she decided not to be too eager, to wait for the right moment — but when it came, she would take off into the bush as fast as she could. Without taking a bullet in the back from either the chauffeur or the engineer. And preferably without encountering any of the animals that were the point of going on a safari.

So when would the right moment be? Not in the morning, when the chauffeur was on his toes and the engineer was still sober enough to manage to shoot something other than himself in the foot. Maybe right after the safari, just before the dinner, when Westhuizen was sufficiently blotto and nervous about the meeting

119

with his president. And when the chauffeur was done being a guide after many hours on the job.

Yes, then the time would be right. She just had to recognize the moment and seize it when it came.

♦ ♦ ♦

They were ready to start the safari. The Chinese official had brought along his own interpreter. It all began in the worst possible way when the interpreter was foolish enough to walk into the tall grass to take a leak. It was even more foolish to do this in sandals.

"Help, I'm dying," he said as he felt a sting on his left big toe and saw a scorpion crawling away in the grass.

"You shouldn't have walked into five-inch grass without real shoes — or at all, really. Especially not when it's windy," said Nombeko.

"Help, I'm dying," the interpreter said again.

"Why not when it's windy?" wondered the engineer, who didn't care about the interpreter's health but was curious.

Nombeko explained that insects take shelter in the grass when the wind blows, and this means that the scorpions crawl out of their holes for a bit of food. And today there was a big toe in the way.

"Help, I'm dying," the interpreter said once more.

Nombeko realized that the whimpering interpreter actually believed what he was saying.

"No, I'm pretty sure you're not," she said. "The scorpion was little, and you're big. But we might as well send you to the hospital so they can wash your wound properly. Your toe will soon swell up to three times its size and turn blue, and it will hurt like hell, if you'll pardon my language. You're not going to be much good as an interpreter, anyway."

"Help, I'm dying," said the interpreter for a fourth time.

"Soon I'm going to start wishing you were right," said Nombeko. "Instead of sniffling that you're dying when you aren't, look on the bright side — it was a scorpion and not a cobra. And now you know that in Africa you can't just pee however and wherever you want and go unpunished. There are sanitary facilities everywhere. Where I'm from, they even come in rows."

The interpreter went quiet for a few seconds, shocked that the scorpion he was about to die from could have been a cobra that he *definitely* would have died from. Meanwhile the guide found a car and a chauffeur that could take the man to the hospital.

The scorpion-afflicted man was placed in the back seat of a Land Rover, where he resumed his repetition of the path he expected his health to take. The chauffeur rolled his eyes and departed.

This left the engineer and the Chinese man to stand there and look at each other.

"How is this going to work?" the engineer muttered in Afrikaans.

"How is this going to work?" the Chinese official muttered in his Wu Chinese dialect.

"Might you be from Jiangsu, Mr Chinese Official?" Nombeko said in the same dialect. "Possibly even from Jiangyan?"

The Chinese official, who had been born and raised in Jiangyan in Jiangsu Province, couldn't believe his ears.

How could that cursed whatshername always be so incredibly irritating? thought Engineer Westhuizen. Now she was standing there speaking some totally useless language with the Chinese guest, and the engineer had no control over what was being said.

"Excuse me, but what's going on?" he said.

Nombeko explained that it just so happened that she and their guest spoke the same language, so it didn't matter that the interpreter would soon be lying there whimpering in a hospital with a blue toe instead of doing his job. If the engineer would allow them to speak, of course. Or perhaps he would prefer that they sit in silence all day and night?

No, the engineer would not. But he would ask whatshername to stick to interpreting and say nothing else. It would not be appropriate for her to make small talk with the Chinese official.

Nombeko promised to do as little small-talking as possible. She just hoped that the engineer would understand if she happened to answer the Chinese official if he spoke to her. That was what the engineer himself had always said she should do. Furthermore, one might say that things had worked out for the best:

"Now you can say whatever you want about advanced weapons technology, Engineer, and other things you don't quite have a grasp on. Should you say the wrong thing — and we can't rule that out, can we? — well, then I can just adjust it in translation."

Essentially, whatsername was right. And since she was utterly below him, he didn't have to feel distaste. One does what one must to survive, thought the engineer. He felt that luck had increased his chances of making it through tonight's dinner with the Chinese official and the president.

"If you take care of this, I'll see if I can't order a new scrubbing brush for you after all," he said.

The safari was a success: they had close encounters with all of the big five. In between, they had time for coffee and small talk. Nombeko took the opportunity to tell the Chinese official that President Botha would happen to run into them five hours later. The Chinese official thanked her for the information and promised to look as surprised as he could. Nombeko did not say that they would probably all be plenty surprised when the acting interpreter suddenly disappeared in the middle of dinner at the safari lodge. Then they could all sit there, staring at one another.

Nombeko climbed down from the Land Rover to walk into the restaurant with the engineer. She was fully focused on her approaching escape. Could she go through the kitchen and out the back? Some time between the main course and dessert?

Her thoughts were interrupted when the engineer stopped short and pointed at her.

"What is that?" he said.

"That?" said Nombeko. "That's me. Whatever my name is."

"No, you idiot, what you're wearing."

"It's a jacket."

"And why are you wearing it?"

"Because it's mine. Have you had a bit too much brandy today, Engineer, if I may ask?"

The engineer no longer had the energy to reprimand his cleaning woman.

"My point, if you even have sense enough to listen, is that that jacket looks awful."

"This is the only jacket I have, Engineer."

"Doesn't matter. You can't look like you come from a shantytown when you're about to meet our country's president."

"Although, to be precise, I do," said Nombeko.

"Take off that jacket at once and leave it in the car! And hurry. The president is waiting."

Nombeko realized that her planned escape had just been cancelled. The seam of her only jacket was full of diamonds, which she was to live on for the rest of her life — if circumstances allowed her to have one. Without them, fleeing South African injustice . . . no, she might as well stay where she was. Among presidents, Chinese officials, bombs, and engineers. Awaiting her fate.

◆ ◆ ◆

Dinner began with Engineer Westhuizen explaining the day's scorpion incident to his president; it was no big deal, he added, because the engineer had had the foresight to bring along one of the servants, who happened to speak the Chinese official's language.

A black South African woman who spoke Chinese? And wasn't that the same person who had both served bubbly and discussed the tritium problem during the president's most recent visit to Pelindaba? P. W. Botha decided not to investigate this any further; he already had enough of a headache. Instead he let himself be satisfied with the engineer's word that the interpreter wasn't a security risk for the very simple reason that she otherwise never left the facility.

P. W. Botha took command of the dinner conversation, president that he was. He began by telling them about South Africa's proud history. Interpreter Nombeko had resigned herself to the thought that her nine years of imprisonment would not end there. Thus, in the absence of any new, spontaneous ideas to the contrary, she interpreted word for word.

The president went on to say more about South Africa's proud history. Nombeko interpreted word for word.

The president went on to say even *more* about South Africa's proud history. At that point, Nombeko grew tired of giving the Chinese official more of something he could do without. Instead she turned to him and said, "If you would like, Mr Chinese Official, I can say even more of the president's self-righteous nonsense. Otherwise I can tell you that what they're getting at is that they are very good at building advanced weapons and that you Chinese ought to respect them for that reason."

125

"I thank you for your honesty, miss," said the Chinese official. "And you're quite right that I don't need to hear more about your country's excellence. But please translate now and say that I'm grateful for this vivid account of your history."

The dinner continued. When the main course arrived, it was time for Engineer Westhuizen to say something about how gifted he was. What he came up with was a mishmash of technical lies that didn't make any sense whatsoever. But Westhuizen got so entangled in what he was saying that even the president could no longer follow (the thing about the engineer's luck was that it lasted all the way up until it ran out). The engineer's muddled tale would have been difficult for Nombeko to translate, even if she had tried. Instead, she said, "I'm going to spare you the nonsense the engineer just spouted, Mr Chinese Official. Basically, it's like this: they've figured out how to build nuclear weapons, and they've already completed several — despite the engineer. But I haven't seen any Taiwanese sneaking around and I haven't heard anyone say that they're going to export any of the bombs. Might I recommend that you answer politely now, and then suggest that the interpreter be given some food? Because I'm about to starve."

The Chinese messenger thought that Nombeko was absolutely charming. He gave a friendly smile and said that he was impressed by Mr Westhuizen's knowledge, and that it demanded respect. Beyond that, he didn't want to show disrespect for South African traditions, not at all, but in China it simply wasn't right for

126

someone to sit at a table without being served just like everyone else. The Chinese official said he was uncomfortable because the superb interpreter hadn't had anything to eat, and he wondered if the president would allow the official to share some of his food with her.

President Botha snapped his fingers and ordered a plate for the native. It wasn't the end of the world if she got something in her stomach, as long as it made their guest happy. Moreover, the conversation seemed to be shaping up for the best; the Chinaman was looking pretty docile.

By the time dinner was over, several things had happened:

1. China knew that South Africa was a nuclear nation
2. Nombeko would for ever have a friend in the secretary-general of Guizhou Province in China
3. Engineer van der Westhuizen had survived yet another crisis, because . . .
4. P. W. Botha was generally pleased with the way things had gone, because the president didn't know any better.

And last but not least:

5. Twenty-five-year-old Nombeko Mayeki was still a prisoner at Pelindaba, but for the first time in her life she had been able to eat until she was completely full.

CHAPTER
SIX

On Holger and Holger and
a broken heart

Part of Ingmar's plan had always been that Holger would be drilled in the spirit of republicanism from birth. On one wall of the nursery he put up side-by-side portraits of Charles de Gaulle and Franklin D. Roosevelt, without stopping to think about how neither of them could stand the other. On another wall he put up Finland's Urho Kekkonen. The three gentlemen earned these places because they had been elected by the people. They were presidents.

Ingmar shuddered at the dreadful idea that someone could be born into one day being the formal leader of an entire nation, not to mention the personal tragedy of having certain values drilled into one's head from day one, without being able to defend oneself. That ought to be considered child abuse, he thought, and to be on the safe side he also put up former Argentinean president Juan Perón on the still-gestating Holger's wall.

One thing that concerned Ingmar, who was always getting ahead of himself, was that the law said that

128

Holger must go to school. Of course the boy needed to learn to read and write, but in addition to that children were force-fed Christian knowledge, geography and other nonsense — things that only took time away from a true education, the important home education: that the king, possibly by democratic means, must be deposed and replaced by a representative elected by the people.

"*Possibly* by democratic means?" said Henrietta.

"Don't quibble now, my dear," Ingmar replied.

At first, the logistics were made even more difficult when Holger came into the world not only once but twice in a matter of minutes. But as he had so often before, Ingmar managed to turn lemons into lemonade. He had an idea so revolutionary that he thought it through for forty seconds before making up his mind and presenting his decision to his wife.

What he had figured out was that Holger and Holger could divide their time at school. Since the birth had happened at home, all they had to do was register the birth of one of them, whichever one they wanted, and keep the other one a secret. One fortunate fact of their situation was that Ingmar had yanked the telephone cord out of the wall, which meant that the midwife-slash-witness had never been summoned.

Ingmar's idea was for Holger One to go to school on Mondays, while Holger Two stayed at home to be drilled in republican knowledge by his father. On Tuesdays, the boys would switch, and they would keep going like this. The result was meant to be an adequate dose of general school-learning along with sufficient amounts of something that *meant* something.

Henrietta hoped she had misheard. Did Ingmar mean that they should keep one of the boys a secret all his life? From the school? From the neighbours? From the world?

"More or less." Ingmar nodded. "In the name of the Republic."

Incidentally they should watch out for the school, because too many books could make a person stupid. After all, he'd become an accountant without reading too much along the way.

"Accountant's assistant," Henrietta corrected him, and was told that she was quibbling again.

What else was she worried about? What the neighbours and the world would say? Please. They didn't have any neighbours to speak of, out there in the forest. Except Johan on the hill, but what did he do besides poach moose? And without sharing, to boot. And surely the world in general didn't deserve much respect. Monarchies and dynasties everywhere.

"What about you?" said Henrietta. "Are you going to give up your job at the post office to stay home with one of the boys full-time? Were you planning for me to bring in every single krona our family needs?"

Ingmar pitied Henrietta for being so narrow-minded. Of course he had to give up his job at the post office; he couldn't have two full-time jobs, after all. But that didn't mean he wasn't going to take responsibility for his family. He was happy to help in the kitchen, for

130

example. It was no longer important for his scrotum to remain cool.

Henrietta replied that the only reason Ingmar could even find his way to the kitchen was because their house was so small. She supposed she could manage her seamstress work, her cooking, and all the nappies if Ingmar and his scrotum would just stay away from her oven.

And then she smiled, in spite of everything. To say that her spouse was full of life would be an understatement.

Ingmar gave notice at work the next day. He was allowed to leave that very day, with full pay for three months, and his departure led to a spontaneous party that night among the otherwise so quiet and dull men and women in the accounting department of the post office.

The year was 1961. Incidentally, that was the same year an unusually gifted girl was born in a shack in Soweto, half an eternity away.

◆ ◆ ◆

During Holger and Holger's early years, Ingmar divided his days between being in his wife's way at home and heading off to pull pranks of varying but republican quality.

He also joined the Republican Club, under the moral leadership of the great Vilhelm Moberg. Moberg, the legendary author, was angry with all the treacherous

131

socialists and liberals who had written "republic" into their party platform without doing anything about it.

But because Ingmar didn't want to overstep the mark too soon, he waited until the club's second meeting before he suggested that he himself could administer the club's considerable funds, with the intention of kidnapping and hiding the crown prince, thus cutting off the constant stream of claimants to the throne.

After a few seconds of shocked silence around the republican table, Moberg had personally sent Ingmar packing, with a well-aimed kick to the backside as a farewell.

Moberg's right foot and the subsequent fall down the stairs had hurt, but otherwise no damage had been done, Ingmar thought as he limped away. They could keep their Republican Club for Mutual Admiration. Ingmar had other ideas.

For example, he joined the spineless Social Democratic Party. The Social Democrats had been in power in Sweden since Per Albin Hansson had guided the nation through the horrors of the Second World War with the help of horoscopes. Hansson himself had made a career out of demanding a republic before the war, but once the old champion of temperance rose to a position where he could do something about it, he prioritized poker and whisky with the boys over following his own convictions. This was even more tragic, considering that Hansson was talented as a matter of record — otherwise, he would never have managed to keep both wife and mistress happy for years, with two children in each camp.

Ingmar's plan was to climb so high in the Social Democratic hierarchy that he would one day have the power to send the damn king as far away as possible by parliamentary means. The Soviets had already managed to launch a dog into space; next time they were welcome to take the Swedish head of state instead, he thought as he made his way to the district office in Eskilstuna, since the Social Democrats of Södertälje had an office next door to his father-in-law's Communists.

But Ingmar's political career turned out to be even shorter than his career in the Republican Club. He was registered as a party member on a Thursday and immediately received a bundle of leaflets to hand out outside the off-licence on the next Saturday.

The problem was that the internationally oriented Eskilstuna district was demanding the resignation of Ngo Dinh Diem in Saigon. But Diem was a president! After a thousand years of imperial dynasty, no less.

Sure, not everything had been done quite correctly. It was said, for example, that his brother had smoked his brain out on opium and then, in the capacity of vote counter in charge of the Vietnamese presidential election, hallucinated two million extra votes for Diem.

Of course that wasn't how things should be done, but to demand the president's resignation because of it would be to take things too far.

So Ingmar threw the leaflets he had been given into the Eskilstuna River. Instead he printed his own, in which he applauded Diem and the efficiency of the American military in the name of social democracy. The damage to the Social Democratic Party was limited, however, because three of the four members of the district leadership happened to have business to take care of at the off-licence that Saturday morning. Ingmar's leaflets ended up in the rubbish instead of in the hands of potential voters, while Ingmar himself was asked to hand over immediately the party book he hadn't yet had time to receive.

◆ ◆ ◆

The years went by. Holger and Holger grew and became, in accordance with their papa Ingmar's plan, nearly identical.

Mama Henrietta devoted her days to sewing clothes, smoking calming John Silvers, and showering all three of her children with love. The oldest of them, Ingmar, spent a great deal of his time singing the praises of republicanism to his boys, and he spent the rest of it on sporadic missions to Stockholm to throw the monarchical ranks into chaos. Each time the latter happened, Henrietta had to start all over again with her collection of money in the sugar bowl she never managed to hide well enough.

Despite certain personal setbacks, one could still count the 1960s as a relatively good decade for Ingmar and his cause. For example, a military junta took over

134

in Greece and chased King Constantine II and his court all the way to Rome. There was every indication that the Greek monarchy was history and that the country was headed for a flourishing economic future.

The experiences of Vietnam and Greece showed Ingmar that, when all was said and done, violence could bring about change. So he had been right, and Vilhelm Moberg was wrong. He could still feel that kick to the backside, several years later. Author bastard.

For that matter, the Swedish king might as well move to Rome, too, if it didn't work out for him to keep Laika company in space. Then he would have people to spend time with in the evenings. Those confounded royals were all related to each other anyway.

And now a new year, 1968, was just round the corner. It would be Ingmar's year, he proclaimed in front of his family that Christmas. And the Republic's.

"That's nice," said Henrietta, opening her Christmas present from her beloved husband. She hadn't expected much, but still: a framed portrait of the Icelandic president, Ásgeir Ásgeirsson.

"To Henrietta, who was planning to stop smoking."

In the autumn of 1968, Holger and Holger entered the Swedish educational system according to the every-other-day principle Ingmar had decided upon on the same day they had turned out to be more than one person.

At school, the teacher thought it was strange that whatever Holger had learned on Monday was already

135

forgotten the next day, and that Tuesday's lessons were lost the day after that, while Monday's had returned.

Oh well, the boy still seemed to function well for the most part, and despite his young age he seemed interested in politics, so there was probably nothing to worry about.

In the years that followed, the general craziness was put on the back burner to such an extent that Ingmar prioritized education in the home above fluttering around in public. When he did go out, though, he always took the children with him. One of them in particular needed extra supervision: the one who was originally called Holger Two showed signs early on of wavering in his faith. That didn't seem to be the case for One.

It so happened that Holger One was the one who was registered — he was the one, for example, with a passport, while Two didn't legally exist. It was as if he were a spare. The only thing Two seemed to have that One didn't was a gift for studying. So it was always Holger Two who went to school when it was time for an exam, no matter whose turn it was according to the schedule. Except for one time when Two had a fever. He was called to the front to talk to his geography teacher a few days later, to explain how he had managed to place the Pyrenees in Norway.

Henrietta noticed Two's relative misery, and through him she became more and more miserable herself. Could it really be the case that her beloved fool had no limits whatsoever?

"Of course I have limits, dear Henrietta," said Ingmar. "I've actually been doing some thinking on that topic. I'm no longer certain that it's possible to take over the whole country at once."

"Take over the whole country?" said Henrietta.

"At once," said Ingmar.

Sweden was, after all, an impressively oblong country. Ingmar had started to entertain the notion of converting the nation bit by bit, starting in the south and working his way up. He could have started at the other end, of course, but it was so damned cold up in the north. Who could transform the government when it was forty below zero?

What was even worse for Henrietta was that One didn't seem to have any doubts at all. His eyes would just shine and shine. The crazier the things Ingmar said, the more his eyes shone. She decided she would not accept any more madness, otherwise she would go mad herself.

"That's it, you need to stay at home. Or else you're out of here!" she said to Ingmar.

Ingmar loved his Henrietta and respected her ultimatum. The boys' schooling continued according to the every-other-day principle, as did the never-ending accounts of different presidents past and present. The madness remained and continued to torment Henrietta. But Ingmar's various excursions ceased, up until the children neared graduation.

Then he had a relapse and took off to demonstrate outside the Royal Palace in Stockholm, for within its walls a crown prince had just been born.

With that, enough was enough. Henrietta called Holger and Holger over and asked them to sit down in the kitchen with her.

"Now I'm going to tell you everything, my dear children," she said.

And so she did.

Her story ended up being twenty cigarettes long, starting with the very first time she and Ingmar met in Södertälje District Court in 1943.

She avoided a value judgement of their father's life work; she just described what had happened up to that point — including how he mixed up the newborns so it was impossible to say which of them had come first.

"It's possible that you're Two, One, but I don't know — no one knows," said Henrietta.

She thought that the story spoke for itself and that her sons would come to the correct conclusions when she was finished.

She was precisely half right.

The two Holgers listened. To one of them, it sounded like a heroic tale, a description of a man who was driven by a passion — someone who fought tirelessly against a constant headwind. To the other, it seemed to be the opposite: the story of a portended death.

"That's all I had to say," Henrietta concluded. "It was important for me to have it said. Think about what I've told you; think about where you want life to take you — and then let's talk about it again at breakfast tomorrow, okay?"

138

That night, Henrietta prayed to God, however much the daughter of a local Communist leader she was. She prayed that her two sons would forgive her, would forgive Ingmar. She prayed that her children would understand, that things could be set right, that they could start a normal life. She asked for God's help in the task of going to the authorities and requesting citizenship for an eighteen-year-old newborn man. She prayed that everything would turn out okay.

"Please, please, God," said Henrietta.

And she fell asleep.

The next morning, Ingmar was still gone. Henrietta felt tired as she made porridge for herself and the children. She was only fifty-nine years old, but she looked older.

Things were difficult for her, in every way. She felt anxious about everything. Now the children had heard her side of the story. All that remained was their judgement. And God's.

Mother and sons sat down at the kitchen table again. Holger Two saw, felt and understood. Holger One didn't see and didn't understand. But he did feel. He felt that he wanted to console Henrietta.

"Don't worry, Mum," he said. "I promise never to give up! As long as I live and breathe I will keep fighting in Dad's name. *As long as I live and breathe!* Do you hear me, Mum?"

Henrietta did hear. And what she heard was too much for her. Her heart broke. Because of sorrow. Because of guilt. Because of repressed dreams, visions and fantasies. Because almost nothing in her life had gone as she'd hoped. Because she had lived with anxiety for thirty-two years. And because one of her sons had just sworn that the madness would continue until the end of time.

But above all, because of 467,200 unfiltered John Silvers since the autumn of 1947.

Henrietta was a warrior. She loved her children. But when a heart breaks, that's it. The massive heart attack took her life in just a few seconds.

♦ ♦ ♦

Holger One never understood that he, along with Ingmar and the cigarettes, had killed his mother. Two considered telling him, but he didn't think it would make anything better so he refrained. When he read the obituary in the Södertälje county paper, he realized for the first time just how much he really didn't exist.

OUR BELOVED WIFE
AND MOTHER
HENRIETTA QVIST
HAS LEFT US
IN ENDLESS SORROW AND LOSS
SÖDERTÄLJE, THE FIFTEENTH OF MAY 1979
INGMAR
HOLGER
——

VIVE LA RÉPUBLIQUE

CHAPTER
SEVEN

On a bomb that didn't exist and an engineer who soon didn't, either

Nombeko was back inside the twelve-thousand-volt fences and life went on. Her realization that, in practice, there was no outer limit to her sentence was still less bothersome to her than the fact that she hadn't realized this from the start.

After bomb one, bombs two and three were built simultaneously and finished a few years later. After another twenty months, bombs four and five were ready, too.

These days the teams were completely separate; neither even knew that the other existed. The engineer alone was still the one who did the final inspection of each finished bomb. Since they were stored in one of the armoured storerooms within the engineer's office, he was able to be alone for each inspection. Thus he could allow himself to be assisted by his cleaning woman without any raised eyebrows. Though the question was, who was assisting whom?

Again, an order for six three-megaton bombs in all had been agreed upon and budgeted. But the project's top man, Engineer Engelbrecht van der Westhuizen, no longer had control over what went on, if he'd ever had it in the first place, because as a rule he was incredibly drunk by ten o'clock each morning. And his servant was too busy cleaning and reading on the sly in the library to be able to cover for him at all times. Furthermore, she never received a new scrubbing brush, so it took much longer to clean the floors.

As a result, as luck would have it, the double production continued after numbers four and five, which meant bombs six — *and seven!*

One atomic bomb too many had been produced by mistake. It was a bomb outside protocol.

A bomb that didn't exist now existed.

When the engineer's cleaning woman discovered this snafu, she informed her boss, who became just as concerned as he had reason to be. Bombs that didn't exist ought to stay that way, otherwise problems might arise. The engineer couldn't exactly start the dismantling process in secret, behind the backs of the president and the government. Anyway, he didn't know how to. And he had no intention of revealing the miscalculation to the research team.

Nombeko consoled Engineer Westhuizen by saying that more bombs might be ordered in time, and that the one that didn't exist could just continue to do so where no one would find it until it was allowed to exist.

"I was just thinking the same thing," said the engineer, when what he had really been thinking was that the cleaning woman had grown up nicely and was really a looker.

So the bomb that didn't exist was locked up in an empty storeroom next to its six fully existing sibling bombs. No one but the engineer himself had access to it. Except for whatshername, of course.

After more than a decade within the double fences of the research facility, Nombeko had read everything that was worth reading in Pelindaba's limited library. And most of what wasn't worth reading.

It didn't help that she'd had time to grow into a real woman; she would soon be twenty-six. At the same time, as far as she knew, blacks and whites were still not allowed to mix, because God had decreed it so according to Genesis, according to the Reformed Church. Not that she'd found anyone interesting to mix with at the facility, but still. She did dream of a man, about what they could do together. Not least from certain perspectives. She had seen pictures of it, in literature that was of a negligibly higher quality than what the British peace-on-earth professor had produced in 1924.

Oh well, better to be without something that resembled love inside the fence at the research facility than to be without life itself outside that same fence. Otherwise she wouldn't be close to anything but the worms in the earth she was buried in.

So Nombeko obeyed herself and continued not to remind the engineer that her seven years had already turned into eleven years. She stayed where she was.

For a little while longer.

◆　◆　◆

The South African armed forces received ever-higher amounts of funding from an economy that couldn't afford it. In the end, a fifth of the country's hopelessly unbalanced budget was going to the military, all while the rest of the world came up with new embargoes. One of the most painful results for the soul of the South African people was that the country had to play cricket and rugby with itself, because no one else wanted to play with it.

But the country still managed to get on, because the trade embargo was far from global. And there were many who argued *against* increased sanctions. Prime Minister Thatcher in London and President Reagan in Washington expressed roughly the same opinion on this matter: that each new embargo ought to have the greatest effect on the poorest citizens. Or as Ulf Adelsohn, party leader of the Swedish Moderates, so elegantly put it, "If we boycott goods from South Africa, the poor Negroes down there will become unemployed."

In reality, the shoe was pinching elsewhere. The thorny issue for Thatcher and Reagan (and Adelsohn, for that matter) wasn't a dislike of apartheid; racism hadn't been politically marketable for several decades. No, the problem was what would appear in its place. It wasn't easy to choose between apartheid and Communism, for instance. Or rather: of course it was, not least for Reagan, who had already fought to make sure that no Communists would be let into Hollywood during his time as a union leader for the Screen Actors Guild. What would people think if he spent billions upon billions of dollars arms-racing Soviet Communism to death while simultaneously allowing a variant of the same to take over in South Africa? Plus, the South Africans had nuclear weapons now, those bastards, even if they denied it.

Among those who didn't agree one bit with Thatcher's and Reagan's hemming and hawing when faced with apartheid politics was the Swedish prime minister, Olof Palme, and Libya's guide through socialism, Muammar Gaddafi. Palme roared, "Apartheid cannot be reformed; apartheid must be eliminated!" Soon after that he himself was eliminated by a confused man who didn't fully comprehend where he was or why he did what he did. Or by the exact opposite of that man; the mystery was never quite solved.

Gaddafi, on the other hand, would remain in good health for many more years. He allowed tons of weapons to be shipped to the South African resistance movement ANC, and he spoke vociferously about the noble fight against the white regime of oppression in Pretoria, all while hiding mass murderer Idi Amin in his very own palace.

This was more or less the way things stood when the world showed once more how strange it can be when it wants to. In the United States, the Democrats and Republicans joined forces and threw in their lot with Palme and Gaddafi, simultaneously creating a congressional revolt against their president. Congress passed a law that forbade all forms of trade with South Africa, as well as all types of investments in it. It was no longer even possible to fly directly from Johannesburg to the

United States; anyone who tried to do so could choose between turning back or being shot down.

Thatcher and other leaders in Europe and the rest of the world realized what was about to happen. No one wants to be on a losing team, of course; more and more countries got behind the United States, Sweden and Libya.

South Africa as the world knew it was starting to crack at the edges.

From her house arrest at the research facility, Nombeko's ability to follow the developments in the outside world was limited. Her three Chinese friends still didn't know much other than that the pyramids were in Egypt and had been there for quite some time. The engineer was no help, either. His analysis of the outside world was increasingly restricted to random grunting:

"Now those queers in the American Congress are starting an embargo, too."

And naturally there were limits to how often and how long Nombeko could scrub the overscrubbed floor in the waiting room with the TV.

But in addition to what she managed to catch from the TV news, she was observant. She noticed that things were happening. Not least because nothing seemed to be happening at all any more. No one rushed through the corridors; no prime ministers or presidents came to visit. Another hint was that the engineer's alcohol intake had started to go from a lot to even more.

Nombeko imagined that the engineer might soon be able to devote himself to his brandy full-time; he could sit and dream his way back to the years when it was possible to convince those around him that he had a clue. His president could sit in the chair next to him, for that matter, muttering that it was the blacks' fault that the country had capsized and gone under. What might happen to her in that situation was something she chose to repress.

"I'm starting to wonder if reality is catching up with the Goose and his ilk," Nombeko said one evening to her three Chinese friends.

She said this in fluent Wu Chinese.

"It would be about time," said the Chinese girls.

In Xhosa that wasn't half bad.

◆　◆　◆

Times got tougher and tougher for P. W. Botha. But, big crocodile that he was, he could stand being in deep water, with just his nostrils and eyes above the surface.

He could entertain the notion of reform, of course: he had to keep up with the times. People had been divided into blacks, whites, coloureds and Indians for a long time. Now he made sure to give the latter two the right to vote. And the blacks, too, for that matter, but not in South Africa — in their homelands.

Botha also eased the restrictions on the general relations between races. Nowadays, blacks and whites could — at least theoretically — sit on the same park bench. They could — at least theoretically — go to the same cinema and see the same film at the same time. And they could — at least theoretically — share bodily fluids (they could do this in practice, too, but in that case either money or violence would be involved).

In addition, the president made sure to centre the power on himself, thin out some human rights, and introduce censorship of the press. The newspapers had only themselves to blame if they didn't have the sense to write anything sensible. A country that is being rocked to its core requires clear leadership, not page after page of this let's-all-hug-each-other journalism.

But no matter how Botha spun things, they turned out all wrong. The country's economy had hardly started moving before it stopped short and then began going in the other direction. It wasn't exactly cheap for the military to subdue every bit of unrest in practically every single shantytown. The darkies simply weren't satisfied with anything. Just think about the time Botha offered to free that damned Nelson Mandela if he promised in return to comply with the government. "Stop being difficult" was the only demand Botha made. "No, I'd rather stay where I am," that fucker said after twenty years on his prison island, and so he did.

As time passed, it became clear that the greatest change P. W. Botha had managed to bring about with his new constitution was to turn himself from prime minister into president. And Mandela into a bigger icon than ever.

Otherwise, everything was the same. No, incorrect. Otherwise, everything was worse.

Botha was starting to tire of it all. He realized that things might really end with the ANC taking over. And in that case . . . well, who would voluntarily put six nuclear weapons into the hands of a Communist Kaffir organization? Better to dismantle the weapons, and make a PR spectacle out of it! "We are taking responsibility" and all that, while the IAEA looked on.

Yes, that might actually work. The president still wasn't ready to make a decision about it, but he personally called the engineer in charge at Pelindaba to put him on standby. Wait, was he already slurring his words at nine in the morning? No, that couldn't be.

◆ ◆ ◆

Engineer van der Westhuizen's little mathematical error (the one that turned six bombs into seven) suddenly turned into an extremely atrocious secret. The president had mentioned the possibility that the six atomic bombs would be destroyed. The *six* bombs. Not the seventh one. Because, of course, it didn't exist.

Now the engineer either had to admit his mistake, confess that he had kept it secret for over a year and receive a disgraceful dismissal and a minimal pension — or he could make things work out to his own advantage. And become financially independent.

The engineer was full of anxiety. But only until the last half litre of Klipdrift made it into his blood. After that, the decision was easy.

He could tell the time. He knew that his was up. Time to have a serious chat with Mossad Agents A and B.

"Hey, whatsyourname," he slurred. "Can you get both of the Jews in here. We've got some business to discuss!"

Engelbrecht van der Westhuizen had worked out that his task was about to come to an end, that the ANC would soon take over the country, and that he could not expect to have a career left. So he had to put his house in order while he still had a house to see to.

Whatshername went to find the agents, who had overseen the entire process off and on, on behalf of South Africa's partner Israel. As she wandered through the corridors, she thought that the engineer was about to go at least one step too far. Probably two.

Mossad Agents A and B were shown into the engineer's office. Nombeko stood in the corner where the engineer always wanted her to be when things heated up.

Engineer Westhuizen set the tone.

"Ah, Jew One and Jew Two, shalom! Have a seat. May I offer you a morning brandy? You, whatsyourname, get our friends a drink!"

Nombeko whispered to the agents that water was available should they prefer it. They did.

Engineer van der Westhuizen told it like it was, saying that he had always been lucky in life and that it just so happened that this luck had placed a nuclear weapon in his lap, an atomic bomb that no one knew existed and thus no one would miss. Really, the engineer said, he ought to keep it for himself and fire it straight into the presidential palace once Mandela was inaugurated, but he was a bit too old to wage a war on his own.

"So now I'm wondering, Jew A and Jew B, if you might want to check with the head Jew in Jerusalem about buying one bomb of the more potent sort. I'll give you the friends-and-family discount. No, wait a second, never mind. I want thirty million dollars. Ten million per megaton. Cheers!" said the engineer, and he drained his brandy and then looked with displeasure at the now-empty bottle.

Mossad Agents A and B thanked him politely for the offer and promised to check with the government in Jerusalem to see how it felt about this sort of business deal with Mr Westhuizen.

"Well, I kowtow to no one," said the engineer. "If this doesn't work I'll sell it to someone else. Now, I don't have time to sit here jabbering with you."

The engineer left both his office and the facility, on the hunt for more brandy. He left behind the two Mossad agents and whatshername. Nombeko realized what was at stake for the Israelis.

"Please excuse me for saying so," she said, "but I'm wondering if the engineer's luck didn't run out just about now."

She didn't add "And mine, too." But she was thinking it.

"I've always been impressed by your cleverness, Miss Nombeko," said Mossad Agent A. "And I thank you in advance for your understanding."

He didn't add "Things aren't looking so good for you, either." But he was thinking it.

It wasn't that Israel didn't want what the engineer was offering; they did. It was just that the seller was a serious alcoholic and a very erratic man. If they made a deal, it would be perilous to have him walking around

151

free on the streets, slurring and chattering about where all his money had come from. On the other hand, they couldn't just say no to the offer, because then what would happen to the bomb? The engineer was likely in a condition to sell it to anyone at all.

So they had to do what they had to do. Mossad Agent A hired a beggar from the slum in Pretoria to steal a car for him the next night; it was a 1983 Datsun Laurel. As thanks, the beggar received fifty rand (according to their agreement) as well as a shot to the temple (on the agent's own initiative).

Agent A planned to use the car to bring the engineer's endless luck to an end by running him over a few days later, as he was on his way home from the bar he always frequented when his personal supply of Klipdrift was gone.

The engineer's new-found bad luck was such that he was run over a second time when A stopped and reversed, and a third time when the agent roared off as fast as he could.

Ironically enough, the engineer had been walking on the pavement when it happened.

Was that all? he thought between the second and third times he was run over, just as Nombeko had done in a similar situation eleven years earlier.

And it was.

♦ ♦ ♦

Mossad Agent B went to find Nombeko just after the news of the death had come to the research facility. The incident was still being classified as an accident, but that would change when witnesses and various technicians on the scene had had their word.

"We might have something to discuss, you and I, Miss Nombeko," he said. "And I'm afraid it's urgent."

Nombeko said nothing at first, but she was thinking very hard. She was thinking that the guarantor of her physical well-being, the eternally drunk Westhuizen, was now dead. She was thinking that she herself might very soon be in a similar condition. If she didn't think quickly.

But she did. So she said, "Yes, we do. May I therefore ask you, Mr Agent, to bring your colleague here for a meeting in the engineer's office in exactly thirty minutes?"

Agent B had long since learned that Miss Nombeko had her head on straight. He knew that she understood that her situation was precarious. This put him and his fellow agent in a position of power.

Miss Nombeko was the one who had the keys and the permission to enter the most forbidden of corridors. She was the one who would make sure that the agents got their hands on the bomb. In return, they would offer her a white lie.

The promise that she would be allowed to live.

But now she had bought herself half an hour. Why? The agent understood most things, but not this. Oh well, half an hour was just half an hour, after all, even if they were in a hurry. The South African intelligence service might realize at any moment that the engineer had been murdered. Soon after that it would become

153

considerably harder to carry a three-megaton bomb out of the facility, even for an agent from a collaborating intelligence agency.

Oh well, half an hour was still just half an hour. Agent B nodded in reply.

"Then we'll meet here at twelve-oh-five."

"Twelve-oh-six," said Nombeko.

During those thirty minutes, all Nombeko did was wait for time to pass.

The agents were back exactly when they were meant to be. Nombeko was sitting in the engineer's chair, and she kindly asked them to sit down on the other side of the desk. It was a strange scene. A young black woman in the director's chair, in the heart of the South African system of apartheid.

Nombeko began the meeting. She said that she understood that the Messrs Mossad Agents were out to get the seventh atomic bomb, the one that didn't exist. Or had she misunderstood?

The agents didn't say anything: they didn't quite want to put the truth into words.

"Let us be honest in this meeting," Nombeko urged them. "Otherwise we won't get anywhere before it's too late."

Agent A nodded and said that Miss Nombeko had understood things correctly. If she could help Israel get its hands on the bomb, they would help her get out of Pelindaba in return.

"Without causing me to end up just as run over as the engineer afterwards?" Nombeko asked. "Or shot and buried in the nearest savannah?"

154

"Why, Miss Nombeko, please!" Agent A lied. "We aren't planning to harm a hair on your head. What do you think we are?"

Nombeko seemed to be satisfied with the agent's lie. She added that for the record she had already been run over once in her life, and that would suffice.

"How are you planning on getting the bomb out of here, if I may ask? Assuming I give you access to it."

Agent B replied that it ought to be relatively easy, if they only hurried. The crate containing the bomb could be addressed to the Israeli Foreign Office in Jerusalem, and here on the base it could be supplied with documentation to class it as diplomatic post. Diplomatic letters were sent via the embassy in Pretoria at least once a week; a largish crate wouldn't make any difference that way. As long as the South African intelligence service didn't ramp up their security and open the crate — and Nombeko and the agents could count on this happening as soon as they realized how the engineer had really died.

"Yes, Messrs Agents, I owe you special thanks for that measure," Nombeko said, simultaneously honestly and treacherously. "Which of you did the honours?"

"I don't think that matters," said Agent A, who was the guilty party. "What's done is done, and we know you understand that it was necessary, Miss Nombeko."

Oh yes, Nombeko understood. She understood that the agents had just fallen into her trap.

"So how are you planning to make sure that little old me is safe?"

The agents' plan was to hide Nombeko in the boot of their car. There would be no risk of detection as long as the security measures remained at their current level. The Israeli intelligence agency at Pelindaba had remained above suspicion for all these years.

Once out in the open, all they had to do was drive straight out into the bush, pull the woman from the boot and give her a shot to the forehead, temple or back of the neck, depending on how much she struggled.

It was a bit sad: Miss Nombeko was an exceptional woman in many ways and, just like the agents, she had been subjected to Engineer Westhuizen's ill-disguised scorn, based on nothing more than the engineer's muddled idea that he represented a superior people. Yes, it was a bit sad, but they had more important things to worry about.

"Our idea is to smuggle you out of here in the boot of our car," said Agent A, leaving out what would happen afterwards.

"Good," said Nombeko. "But insufficient."

She continued, saying that she did not intend to lift a finger to help the Messrs Agents until they had handed her an airline ticket, Johannesburg-Tripoli.

"Tripoli?" said Agents A and B in unison. "What are you going to do there?"

Nombeko didn't have a good answer. For all these years, her goal had been the National Library in Pretoria. But she couldn't go there now. She had to leave the country. And Gaddafi in Libya was on the ANC's side, wasn't he?

Nombeko said that she wanted to go to a friendly country for a change, and that Libya seemed like a good choice in this situation. But by all means, if the Messrs Agents had a better idea, she was all ears.

"Just don't try to say Tel Aviv or Jerusalem. Because my plan includes surviving the week, at least."

Mossad Agent A was becoming increasingly enchanted with the woman in the chair in front of him. They had to be on their guard to make sure she didn't get her way. She had to realize that her bargaining position was weak — that in order to be smuggled off the base, she had no choice but to trust the agents she couldn't trust. But after that, at least, she could make the situation work to her advantage. Her problem was that there would never be any step two or three. As soon as the boot was closed, she would be on her way to her own grave. And then it wouldn't matter what it said on the ticket. Tripoli, why not? Or the moon.

But first they had to play the game.

"Yes, Libya would probably work," said Agent A. "Along with Sweden, it's the country that is loudest in protesting against the South African system of apartheid. You would be granted asylum there within ten seconds if you asked, miss."

"Well, there you go!" said Nombeko.

"But Gaddafi does have his drawbacks," the agent went on.

"Drawbacks?"

Agent A was happy to tell her all about the lunatic of Tripoli, who had once attacked Egypt with grenades just because its president had chosen to answer when

157

addressed by Israel. It couldn't hurt to show some concern for Miss Nombeko. To build up trust until the necessary shot to the back of the head.

"Yes, Gaddafi is out fishing for nuclear weapons as much as South Africa; it's just that he hasn't fished as successfully so far."

"Oh dear," said Nombeko.

"Anyway, he can take solace in the fact that he must have at least twenty tons of mustard gas in storage, and the world's largest chemical weapons factory."

"Oh my," said Nombeko.

"And he has forbidden any opposition, and all strikes and demonstrations."

"Oh no," said Nombeko.

"And he has anyone who disagrees with him killed."

"Does he have any humane side at all?" said Nombeko.

"Oh yes," said the agent. "He took good care of the ex-dictator Idi Amin when Amin was forced to flee from Uganda."

"Yes, I read something about that," said Nombeko.

"There is more to tell," said Agent A.

"Or not," said Nombeko.

"Don't get me wrong, Miss Nombeko. We are concerned about your well-being, and we don't want anything to happen to you, even if you recently insinuated that we are not to be trusted. I confess that we were both hurt by that insinuation. But if you want to go to Tripoli, we will certainly arrange it."

That sounded perfect, thought Agent A.

That sounded perfect, thought Agent B.

That is the stupidest thing I have heard in my entire life, thought Nombeko. And I have spent time with assistants from the sanitation department of the City of Johannesburg *and* alcoholic engineers with distorted self-images.

The agents were concerned about her well-being? She might have been born in Soweto, but it hadn't happened yesterday.

Libya didn't seem as much fun any more.

"What about Sweden?" she said.

Yes, it would probably be preferable, the agents thought. Of course, they had just killed their prime minister, but at least ordinary people could walk down the street unharmed. And, as they'd said, the Swedes were quick to accept South Africans, as long as they said they were against the apartheid regime — and the agents had reason to believe that Nombeko was.

Nombeko nodded. Then she sat there in silence. She knew where Sweden was. Almost at the North Pole. Far from Soweto, and that was obviously a good thing. Far from everything that had been her life so far. What, she wondered, might she miss?

"If there's anything you want to take to Sweden, Miss Nombeko, we will certainly do our best to help you get it," said Agent B, in order to build up more trust with zero substance.

If you keep on like this I might almost start believing you, Nombeko thought. But only almost. It would be exceedingly unprofessional of you not to try to kill me as soon as you've got what you want. "A carton of dried antelope meat would be nice," she said. "I can't imagine that they have antelope in Sweden."

No, A and B didn't think so either. The agents would arrange address labels for one small and one large package right away. The bomb in the crate would go to the Foreign Office in Jerusalem, via the embassy in Pretoria. And Miss Nombeko could sign for the carton of antelope meat at the Israeli embassy in Stockholm in just a few days.

"Do we have an agreement, then?" said Agent A, thinking that everything was working out for the best.

"Yes," said Nombeko. "We have an agreement. But there's one more thing."

One more thing? Agent A had a well-developed sense for the sort of business he did. He suddenly suspected that he and his colleague had counted their chicks before they hatched.

"I realize we don't have much time," said Nombeko. "But there's something I need to take care of before we can leave."

"Take care of?"

"We'll meet here again in one hour, at one twenty; you probably ought to hurry if you're going to have time to get both an airline ticket and antelope meat before then," she said, and she left the room through the door behind the engineer's desk, to the room the agents didn't have access to. The agents were left alone in the office.

"Have we underestimated her?" said A to B.

B looked concerned.

"If you get the ticket I'll get the meat," he said.

160

◆ ◆ ◆

"Do you see what this is?" Nombeko said when the meeting resumed and she placed a rough diamond on Engineer Westhuizen's desk.

Agent A was a multifaceted man. He had, for instance, no problem dating a pottery goose from the Han dynasty to 1970s South Africa. And he could immediately tell that the object before him now was probably worth about a million shekels.

"I see," he said. "Where are you trying to go with this, Miss Nombeko?"

"Where am I trying to go? I want to go to Sweden. Not to a hole behind a bush on the savannah."

"And for that reason you want to give us a diamond?" said Agent B, who, unlike Agent A, might have still been underestimating Nombeko.

"What kind of person do you think I am, Mr Agent?" she said. "No, I just want to use this diamond to make it seem plausible that I managed to get a small package out of the facility since we last saw one another. Now you must decide whether you believe I succeeded in doing so, for example with the help of another diamond like this. And whether I subsequently received confirmation that the package in question reached its destination with the help of yet another diamond. And whether you believe that one of the two hundred and fifty proud and constantly underpaid workers at Pelindaba might have agreed to such an arrangement. Or whether you don't believe it."

"I don't understand," said Agent B.

161

"Well, *I* suspect the worst," Agent A mumbled.

"That's right," said Nombeko, smiling. "I recorded our last conversation, in which you confessed to murdering a South African citizen, as well as to the theft of one South African weapon of mass destruction. I am sure that both of you understand the consequences you and your nation would face if the tape were to be played in . . . well, who knows? I'm not going to tell you where I sent it. But the recipient has confirmed via the messenger I bribed that it is where I want it to be. In other words, it is no longer here on the base. If I pick it up within twenty-four — no, sorry, twenty-three hours and thirty-eight minutes — time flies when you're having fun — you have my word that it will disappear for ever."

"And if you don't pick it up, it will become public?" A filled in.

Nombeko didn't waste time on a reply.

"Well, I think this meeting is over. It'll be exciting to see if I survive my trip in the boot. It certainly feels like my chances have increased. From zero."

And then she stood up, said that the package of antelope meat should be delivered to the department of outgoing post within thirty minutes, and that she herself would make sure the same went for the larger crate; after all, it was in the next room. Beyond that she was looking forward to receiving proper documentation: stamps and forms and whatever else was necessary for the crate would be sufficiently inaccessible to each and every person who didn't want a diplomatic crisis on his hands.

A and B nodded sullenly.

162

♦ ♦ ♦

The Israeli agents analysed the situation. They considered it likely that the damned cleaning woman did have a tape of their earlier conversation, but they weren't so sure that she had managed to smuggle it out of Pelindaba. There was no question that she had at least one rough diamond in her possession, and if she had one she could have more. And if she did have more of them, it was possible that one of the many workers with high security clearance at the facility had fallen into temptation and secured his family's financial position for the rest of his life. Possible, but not certain. On the one hand, the cleaning woman (they no longer called her by name — they were far too annoyed to do so) had been at the facility for eleven years; on the other hand the agents had never seen her with a single white person, except for the late engineer and the agents themselves. Had one of the 250 workers really sold his soul to the woman they called Kaffir behind her back?

When the agents added the dimension of sex — that is, the possibility, or rather the risk, that the cleaning woman had added her body to the pot — the odds were shifted to the agents' disadvantage. Anyone who would be immoral enough to run errands for her for the sake of a diamond would also be immoral enough to report her. But anyone who could expect the added possibility of future sexual adventures would just be biting himself in the arse. Or somewhere else, if only he could reach.

All in all, Agents A and B figured that there was a 60 per cent chance that Nombeko really was sitting on the

163

trump card she claimed to have, and a 40 per cent chance that she wasn't. And those odds were too poor. The harm she could bring them and — above all! — the country of Israel was immeasurable.

Thus their decision had to be that the cleaning woman would come along in the boot as planned, that she would receive a ticket to Sweden as planned, that her twenty pounds of antelope meat would be sent to Stockholm as planned — and that she would *not* receive the shot to the back of the head as planned. Or to the forehead. Or anywhere else. She was still a risk as long as she was alive. But now she was an even greater risk if she was dead.

Twenty-nine minutes later, Nombeko received airline tickets and the antelope meat Agent A had promised her, as well as duplicate copies of properly filled-in forms for the diplomatic post. She thanked them and said that she would be ready to leave within fifteen minutes; she just wanted to make sure that both packages were handled correctly. What she meant by this — but didn't say — was that she was going to have a serious talk with the Chinese girls.

"One large and one small package?" said the little sister, who was the most creative of them. "Would Miss Nombeko mind if we . . ."

"Yes, that's just it," said Nombeko. "These packages must *not* be sent to your mother in Johannesburg. The small package is going to Stockholm. It's for me, and I

164

hope that's reason enough not to touch it. The large one is going to Jerusalem."

"Jerusalem?" said the middle sister.

"Egypt," the big sister explained.

"Are you leaving?" said the little sister.

Nombeko wondered how the engineer could ever have come up with the idea of putting these three girls in charge of the post.

"Yes, but don't say anything to anyone. I'm going to be smuggled out of here in a little bit. I'm going to Sweden. I guess we have to say goodbye now. You've been good friends."

And then they hugged one another.

"Take care of yourself, Nombeko," the Chinese girls said in Xhosa.

"再见," Nombeko replied. "Farewell!"

Then she went to the engineer's office, unlocked his desk drawer and took her passport.

"Market Theatre, please, the marketplace, downtown Johannesburg," Nombeko said to Agent A as she crawled into the boot of the car with its diplomatic plates.

She sounded like any old customer talking to any old taxi driver. It also seemed as if she knew Johannesburg inside out — and as if she knew where she was going. The truth was that a few minutes earlier she had paged through one last book among those in the Pelindaba library and found what was probably the most crowded place in the whole country.

"I understand," said Agent A. "Will do."

And then he closed the boot.

What he understood was that Nombeko wasn't planning to let them drive her to the person who held the tape so that they could kill them both. He also understood that once they had arrived, Nombeko would manage to disappear in the crowd in under two minutes. He understood that Nombeko had won.

Round one.

But as soon as the bomb had arrived in Jerusalem, there would no longer be any physical evidence on the loose. After that, the tape could be played any number of times, anywhere at all; all they had to do was deny it. Everyone was against Israel anyway; of course there were tapes of that nature circulating. Believing them just because they existed, however, would be silly.

Then it would be time for round two.

Because you don't mess with the Mossad.

◆ ◆ ◆

The agents' car left Pelindaba at 2.10p.m. on Thursday, 12 November 1987. At 3.01 the same day, the day's outgoing post was transported through the same gates. It was eleven minutes late because they'd had to switch vehicles due to an extra-large item.

At 3.15 the director of the investigation surrounding the death of Engineer van der Westhuizen confirmed that he had been murdered. Three independent witnesses had given similar testimonies. Furthermore, two of them were white.

Their testimonies were corroborated by the observations the director of investigation made at the scene. There were traces of rubber at three points along the engineer's demolished face. It must have been run over by at least three tyres — that is, one tyre more than a normal car has on each side. Thus the engineer had either been run over by more than one car, or — as the witnesses unanimously agreed — several times by the same car.

It took another fifteen minutes, but by 3.30 security at the research facility was increased by one level. The black cleaning woman in the outer perimeter was to be dismissed immediately, along with the black cleaning woman in the central G wing and the three Asians in the kitchen. All five would be subjected to the intelligence service's risk analysis before they were at the most *possibly* set free. All entering and exiting vehicles would be checked, even if the commander of the army himself were behind the wheel!

♦ ♦ ♦

Nombeko asked her way around the airport, followed the stream of people and was past the security check before she even understood that it existed and that she had been subjected to it. She realized after the fact that diamonds in the lining of a jacket won't set off a metal detector.

Because the Mossad agents had had to buy tickets at such short notice, only the most expensive seats were available. Her seat in the cabin was, accordingly, a good one. It took the staff quite some time to convince Nombeko that the glass of Champagne de Pompadour Extra Brut she was offered was included in the price. Just as was the food that followed. She was also kindly but firmly shown back to her seat when she tried to help clear the other passengers' trays.

But she had figured it out by the time she received dessert, which consisted of almond-baked raspberries, and which she washed down with a cup of coffee.

"May I offer you some brandy with your coffee?" the flight attendant offered kindly.

"Yes, please," said Nombeko. "Do you have Klipdrift?"

Soon thereafter she fell asleep. She slept serenely and well — and for a long time.

When she arrived at Stockholm Arlanda airport, she followed the instructions of the so elegantly duped Mossad agents. She went up to the first border policeman she saw and asked for political asylum. The reason she gave was membership of the banned organization the ANC, which sounded better than saying she had just helped another nation's intelligence agency steal a nuclear weapon.

Her initial interrogation with the Swedish border police took place in a bright room with windows looking out onto the runway. Something was happening out there, something Nombeko had never before experienced. It was snowing. It was the first snow of winter, right in the middle of the South African spring.

168

CHAPTER
EIGHT

On a match that ended in a draw and an entrepreneur who didn't get to live his life

Ingmar and Holger One were in agreement that the best way to honour Mum was to continue their fight. Two was sure that his father and brother were wrong about that, but he settled for asking who they thought was going to bring money into the household, in that case.

Ingmar frowned and admitted that he hadn't prioritized that part, in the midst of everything he'd had to consider recently. There were still a few hundred-krona notes left in Henrietta's sugar bowl, but they would soon be just as gone as Henrietta herself.

For lack of a better idea, the former postal clerk decided to reapply for his job as assistant to the accountant, who now had only two years left until retirement. And who replied that under no circumstances was he planning to let Mr Qvist spoil them.

The situation was rather troublesome — for another few days. And then Ingmar's father-in-law died.

The angry Communist who had never met his grandchildren (and who couldn't get his hands on Ingmar) died at the age of eighty-eight, full of bitterness, with a lost daughter, a wife who had disappeared, and capitalism blooming around him. At least he didn't have to watch everything he owned be taken over by the Holgers and Ingmar, though, since he no longer existed. Holger One, the one who did exist, inherited it all.

Alongside his political activities, the leader of Södertälje's Communists had imported and sold products from the Soviet Union. Until the very end he had travelled around Swedish marketplaces to promote his goods along with his opinions of the greatness of the Soviet Union. Things went so-so with both the former and the latter, but in any case, his profits were enough to cover the bare necessities of life plus a colour TV, two visits a week to the off-licence and three thousand kronor per month as a gift to the party.

Included in One's inheritance from his grandfather was a truck in good condition and a garage-slash-warehouse bursting with stuff; for all these years the old man had made purchases at a slightly greater pace than he had managed to sell them.

Among the goods were black and red caviar, pickles and smoked krill. There was Georgian tea, Belarusian linen, Russian felted boots and Inuit sealskins. There were all sorts of enamel containers, including the classic green rubbish bin with a pedal. There were furashki, the Russian military caps, and ushanki, the fur hats that are impossible to freeze in. There were rubber hot-water bottles, and shot glasses with mountain-ash berries painted on them. And size forty-seven braided straw hats.

There were five hundred copies of *The Communist Manifesto* in Russian and two hundred goat-hair shawls from the Urals. And four Siberian tiger traps.

Ingmar and the boys found all of this and more in the garage. And, last but not least:

An eight-foot-tall statue of Lenin, made of Karelian granite.

If Ingmar's father-in-law had still been alive, and if moreover he had wished to converse with his son-in-law instead of strangling him, he could have told him that he had bought the statue on the cheap from an artist in Petrozavodsk who had made the mistake of giving the great leader human features. The steely grey gaze of Lenin had turned out somewhat abashed, and the hand that was meant to point straight into the future seemed to be *waving* at the people Lenin was meant to lead. The mayor of the city, who had ordered the statue, became upset when he saw the result, and he told the artist to vanish immediately, or else the mayor would see to it that he did.

Just then Ingmar's father-in-law had shown up on one of his shopping rounds. Two weeks later, the statue was lying there and waving straight at a garage wall in Södertälje.

Ingmar and One browsed through the riches as they chuckled happily. This would be enough to support the family for years!

Two was not as delighted about this development. He had been hoping that his mother hadn't died in vain, and that things would change for real.

"Lenin might not have the world's highest market value," he tried, but he was immediately snapped at.

"God, you're so negative," his father, Ingmar, said.

"Yeah, God, you're so negative," said Holger One.

"Or *The Communist Manifesto* in Russian," Two added.

◆ ◆ ◆

The goods in the garage were enough to support the family for eight whole years. Ingmar and the twins followed in Ingmar's father-in-law's footsteps from marketplace to marketplace, making enough to support a tolerable standard of living by a certain margin. This was in large part because the Communists in Södertälje no longer received a portion of this income. Neither did the tax authorities, for that matter.

Two constantly longed to get away, but he took comfort in the fact that during their years of marketing, at least there wasn't any extra time for the republican tomfoolery.

After those eight years, all that remained was the eight-foot-tall Lenin statue in Karelian granite as well as 498 of the 500 copies of *The Communist Manifesto* in Russian. Ingmar had managed to sell one copy to a blind man during the market days in Mariestad. They had needed the other on the way to Malma Market, when Ingmar got a stomach bug and had to stop the car to squat in a ditch.

To some extent, then, Holger Two had been correct.

"What do we do now?" said Holger One, who had never had an idea in all his life.

"Anything you want, as long as it has nothing to do with the royal family," said Holger Two.

"No, that's exactly what it has to do with," said Ingmar. "There's been far too little of that sort of thing recently."

Ingmar's idea for continued survival involved modifying the statue of Lenin. The fact was, he had recently realized that this particular Lenin and the King of Sweden had a considerable number of common features. All they had to do was hack the moustache and beard off the old man, tap a little here and there at his nose, and turn his cap into wavy hair — and presto! Vladimir Ilyich would be the spitting image of His Majesty!

"You're planning on selling an eight-foot-tall statue of the king?" Holger Two said to his father. "Have you no principles?"

"Now, don't be cheeky, my dear renegade of a son. Necessity knows no law. I learned that back when I was young and strong and had no choice but to commandeer a Salvationist's new bicycle. Incidentally, his name was Holger, too."

And then he went on, saying that the Holgers had no idea how many wealthy royalists there were in this country. A statue of the king could go for twenty or thirty thousand. Maybe forty. And then all they had to do was sell the truck.

Ingmar got to it. He hacked and filed and polished for an entire week. And he succeeded beyond all expectations. When Holger Two saw the result, he thought that one could say a lot of things about his father, but irresolute he was not. Neither did he lack a gift for artistry.

The sale itself remained. Ingmar's idea was to winch the statue into the back of the truck and then drive around to all the counts and barons in all the manors around Stockholm until one of them realized that he could not live without a Swedish-Karelian granite king in his very own garden.

But the winching was a delicate operation; after all, the king mustn't fall on his arse. Holger One was eager to help, if his father would just tell him what to do. Two stood with his hands in his pockets and didn't say anything.

Ingmar looked at his boys and decided that, this time, he couldn't afford for one of them to bungle things. Dad would take care of it himself.

"Just take a few steps back and don't pester me," he said, fastening cables here and there in his advanced pulley system.

And then he started winching. And he actually managed to lift the statue of the king all the way up to the edge of the truck bed, all on his own.

"All that's left is the rest," said the pleased king-hater, a split second before one of the cables snapped.

174

Then and there, Ingmar Qvist's lifelong struggle came to an end.

For the king bowed humbly towards him, met his gaze for the first time, and fell slowly but inevitably right on top of his creator.

Ingmar died instantly under the weight of the king, while the king himself broke into four pieces.

Holger One was completely stricken with grief. Two stood next to him, ashamed that he couldn't seem to feel anything at all. He looked at his dead father, and next to him, the pieces of the king.

The match seemed to have ended in a draw.

A few days later, one could read in *Länstidningen Södertälje*:

MY BELOVED FATHER
INGMAR QVIST
HAS LEFT ME
IN ENDLESS SORROW AND LOSS
SÖDERTÄLJE, 4 JUNE 1987
HOLGER

—

VIVE LA RÉPUBLIQUE

♦ ♦ ♦

Holgers One and Two were identical copies of one another. And they were each other's opposites.

One had never questioned his father's calling for a second. Two's doubt had manifested itself when he was only seven, and it continued to grow. By the time Two was twelve, he knew that things just weren't right in his father's head. Beginning with his mother's death, he questioned Ingmar's ideas more and more often.

But he never left. As the years went on, he felt an ever-greater sense of responsibility towards his father and brother. And then there was the fact that One and Two were twins. That was a bond that was not easy to break.

It was hard to say why the brothers had turned out so differently. Perhaps it had something to do with the fact that Holger Two — the one who didn't really exist — was generally gifted in a way that the first brother was not.

So it was natural that Two was the one who took care of essays and exams during their school years, and that it was Two who passed his brother's driving test and taught him the art of driving. And what's more, it was a truck-driving licence. Their grandfather's Volvo F406 was the brothers' only possession worth mentioning. That is to say, it was Holger One who owned it. Because to own something, one must exist.

Once their father was gone, Two thought about going to the authorities to let them know he existed, so that he might be able to apply to a school of higher education. And find a girl to love. And make love with. Wonder what that would feel like?

But when Two thought about it, he realized it wasn't quite that simple. Could he even make use of the good grades he'd got in upper secondary school? Didn't they

176

belong to his brother? By definition, Holger Two hadn't even finished his basic schooling.

Besides this, there were more immediate issues to deal with. Such as how the Holgers could afford enough food to eat. Holger One existed for real: he had a passport and a driver's licence, and he ought to be able to look for a job.

"A job?" said One when the matter came up.

"Yes, as in employment. It's not unusual for people who are twenty-six years old to pursue such a thing."

Holger One suggested that Two could have a go at that instead, in One's name. Pretty much like the way they had done it during all those years of school. But Two said that now the king had killed their father, it was time to leave their youth behind. Two had no intention of running his brother's errands — and definitely not his father's.

"It wasn't the king, it was Lenin," Holger One said sulkily.

Two said that the person who had fallen on top of Ingmar could be anyone One wanted it to be, including Mahatma Gandhi. That was history. Now it was time to build a future. He would prefer to do so with his dear brother, but only if One promised to drop all of his ideas involving a change of government. One mumbled that he didn't have any ideas anyway.

Holger Two was content with that answer and spent the next few days thinking about what their next step in life should be.

The most pressing issue was putting food on the table.

The solution would have to be to sell the table in question. The whole house, in fact.

The family plot outside Södertälje changed ownership, and the brothers moved into the back of the Volvo F406 truck.

But they had sold a cottage, not a castle, and it had, to all intents and purposes, not been maintained since Ingmar had started losing his mind forty years earlier. Holger One, the formal owner, received only 150,000 kronor for his parental home. The money would soon be gone again if the Holgers didn't do something about it.

One wondered what Two thought the top quarter of Dad's statue might be worth. To make sure that One never brought it up again, Two took out a chisel and a hammer and hacked it to pieces. When he was done, he promised that he would also burn the 498 remaining copies of *The Communist Manifesto* in Russian, but first he was going to take a walk because he needed some time to himself.

"Please don't think too much while I'm gone."

◆ ◆ ◆

Holger & Holger Incorporated? Would that work? A transport service? They did have a truck, after all. That was all they had. A truck.

Holger Two placed an ad in the paper for a SMALL TRANSPORT SERVICE SEEKING JOBS and was immediately contacted by a pillow entrepreneur in Gnesta who needed help because the distributor he'd been using until now had forgotten to complete not only every fifth transport but also every other tax payment, so he'd been forced to move into the Arnö Prison for rehabilitation. The state believed it would take the distributor eighteen months to be rehabilitated. The pillow entrepreneur, who knew the true nature of the distributor, thought that it might take longer than that. In any case, the distributor was where he was and the entrepreneur needed an immediate substitute.

Gnesta Down & Featherbed Inc. had made pillows for the hotel industry as well as various county councils and authorities for ages and ages. At first things had gone well for the company, then less well, and finally things didn't go at all. Then the entrepreneur had fired his four employees and started importing pillows from China instead. This made his life more tolerable, but it was hard work, and he was starting to feel old. The overworked man was tired of everything, and he only kept going because he had long since forgotten that life could consist of anything else.

Holgers One and Two met the entrepreneur at his industrial building on the outskirts of Gnesta. It looked like a miserable area, with a warehouse and a condemned building facing a yard, and on the other side of the street there was a pottery factory that had been abandoned many years ago. The closest neighbour was a scrapyard; other than that, the area was deserted.

Because Holger Two could speak for himself and because Holger One remained silent on Two's orders, the entrepreneur felt that he could trust this potential new distribution solution. The apartments in the condemned building weren't the world's greatest, but if the brothers wanted to move into one of them, or two of them, that would be fine. The entrepreneur himself lived in the centre of the small town.

Everything seemed to be working out for the best, but then the pension board sent a letter saying that the entrepreneur was about to turn sixty-five and thus had the right to start drawing a pension. He hadn't thought of that. What luck! Now it was time to enjoy the life of a pensioner. Doing nothing full-time — that was something the entrepreneur was looking forward to. And maybe even some boogie-woogie? He hadn't tried to kick up his heels since the late summer of '67 when he went to Stockholm to visit Nalen, only to find that the famous dance hall had closed and become a Free Church.

The information about his upcoming pension was nice for the entrepreneur. For Holger and Holger it was more problematic.

Oh well, the brothers had nothing to lose, so Two decided to move forward aggressively. He suggested that Holger & Holger AB take over the entrepreneur's entire business, including the warehouse, the condemned building and the pottery. In return, the entrepreneur would receive 35,000 kronor per month from the brothers for as long as he lived.

"As an extra pension," Holger Two said. "We don't exactly have any cash to buy you out with right now, Mr Entrepreneur."

The newly minted pensioner thought this through. And he thought some more. And then he said, "Done! But let's say thirty thousand rather than thirty-five thousand. And on one condition!"

"Condition?" said Holger Two.

"Well, the thing is . . ." the entrepreneur began.

The lowered price took into account the fact that Holger and Holger promised to take over responsibility for the American engineer whom the entrepreneur had found hiding in the pottery fourteen years earlier. The American had built military tunnels during the Vietnam War; he had been under constant attack by the Viet Cong and ended up seriously injured. He had received care at a hospital in Japan, become healthy again, dug his way out of his hospital room through the floor, fled to Hokkaido, hitched a ride to the Soviet border on a fishing trawler, switched to a Soviet coast-guard vessel, ended up in Moscow and then in Helsinki, and had made his way to Sweden and Stockholm. There he was granted political asylum.

But the Vietnam deserter thought he saw the CIA everywhere in Stockholm; he was a nervous wreck, and he was sure that they would find him and take him back to the war. So he went wandering around the countryside, ended up in Gnesta, happened to see an abandoned pottery, sneaked in and lay down to sleep under a tarp. It was a little more than just coincidence that he ended up where he did, because a potter was what the American was deep down in his heart. He had

181

become an engineer and a military man on his father's orders.

The pillow entrepreneur didn't have much in the way of pots in his pottery; instead that was where he kept the parts of the pillow firm's bookkeeping that didn't do well in the light of day. For that reason he had to go there several times a week. One day, a terrified face popped up among the binders — it was the American — and the entrepreneur took pity on him. He was allowed to stay, but only if he moved into one of the apartments in the condemned house at Fredsgatan 5. If the American wanted to revive the pottery factory, that was fine, but the door to the windowless room over there must be kept closed.

With a certain amount of alarm, the American had accepted the offer, at which point he immediately, and without permission, started building a tunnel from his apartment on the ground floor of Fredsgatan 5 all the way to the pottery on the other side of the road. When the entrepreneur caught him at it, he said that he had to have an escape route when the CIA came knocking at his door. It took him several years to finish digging the tunnel. By the time it was ready, the Vietnam War had been over for a long time.

"He's not quite right, he certainly isn't, but he's part of the deal," said the overworked entrepreneur. "But he doesn't bother anyone, and as far as I know he lives on the pottery he can throw and sell at the markets in the area. Crazy, but he won't harm anyone except himself."

Holger Two was hesitant. He felt that he didn't need to surround himself with any more craziness. His brother and what he'd inherited from his father were enough. On the other hand, this arrangement would allow the brothers to move into the condemned building just as the American had done. A real house, instead of a mattress in the back of the truck.

He decided to agree to take responsibility for the nervous wreck of an American potter, so everything the former entrepreneur owned and had was signed over to One's newly incorporated business.

Finally, the overworked man could relax! He travelled to Stockholm the next day in order to enjoy himself and bathe at the classic Sturebadet spa and bathhouse; after that he would have pickled herring and schnapps at Sturehof!

But he forgot that the country had switched to driving on the right since the last time he visited the bustling capital. He had never even noticed that the same went for Gnesta. And so he was looking in the wrong direction as he stepped out into Birger Jarlsgatan.

"Life, here I come!" he said.

And was immediately and fatally run over by a bus.

"That's really sad," said Holger One when the brothers learned what had happened.

"Yes. And cheap," said Holger Two.

Holger and Holger went to visit the American potter to tell him about the very tragic fate of the pillow entrepreneur and to say that he was allowed to continue living there, because it was part of the agreement with the now-dead man, and agreements were meant to be kept.

Holger Two knocked on the door.

It was quiet in there.

Holger One knocked, too.

"Are you from the CIA?" they heard a voice say.

"No, from Södertälje," said Holger Two.

After that it was quiet for a few more seconds. Then the door was cautiously opened.

The meeting between the men went well. It started off a bit hesitantly, but things went better after Holger and Holger insinuated that at least one of them had a somewhat complicated relationship with society as well. It was true that the American had been granted asylum, but since then he had not been in contact with the Swedish authorities, so he didn't dare guess how much his asylum was worth today.

The potter could tolerate the new ownership of the condemned building; he decided to stay put, telling himself that there really weren't enough indications to suggest that Holger and Holger were doing errands for the American intelligence agency. Actually, there were almost no indications because, no matter how crafty the CIA was, they would never think of sending two identical agents with the same name.

The American even considered Holger Two's offer of jumping in now and then to take care of pillow deliveries. But in that case he demanded that the truck be given fake licence plates so that the CIA couldn't locate him in the event that he should be captured in a picture taken by one of the organization's thousands of hidden cameras, which were all over the country.

Holger Two shook his head, but he sent One out on a night-time assignment to steal a set of licence plates. But when the potter further demanded that the truck be painted black so that he could more easily shake off the American intelligence agency along some dark forested road on the day they managed to catch up with him, Two had had enough.

"We'll deliver our pillows ourselves, come to think of it. But thanks anyway."

The potter gazed after him for a long time. Why had he changed his mind so quickly?

◆ ◆ ◆

Holger Two felt that, on the whole, life had turned out to be relatively miserable, despite the arrangement with the pillow company and the condemned house. Furthermore, he was forced to note jealously that One had acquired a girlfriend. She was crazy, too, in Two's opinion, but then birds of a feather tend to flock together. She was a young girl of perhaps seventeen, and she seemed to be angry with everything, with the possible exception of Holger One. The two of them had met in central Gnesta, where the angry young woman had arranged a one-person demonstration against the corrupt banking system. As a self-designated representative of Daniel Ortega in Nicaragua, she had applied for a loan of half a million kronor, but the manager of the bank — who happened, incidentally, to be the angry young woman's father — had said that loans couldn't be granted via a delegate, and that President Ortega would have to come to Gnesta himself, show identification, and argue for his own creditworthiness.

Creditworthiness? How worthy was the bank manager himself, turning his back on his own daughter like this?

Thus the demonstration. Which had limited impact, because the audience consisted only of the girl's father, who was standing at the door of the bank, two scruffy men on a bench, who were waiting for the clock to strike ten so the Systembolaget off-licence would open — and Holger One, who was in town on an errand to buy bandages and antiseptic because he had hammered his thumb early that morning when he set about fixing a hole in the floor in his and his brother's apartment.

It was easy to see what the girl's father was thinking. The two scruffy men were mostly imagining what one could buy in Systembolaget for half a million kronor (the bolder one guessed one hundred bottles of Explorer vodka), while Holger One was completely blinded by the girl. She was fighting for a *president* who was, in turn, fighting an uphill battle, to say the least, in that he was an enemy of the United States and most of the rest of the world.

When the girl had finished demonstrating, he introduced himself and told her about his dream of deposing the Swedish king. Within five minutes they had realized they were made for each other. The girl went up to her unhappy father, who was still standing at the door of his bank, and informed him that he could go to hell because she was going to move in with . . . uh, what was his name? Holger!

Two was driven out of his and One's shared home; he had to make his own in the even more run-down apartment across the hall. All while life continued on its ill-fated path.

Then one day there was a delivery to Upplands Väsby, north of Stockholm — to the refugee camp run by the Immigration Board. Holger Two drove into the compound, parked outside the camp's storeroom, saw a solitary black woman, surely a new arrival, sitting on a bench at a distance, didn't think twice about it, and carried in the pillows he had brought. When he came out again, the woman suddenly spoke to him. He answered her politely and in return he heard her spontaneously marvel that men like him could exist.

He felt this comment so deeply in his heart that he couldn't help the reply that came out of him, namely, *"The problem is, I don't."*

He might have run far away instead, if he had known what was going to happen.

PART THREE

Present — That part of eternity dividing the domain of disappointment from the realm of hope.

Ambrose Bierce

CHAPTER
NINE

On a meeting, a mix-up and an unexpected reappearance

Nombeko had described herself as a South African freedom fighter with a price on her head. Sweden liked that sort of person and, sure enough, she was immediately admitted to the country. First stop: the transit camp of Carlslund in Upplands Väsby, just north of Stockholm.

Now, for the fourth day in a row, she was sitting on a bench in the cold outside camp building number seven, wrapped in a brown blanket with IMMIGRATION BOARD written on it, thinking about what she was going to do with the surplus of freedom she suddenly found herself possessing.

She was now twenty-six years old. Meeting a few nice people might not be a bad idea. *Normal* people. Or at least one normal person. Someone who could teach her about Sweden.

And what else? Well, one could assume there was probably a national library in this country, too. Even if most of what was on the shelves would be in a language she didn't understand. The normal person who taught her about Sweden would just have to teach her Swedish as well.

Nombeko had always done her best thinking when she had some dried antelope meat to chew on. There hadn't been any at Pelindaba. That might explain why it took her eleven years to figure out how to escape from there.

What if the antelope meat had already arrived at the Israeli embassy? Did she even dare to go there? Why not? That tape she had used as a threat against the agents would still serve its purpose, even if it was just as nonexistent now as it had been then.

At that moment, a truck with a red cargo box pulled into the yard. It backed up to a storehouse and a man of about Nombeko's age hopped out and started carrying plastic-wrapped pillows from the truck to the storehouse. Again and again, until the truck was empty and he got a signature from a woman who was apparently in charge of the storehouse in question. A *woman* who was in charge. OK, she was white, but still.

Nombeko walked up to the man and said that she had a question. But it would have to be in English, because she didn't speak any Swedish. Unless by chance the man spoke Xhosa or Wu Chinese?

The man looked at Nombeko and said that English would be fine. He had never heard of the other languages. How could he help her?

"Hello, by the way," he said, extending his hand. "My name is Holger."

An astounded Nombeko took Holger's hand. A white man with manners.

"Nombeko," said Nombeko. "I'm from South Africa. I'm a political refugee."

Holger was sorry to hear about Nombeko's bad fortune, but he welcomed her to Sweden all the same. She wasn't cold, was she? If she wanted, he could ask for another blanket for her from the storehouse.

Was she cold? Ask for a blanket? What was going on? Had Nombeko already managed to meet the normal person she had never met thus far, just a few seconds after she had dared to hope for such a thing? She couldn't help uttering her appreciative surprise:

"Imagine that people like you exist after all."

Holger gave her a melancholy look.

"The problem is, I don't," he said.

Don't what? Nombeko wondered. And she said just that: "What don't you do?"

"Exist," Holger replied. "I don't exist."

Nombeko looked him up and down and down and up. And she thought it certainly was typical that just when someone who seemed worth her respect showed up in her life — he didn't exist.

Nombeko let Holger's statement go and asked instead if he might know where the Israeli embassy was.

The man who didn't exist didn't quite see the connection between a South African refugee and the Israeli embassy, but he didn't think it was any of his business.

"It's in the centre of town, if I remember correctly. I'm going that way anyway. Would you like a ride, Miss

Nombeko? If you don't think I'm being too forward, that is."

He was being all normal again. He was practically apologizing for existing. Which was, of course, rather contradictory if he didn't exist.

Nombeko became vigilant. She studied the man. He looked nice. And the way he expressed himself was both intelligent and friendly.

"Yes, please," she said at last. "If you can wait a moment. I'm just going to go up to my room to get my scissors."

They drove south towards central Stockholm. The man turned out to be easy to talk to — what was his name, Holger? He told her about Sweden, about Swedish inventions, the Nobel Prize, Björn Borg . . .

Nombeko had many questions. Had Björn Borg really won five straight Wimbledons? Fantastic! What was a Wimbledon?

The red truck arrived at Storgatan 31, and Nombeko climbed down from the cab, went to the gate of the embassy, introduced herself and asked if a package from South Africa addressed to her had shown up.

Yes, it had just arrived, and it was a good thing that she was already here: the embassy couldn't have deliveries like this one just sitting around. The gatekeeper turned to Nombeko's chauffeur and asked him to back up to the loading bay around the corner. It was best for the miss to stay here: there were a few papers she had to sign. Now where were they?

Nombeko tried to protest. The package wasn't going with the truck; she had been planning to carry it herself, under her arm. She would make her way back to the camp somehow. But the guard just smiled as he waved Holger away. And then his nose was back in his pile of papers.

"Let's see here . . . I'm not very organized, you see, miss. Not this one . . . this one?"

It took some time. By the time the formalities had been taken care of, the package had already been loaded into the back of the truck and Holger was ready to leave. Nombeko said goodbye to the gatekeeper and climbed back up into the cab. "You can just let me out at a bus stop, I guess," she said.

"I don't quite understand," said Holger.

"What do you mean?"

"I thought you said there were twenty pounds of antelope meat in your package."

"Yes?" said Nombeko, gripping the scissors that were in her pocket.

"I would guess it's more like a ton."

"A ton?"

"Good thing I have a truck."

Nombeko didn't say anything for a few seconds. She let this information sink in. Then she said, "This isn't good."

"What isn't good?" Holger wondered.

"Everything, actually," said Nombeko.

◆ ◆ ◆

Mossad Agent A was in a good mood. It was morning in his hotel room in Johannesburg. His colleague from his years at Pelindaba was already on his way to a new post in Buenos Aires. A himself was planning on going to Jan Smuts International right after breakfast to fly home; he had a few weeks of well-deserved vacation in front of him before he found the cleaning woman in Sweden and did with her what he must do (and was happy to do).

The room phone rang. A was surprised, but he answered anyway. It was none other than Foreign Minister Peres, who was famous for getting straight to the point.

"Why on earth have you sent me twenty pounds of horse meat?" the foreign minister said to his agent.

Mossad Agent A was quick on the uptake. He immediately realized what had happened.

"I am terribly sorry, Mr Minister. There's been a horrible mix-up. I will take care of it right away!"

"How the hell is it possible to mix up what I was supposed to receive with twenty pounds of horse meat?" said Shimon Peres, who didn't want to say the words *atomic bomb* over the telephone.

"Actually, it's antelope meat," said Agent A, who immediately regretted saying it.

Mossad Agent A managed to shake off his angry foreign minister for the time being, and he called the Israeli embassy in Stockholm. Transferred to the gatekeeper, he said, "For God's sake, don't let the seventeen-hundred-pound delivery from South Africa leave the embassy. *Don't even touch it* until I get there!"

"What a nuisance," said the gatekeeper. "A nice black woman was just here with a truck, and she signed for it. Unfortunately, I can't see what her name is, because I don't seem to be able to find the receipt."

Mossad Agent A never swore. He was deeply religious and had been brought up with strict guidelines on what one could and could not say. He put down the receiver, sat on the bed, and said, "Fucking hell."

Agent A painted mental pictures of the ways he would kill Nombeko Mayeki. The slowest options felt best.

♦ ♦ ♦

"An atomic bomb?" said Holger.

"An atomic bomb," said Nombeko.

"A nuclear weapon?"

"That, too."

Nombeko thought that Holger deserved to hear the whole story, now that things had gone the way they had. So she told him about Pelindaba, the secret nuclear weapons project, and the six bombs that had turned into seven; about Engineer Westhuizen, his luck, his Klipdrift and his unfortunate demise; about the two Mossad agents, the box of antelope meat that was meant to go to Stockholm, and the considerably larger package — the one that Holger and Nombeko were driving around with right now, which was meant to go to Jerusalem. Although she didn't go into detail, Holger soon had a rough idea of what had happened.

And he understood it all, except for how things could have gone so wrong. Nombeko and the agents had had two packages to keep track of, one small one and one gigantic one. How hard could it be?

Nombeko wasn't sure, but she had her suspicions. The fact was that three nice but slightly flighty Chinese girls with poor judgement were in charge of the post at the research facility. Nombeko believed that the labelling of two packages at the same time had been one package too many. And so things had got mixed up.

"Yes, that's the least one can say," said Holger, feeling chilled through.

Nombeko said nothing for a moment. Holger went on: "So you and representatives from what is possibly the world's most capable intelligence agency put address labels in the hands of three flighty girls with poor judgement?"

"That's what happened," said Nombeko. "If we want to be critical, and perhaps we should, given the situation."

"Who puts people that can't be trusted in charge of outgoing post?"

"And incoming," said Nombeko. "Well, that was all the engineer's doing. He was truly one of the stupidest people I've ever met. He could read, but that was about it. He reminded me of a terribly dense assistant from the sanitation department of the City of Johannesburg I once had to deal with as a teenager."

Holger didn't say anything, but he let his brain go in four different directions at the same time. Anyone who has involuntarily driven around with an atomic bomb in the back of his truck knows the feeling.

"Should we turn round and give the bomb back to the Israelis?" said Nombeko.

This jolted Holger out of his mental paralysis.

"Never!" he said.

He, too, had a rather unusual life story. The fact was, Miss Nombeko understood, that he didn't exist in some ways; he had, of course, already mentioned this. But he still loved his country. And there was no way he could even consider voluntarily handing over an atomic bomb to any intelligence agency — Israeli or otherwise — *on Swedish soil.*

"Never!" he said again. "And you can't stay at the refugee camp. I'm sure the Israelis will try to find both you and the bomb."

Nombeko took in what Holger had just said. But what captured her interest more than anything else was his repeated assertions that he didn't exist.

"It's a long story," Holger mumbled.

Nombeko thought some more. All she had figured out so far regarding her future as a free woman was that she wanted to meet some normal people, because she had no experience of that at all. And then a seemingly normal Swedish man had shown up. Nice. Considerate. Well read. Who claimed that he didn't exist.

This was as far as she got before Holger said, "I live in a condemned building in Gnesta."

"That's nice," said Nombeko.

"What if you move into the same building?"

Nombeko had decided that she wouldn't need her scissors in Holger's company. A condemned building in . . . what was it called? Gnesta?

Well, she thought. She had lived in a shack for half her life, and she'd been locked up behind a fence for the other half. A condemned building would probably be an improvement.

But was Mr Holger sure that he wanted to be saddled with a refugee and a nuclear weapon? And another country's intelligence agency on his heels?

Holger wasn't sure of anything. But he found himself liking this person. He couldn't imagine sending her into the clutches of the Israeli Mossad without a second thought.

"No," he said. "I'm not. But the offer stands."

Nombeko liked Holger in return. If there was in fact someone there to like.

"You're not angry with me because of this thing about the atomic bomb, then?"

"Nah," said Holger. "Such things happen."

The drive from the Israeli embassy in Östermalm out to the E4 highway and south took them through Norrmalm and Kungsholmen. Through the windscreen, Holger and Nombeko could see Sweden's tallest building, the 275-foot-tall *Dagens Nyheter* tower. Holger couldn't help imagining what might happen to it if the bomb went off. Finally he had to ask:

"How bad would it be if things went badly?" he said.

"What do you mean?" said Nombeko.

"Well, if I drive into a lamppost here and the bomb goes off . . . exactly what would happen? I assume you and I would be in bad shape, but what about the skyscraper over there, for instance — would it collapse?"

Nombeko replied that Holger had guessed correctly that they probably wouldn't make it. Neither would the skyscraper. The bomb would destroy almost everything within a radius of . . . say . . . thirty-eight miles.

"Almost everything within a radius of thirty-eight miles?" said Holger Two.

"Yes. Or, really, everything."

"Within thirty-eight miles? All of Greater Stockholm?"

"Well, I don't know how big Greater Stockholm is, but it does sound big. Then there are other factors to consider . . ."

"Factors?"

"Besides the fireball itself. Shock waves, immediate radioactivity, wind direction. And things like . . . Say you drive into a lamppost here and now and the bomb goes off . . ."

"Or say I *don't*, on second thoughts," said Holger, gripping the wheel tightly with both hands.

"But just as an example. What would happen, I would guess, is that all the major hospitals in the Stockholm area would immediately go up in flames. So who would take care of the several hundred thousand severely injured people from the edges of the bomb's radius?"

"Yes, who would do that?" said Holger.

"Not you or me, anyway," said Nombeko.

Holger, wanting to get out of that thirty-eight-mile radius as quickly as possible, drove onto the E4 and speeded up. Nombeko had to remind him that no matter how fast and far he drove it would still be thirty-eight miles to safety as long as he had what he did in the truck.

Then he slowed down again, thought a little more, and asked if Miss Nombeko couldn't disarm the bomb herself, given that she'd been there when it was built. Nombeko replied that there were two types of atomic bomb: operative ones and inoperative ones. As luck would have it, the bomb they were driving around with was an operative one; it would take four or five hours to render it harmless. There hadn't been enough time for this when things had suddenly got rushed down there in South Africa. And unfortunately, this particular bomb's unique disarming diagram was in the hands of the Israelis. They were — as Holger could surely understand — not in any position to call Jerusalem and ask them to fax it over.

Holger nodded, looking anxious. Nombeko consoled him by saying that she thought the bomb could tolerate a great deal, so even if Holger slid off the road, chances were that he, she and Greater Stockholm would survive.

"You think so?" said Holger.

"Of course, it would be best not to find out," said Nombeko. "Where did you say we're going, by the way? Gnesta?"

"Yes. And once we get there, our main task will be to get my brother to understand that he can't use what we have in the truck to bring about a revolution."

♦ ♦ ♦

Sure enough, Holger lived in a condemned building. Nombeko thought it was quite charming. It was an L-shaped four-storey structure, and it was connected to a warehouse that was also L-shaped. Together the buildings formed a square or courtyard with a narrow entryway that led out to the street.

Nombeko thought it would be a waste to tear down the building. Yes, there was the occasional hole in the wooden stairs up to the floor where she had been told she could live. And she had been forewarned that several of the windows in her new apartment were covered with boards instead of glass. And that there was a draught from the cracks in the wooden walls. But all in all, it would be an enormous improvement on her shack in Soweto. Just take the fact that there were real boards for a floor in the condemned building, rather than trampled earth.

Using skids, hard work and ingenuity, Holger and Nombeko managed to get the atomic bomb out of the back of the truck and into a corner of the warehouse, which otherwise housed an awful lot of pillows. She and Holger hadn't discussed it, but one didn't need to be nearly as gifted as Nombeko possibly was to realize that he was in the pillow-selling and pillow-distributing business.

The bomb now stood crammed into a corner of the warehouse, posing no immediate threat. As long as none of the thousands of easily ignited pillows caught fire, there was reason to believe that Nyköping, Södertälje, Flen, Eskilstuna, Strängnäs and Stockholm and its environs would endure. Not to mention Gnesta.

As soon as the bomb was in the warehouse, Nombeko had a few questions. First this nonsense about Holger's nonexistence. Then the part about Holger's brother. What made Holger think that his brother would be tempted to use the bomb to bring about a revolution? And who was he, by the way? Where was he? And what was his name?

"His name is Holger," said Holger. "And he's around here somewhere, I imagine. It's sheer luck he didn't show up as we were dealing with the crate."

"Holger?" said Nombeko. "Holger and Holger?"

"Yes. He is me, you could say."

Holger had to straighten things out this instant, otherwise Nombeko would leave. He could keep the bomb, though; she had had enough of it.

She piled pillows onto the crate in the warehouse, climbed up, and sat in one corner. Then she ordered Holger, who was still on the floor, to explain. Or, as she put it:

"Explain!"

She didn't know what to expect, but forty minutes later, when Holger was finished, she felt relieved.

"Well, that doesn't matter. If you don't exist just because you don't have any papers that say you do, you have no idea how many South Africans don't either. I only exist because the numbskull of an engineer I slaved for needed me to, for his own convenience."

Holger Two accepted Nombeko's comforting words and climbed onto the crate himself; he lay down among the pillows in another corner and just breathed. It was all too much — first the bomb in the crate under them and then sharing his life story. For the first time, an outsider had heard the whole truth.

"Are you staying or going?" said Holger Two.

"I'm staying," said Nombeko. "If I may?"

"You may," said Holger Two. "But now I think I need some peace and quiet."

"Me, too," said Nombeko.

And then she settled down across from her new friend, so that she could just breathe, too.

At that moment, there was a cracking sound as a board came loose on one of the short ends of the crate containing the bomb.

"What was that?" said Holger Two, at the same instant that the next board fell to the ground and a woman's arm stuck out.

"I have my suspicions," said Nombeko, and they were immediately confirmed as three Chinese girls crawled out, blinking.

"Hi," said the little sister when she caught sight of Nombeko.

"Do you have anything to eat?" said the middle sister.

"And drink," suggested the big sister.

CHAPTER
TEN

On an unbribable prime minister and a desire to kidnap one's king

Would this absurd day never end? Two was now sitting up in his bed of pillows, looking at the row of three girls who had just crawled out of the crate.

"What is happening?" he said.

Nombeko had been a bit worried about the girls, and about what would happen when the security arrangements were tightened up at Pelindaba. She was afraid that they would receive the fate that had been meant for her.

"I don't know what will happen next," she said, "because that's apparently how life is. But what just happened was that we found out how the large package and the small package happened to switch places. Nice escape, girls!"

The Chinese girls were hungry after four days in the crate along with the bomb, four pounds of cold rice and five litres of water. They were escorted to Holger's apartment, where they tasted blood pudding with lingonberries for the first time in their lives.

"Reminds me of the clay we used to make geese out of," the middle sister said between mouthfuls. "Can I have seconds?"

When they were full, all three of them were tucked into Holger's wide bed. They learned that they had been assigned the last somewhat functional apartment in the building, the one on the top floor, but it wouldn't be habitable until a large hole in the wall of the living room had been taken care of.

"I'm sorry you have to sleep in such crowded conditions tonight," said Holger Two to the girls, who had already fallen asleep.

◆ ◆ ◆

A condemned building gets its name because it should and will be torn down. Only in exceptional cases do people reside in condemned buildings.

So one could say it was noteworthy that a single condemned building in Gnesta, Sörmland, now housed the following: one American potter, two very similar and dissimilar brothers, one angry young woman, one escaped South African refugee and three Chinese girls with poor judgement.

All of these people found themselves in nuclear-weapons-free Sweden. Right next door to a three-megaton atomic bomb.

Thus far, the list of nuclear nations had included the United States, the Soviet Union, Great Britain, France, China and India. Experts estimated their combined number of warheads at about sixty-five thousand. The same experts were in less agreement on how many times over these could destroy the Earth; after all, the strength of the loads varied. The pessimists guessed fourteen to sixteen times. The optimists guessed it was more like two.

South Africa could be added to the above list. So could Israel, although neither of them wanted to explain how that had come to pass. Perhaps Pakistan could be added, too: they'd been promising to develop their own nuclear weapons ever since India had set one off.

And now Sweden. If involuntarily. And without knowing it.

◆ ◆ ◆

Holger and Nombeko left the Chinese girls where they were and went to the warehouse to have a talk in peace and quiet. There was the bomb, in its crate, with the pillows on top of it making it seem like a cosy corner, even though the situation wasn't particularly cosy.

They climbed up on the crate again and sat at either end.

"The bomb," said Holger Two.

"We can't just keep it here until it no longer poses a danger to the general public," said Nombeko.

Two felt hope igniting inside him. How long would that take?

"Twenty-six thousand and two hundred years," said Nombeko. "Plus or minus three months."

Two and Nombeko agreed that 26,200 years was too long to wait, even if luck was on their side when it came to the margin of error. Then Two explained what a political stick of dynamite the bomb was. Sweden was a neutral country and — according to itself — the world's foremost representative of good ethics. The country believed itself to be absolutely free of nuclear weapons, and it hadn't been involved in a war since 1809.

According to Holger Two, two things must happen: they had to hand the bomb over to the country's leaders, and they had to do it so deftly as to avoid starting any rumours. Furthermore, there was a third thing — this manoeuvre should happen so quickly that Two's brother and company didn't have time to mess anything up.

"So let's do it," said Nombeko. "Who is your head of state?"

"The king," said Holger. "But he's not the one in charge."

A boss who wasn't in charge. Rather like Pelindaba. The engineer there had essentially done what Nombeko told him to, without understanding it himself.

"So who is in charge, then?"

"Well, the prime minister, I suppose."

Holger Two told her that Sweden's prime minister was named Ingvar Carlsson. He had become prime minister overnight after his predecessor, Olof Palme, was murdered in central Stockholm.

"Call Carlsson," Nombeko suggested.

So Holger did. Or at least the government offices, where he asked for the prime minister and was transferred to his assistant.

"Hello, my name is Holger," said Holger. "I would like to speak to Ingvar Carlsson about an urgent matter."

"I see, what might that be?"

"Unfortunately I can't say. It's a secret."

In his day, Olof Palme had been listed in the phone book. Any citizen who wanted something from his prime minister could just call him at home. If it wasn't the children's bedtime or the middle of dinner, he would simply pick up the phone.

But that was in the good old days. And those days had ended on 28 February 1986, when the bodyguard-less Palme was shot in the back after a trip to the cinema.

His successor was protected from the average Joe. His assistant replied that Mr Holger must certainly understand that under no circumstances could she allow unknown people to speak to the head of state.

"But it's important."

"Anyone could say that."

"Really important."

"No, I'm sorry. If you like you can write a letter to —"

"It's about an atomic bomb," said Holger.

"I beg your pardon? Was that a threat?"

"No, for Heaven's sake. It's the other way round. Or, well, the *bomb* is a threat, of course — that's why I want to get rid of it."

"You want to get rid of your atomic bomb? And you're calling the prime minister to give it away?"

"Yes, but —"

"I can tell you that people very frequently try to give things to the prime minister. Just last week there was an obstinate appliance dealer who wanted to send over a new washing machine. But the prime minister does not accept that sort of gift, and that also goes for . . . atomic bombs? Are you quite sure this isn't some sort of threat?"

Holger assured her once more that he didn't mean any harm. He realized he wasn't going to get any further, so he thanked her for nothing and said goodbye.

Then, at Nombeko's urging, he called the king as well, and he spoke to a court secretary who answered in a similar fashion to the prime minister's assistant, only snootier.

In a perfect world, the prime minister (or at least the king) would have answered, received the information, immediately travelled to Gnesta and taken away the bomb and its container. All before Holger's potentially revolutionary brother had even had time to discover the crate, started to ask questions, and — God forbid — started thinking for himself.

Again, that would have been in a perfect world.

In the real world, what happened instead was that One and the angry young woman walked through the door of the warehouse. They were there to find out how it happened that the blood pudding they had been planning on taking from Two's refrigerator was gone and the apartment was full of sleeping Chinese people. Now they had a few more questions, such as who the black woman on the crate in the corner was. And what that crate she was sitting on was.

From the new arrivals' body language, Nombeko realized that she and the crate were the centre of attention, and she said that she would be happy to participate in the conversation if only it could be conducted in English.

"Are you an American?" said the angry young woman, adding that she hated Americans.

Nombeko said that she was South African, and that she thought it sounded laborious to hate all Americans, given how many of them there were.

"What's in the crate?" said Holger One.

Holger Two answered by not answering. Instead he told them that the three Chinese girls in the apartment and this woman right here were all political refugees, and that they would be staying in the condemned building for a while. On a related note, Two apologized that his blood pudding had been eaten before One had time to steal it.

Yes, his brother did find this irritating. But what about the crate? What was in it?

"My personal belongings," said Nombeko.

"Your personal belongings?" the angry young woman repeated, in a tone that said she expected a more thorough explanation.

Nombeko noticed that curiosity had taken a hopelessly strong hold in both One's and his girlfriend's eyes. Might as well mark her territory:

212

"My personal belongings," she said again, "all the way from Africa. Just like me. And I'm both nice and unpredictable. I once planted a pair of scissors in the thigh of a man who couldn't behave himself. Another time . . . it happened again. The same man, actually, but a new pair of scissors and the other thigh."

These circumstances were too difficult for Holger One and his girlfriend to grasp. The woman on the box had a friendly-sounding voice, but at the same time she was hinting that she might attack them with scissors if her crate wasn't left in peace.

So One took the angry young woman under his arm, mumbled goodbye on behalf of both of them, and left.

"I think I have a Falu sausage in the bottom drawer of the fridge," Two called after him. "If the two of you aren't planning to buy your own food."

Holger Two, Nombeko and the bomb were alone in the warehouse. Two said that Nombeko, as she probably understood, had just met his brother the republican and his ill-tempered girlfriend.

Nombeko nodded. It seemed precarious to have those two and an atomic bomb on the same continent. Much less in the same country. And now they lived in the same property. They would have to do something about that as soon as possible, but now it was time for some rest and relaxation. It had been a long and eventful day.

Holger Two agreed. Long and eventful.

Nombeko received a blanket and pillow from Two before he took a mattress under his arm and showed her the way to her apartment. He opened the door, put down what he was carrying and said that what he had to offer was not exactly a palace, but he hoped that she would feel at home.

Nombeko thanked him, said goodbye for the time being, and stood there in the doorway, alone. She remained there for some time, philosophizing.

On the threshold of one's own life, she thought. But it was a life with impediments, considering that she had an atomic bomb in tow and probably one or two single-minded Mossad agents on her heels.

But still. She had her own apartment now, instead of a shack in Soweto. She would never again have to administer shit, and she was no longer locked up behind double fences along with an engineer who was practically single-handedly responsible for keeping an entire brandy industry in business.

The National Library in Pretoria was lost to her. Instead, its counterpart in Gnesta would have to do. It was pretty extensive, according to Holger Two.

What about everything else?

What she would have liked to do most of all was take the damn bomb and drive back to the Israeli embassy. And maybe she would just set it on the street outside, tell the gatekeeper, and run away. Then she could have re-entered the Swedish immigration process, received a residence permit, studied at a university and eventually become a Swedish citizen.

And after that? Well, being a Swedish ambassador in Pretoria wasn't a bad idea. The first thing she would do was invite President Botha to a dinner without food.

Nombeko smiled at her fantasies.

But the reality was that Holger refused to hand the bomb over to anyone but the prime minister of Sweden. Or possibly the king. And neither of them would answer the phone.

Holger was the most normal person she had met in her life so far. He was actually quite pleasant. Nombeko felt that she wanted to respect his decisions.

But aside from him, it seemed to be her fate to be surrounded solely by fools. Was it even worth fighting? On the other hand: how can one accept fools as they are?

The American potter, for example, whom Holger had told her about. Should she let him take care of himself in his general insanity? Or should she seek him out and make him understand that she wasn't automatically from the CIA, just because she spoke English?

And the Chinese girls, who had long since become full-grown women, even if they didn't always act like it. Soon they would regain their energy after the journey, the blood pudding and their sleep, and they would start looking around. In what way was their future Nombeko's responsibility?

Holger's brother, the one with the same name, was easier. The brother must be kept away from the bomb. Along with his girlfriend. The responsibility for making sure that that actually happened could not be passed off.

The cleaning woman from Pelindaba realized that even in Sweden there were things that had to be tidied up and decisions that had to be made before she could start living life for real. Learning Swedish was high on the list, of course: Nombeko couldn't bear the thought of living a mile from a library without making use of it. Protecting the bomb was at least as important. And it couldn't be helped — she didn't think she would have any peace of mind if she didn't deal with the crazy potter and the three happy-go-lucky, injudicious girls. Beyond that, she hoped there would be enough time left over for the only company she felt she could appreciate — that of Holger Two.

But first of all: sleep. Nombeko stepped into her apartment and closed the door.

♦ ♦ ♦

When she took inventory of the situation the next morning, she found that Holger One had left early to deliver pillows in Gothenburg and had taken the angry young woman with him. The three Chinese girls had awoken, eaten up the Falu sausage and fallen asleep again. Holger Two was sitting in the cosy corner of the warehouse with some administrative work (and simultaneously guarding the bomb), and because most of what he had to work on was in Swedish, Nombeko couldn't help him.

"Should I go and get to know the potter in the meantime?" she said.

"I wish you the best of luck with that," said Holger Two.

216

"Who is it?" the potter said through the door.

"My name is Nombeko," said Nombeko. "I'm not from the CIA. However, Mossad is on my heels, so please let me in."

Because the potter's neurosis concerned the American intelligence agency and not the Israeli one, he did as she asked.

The fact that his visitor was both black and a woman mitigated the way he viewed the circumstances. Certainly the American agents that were out in the world assumed every conceivable colour and shape, but the archetype was a white man in his thirties.

The woman also displayed evidence that she knew an African tribal language. And she could account for so many details from her alleged childhood in Soweto that it was impossible to rule out that she'd actually lived there.

Nombeko, for her part, was rather fascinated by how much of a nervous wreck the potter seemed to be. Her tactic would have to be frequent but short visits in order to build up trust.

"See you tomorrow," she said when she left.

One floor up, the Chinese girls had woken up again. They had found *knäckebröd* in the pantry, and they were sitting there crunching on it when Nombeko joined them.

Nombeko asked what the girls were planning to do next, and heard in reply that they hadn't had time to think about it much. But they might go to see their uncle Cheng Tao, since he lived nearby. In Basel. Or maybe it was Bern. Or Bonn. Possibly Berlin. Their uncle was an expert at creating antiques, and they were sure he wouldn't say no to some help.

Among all the things Nombeko had absorbed from the library in Pelindaba was a certain amount of knowledge about the European continent and its cities. So she considered herself to have every reason to guess that neither Basel, Bern, Bonn nor Berlin was exactly next door. And she thought it might not be easy to find the uncle even if they managed to figure out which city he was in. Or at least which country, for starters.

But the girls replied that all they needed was a car and some money; the rest would take care of itself. It wasn't important whether it was Bonn or Berlin; they could always ask their way. In any case, it was Switzerland.

Nombeko had an abundance of money for the Chinese girls, of course. At least in an indirect form. The seam of what had been her only jacket since her adolescence in Soweto still contained a fortune in diamonds. She fished one out and went to the local jeweller in Gnesta to get it appraised. But the jeweller had previously been cheated by an assistant of foreign extraction, and for this reason had found himself concurring with the global opinion that foreigners cannot be trusted.

So when a black woman came into his shop and spoke English as she placed a rough diamond on the counter, he asked her to go away, otherwise he would call the police.

Nombeko had no desire for close contact with representatives of Swedish law and order, so she picked up her diamond, apologized for the bother and left.

No, the girls would have to earn their own money and get their own car. If Nombeko could be of help with the little things, then she absolutely would, but no more than that.

The same afternoon, Holger One and the angry young woman came back. One discovered that his brother's pantry was bare, and he had no choice but to go to the shop. This gave Nombeko the opportunity to have her first private conversation with the angry young woman.

Her plan was twofold. First get to know the enemy — that is, the angry young woman and Holger One — so that she could then lead them away from the bomb, figuratively and preferably also literally.

"Aha, the American," the angry young woman said when she saw who was knocking at her door.

"I told you, I'm South African," said Nombeko. "Which origin, above all others, are *you*?"

"I'm Swedish, of course."

"Then you must have a cup of coffee to offer me. Or even better, tea."

She could probably fix some tea, even if coffee was preferable because she'd heard there were better working conditions on the South American coffee plantations than on the Indian tea ones. Or else that was just a lie. People told so many fucking lies in this country.

Nombeko sat down in the angry young woman's kitchen and said there was probably an awful lot of lying in every country. And then she opened the conversation with a simple and general question:

"So how are things with you?"

The angry young woman turned out to be angry about everything. She was angry about the country's continued dependence on nuclear power. And oil. About all the rivers harnessed for hydro-electric power. About the noisy and ugly wind power. About how they were going to build a bridge to Denmark. With all the Danes, because they were Danes. With mink farmers because they were mink farmers. With animal breeders in general, actually. With everyone who ate meat. With everyone who didn't (she lost Nombeko here for a moment). With all the capitalists. With almost all the Communists. With her father because he worked at a bank. With her mother because she didn't work at all. With her grandmother because she had some noble blood. With herself because she was forced to be a wage slave instead of changing the world. And with the world, which didn't have any good wage-slavery to offer.

She was also angry because she and Holger lived in the condemned building for free, because this meant there wasn't any rent she could refuse to pay. God, she so longed for a protest! What made her angriest of all was that she couldn't find a single good protest to go to.

Nombeko thought that the angry young woman ought to take a job as a black person in South Africa for a few weeks, and maybe empty a latrine barrel or two in order to get some perspective on her life.

"And what is your name?"

Imagine that; the angry young woman could become even angrier. The fact was, her name was something so horrid that she couldn't say it.

But Nombeko insisted, and she finally managed to get the name out.

"Celestine."

"Wow, that's so beautiful," said Nombeko.

"It was my father's idea. That bank manager. Damn him!"

"What may I call you without risking my neck?" Nombeko wondered.

"Anything but Celestine," said Celestine. "What's your name?"

"Nombeko."

"Well, that's a hell of a name, too."

"Thanks," said Nombeko. "May I have a little more tea?"

Because Nombeko had the name she did, she was given permission after her refill to call Celestine Celestine. And to shake her hand as she left, as thanks for the tea and the conversation. On the stairs as she left she decided to wait until the next day for Holger One. It was taxing to get to know the enemy.

The best thing that came out of her meeting with the girl who didn't want to be named what she was named was that she didn't mind if Nombeko used her Gnesta library card. The defected political refugee was in need of a library card, while the angry young woman had realized that all you could borrow was bourgeois propaganda of one sort or another. Except *Das Kapital* by Karl Marx. That was only half-bourgeois, but they only had it in German.

During her first time at the library, Nombeko borrowed a Swedish language course with accompanying cassettes.

Holger Two had a tape player, and they did the first three lessons among the pillows on the crate in the warehouse.

"*Hi. How are things? How are you? I am well,*" said the tape player (in Swedish, of course).

"Me, too," said Nombeko, who was a quick learner.

Later that same afternoon, she felt ready to take on Holger One. She found him and got straight to the point.

"So I hear you're a republican?"

Yes, Holger One said that he was. Everyone ought to be. The monarchy was depraved. The problem was that he was so desperately empty of ideas.

Nombeko said that even a republic can have its downsides, like for instance the South African one, but by all means. She was there to try to help.

What she meant was that she wanted to help One stay away from the bomb, but she left plenty of room for other interpretations.

"It would be terribly nice of you to help, Miss Nombeko," he said.

222

In accordance with the plan she had started to formulate, she asked Holger to tell her about the republican thoughts he had had in the months since the king had fallen on his father.

"Not the king! Lenin."

Holger One admitted that he wasn't as clever as his brother, but that he still had an idea to bring to the table. It was to kidnap the king by helicopter, get him onboard while leaving his bodyguards behind, take him to some sort of place and then get him to abdicate.

Nombeko looked at One. Was *that* what he had managed to think up?

"So. What do you think, Miss Nombeko?"

Nombeko couldn't say what she thought. Instead she said, "That idea might not be quite complete, don't you think?"

"What do you mean?"

Well, where had he been planning to get a helicopter, for example? Who would fly it, where would they kidnap the king, where would they take him, and what was their argument for why he should abdicate? Among other things.

Holger One sat there without saying anything. He lowered his eyes.

It was becoming more and more obvious to Nombeko that Two hadn't received the short end of the stick when the combined amount of general intelligence had been divided between the brothers. But she didn't say that, either.

"Let me think it over for a week or two, and then I'm sure everything will work out, but right now I want to go and find your brother. As a change of pace."

"Thank you so much, Miss Nombeko," said Holger One. "Thank you so much!"

Nombeko went back to Two and told him she had started a conversation with his brother and that her plan was to think of a way to get him to think of other things besides crates with secret contents. Her half-finished idea involved making One believe that he was getting closer to a revolution, when in reality he was just getting farther away from the bomb.

Holger Two nodded his approval and said it sounded like everything would work out for the best.

CHAPTER
ELEVEN

On how everything temporarily worked out for the best

The Chinese girls, who had been responsible for the kitchen at Pelindaba, soon grew tired of blood pudding, Falu sausage and *knäckebröd*, and they opened a cafeteria for themselves and everyone else living at Fredsgatan. Since they really could cook, Holger Two was happy to finance their operation with the pillow-sale profits.

At the same time, and on Nombeko's initiative, Two managed to get the angry young woman to agree to taking over responsibility for the distribution, even if their negotiations were difficult at first. Not until the latter understood that she would be forced to illegally drive a truck with stolen licence plates did she become curious enough to hear more.

There were, of course, three megatons of reasons for the angry young woman *not* to draw the attentions of the police to Fredsgatan (even if she herself didn't understand this). The licence plates on the otherwise unremarkable truck had already been stolen, so the truck couldn't be traced back to Gnesta. But that didn't mean its driver should be seventeen years old and without a licence. So she was instructed not to say anything, above all not her name, if she were pulled over.

The angry young woman didn't think that she could manage to remain silent if faced with the police. She hated them far too much for that. So Holger Two suggested that she could sing a little tune instead; that would be sure to irritate them while also making sure that nothing was said.

When all was said and done, Two and the angry young woman had agreed that Celestine, should she be stopped by the police, would call herself Édith Piaf, look a little crazy (Two thought she had it in her), and start singing "*Non, je ne regrette rien.*" She would do no more than that before she got the chance to borrow a phone and call Holger. And their conversation could consist of the same melody; Holger would understand.

Holger Two stopped there, letting the angry young woman interpret this to mean that he would immediately come to her aid, when in reality he planned to spirit the bomb out of the warehouse while she was safely in custody.

The angry young woman liked what she heard.

"God, it'll be so cool to mess with the pigs. I hate Fascists," she said, promising to learn the lyrics to the French classic by heart.

She looked so full of expectation that Holger Two had to emphasize that being taken into custody by the police was not an end in itself. Rather the opposite: part of being a pillow deliverywoman was to try *not* to end up in jail.

226

The angry young woman nodded. She was no longer as pleased.

Did she understand?

"Yes, for fuck's sake. I understand."

At about the same time, Nombeko managed beyond expectations to get Holger One to think about something other than the crate in the warehouse. She had investigated the idea of enrolling him in classes to get a helicopter pilot certificate as a distraction. She could see no danger in it; the chances that he'd ever succeed in carrying out his so-called idea were infinitesimal.

The path to a certificate would take a normal student at least one year; that is to say, it would take this student almost four. This was a length of time that was likely to be more than sufficient for Nombeko, Two and the bomb.

Upon closer inspection, however, it turned out that One would have to be examined in aviation systems, flight safety, performance, flight planning, meteorology, navigation, operating procedures and aerodynamics — eight things that, in Nombeko's opinion, he could not manage. Instead he would get tired of it in a few months, if he hadn't already been kicked off the course by then.

Nombeko reconsidered. And Two helped her. They read employment ads in the newspapers for several days before they found something that might work.

All that was left to do was a small cosmetic operation. Or "forgery of documents", as it is otherwise known. They had to get Two's exceedingly unqualified brother to appear to be something else. Two drafted, cut, and pasted according to Nombeko's instructions. When she was satisfied, she thanked him for his help, took the finished product under her arm, and went to find Holger One.

"What if you went out and looked for a job?" she said.

"Ugh," said One.

But Nombeko hadn't meant just any job. She explained that Helicopter Taxi Inc. in Bromma was looking for a customer service representative and jack-of-all-trades. If One were to get the job, he would both make contacts and learn a bit about how to fly a helicopter. When the time was right, he would be ready.

She said, without believing a word of it.

"Brilliant!" was Holger One's opinion.

But how was Miss Nombeko thinking he would get the job? Well, the thing was that the library in Gnesta had just procured a new copy machine, one that made fantastic four-colour copies of anything one asked it to.

And then she showed him ready-made certificates of employment and strong recommendations in One's (and for that matter Two's) name. It had taken a good deal of fiddling and many torn-out pages from publications at KTH, the Royal Institute of Technology in Stockholm. But on the whole, it looked impressive.

"The *Royal* Institute of Technology?" Holger One wondered.

Nombeko said none of what she was thinking. Instead she went on:

"Here's your degree from KTH, the royal department of engineering; you're an engineer and you know a great deal about aircraft in general."

"I do?"

"Here you have four years as an assistant air traffic controller at Sturup Airport outside Malmö. And here you have four years as a receptionist at Taxi Skåne."

"But I've never —" One began, but he was immediately cut off.

"Now go and apply for the job," said Nombeko. "Don't think. Apply."

So he did. And sure enough, he got the job.

Holger was satisfied. He hadn't kidnapped the king with a helicopter, and he still didn't have a helicopter certificate, an aircraft, or an idea. But he worked next to a helicopter (or three), he was learning, he got free lessons now and then from the taxi pilots, and he was — completely in line with Nombeko's plan — keeping his muddled dream alive.

When he began his duties, he also moved into a roomy studio apartment in Blackeberg, which was several lengthy stone-throws away from Bromma. The gaze of Holger Two's simple-minded brother had been drawn away from the bomb for the foreseeable future. It would have been optimal if his possibly even more simple-minded girlfriend had gone with him, but she had exchanged the energy issue (where all known forms of energy were evil) for women's liberation. She considered this to include the right, as a woman, to drive a truck before one was old enough to get a licence and to carry more pillows at one time than any man could. So she remained in the condemned building and kept at her wage slavery; she and her beloved Holger commuted to see each other.

The potter's general condition was also among the things that seemed to be going well for the time being. Nombeko noticed that he grew less tense every time they met. And that it also helped him to have someone to talk to about the threat from the CIA. She was happy to help, because it was as interesting to listen to him as it had once been to hear Thabo's tales of his many grand exploits in Africa. According to the potter, the American intelligence agency was pretty much everywhere. Nombeko learned that the new automatic taxi dispatch systems all over the country were produced in San Francisco. The potter thought that said it all. But calling around from a telephone booth had taught him that at least one company had refused to fall into line with the American intelligence agency. Borlänge Taxi was still sticking to manual service.

"That might be good to know, Miss Nombeko, if you're travelling anywhere in the future."

Unlike many other things he said, the potter got away with this stupid remark, since Nombeko didn't know where Borlänge was in relation to Gnesta.

So the old Vietnam deserter was deeply mentally unstable and full of delusions. But he was also completely exceptional when it came to creating beauty out of clay and porcelain, with glazes in various shades of napalm yellow. This was what he sold at marketplaces here and there. Every time he needed money, he took the bus or Borlänge Taxi to the marketplace in question. He never took the train, because everyone knew that the CIA and Swedish Railways were hand in hand. With him he brought two cumbersome suitcases full of his collection. And then he would sell out of everything in a few hours, because he charged shamefully low prices. Any time he travelled by Borlänge Taxi, his trip always involved a loss. Taxi trips of 130 miles were not free, after all. Debit, credit and his own talent were among the many things the potter didn't understand.

◆ ◆ ◆

After some time, Nombeko spoke passable Swedish with the Holgers and Celestine, Wu Chinese with the girls, and English with the American potter. And she borrowed so much literature from the library in Gnesta that she had to decline, in Celestine's name, a position on the board of the Gnesta Literary Society (GLS).

She spent as much of the rest of her time as possible with the comparatively normal Holger Two. She assisted him with the bookkeeping for the pillow company and suggested efficiency improvements in purchasing, sales and delivery. Two was happy for the help, but it took until the early summer of 1988 before he realized that she could count. That is: *count*.

It happened one beautiful June morning. When Holger arrived in the warehouse, Nombeko welcomed him by saying, "Eighty-four thousand four hundred and eighty."

"And good morning to you," said Holger. "What did you say?"

It so happened that he had been running around cursing because the burned-out entrepreneur had upped and died before he had completed a proper handover of the company. For example, it was impossible to know the extent of the pillow stock.

But now Nombeko was placing four pieces of paper in his hands. What she had been doing while Holger was lolling in bed was to pace off the area, measure the volume of one pillow, and calculate the correct number based on that.

$$\frac{\left([20 \cdot 7 \cdot 6 \cdot \frac{1.6}{2}] + [7 \cdot 12 \cdot 6 \cdot \frac{1.6}{2}] + \left[\left(\frac{(9 \cdot \frac{1.6}{2}) + (6 \cdot \frac{1.6}{2})}{2}\right) \cdot 7 \cdot (20 + 12)\right] - 3 \cdot 3 \cdot 9 \cdot \frac{1.6}{2} - 2 \cdot 3 \cdot 2\right)}{0.5 \cdot 0.6 \cdot 0.06} =$$

$$\frac{672 + 403.2 + 1.2 \cdot 7 \cdot 32 - 3 \cdot 3 \cdot 9 \cdot \frac{1.6}{2} - 2 \cdot 3 \cdot 2}{0.5 \cdot 0.6 \cdot 0.05} =$$

$$\frac{672 + 403.2 + 268.8 - 64.8 - 12}{0.015} =$$

$$\frac{1267.2}{0.015} = 84,480$$

Holger looked at the top piece of paper and didn't understand a thing. Nombeko said that wasn't so strange: one had to look at the equation as a whole.

"Look here," she said, turning the page.

$$\text{Volume of the warehouse} = (A*B+C*D)*E+\left(\frac{(F-E)*C}{2}\right)*(A+D)$$

$$(A*C+B*D)*\text{Shadow } E*\frac{G}{H}+\left(\frac{\left(\left(\text{Shadow } F+\frac{G}{H}\right)-\left(\text{Shadow } E+\frac{G}{H}\right)\right)*C}{2}\right)$$

$$*(A+D)=$$

$$\left[A*C\ \text{Shadow } E*\frac{G}{H}\right]+$$

$$\left[B*D\ \text{Shadow } E*\frac{G}{H}\right]+$$

$$\left[\left(\frac{\left(\text{Shadow } F*\frac{G}{H}\right)-\left(\text{Shadow } E*\frac{G}{H}\right)}{2}\right)*C*(A+D)\right]$$

"Shadow E?" said Holger Two, for lack of anything better to say.

"Yes, I measured the volume of the loft while the sun was out."

And she turned the page again.

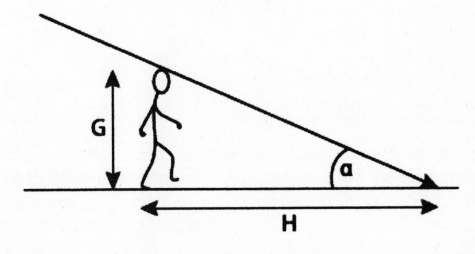

"Who's the stick man?" said Holger Two, still for lack of anything better.

"That's me," said Nombeko. "A bit white in the face, but otherwise quite accurate, if I do say so myself. Ever since the engineer was kind enough to supply me with a passport, I have known how tall I am. So all I had to do was measure my shadow in relation to the loft. After all, the sun stays admirably low in this country. I don't know what I would have done at the equator. Or if it had been raining."

When Holger still didn't understand, Nombeko tried a different tactic.

"It's very simple," she said, and she was just about to turn the page again when Holger interrupted.

"No, it's not. Did you count the pillows on the crate?"

"Yes. All fifteen of them."

"And the one on the bed in your room?"

"I forgot that one."

CHAPTER
TWELVE

On the love of an atomic bomb and differential pricing

Life was complicated for Holger Two and Nombeko. But they weren't the only ones having a tough time just then. Countries and television companies all over the world were mulling over what attitude they should take towards the birthday concert that had been arranged in honour of Nelson Mandela on his seventieth birthday in June 1988. Mandela was a terrorist, after all, and he would have stayed that way if only superstar after superstar hadn't thought otherwise and made it known that they wanted to attend the concert, which was to be held at Wembley Stadium in London.

For many, the solution was to recognize the event and yet not. It was said, for example, that the American Fox Television, which broadcast the concert after the event, first edited out any part of the speeches and songs that might seem political in order to avoid irritating Coca-Cola, which had bought advertising slots during the programme.

Despite all of this, more than six hundred million people in sixty-seven countries ended up watching the concert. There was really only one country that completely quashed any news of what was going on.

South Africa.

◆　◆　◆

In the elections for the Swedish Parliament a few months later, the Social Democrats and Ingvar Carlsson managed to remain in power.

Unfortunately.

Not that Holger Two and Nombeko were letting any ideological opinion colour their view of the results, but the fact that Carlsson remained where he was meant that there was no point in calling up his government offices again. The bomb stayed put.

Beyond that, the most remarkable thing about the recent election was that the Environmental Party, a new political movement, won seats in Parliament. Less attention was given to the fact that the one vote cast for the nonexistent "Tear All This Shit Down" Party was declared invalid; it had been turned in by a girl in Gnesta who had just turned eighteen.

On 17 November 1988, Nombeko had been a member of the condemned building for exactly one year. For that reason, she was surprised with a cake in the warehouse. The three Chinese girls had arrived on the same day, of course, but they were not invited. It was just Holger and Nombeko; that's how he wanted it. She did, too.

He certainly is sweet, that Holger, she thought, giving him a kiss on the cheek.

For his entire adult life, Holger Two had dreamed of being able to exist, and of doing so as part of a larger whole. He longed for a normal life, with a wife and kids and honest work — anything at all, as long as it had nothing to do with pillows. Or the royal family.

Mum, dad and kids . . . that would be something. He hadn't had a childhood himself. While his classmates had put up pictures of Batman and Sweet on the walls of their bedrooms, Holger had portraits idolizing the Finnish president.

But would it ever be possible to find a prospective mother for the potential children in a hypothetical family? Someone who would be satisfied with a dad who existed for her and the kids, but not for the rest of society? And with living in a condemned building for that very reason? And with the fact that the family game they were best equipped for was the children having pillow fights around an atomic bomb?

No, of course that wouldn't happen.

All that would happen was that time would go on.

But with that, a thought was born, a sneaking suspicion that . . . Nombeko . . . in some ways, she existed just as little as he did. And she was even more mixed up with the bomb than he was. And on the whole, she was pretty . . . wonderful.

And then that kiss on the cheek.

Two made up his mind. She wasn't just the one person he wanted above all others, she was also the only one available. So if he didn't give it a chance, he didn't deserve any better.

"So, Nombeko," he said.

"Yes, dear Holger?"

Dear? There was hope!

"If I . . . If I were to think about moving a little closer . . ."

"Yes?"

"Would the scissors come out?"

Nombeko said that the scissors were in a box in the kitchen, and she thought that was a good place for them. In fact, she said, she had been wishing for a long time that Holger would want to do just that — move a little closer. Both of them were about to turn twenty-eight, and Nombeko admitted that she'd never been with a man. In Soweto she had been a child, and then she was locked up for eleven years, surrounded by men who were essentially repulsive in every way, and of a forbidden race. But happily, what was forbidden there wasn't forbidden here. And Nombeko had felt for a long time that Holger was the exact opposite of his brother. So if he wanted to . . . she did, too.

Holger almost couldn't breathe. That he was the exact opposite of his brother was the nicest thing anyone had ever said to him. He said that he didn't have any experience with . . . that, either. It just hadn't . . . there was all that stuff with Dad . . . did Nombeko really mean that . . .

"Can't you just be quiet and come here?" said Nombeko.

238

Naturally, a person who doesn't exist does best with someone who also doesn't exist. Nombeko had left the refugee camp in Upplands Väsby after just a few days, and since then she had disappeared from the face of the Earth and had been listed as "missing" for a year; she was a parenthetical line in a Swedish register. She hadn't had time to get any sort of formal residence permit.

Holger, for his part, still hadn't done anything about his continued nonexistence. It was such a complicated matter. And his interest in Nombeko made it even more so. Anything might happen if the authorities started investigating him in order to corroborate his story, including that they might find both Nombeko and the bomb. In both cases, he risked losing the joy of a family before it had even had time to begin.

Given the situation, it might seem contradictory that Holger and Nombeko decided early on that if they had a child, then so be it. And then, when they didn't have one, they longed for it to happen.

Nombeko would have liked a daughter who didn't have to carry shit starting when she was five and who didn't have a mother who lived on thinner until she was no longer alive. Holger didn't care which sort of child it was; the important thing was that the child would be allowed to grow up without being brainwashed.

"A girl who can think whatever she wants about the king, you mean?" Nombeko summarized, snuggling closer to her Holger among the pillows on the crate.

"With a dad who doesn't exist and a mum who's on the run. What a great start to life," said Holger.

Nombeko snuggled even closer.

"Again?" said Holger.

"Yes, please."

But on the crate? It seemed troubling, until Nombeko promised that the bomb wouldn't explode, no matter how many times she did.

♦ ♦ ♦

The Chinese girls' cooking was truly something special. But the cafeteria in the living room of the fourth-floor apartment was seldom full. Holger One worked in Bromma. Celestine was often out delivering pillows. The American potter kept to his pantry of preserves so as not to put himself in unnecessary danger (only he understood what this danger might consist of). Occasionally there were times when even Two and Nombeko preferred to go somewhere in downtown Gnesta to be a bit romantic.

If the concept of "pissing into the wind" had existed in Wu Chinese, it would have been what the girls felt like they were doing, off and on. And it wasn't as if they were paid for their work; they weren't getting even a tiny bit closer to their uncle in Switzerland.

In all their cluelessness, the girls decided to start a restaurant for real. The idea was fuelled by the fact that so far the only Chinese restaurant in Gnesta was run by a Swedish man, who had two Thai employees in the kitchen to increase his credibility. It ought to be illegal

240

to let Thais make Chinese food, the girls thought, and they put an ad in the local advertising flyer to say that the restaurant Little Peking had opened its doors on Fredsgatan.

"Look what we did!" they said proudly when they showed the ad to Holger Two.

When Two had recovered, he explained that what they had done was start an unlicensed business in a condemned building they were not allowed to live in, in a country they were not allowed to be in. And what's more, they were about to break at least eight of the National Food Administration's strictest regulations.

The girls gave him a strange look. Why would the authorities have any opinion on where and how they made food and whom they sold it to?

"Welcome to Sweden," said Two, who knew the country that didn't know him.

◆　◆　◆

Luckily the ad had been small and also in English: the only person who showed up that evening was the municipal environment director — not to eat, but to close down what had apparently just opened.

But she was blocked at the door by Holger Two, who reassured her that the ad had just been a prank. Of course no one was serving food in the condemned building, and obviously no one lived in it. Pillows were warehoused and distributed here, and that was it.

Would the environment director like to buy two hundred pillows, by the way? That might sound like a lot for an environment department, but, Holger was afraid, that's how they were sold, as a unit, and there was no way to buy fewer pillows.

No, the municipal official did not want any pillows. The people at the environment department in Gnesta prided themselves on staying awake during working hours, and apparently just afterwards as well. However, she was satisfied with Holger's prank explanation, and she returned home.

With that, the immediate danger had passed. But Holger Two and Nombeko realized they had to do something about the Chinese girls, who had started to become impatient about their next step in life.

"We've tried distraction before," said Two, referring both to One's helicopter work and his girlfriend's joy over illegally driving a truck with stolen plates. "Couldn't we try that again?"

"Let me think," said Nombeko.

◆　◆　◆

The next day, she went to visit the American potter for yet another chat. On this particular morning she got to listen to his proven truth about how all phone calls in Sweden were recorded and analysed by personnel who took up an entire floor of the American intelligence headquarters in Virginia.

"It sounds like a large floor," said Nombeko.

While the potter expounded upon the subject beyond all rhyme and reason, Nombeko's thoughts moved in the direction of the Chinese girls. What *could* they do, if they couldn't start a restaurant? What were they good at?

Well, poisoning dogs was one thing. But they were a bit *too* good at that. And Nombeko couldn't see any immediate financial application in Gnesta and its environs for such a talent.

And they could make geese from the Han dynasty. Maybe that would work. There was a pottery studio on the other side of the street. And a crazy potter. Could one bring him and the girls together somehow?

An idea began to germinate.

"Meeting this afternoon at three," she said while the potter was still going through his phone-tapping argument.

"About what?" said the potter.

"At three," Nombeko replied.

At exactly the appointed time, she knocked once again on the door of the nervous American. With her she had three South African Chinese girls.

"Who's there?" the potter said through the door.

"The Mossad," said Nombeko.

The potter had no sense of humour, but he recognized her voice and opened the door.

The American and the Chinese girls had hardly even met each other, because for reasons of safety the former preferred his own preserves to the girls' delicious lunches and dinners. In order to get them to hit it off, Nombeko convinced the potter that the girls belonged to a minority group from Cao Bằng in North Vietnam, where they had devoted themselves to the peaceful cultivation of opium before the horrible Americans hounded them out of there.

"I am truly sorry," said the potter, apparently buying that the girls were not who they were.

Nombeko turned things over to the big sister, who explained how good they had once been at making two-thousand-year-old pottery. But now they no longer had access to a work area, and their mother the designer was back in South Africa.

"South Africa?" said the potter.

"Vietnam."

The big sister rushed to continue. If Mr Potter might consider giving the girls access to his pottery factory and being the one who created the planned Han dynasty pieces, the girls promised to help by giving him advice about how the pieces should look. In addition, they knew all about the final stage of the process: treating the clay surface so that what one ended up with really was a genuine Han dynasty goose. Or half genuine.

Yes. The potter was with them up to this point. Their subsequent conversation on pricing, however, was a rough one. The potter thought that thirty-nine kronor would be a good price, while the girls were thinking more like thirty-nine thousand. Dollars.

Nombeko didn't really want to get involved. But at last she said, "Perhaps you could meet halfway?"

The collaboration actually ended up working. The American was quick to learn how the geese should

244

look, and in addition he got so good at making Han dynasty horses that they had to knock one ear off each horse to make it more authentic.

Every finished goose and horse was then buried in the dirt behind the pottery, and the girls tossed hen droppings and urine on top of the pieces so that they would age two thousand years in three weeks. When it came to pricing, the group eventually agreed on two different categories. One was the thirty-nine-krona category; those pieces would be sold at marketplaces all over Sweden. The other, the thirty-nine-thousand-dollar category, would be supplied with certificates of authenticity created by the big sister, who had learned how to make them from her mother, who in turn had learned from her brother, the master of all masters: Cheng Tao.

Everyone thought this was a good compromise. And their first sales went superbly. In their first month, the girls and the potter together found buyers for nineteen pieces. Eighteen of them were sold at the Kivik market, and the nineteenth was sold at Bukowskis auction house.

But putting the pieces up for sale at the fine old firm in Stockholm wasn't without complications, not if one didn't want to be locked up — and Nombeko and the girls had already tried that once. So they made sure to locate a retired gardener via the Chinese Society in Stockholm. He was about to move home to Shenzhen after thirty years in Sweden, and he received a 10 per cent commission to act as the seller to the auction firm. Even if the big sister's certificate of authenticity was a good one, there was always the risk that the truth would come out after a year or two. If this happened, the long arm of the law would have a hard time reaching all the way to Shenzhen. Furthermore, eleven million people lived there, so it was a dream for any Chinese person who had reason not to be found by the Swedish police.

Nombeko was the one who took care of the bookkeeping. She was also on the unofficial company's even more unofficial board.

"In summation, we have taken in seven hundred and two kronor in market sales and two hundred and seventy-three minus commission at auction during our first month of accounting," she said. "The costs were kept down to six hundred and fifty kronor for travel to Kivik market, there and back."

The potter's financial contribution to the endeavour in that first month was thus a net profit of fifty-two kronor. Even he realized that one branch of sales was more profitable than the other. On the other hand, they couldn't use Bukowskis too often. The auction firm would soon grow suspicious if a new Han dynasty goose were to show up as soon as the last one had come under the hammer, no matter the quality of the certificate of authenticity. Once a year would have to do. And only if they could obtain another homeward-bound decoy.

The Chinese girls and the American bought a decent secondhand Volkswagen bus with their first month's profits, and then they adjusted the market selling price to ninety-nine kronor; they couldn't get the potter to agree to go any higher. He did, however, add his

246

napalm-yellow Saigon collection to the joint venture, and all in all the girls and the potter took in about ten thousand kronor per month through their business, while waiting for Bukowskis to be ready again. This was more than enough money for all of them. They did live cheaply, after all.

CHAPTER
THIRTEEN

On a happy reunion and the man who became his name

It would still be a while before it was time for one of the tenants at Fredsgatan 5 to die.

Holger One was happy at Helicopter Taxi Inc. He managed answering the telephone and brewing coffee splendidly. In addition, he was allowed a practice flight now and then in one of the three helicopters, and each time he imagined that it was bringing him one step closer to kidnapping the king.

At the same time, his young and angry girlfriend was travelling around Sweden in a truck with stolen plates, and she kept herself in good spirits by way of her hope that she would one day be caught in a routine traffic stop.

The three Chinese girls and the American went from market to market, selling antique items for ninety-nine kronor apiece. At first Nombeko went along to keep an eye on everything, but when it turned out that it went well, she stayed at home more and more often. As a supplement to the market sales, Bukowskis was subjected to a new Han dynasty goose about once a year, and it was sold just as easily each time.

The Chinese girls' plan was to fill the VW bus with pottery and take off to see their uncle in Switzerland once they had saved up a little money. Or a lot. They were no longer in any rush. After all, they found life to be both lucrative and rather pleasant in this country (whatever it was called).

The potter worked alongside the girls, suffering only from a few exaggerated neuroses, and only now and again. For example, once a month he went through the pottery studio looking for hidden microphones. He didn't find any. Not a single one. Not ever. Strange.

In the parliamentary election of 1991, the "Tear All This Shit Down" Party received another invalid vote. But many more went to the Moderate Party. Sweden got a new prime minister, and Holger Two had reason to make another call to offer him something he surely didn't want but ought to accept just the same. Unfortunately, Prime Minister Bildt never got the chance to say yes or no, because his assistant had the same idea as her predecessor about which calls could be put through and which couldn't. And when Holger tried to contact the same king as four years earlier, the same court secretary said the same thing she had last time. And she may have said it a bit more snootily.

Nombeko understood Two's demand that the bomb should be handed over to the prime minister or no one at all. The only exception being if the king happened to get in their way.

But after nearly four years and a change of government, she realized that one had to *be* someone in order to get close enough to the Swedish prime minister without causing alarms to go off. It would be best to be a president of another country or at least the CEO of a company with thirty or forty thousand employees.

Or an artist. Earlier that year, a girl named Carola had sung about being "captured by a storm wind" and won a song competition because of it, and it had been shown all over the world. Nombeko didn't know whether she had met the prime minister afterwards, but he had at least sent her a telegram.

Or a sports star. That Björn Borg probably could have been granted an audience whenever he wanted in his glory days. Maybe he still could. You had to *be* someone. That is, you had to be exactly what Holger Two was not, while she herself was illegal.

On the other hand, she hadn't been locked up behind an electric fence for four years now. And she very much wanted to keep it that way in the future. So Nombeko was able to reconcile herself to the fact that the bomb remained where it was for a little longer, if it absolutely had to stay there, while she browsed through a new shelf each week at the local library.

Meanwhile, Holger Two grew his import business to include hand towels and hotel soaps.

Pillows, hand towels and soaps were not what he had had in mind when, in his youth, he dreamed of getting away from his father, Ingmar, but they would have to do.

◆ ◆ ◆

In early 1993, contentment spread throughout both the White House and the Kremlin. The United States and Russia had just taken another step in their joint efforts on mutual control of the two superpowers' nuclear weapons arsenals. Moreover, with the new START II treaty, they had agreed to further arms reductions.

Both George Bush and Boris Yeltsin thought that the world had become a safer place to live.

Neither of them had ever been to Gnesta.

That same summer, the Chinese girls' chances of continued lucrative employment in Sweden grew dimmer. It all started when an art dealer in Södertälje discovered that authentic Han dynasty geese were being sold at markets around the country. He bought twelve of them and took them to Bukowskis in Stockholm. He wanted 225,000 kronor for each, but instead he found himself in handcuffs and jail. No one could believe in twelve Han dynasty geese in addition to the five the firm had sold in as many years.

The attempted fraud was reported in the papers, where Nombeko noticed it and immediately told the girls what had happened and said that they must absolutely not approach Bukowskis again, with or without a decoy.

"Why not?" wondered the little sister, who lacked the ability to see the danger in anything.

Nombeko told her it was probably impossible to explain that to anyone who didn't already understand, but that they must still do as she said.

At this point, the girls felt they'd had enough of their ongoing adventure. They had already collected a decent amount of money, and they wouldn't get much more if they were reduced to accepting the American potter's pricing.

Instead they filled the VW bus with 260 newly made pieces of pottery from the time before Christ, hugged Nombeko goodbye, and took off for Switzerland, their uncle Cheng Tao and his antiques store. They would sell the pieces they took with them for $49,000 per goose or $79,000 per horse; they also had a handful of other things that were so unfortunate they could be considered more than unique and had therefore received price tags between $160,000 and $300,000. Meanwhile, the American potter resumed his trips from market to market, selling his own copies of the same items for thirty-nine kronor, pleased that he no longer had to compromise on the price.

In her goodbye, Nombeko had said that the price level the girls had chosen was undoubtedly fair, considering how old and lovely the pieces were — especially to an untrained eye. But just in case the Swiss weren't as easily fooled as the Swedes, she wanted to send them off with the advice not to be careless with the certificates of authenticity.

To this the big sister replied that Nombeko shouldn't worry. Their uncle had his weak points like anyone else, but when it came to the art of creating fake certificates of authenticity, he was a match for anyone. Yes, he had spent four years in prison in England once, but the fault for that lay squarely with that bungler in London who had drawn up such a slipshod authentic certificate of authenticity that their uncle's fake one looked too good in comparison. That bungler had even been locked up for three months before Scotland Yard figured out how things really stood: that is, that the fake, unlike the original, wasn't a fake.

Since then, Cheng Tao had learned his lesson. These days he made sure not to make his work too perfect. Kind of like when the girls knocked off one ear on the Han dynasty horses in order to up the price. Things would go well, they promised.

"England?" Nombeko wondered, mostly because she wasn't sure the girls understood the difference between Great Britain and Switzerland.

No, that was history. During his time in prison, their uncle had shared a cell with a Swiss "sweetheart swindler" who had done his job so damned well that he was in for twice as many years as their uncle. As a result, the Swiss man didn't need his identity for a while, so he had lent it to their uncle, possibly without being asked first. Their uncle didn't always ask before he borrowed things. On the day he was released, the police stood waiting outside the gates. They had planned to deport him to Liberia, because that was the last place he had been. But then it turned out that the Chinese man wasn't African but Swiss, so they sent him to Basel instead. Or maybe it was Bern. Or Bonn. Possibly Berlin. In any case, as she'd said, it was Switzerland.

"Goodbye, dear Nombeko," said the girls in the little Xhosa they still remembered, and then they left.

"祝你好运," Nombeko called after the VW bus. "Good luck!"

As she watched the girls disappear, she spent a few seconds calculating the statistical probability that three illegal Chinese refugees who couldn't tell Basel from Berlin would make it through Europe in an uninsured VW bus, find Switzerland, get into the country and then run into their uncle. Without being discovered.

Since Nombeko didn't meet the girls ever again, she never knew that they decided early on to drive straight through Europe until they got to the country they were looking for. Straight through was the only right way, the girls thought, because there were road signs all over the place that no one could understand. Nombeko also never knew that the Swedish-registered, touristy VW bus was waved through each and every border control along the way, including the one between Austria and Switzerland. And she never knew that the first thing the girls did after that was go into the nearest Chinese restaurant to ask if the owner might know Mr Cheng Tao. The owner didn't, of course, but he knew someone who might know him, who knew someone who might know him, who knew someone who said he had a brother who might have a tenant by that name. The girls really did find their uncle, in a suburb of Basel. Their reunion was a happy one.

But, of course, Nombeko never knew this.

◆ ◆ ◆

All of the remaining tenants at Fredsgatan were still alive. Holger Two and Nombeko clung to one another more and more. The latter noticed that just being near her Holger made her happy, while Holger himself felt immensely proud every time she opened her mouth. She was the smartest person he knew. And the most beautiful.

They still had lofty ambitions among the pillows in the warehouse, in their endeavour to have a child together. Despite the complications that would arise should it really happen, the couple's frustrations grew when it didn't. It was as though they had got stuck in life and a little baby was what would unstick them.

Their next step was to blame the bomb. If they could just get rid of it, a baby would probably turn up out of sheer momentum. Intellectually, they knew that there was no direct connection between the bomb and a baby, but it increasingly became a matter of emotion rather than reason. Take, for example, the way they moved their erotic activities to the pottery once a week. New place, new possibilities. Or not.

Nombeko still had twenty-eight rough diamonds in the lining of the jacket she no longer wore. After her first failed attempt a few years earlier, she hadn't wanted to subject herself and the group to the risk involved in travelling around and selling them. But now she was starting to entertain the idea again. Because if she and Holger had a lot of money, it might be possible to find new ways to reach the troublesome prime minister. It was too bad that Sweden was so hopelessly uncorrupt, otherwise they could have bribed their way to him.

Holger nodded thoughtfully. Maybe that last part wasn't such a bad idea after all. He decided to try it right away. He found the number to the Moderate Party, called it, introduced himself as Holger, and said he was thinking of donating two million kronor to the party, on the condition that he got to have a one-on-one meeting with the party leader (slash prime minister).

The people at the party headquarters were more than interested. It would surely be possible to arrange a meeting with Carl Bildt if Mr Holger would just state who he was and what his business was, as well as his full name and address.

"I would prefer to keep that private," Holger tried, and was told in reply that he was certainly welcome to do so, but that it was still necessary to maintain a certain degree of security surrounding the party leader, who was moreover the country's head of government.

Holger thought quickly; he could pretend to be his brother with an address in Blackeberg and a job at Helicopter Taxi Inc. in Bromma.

"Then will I be guaranteed a meeting with the prime minister?" he said. The office couldn't promise anything, but they would do their best. "So I'm going to donate two million kronor and then *possibly* get to meet him?" said Holger.

That was more or less correct. Surely Mr Holger understood.

No, Mr Holger did not. In his frustration over how damn hard they had to make it to talk to a simple prime minister, he told the Moderates that they could look for someone else to cheat out of his money. Then he wished them the very worst of luck in the next election and hung up.

Meanwhile Nombeko had been thinking. It wasn't as though the prime minister sat around at his government offices all day long until he left office. He did actually go out and meet people. Everyone from other countries' heads of state to his own colleagues. Beyond that, he was on TV now and again. And he talked to journalists on the left and right. Preferably right.

It was unlikely that Holger or Nombeko could transform him- or herself into a head of state from a foreign country. It sounded easier to get a job in the government offices or somewhere nearby, although that would be quite difficult enough in itself. Two could start by applying to a university; all he had to do was dash off some entrance exams first. Then he could study whatever he wanted in his brother's name, as long as it would eventually bring him into the vicinity of the prime minister. They wouldn't need the pillow business any more if they could just sell the fortune in Nombeko's jacket.

Two absorbed what Nombeko had said. Political scientist? Or economist? It would take several years at a university. And it might not even lead anywhere. But the alternative seemed to be to stay where they were until the end of time, or at least until One realized that he would never learn to fly a helicopter or until the angry young woman grew tired of never being arrested by the police. If the disturbed American hadn't already messed something up by then.

Furthermore, Two had always loved the idea of higher education. Nombeko gave her Holger a hug to acknowledge that if they didn't have a child, at least they had a semblance of a plan. It felt good.

They just had to find a safe way to sell the diamonds.

◆ ◆ ◆

While Nombeko was still pondering how and where she would approach which diamond merchant, she walked straight into the solution. It happened on the pavement outside the library in Gnesta.

His real name was Antonio Suarez, and he was a Chilean who had fled to Sweden along with his parents because of the *coup d'état* in 1973. But hardly anyone in his circle of acquaintances knew his name. He was simply called "the Jeweller", even though he was anything but. He had, however, once been a shop assistant at the only jeweller's in Gnesta, where he'd arranged for the entire contents of the shop to be robbed by his own brother.

The robbery went well, but his brother went on a binge all by himself the next day, got in his car while extremely drunk, and was stopped by a police patrol that couldn't help but notice that he was both speeding and swerving from side to side.

The brother, who was romantically inclined, began by admiring the shape of the female police inspector's breasts, upon which he received a bop to the nose. This in turn made him fall madly in love: nothing was as irresistible as a woman with guts. He put down the breathalyzer the wronged inspector asked him to blow into, took a diamond ring worth 200,000 kronor from his pocket, and proposed.

Instead of the yes he had expected, he received handcuffs and a free ride to the nearest jail cell. When all was said and done, the speeder's brother was behind bars, too. Even though he denied everything.

"I have never seen this man in my entire life," he said to the prosecutor in Katrineholm district court.

"But isn't that your brother?" said the prosecutor.

"Yes, but I've never seen him."

But the prosecutor had a few things up his sleeve. For one, he had photographs of the brothers together, from their childhood on. The fact that they were listed as living at the same address in Gnesta was another matter of aggravation, and then there was the fact that a large part of the spoils from the robbery had been found in the wardrobe they shared. Furthermore, the brothers' honest parents testified against them.

The man who had since been called the Jeweller got four years in Hall Prison, the same as his brother. After that the brother flew back to Chile while the Jeweller supported himself by selling cheap trinkets imported from Bolivia. The plan was to save all the money in a pile until he had a million kronor, at which point he planned to retire to Thailand. He had met Nombeko at the markets. It wasn't as if they actually spent time together, but they nodded at each other in passing.

The problem was that the Swedish market crowd never really seemed to understand the magnitude of silver plastic Bolivian hearts. After two years of hard work, the Jeweller was struck by depression; he thought that everything was just shit (which it essentially was). He had made it to 125,000 kronor in pursuit of his million, but he couldn't take it any more. Instead he went to Solvalla one Saturday afternoon in his depressed condition and used all his money to place what was by far the biggest bet of all on that week's V75 horse racing, with the intention of losing it all and then going to lie down and die on a park bench in Humlegården.

But then horse after horse performed as it should (but never had before), and when all the races were over, one solitary winner with seven correct picks was able to collect 36.7 million kronor, of which he received 200,000 as cash in hand.

The Jeweller decided to forget about dying on a park bench in Humlegården; instead he went to the Café Opera and drank himself silly.

In this he succeeded beyond expectations. He woke up the next afternoon in a suite at the Hilton at Slussen, naked except for his socks and underwear. His first thought, given the presence of his underwear, was that he might not have had as much fun as last night's circumstances called for, but he couldn't say for sure because he didn't remember.

He ordered breakfast from room service. While eating his scrambled eggs and drinking his champagne, he decided what he wanted to do with his life. He put aside the Thailand idea. Instead he would stay in Sweden and invest in a business of his own for real.

The Jeweller would become . . . a jeweller.

Out of pure malevolence, he set up shop next door to the boutique in Gnesta where he had once been trained and that he later robbed. Because Gnesta is Gnesta, where one jeweller is almost too many, it took the Jeweller less than six months to drive his former boss out of business. Incidentally, this was the same man who had nearly called the police that time Nombeko had paid a visit.

Then one day in May 1994, the Jeweller ran into a black woman outside the library on his way to work. Where had he seen her before?

"The Jeweller!" said Nombeko. "It's been a long time. How is life treating you today?"

Oh yes, she was the woman who had gone around with that screwy American and those three Chinese girls who were impossible to get anywhere with.

"Fine, thanks," he said. "I've exchanged silver plastic Bolivian hearts for the real thing, you could say. I'm a jeweller here in town these days."

Nombeko thought this was extraordinary. Suddenly and strangely, she had a contact in Swedish jewellers' circles. And one who seemed to have flexible morals, or possibly no morals at all.

"Fantastic," she said. "I guess it's *Mr* Jeweller from now on. Might you have any interest in making a deal

261

or two? I happen to have some rough diamonds to hand, and I would be happy to exchange them for money."

The Jeweller thought about how impossible God was to understand. On the one hand, he had always prayed to him; on the other hand, he had seldom received anything in return. And then there was that ill-fated robbery, which ought to work against him when it came to the divine. Instead, the Lord was dropping riches straight into his lap.

"My interest in rough diamonds is very keen, Miss . . . Nombeko, was it?"

So far, business hadn't gone at all as the Jeweller had planned. But now he could start planning to rob himself on the side once more.

Three months later, all twenty-eight diamonds had been traded in and sold on. Instead, Nombeko and Holger had a backpack full of money. Nineteen point six million kronor, which was probably 15 per cent less than if the deal hadn't had to be carried out so discreetly. But, as Holger Two said, "Nineteen point six million is still nineteen point six million."

He had just signed up to take the autumn university entrance exams. The sun was shining and the birds were chirping.

PART FOUR

Life need not be easy,
provided only that it is not empty.

Lise Meitner

CHAPTER
FOURTEEN

On an unwelcome visitor and a sudden death

In the spring of 1994, South Africa became the first and, up to then, the only country in the world to develop its own nuclear weapons and then relinquish them. It voluntarily allowed its nuclear programme to be dismantled just before the white minority was forced to hand over power to the blacks. The process took several years and was carried out under the supervision of the International Atomic Energy Agency, which, when everything was officially finished, confirmed that South Africa's six atomic bombs no longer existed.

The seventh, however, the one that had never existed — that one still existed. Furthermore, it would soon be on the move.

It all started when the angry young woman grew tired of never being apprehended by the police. What the hell were they thinking? She drove too fast, she crossed solid lines, she honked at old ladies as they crossed the street. Yet year after year went by in which not a single officer showed any interest in her. There were thousands of police officers in this country, all of whom ought to go to hell, and Celestine hadn't had a chance to inform a single one of them of this fact.

The thought that she might get to sing "*Non, je ne regrette rien*" was still too pleasing for her to stop doing her job, but something really must happen soon, before she woke up to find herself part of the establishment. Just think of what Holger Two had suggested a few days earlier: that she should get an actual driving licence. That would ruin everything!

In frustration, she went up to see Holger One in Bromma and told him they had to make their mark *now*.

"Our mark?" said Holger One.

"Yes. Stir things up."

"Well, what are you thinking?"

The angry young woman couldn't say, exactly. But she went to the nearest store and bought a copy of the shitty bourgeois newspaper *Dagens Nyheter*, which was only there to be the tool of the powers that be. Damn them!

And then she paged through it. And paged through it some more. She found a lot of things that made her even angrier than her base level of anger, but above all it was a short article on page seventeen that really got her going.

"Here!" she said. "We just cannot accept this!"

The article said that the relatively newly formed party the Sweden Democrats was planning a demonstration at Sergels Torg in Stockholm the next day. Almost three years earlier, the party had received 0.09 per cent of the votes in the Swedish parliamentary election and, according to the angry young woman, that was too fucking many votes. She explained to her boyfriend that the party consisted of secret racists and was led by an ex-Nazi, and that they were all crazy about the royal family!

The angry young woman felt that what the Sweden Democrats' demonstration needed more than anything else was . . . a counter-demonstration!

The part about the party's views on the status of the king and queen caused Holger's anger to flare up, too. It would be so wonderful to influence opinions in the spirit of his father, Ingmar, after all these years.

"Well, I do have the day off tomorrow," he said. "Come on, let's go home to Gnesta and get ready!"

Nombeko came across Holger One and the angry young woman as they were making signs for the next day's protest. The signs read SWEDEN DEMOCRATS OUT OF SWEDEN, NO MORE ROYAL FAMILY, SEND THE KING TO THE MOON and SWEDEN DEMOCRATS ARE STUPID.

Nombeko had read a bit about that party, and she nodded in recognition. Being a former Nazi was, of course, not an impediment to having a political career. Almost all the prime ministers of South Africa in the second half of the twentieth century had had that very same background. It was true that the Sweden Democrats had only received a tenth of a per cent of the vote in the last parliamentary election, but their rhetoric was based on fear, and Nombeko believed that fear had a bright future ahead of it; it always had.

So the part about SWEDEN DEMOCRATS ARE STUPID was not something Nombeko could really agree with. It was actually quite clever, as a Nazi, to stop referring to oneself as such.

Upon hearing this, the angry young woman gave a speech, the theme of which was that she suspected Nombeko of being a Nazi herself.

Nombeko left the sign manufacturers and went to find Two to tell him that they might be facing a problem, in that Two's disaster of a brother and his girlfriend were on their way to Stockholm to make trouble.

"Ah well, show me a peace that lasts," said Holger Two, without knowing the extent of the misery that awaited.

◆ ◆ ◆

The main speaker at the Sweden Democrats' demonstration was the party leader himself. He stood on a homemade podium, microphone in hand, and talked about what Swedish values were, and about the threats thereto. He demanded, among other things, an end to immigration and the reintroduction of the death penalty, which had not been practised in Sweden since November 1910.

Before him stood about fifty like-minded people, who applauded. And just behind them were the angry young woman and her boyfriend, whose signs were still under wraps. The plan was to break in with a counter-demonstration just as the party leader finished speaking, so there was no risk of being drowned out.

As the speech went on, however, it turned out that Celestine was not only angry and young but also in need of a toilet. She whispered in Holger's ear that she needed to sneak into Kulturhuset next to the square, but that she would soon be back.

"And then we'll give them more than they can handle," she said, giving her Holger a kiss on the cheek.

Unfortunately, the speaker was soon finished with what he had to say. The audience started drifting in various directions. Holger One felt that he had to act alone, and he tore the protective paper off the first sign to reveal SWEDEN DEMOCRATS ARE STUPID. He really would have preferred SEND THE KING TO THE MOON, but he would have to make do. Plus, this one was Celestine's favourite.

The sign had not been exposed for more than a few seconds before two young Sweden Democrats caught sight of it. They were not pleased.

Even though both of them were on disability benefits, they ran up to Holger, tore the sign from his hands and tried to rip it to pieces. When this didn't work, one of them started to bite the sign, thus suggesting that the wording on the sign had some basis in reality.

When even this did not attain the desired result, the other one began to hit Holger over the head with the aforementioned sign until it broke in half. After that they jumped on him in their black boots until they grew tired. The thoroughly jumped-upon Holger remained on the ground, but he had enough strength to whimper "*Vive la République*" at the men, who immediately felt provoked again. Not that they understood what Holger had said, but he'd said *something*, and for that he deserved another beating.

When they had finished assault number two, they decided to get rid of the wreckage. They dragged Holger by the hair and one arm all the way across the square and into the subway system. There they tossed him on the ground before the turnstile guard and started on assault number three, which consisted of even more kicking, along with the suggestion that Holger, who could no longer move, ought to crawl down into the subway and never again show his ugly mug above ground.

"*Vive la République*," the beaten but valiant Holger repeated as the men walked away mumbling, "Fucking foreigners."

Holger lay where he was, but then he was helped to his feet by a reporter from Swedish Television, who was there with a cameraman to do a segment on marginal extreme-right parties with wind in their sails.

The reporter asked who Holger was and which organization he represented. The completely ruined and confused victim said that he was Holger Qvist from Blackeberg and that he represented all the citizens of this country who suffered under the yoke of the monarchy.

"So you're a republican?" said the reporter.

"*Vive la République*," said Holger for the third time in four minutes.

The angry young woman had done her business and come back out of Kulturhuset, but she didn't find her

Holger until she had followed the mass of people into the subway. She pushed her way through, shoved the TV reporter aside, and pulled her boyfriend down into the underworld for the commuter train journey to Gnesta.

The story might have ended there if it weren't for the cameraman, who had managed to capture the entire assault, beginning with the very first attack on Holger, including the fruitless sign-biting. What's more, he had managed to zoom in on Holger's tortured face at the very moment he had lain on the ground and whispered "*Vive . . . la . . . République*" after the two Sweden Democrats, who were both fit as fiddles and on disability benefits.

In its edited version, the assault was thirty-two seconds long and was broadcast along with the short interview on the news programme *Rapport* that same evening. The dramaturgy of those thirty-two seconds was so exceptional that the TV channel managed to sell broadcast rights to thirty-three countries within twenty-six hours. Soon, more than a billion people all over the world had seen Holger One get beaten up.

♦ ♦ ♦

The next morning, Holger was awakened by the pain throughout his body. But nothing appeared to be broken, and he decided to go to work after all. Two of the three helicopters had missions that morning, and that meant a lot of paperwork.

He arrived ten minutes after the actual start of his working hours, and he was immediately ordered by his boss, who was also one of the pilots, to go home again.

"I saw you on TV last night. How can you even stand up after that beating? Go home and rest — hell, go on holiday," said his boss, taking off in one of the Robinson R66s, destination Karlstad.

"You fucking nut, you're just going to scare people, looking like that," said the other pilot, taking off in turn in the other Robinson R66, destination Gothenburg.

The lonely Holger was left behind, along with the remaining pilotless Sikorsky S-76.

Holger couldn't bring himself to go home. Instead he limped into the kitchen, poured some morning coffee and returned to his desk. He didn't really know how he should feel. On the one hand, he was totally beaten to a pulp. On the other hand, *Rapport*'s video had been an enormous success! Maybe it would lead to a republican movement all over Europe!

Holger had realized that there was hardly a single television station worth its salt that hadn't broadcast the clip of him being beaten up. He had received a sound thrashing. And it was good TV. Holger couldn't help but feel proud of himself.

At that moment, a man stepped into the office. Unannounced.

The customer looked at Holger, who immediately felt that this was a man and a situation he wanted to avoid. But there was no way past the man, and his gaze was so determined that Holger remained seated.

"How may I help you?" he asked nervously.

"Let me introduce myself," the man said in English. "My name is something that is none of your business, and I am a representative of an intelligence agency whose name doesn't concern you. When people steal things from me, I get angry. If the stolen object is an atomic bomb, I get even angrier. And incidentally, my rage has been building up for a long time. In short, I am *very angry*."

Holger Qvist had no idea what was going on. This feeling was not unusual for him, but that didn't mean he was comfortable with it. The man with the determined gaze (who had an equally determined voice) took two enlarged photographs from his briefcase and placed them on the desk in front of him. The first clearly showed Holger Two in a loading bay, and the other showed Two and another man loading a large crate into a truck with the help of a forklift. *The* crate. The photographs were dated 17 November 1987.

"That's you," said the agent, pointing at Holger's brother. "And that is mine," he said, pointing at the crate.

◆ ◆ ◆

Mossad Agent A had spent seven years suffering on account of the missing nuclear weapon. He had spent just as long being determined to locate it. He had started by working along two parallel tracks. One was to find the thief and hope that both thief and stolen property were still in the same place. The other was to keep his ear to the ground, listening carefully in case an atomic bomb in western Europe or elsewhere in the world were to be offered up for sale. If he couldn't get to the bomb via the thief, it might work to go through the fence.

First A travelled from Johannesburg to Stockholm and began by going through the tapes from the security cameras at the Israeli embassy. From the camera at the gate it was easy to see that it was in fact Nombeko Mayeki who had signed for her package in front of the gatekeeper.

Was it possible that it was just a mix-up? No, because why would she have come to the embassy in a truck? Twenty pounds of antelope meat could just about fit in a bike basket, after all.

If it had been a mistake, she would probably have come back when she discovered the mix-up, because in her defence it had to be said that according to the tapes she hadn't been there when the crate was transferred to the back of the truck. At that point she was still with the gatekeeper round the corner, signing the document.

No, there could be no doubt. The secret agent from the Mossad, who had been decorated many times over, had been tricked for the second time in his career. By a cleaning woman. The same cleaning woman who had tricked him the first time.

Oh well, he was a patient man. One day, sooner or later, they would meet again.

"And then, my dear Nombeko Mayeki, you will wish that you were someone else. Somewhere else."

The camera at the embassy gates had also captured the licence plate of the red truck that had been used in the weapons heist. Another camera, the one in the embassy's loading bay, had several clear images of the white man of about Nombeko's age who had helped her. Agent A had printed out and copied several versions.

After that, he had set off at full speed. Further investigation revealed that Nombeko Mayeki had absconded from the refugee camp in Upplands Väsby on the same day she had taken the bomb from the embassy. Since then she had been missing.

The numbers on the licence plate led to an Agnes Salomonsson in Alingsås. There it turned out that the car was still red, but that it was no longer a truck but a Fiat Ritmo. So the plates were stolen. The cleaning woman was acting like a professional through and through.

All that was left for Agent A to do in the very first phase of his work was to share the recent picture of the truck driver with Interpol. This didn't lead anywhere, either. The person was not a known member of any illegal weapons ring. And yet he was driving around with an atomic bomb.

Agent A drew the logical but incorrect conclusion that he had been tricked by someone who knew what she was doing in all respects, that the atomic bomb had already left Swedish territory, and that his focus ought to be on investigating all of the murky international trails he had.

The fact that the South African bomb was joined, throughout the years, by other nuclear weapons that were on the loose made Agent A's job that much harder. In conjunction with the dissolution of the Soviet Union, atomic bombs popped up here and there — both imaginary ones and real ones. Intelligence reports mentioned a missing nuclear weapon in Azerbaijan as early as 1991. The thieves had chosen between two available missiles and taken the one that weighed the least. For this reason, all they ended up with was the shell. At the same time, they proved that nuclear weapons thieves didn't necessarily have an advantage over the general public when it came to brains.

In 1992, Agent A was on the trail of the Uzbek Shavkat Abdoujaparov, a former colonel in the Soviet Army who had left a wife and children in Tashkent, disappeared and then shown up three months later in Shanghai, where he claimed to have a bomb to sell for fifteen million dollars. The price suggested something that could do considerable damage, but before Agent A even made it there, Colonel Abdoujaparov was found in a wet dock in the harbour with a screwdriver sticking out of his neck. His bomb was nowhere to be found, and it hadn't shown up since.

Agent A was stationed in Tel Aviv from 1994 on, and not by choice; it wasn't an unimportant post, but it was much lower than would have been the case if the South African bomb incident hadn't happened. The agent never gave up; he followed various trails from his home base, and he always carried a mental image of Nombeko and the unknown man with the truck.

And then suddenly the night before, during a temporary and far too uninspiring assignment in Amsterdam, after seven years! On the television news. Images from a political disturbance on a square in Stockholm. Members of the xenophobic party the Sweden Democrats carrying away a counter-demonstrator. Dragging him into the subway. Kicking him with their boots. And there! A close-up of the victim.

It's HIM!

The man with the red truck!

According to the news: Holger Qvist, Blackeberg, Sweden.

◆ ◆ ◆

"Excuse me," said Holger, "but what is this atomic bomb you're talking about?"

"Didn't you get enough of a beating yesterday?" said Agent A. "Finish your coffee if you like, but do it now because in five seconds you and I will be on our way to see Nombeko Mayeki, wherever she is."

Holger One thought so hard that his already very sore head hurt even more. So the man on the other side of the table was working for another country's intelligence service. And he thought Holger One was Holger Two. And he was looking for Nombeko. Who had stolen an . . . *atomic bomb* from the man.

"The crate!" Holger One said suddenly.

"Yes, where is it?" said Agent A. "Tell me where the crate with the bomb is!" Holger absorbed the truth that was now dawning on him. The mother of all revolutionary dreams had been in their warehouse on Fredsgatan for seven years without him knowing it. For seven years he had had access to perhaps the only thing that could get the king to abdicate.

"May you burn in Hell," Holger One murmured, in English out of sheer momentum.

"Excuse me?" said Agent A.

"Oh, not you, sir," Holger apologized. "Miss Nombeko."

"I'm with you there," said the agent, "but I don't plan to rely on faith that it will just happen. That's why you must take me to her *now*. Where is she? Answer me!"

Agent A had confidence in his firm voice. Furthermore, he now had a pistol in his hand.

Holger was reminded of his childhood. Of his father's battle. Of how he himself had become a part of it. And of his inability to carry it on.

And now, the realization that the solution had been there all along.

His main concern wasn't that there was an agent from an unknown intelligence agency standing there, ready to shoot him if he didn't take him to Nombeko and her crate. Rather, it was that he had been fooled by his brother's South African girlfriend. And that it was all too late now. For seven years, he had had the opportunity on a daily basis to fulfil his father's mission in life. Without knowing it.

"Perhaps you didn't hear my question," said the agent. "Would a bullet in the knee help you listen better?"

A bullet in the knee, not between the eyes. For the time being, One was useful. But what would happen later? If he brought the agent to Fredsgatan, would the man with the pistol simply take the crate, which might weigh a ton, under his arm and wave goodbye?

No, he wouldn't. On the contrary, he would kill them all. But not before they helped him load the bomb into the back of the red truck.

He would kill them all unless Holger did what he suddenly realized he had to do. Because the only thing he could do was fight for his brother's and Celestine's lives.

"I'll take you to Nombeko, Agent," Holger One said at last. "But it will have to be by helicopter if you don't want to miss her. She and the bomb are about to leave."

This lie about the urgency of the situation had come out of nowhere. One might even say that it was an idea. If so, it was the first of its kind, Holger thought. And the last, because now he was finally going to do something useful with his life.

He was going to die.

Agent A had no intention of letting himself be tricked a third time by the cleaning woman and her crew. What was the catch here?

Had Nombeko realized that Holger Qvist's appearance on TV was a risk? Was that why she was in the process of packing up her things to leave? The agent could tell a Han dynasty goose from junk, and a rough diamond from cheap glass. And a lot of other things besides.

But he could not fly a helicopter. He would have to rely on the pilot — that is, the man across from him.

There would be two people in the cabin: one at the controls, and the other with a weapon in his hand.

A decided to go with the helicopter, but he also decided to let B know first, in case anything were to go wrong.

"Give me the exact coordinates of the place where the cleaning woman is," he said.

"The cleaning woman?" said Holger One.

"Miss Nombeko."

Holger did as he was asked. Using the office's PC and mapping program, it took only a few seconds.

"Good. Now sit still while I send a message to the outside world. Then we'll take off."

Agent A had something as modern as an advanced mobile phone, from which he sent an encrypted message to his colleague B with a complete update on where he was, who he was with, where he was going, and why.

"Departure," he said afterwards.

Over the years, Holger One had racked up at least ninety practice hours with his pilot colleagues at Helicopter Taxi Inc. in Bromma. But this was the first time he would fly the machine by himself. His life was over now; he knew that. He would have loved to take that damned Nombeko with him into death — had the agent called her a cleaning woman? — but not his brother. And not the wonderful Celestine.

As soon as he reached uncontrolled airspace, he levelled out at two thousand feet, at 120 knots. The trip would take just under twenty minutes.

280

When One and the agent were almost at Gnesta, Holger did *not* prepare for landing. Instead, he turned on the autopilot, setting it to go due east and to maintain an altitude of two thousand feet and a speed of 120 knots. And then, as he was used to doing, he unbuckled his seatbelt, hung up his headphones, and crawled to the rear of the cabin.

"What are you doing?" the agent said to Holger, who didn't bother to answer.

As One unlocked the back door of the helicopter and shoved it to the side, the agent remained in the forward seat; he couldn't really turn round to see what Holger was up to without first loosening his own four-point seatbelt. But how did it work? It was difficult and there wasn't much time, but he tried anyway. He twisted his body; the belt tightened, and the agent threatened Holger:

"If you jump I'll shoot!"

Holger One, who was normally anything but quick-witted, surprised himself:

"So I'll definitely be dead before I hit the ground? How do you think that will improve your situation, Mr Agent?"

A was frustrated. He was about to be left alone in midair in an aircraft he couldn't pilot himself. Being talked down to by the pilot, who was about to take his own life into the bargain. He was about to swear for the second time in his life. He twisted his strapped-down body a little more, tried to move his weapon from his right to his left hand, and — dropped it!

The pistol landed on the floor behind the rear seat and slid all the way over to Holger, who was standing there in the buffeting winds, ready to jump out.

One picked up the pistol in surprise and stuck it in his inner pocket. Then he said that he wished the agent good luck learning how an S-76 helicopter works.

"What bad luck that we left the instruction book back in the office."

Holger had nothing more to say. So he jumped. And for a second he felt a certain inner peace. But only for a second.

Then he realized that he could have used the pistol on the agent instead.

Typical, thought Holger One about himself. Usually thinking wrong, and always a little too slowly.

His body accelerated to 150 miles per hour during his two-thousand-foot journey down to rock-hard Mother Earth.

"Farewell, cruel world. I'm coming, Dad," said Holger, without even hearing his own voice in the rushing wind.

Agent A was left behind in a helicopter on autopilot, headed due east straight out above the Baltic Sea at 120 knots, with no idea how to cancel autopilot or what to do if he managed to cancel it. With fuel for about 80 nautical miles. And with 160 nautical miles left to go to the border of Estonia. In between: sea.

Agent A looked at the mess of buttons, lights and instruments before him. Then he turned round. The sliding door was still open. There was no one left to steer the aircraft. That idiot had pocketed the pistol and jumped. The ground under the helicopter was disappearing. It was being replaced by water. And even more water.

The agent had been in tight corners before in his long career. He was trained to keep his cool. So he assessed his situation slowly and analytically. And then he said to himself, "Mummy."

♦ ♦ ♦

The condemned building at Fredsgatan 5 in Gnesta had been a condemned building for nearly twenty years before reality caught up with it. It started when the director of the environment department was out walking her dog. She was in a bad mood after having kicked out her live-in boyfriend the night before, for good reason. And things only got worse when the dog ran away after a stray bitch showed up. Apparently all men were the same, whether they had two legs or four.

So she ended up on a substantial detour on that morning's walk, and before she had caught her horny dog again, the director of the environment department had managed to discover that there seemed to be people living in the condemned building at Fredsgatan 5 — in the same building where that ad from several years ago said a restaurant had opened.

Had the environment director been deceived? There were two things she hated more than anything else: her ex-boyfriend and being deceived. The combination of being deceived by her ex-boyfriend was the worst, of course. But this was bad enough.

The area had been set aside by the city as an industrial zone since 1992, when Gnesta broke away from the Municipality of Nyköping and set out on its own. The municipality had planned to do something with the area, but other things had got in the way. But that didn't mean people could just live wherever they wanted. Furthermore, there seemed to be an unlicensed business in the old pottery factory on the other side of the street. Why else would the dustbin outside the door be full of empty bags of throwing clay?

The director of the environment department was the sort of person who considered unlicensed businesses to be one step away from anarchy.

First she took out her frustrations on her dog, and then she went home, poured bits of meat into a bowl in the kitchen, and said goodbye to Achilles, who, like any man, was asleep after having satisfied his sexual urges. His master went off to work to join her colleagues in putting a stop to the Wild West activities on Fredsgatan.

A few months later, when the official and political mills had finished grinding over the matter, the owner of the property, Holger & Holger Inc., was notified that Fredsgatan 5 was to be seized, emptied and demolished in accordance with chapter two, paragraph fifteen of the constitution. The municipality's obligations were fulfilled as soon as this notice was published in *Post och Inrikes Tidningar*, the government newspaper. But as a humane gesture, the director with the horny dog made sure that a letter was sent to anyone who might be living on the property.

284

★ ★ ★

The letter arrived on the morning of Thursday, 18 August 1994. Along with references to various paragraphs of the law, it said that all tenants, if any, must vacate the premises by 1 December at the latest.

The first to read the letter was the often so angry Celestine. That same morning, she had waved goodbye to her black-and-blue boyfriend, who had insisted on going back up to Bromma to work despite the previous day's battering.

She became angry again and rushed to find Nombeko, waving the horrid letter. Callous authorities throwing average, honest people into the street!

"Well, we're not really average or honest," said Nombeko. "Come with Holger and me to the cosy corner in the warehouse instead of standing there and being angry about every little thing. We're just about to have our morning tea; if you like, you can have coffee for political reasons. It'll be good to talk this through in peace and quiet."

Peace and quiet? When there was finally — *finally* — a protest to see to? Nombeko and Holger could drink their damned tea in their fucking cosy corner, but she was going to protest! Damn the man!

The angry young woman crumpled the letter from the municipality and then, in a fury (what else?), she went down to the yard, unscrewed the stolen licence plates from Holger and Holger's red truck, got into the driver's seat, started the engine, backed up and blocked the entrance that connected the warehouse to the street, and which led into their common yard. Upon doing this, she yanked the handbrake, wiggled her way out through the window, threw the keys into a well, and carefully slashed all four tyres so the truck was sure to stay where it was, effectively blocking any attempt to enter or exit.

After this preliminary act of war against society, she took the licence plates under her arm and went to find Holger and Nombeko to tell them that there would be no more tea in the cosy corner (or coffee, for that matter), because now it was time to occupy their building! On the way she grabbed the potter; she wanted to gather as many people as possible. It was just too bad that her darling Holger was at work. Well, it couldn't be helped. They must fight the fight whenever it happened.

Holger Two and Nombeko were sitting close together on top of the bomb when Celestine stumbled in with the clueless potter in tow.

"There's a war going on!" said Celestine.

"There is?" said Nombeko.

"CIA?" said the potter.

"Why do you have the licence plates to my truck under your arm?" said Holger Two.

"Well, they're stolen property," said the angry young woman. "I was thinking that —"

At that instant, there was a sudden cracking sound above their heads. It was Holger One, who, having fallen at over 120 miles per hour for more than 2,000 feet, came straight through the leaky warehouse roof — and landed on the 50,640 pillows that happened to be in there at the time.

286

"Why, hello, darling!" The angry young woman lit up. "I thought you were in Bromma."

"Am I alive?" said Holger One, touching his shoulder, which was the only part of his body that didn't hurt after his assault, and which had now taken the brunt as he hit the roof, which immediately collapsed under his weight and speed.

"So it seems," said Nombeko. "But why did you come through the roof?"

Holger One kissed his Celestine on the cheek. Then he asked his brother to serve him a double whisky. No, a triple. He needed to throw it back, make sure that none of his internal organs had switched places, gather his thoughts and be left alone for a while. He promised to explain after that.

Holger Two did as One asked, and then he departed with the others, leaving his brother alone with the whisky, the pillows and the crate.

The angry young woman took the opportunity to check if there was any sort of fuss under way out on the street as a result of the occupation. There was not. And that wasn't so strange. For one thing, they lived on a road that saw little traffic at the edge of an industrial area, with only a scrapyard for a neighbour. For another, just because there was a truck with slashed tyres sitting in a driveway, that didn't mean it wasn't clear to everyone that there was an occupation going on.

An occupation that no one cared about was, of course, not worthy of the name. The angry young woman decided to give things a shove in the right direction.

She made some calls.

First to *Dagens Nyheter*, then to Radio Sörmland, and finally to *Södermanland News*. At *DN* she was met with a yawn. From a Stockholm perspective, Gnesta is practically the other side of the world. At Radio Sörmland in Eskilstuna, they transferred her call to Nyköping, where they asked Celestine to call again after lunch. *Södermanland News* appeared the most interested. Until they realized that the action wasn't a police matter.

"Can one even define your occupation as an occupation, if no one on the outside considers anything to be occupied?" said the philosophically inclined (and possibly lazy) editor of the paper.

The angry young woman told all three, in turn, to go to hell. Whereupon she called the police. A poor operator at an exchange in Sundsvall answered:

"Police, how may I be of service?"

"Hello, you cop bastard," said the angry young woman. "We're going to crush the mercenary capitalist society. The power will return to the people!"

"What is this in reference to?" wondered the frightened operator, who was in no way a police officer.

"That's what I'm about to tell you, you old bitch. We have occupied half of Gnesta. And if our demands are not met . . ."

At this point, the angry young woman lost her train of thought. Where had she got "half of Gnesta" from?

And what were their demands? And what were they going to do if their demands weren't met?

"Half of Gnesta?" said the operator. "Let me transfer —"

"Fredsgatan 5," said the angry young woman. "Are you deaf?"

"Why are you occupying . . . Who are you, by the way?"

"The hell with that. If our demands aren't met we will jump from the roof one by one until our blood is flowing through the whole town."

The question is which one of them was more surprised by what Celestine had just said: the operator or Celestine herself?

"Oh, my goodness," said the operator. "Stay on the line and I'll transfer you to —"

This was as far as she got before the angry young woman hung up. It seemed likely that her message to the police had got through. Furthermore, her words hadn't come out exactly as the angry young woman had intended, or to the extent she had intended.

Oh well, now the occupation was for real, and it felt good.

At that moment, Nombeko knocked on Celestine's door. Holger One had drained his double or triple whisky and collected himself. Now he had something to say. Celestine was welcome to come to the warehouse, and she could feel free to grab the potter on the way.

"I know what's in the crate," Holger One began.

Nombeko, who understood most things, could not understand this.

"How could you know that?" she said. "You fall in through the roof and suddenly you say you know something you didn't know for seven years. Did you go to Heaven and come back? And if you did, who did you talk to?"

"Shut up, you goddamned cleaning woman," Holger One said, whereupon Nombeko immediately realized that One had been in direct contact with the Mossad, or else he had run into the engineer on his trip to Heaven. The only thing that suggested it wasn't the latter was that the engineer was probably spending his time somewhere else.

Holger One continued his story, explaining that he had been sitting all by himself at the office even though he had been ordered to go home, when a man from a foreign intelligence agency had stepped through the door and demanded to be taken to Nombeko.

"Or the *cleaning woman?*" said Nombeko.

With a pistol, the man had forced Holger into the only free helicopter and ordered him to fly it to Gnesta.

"Does this mean that an angry agent from a foreign intelligence agency might fall through the roof at any moment?" Holger Two wondered.

No, it didn't. The agent in question was on his way out across the open sea and would crash into that sea as soon as the helicopter ran out of fuel. Holger himself had jumped out of the helicopter with the intent of saving the lives of his brother and Celestine.

290

"And of me," said Nombeko. "As a side effect."

Holger One glared at her and said that he would rather have landed right on Nombeko's head than on the pillows, but he never did have any luck.

"It seems to me you had a *little* luck just now," said Holger Two, who was completely floored by the way things had unfolded.

Celestine hopped into her hero's arms, hugged and kissed him, and said that she didn't want to wait any longer.

"Tell me what's in the crate. Tell me, tell me, tell me!"

"An atomic bomb," said Holger One.

Celestine let go of her rescuer and beloved. And then she thought for a moment before she summed up the situation with an "Oh, wow."

Nombeko turned to Celestine, the potter and Holger One and said that in the light of what they had just learned it was important that they all made sure not to draw attention to Fredsgatan. If people started running around in the warehouse, there could be an accident involving the bomb. And it wouldn't be just any accident.

"An atomic bomb?" said the potter, who had heard but not really understood.

"Considering what I know now, it is possible I have taken some measures that we could have done without," said Celestine.

"How so?" said Nombeko.

Then, from out on the street, they heard a voice come over a megaphone.

"This is the police! If there is anyone inside, please identify yourselves!"

"As I was saying," said the angry young woman.

"CIA!" said the potter.

"Why would the CIA come just because the police did?" said Holger One.

"CIA!" said the potter again, and he immediately said it again.

"I think he's got stuck," said Nombeko. "I once met an interpreter who did the same thing when he was stung in the toe by a scorpion."

The potter repeated himself a few more times, and then he grew silent. He just sat on his chair in the warehouse, staring straight ahead with his mouth half open.

"I thought he was cured," said Holger Two.

The megaphone voice returned.

"This is the police speaking! If there is anyone inside, make yourselves known! The entrance is blocked; we are planning to force our way in. We are taking the phone call we received extremely seriously!"

The angry young woman explained to the group what she had done; that is, started an occupation, a war against society in the name of democracy; she had used the truck, among other things, as a weapon. For informational purposes, she had also called the police. And she had stirred things up quite nicely, even if she did say so herself.

"What did you say you did with my truck?" said Holger Two.

"*Your* truck?" said Holger One.

The angry young woman said that Two mustn't get hung up on the details. This was a matter of defending important democratic principles, and in this context a tiny little tyre-slashing was nothing. And how was she supposed to know that her neighbours were keeping atomic bombs in the storeroom?

"Atomic bomb. Singular," said Holger Two.

"Three megatons," said Nombeko, to balance out Holger's minimization of the problem.

The potter hissed something no one could hear, probably the name of the intelligence service whose bad side he was on.

"I don't think 'cured' is quite the right word," said Nombeko.

Holger Two didn't want to prolong the discussion of the truck, because what's done was done, but he wondered to himself which democratic principle Celestine had in mind. Also, they were talking about *four* tyre-slashings, not one, but he didn't say anything about that either. Anyway, this was a problematic situation.

"It probably can't get much worse than this," he said.

"Don't say that," said Nombeko. "Look at the potter. I think he's dead."

CHAPTER
FIFTEEN

On the murder of a dead man
and on two frugal people

Everyone looked first at the potter and then at Nombeko, except for the potter himself, who was looking straight ahead.

Nombeko realized that, at best, a real life with Two would be postponed once again and, more likely, permanently suspended. But now it was time to take immediate action. The mourning of that which had never been would have to wait for the future, if any.

She told the group that they now had at least two reasons to delay the police. One was the obvious risk that they might choose to break in via the south wall of the warehouse, where they would drill or weld their way into a three-megaton bomb.

"Think how surprised they'd be," said Holger Two.

"No, just dead," said Nombeko. "Our other problem is that we have a corpse sitting on a chair."

"Speaking of the potter," said Holger Two. "Didn't he build a tunnel he could use to escape if the CIA came?"

"Then why didn't he do that instead of sitting down and dying?" said Holger One.

294

Nombeko praised Two for thinking of the tunnel and told One that he would probably understand any day now. And then she assigned herself the task of finding the tunnel, if it existed, seeing where it led, if anywhere, and — not least — if it was big enough for an atomic bomb to fit through. And she had to be quick, because who knew when the people out there would get themselves in gear.

"In five minutes we will start to break in!" the police said into the megaphone.

Five minutes was, of course, an impossibly short amount of time to:

1. find a homemade tunnel
2. find out where it led
3. get skids, ropes, and their imaginations in order so that that bomb could come along on the escape.

If it would even fit.

The angry young woman would probably have felt something like shame if she'd had that basic capability. Her words had come out rather of their own accord when she spoke to the police on the phone.

But then she realized that this could work in their favour.

"I think I know how we can buy some time," she said.

Nombeko suggested that Celestine tell them as quickly as possible, since the police might start drilling into the bomb in four and a half minutes.

Well, the fact was, said Celestine, that she had raised her voice a bit in her conversation with the cops, even if they were the ones who had started it by saying "Police" when they answered the phone. In a very provocative tone.

Nombeko asked Celestine to get to the point.

Yes, the point. The point was that if the group lived up to the threats Celestine happened to have made, it would stop the pigs out there in their tracks. Almost definitely. And quite thoroughly, besides. Of course, it would be . . . what was it called? . . . unethical, but surely the potter had nothing against it.

The angry young woman presented her idea. What did the others think?

"Four minutes left," said Nombeko. "Holger, you get the legs, and you get the head, Holger. I'll help with the middle."

Just as One and Two had taken hold of their respective ends of the two hundred pounds of former potter, there was a ring from the mobile phone Holger One used on behalf of the helicopter taxi service. It was his boss, who delivered the unfortunate news that one of the helicopters had been stolen. Typically enough, it had happened just after Holger had gone home to heal; otherwise, of course, he could have stopped the theft. Might he be available to arrange the police reports and all the insurance contacts? No? Helping a friend move? Well, just don't lift anything too heavy.

◆ ◆ ◆

The commanding officer on the scene had decided that they would use a torch to cut a new entrance into the property through the sheet-metal southern wall of the warehouse. The threat had been dramatic, and it was impossible to know who might be running riot in there. The easiest way to get in would, of course, have been to use a tractor to tow away the truck blocking the entrance. But the truck might be rigged somehow, as might all the windows on the property, for that matter. Thus the decision to go through the wall.

"Light it up, Björkman," said the commanding officer.

At that instant, they caught sight of a person behind the curtain in one of the broken windows in the attic of the condemned building. He could hardly be seen, but he could be heard:

"You'll never get us! If you break in we'll jump one by one! Do you hear me?" said Holger Two in as fierce and desperate a voice as he could manage.

The commanding officer stopped Björkman and his welding unit. Who was that, yelling up there? What was he up to?

"Who are you? What do you want?" the officer asked through his megaphone.

"You'll never get us!" said the voice behind the curtain again.

And then a man stepped up; he seemed to wriggle over the edge, it looked like someone was helping him . . . right? Was he going to jump? Was he going to jump to his death just because . . .

Shit!

The man let go. And sailed down to the asphalt. It was as if he wasn't anxious at all, as if he had decided to do what he was doing. He didn't make a sound as he fell. He didn't try to protect himself with his hands.

He landed on his head. A crack and a thud. Lots of blood. Not a chance he'd survived.

The break-in was immediately halted.

"Oh, shit," said the policeman with the welding unit, starting to feel ill from what he'd seen.

"What do we do now, boss?" said his colleague, who was feeling no better.

"We stop everything," said the commanding officer, who perhaps felt worst of the three. "And then we call the National Task Force in Stockholm."

♦ ♦ ♦

The American potter was only fifty-two years old, and it was true that he had been pursued all his life by his memories of the Vietnam War, and pursued by imaginary pursuers as well. But since Nombeko and the Chinese girls had become part of his life, things seemed to be going in the right direction. He was almost rid of his paranoid anxiety, he no longer had such high levels of adrenalin, and his body had got used to handling the new levels. So when what he assumed was the CIA suddenly knocked on the door for real, everything happened so fast that his adrenalin levels didn't have time to take up their former defensive positions. Instead, the potter was afflicted with ventricular fibrillation. His pupils dilated and his heart stopped.

When this happens, you *look* dead at first, and then you die for real. And then, if you are thrown headfirst from a fourth-floor window — you die again, if you hadn't done so already.

Holger Two ordered them to return to the warehouse, where he held a thirty-second moment of silence for the man who was no longer with them, thanking him for his crucial help during their current difficult situation.

After that, Two handed the command back to Nombeko. She thanked him for his trust and began by saying that she had had time to find and visually inspect the tunnel the potter had dug. It appeared that he would be helping the group not just once after his death, but twice.

"He didn't just build a four-hundred-and-fifty-foot tunnel to the pottery on the other side of the street; he supplied it with electricity and added kerosene lamps for backup. There's a cupboard of food that would last several months, and bottles of water . . . In short, he was really, really crazy."

"May he rest in peace," said Holger One.

"How big is the tunnel?" said Holger Two.

"The crate will fit," said Nombeko. "Not by a wide margin, but a small one."

So Nombeko delegated tasks. Celestine was assigned to go through the apartments, remove anything that could lead to the various inhabitants and leave the rest.

"Except one thing," Nombeko added. "In my room there's a backpack that I want to bring along. It contains things that will be important in the future."

Nineteen point six million important things, she thought.

Holger One was assigned to go through the tunnel to get the hand cart that stood in the pottery, while Two was kindly ordered to transform the bomb's container from a cosy corner back to a regular old crate.

"Regular?" said Holger Two.

"Please get going, my dear."

The division of labour was over; everyone attended to his or her own task.

The tunnel was a dazzling example of paranoid engineering. Its ceiling was high, and it had straight walls and an apparently stable system of joists that locked into each other and kept it from collapsing.

It led all the way to the cellar of the pottery, and it had an exit at the back of the property, out of sight of the steadily increasing crowd of people outside Fredsgatan 5.

It is as difficult as it sounds to handle 1700 pounds of atomic bomb on a four-wheeled hand cart. And yet, in under an hour, the bomb was on a street off Fredsgatan, only two hundred yards from the hive of activity outside the condemned building, where the National Task Force had just arrived.

"I think it's time to roll out of here," said Nombeko.

*   *   *

The Holgers and Nombeko pushed from behind while the angry young woman took care of steering up front.

Their journey progressed slowly along a small, paved road straight into the Sörmland countryside. Half a mile away from the besieged Fredsgatan. One mile. And so on.

It was, at times, hard work for everyone but Celestine. But after one and a half miles, as soon as they had pushed the cart over an invisible crest, it was easier. And with that, for the first time, they were on a slight downhill slant. One, Two and Nombeko got some well-deserved rest.

For a few seconds.

Nombeko was the first to realize what was about to happen. She ordered the Holgers to push from the other side instead. One of them understood and obeyed her immediately; the other eventually understood, too, but he had just stopped and lagged behind to scratch his behind.

One's temporary departure did not make any difference, however. It was too late as soon as the 1700 pounds started rolling on its own.

The last to give up was Celestine. She ran ahead of the bomb and tried to guide it along the right path until it was moving too quickly even for her. Then she locked the handle and jumped aside. With that, there was nothing more to do other than watch three megatons of weapon of mass destruction roll down the increasingly steep hill of the narrow country road. On one side of

301

the crate: a lashed-down backpack containing 19.6 million kronor.

"Anyone have any idea how to get thirty-eight miles away from here in ten seconds?" said Nombeko as her gaze followed the runaway bomb.

"Ideas aren't my strong suit," said Holger One.

"No, but you're good at scratching your arse," said his brother, thinking that these were peculiar last words.

Two hundred yards on, the road made a slight jog to the left. Unlike the wheel-borne atomic bomb, which kept going straight ahead.

◆ ◆ ◆

Mr and Mrs Blomgren had found in each other a person who felt that thrift was the finest virtue of them all. For forty-nine years, Margareta had been holding tight to her Harry, who held even tighter to all the couple's money. They considered themselves responsible. Any outside observer would more likely have called them stingy.

Harry had been a scrap dealer all of his working life. He had inherited the business from his father when he was only twenty-five. The last thing his father did before a Chrysler New Yorker fell on top of him was to hire a young girl to handle the company's bookkeeping. Heir Harry thought that this was an unfathomable waste of money until the girl, Margareta, invented something she called invoice fees and overdue interest. Then, instead, he fell madly in love, proposed and got a yes. The wedding was held at the scrapyard, and the three other employees were invited via a notice on the bulletin board in the hall. To a pot luck.

They never had any children. That was a cost Henry and Margareta calculated continuously until they no longer had any reason to calculate it.

On the other hand, their living situation worked itself out. For the first twenty years they lived with Margareta's mother in her house, Ekbacka, until the old woman died — what luck. She was sensitive to cold and had spent all those years complaining that Harry and Margareta refused to keep the house warm enough in the winter to keep frost from forming on the insides of the windows. She was in a better place now, lying there at a frost-free depth in the cemetery in Herrljunga. Neither Harry nor Margareta saw the point in wasting money on flowers for her grave.

As a nice hobby, Margareta's mother kept three ewes, which grazed in a small pasture along the road. But before the woman was even cold, even though she had been rather cold from the start, Harry and Margareta slaughtered the animals and ate them. A leaky sheep shed remained; they let it rot.

Then the couple retired, sold the scrapyard, and made it past both seventy and seventy-five years of age before they decided one day to actually do something about that ramshackle shed in the pasture. Harry tore it down and Margareta piled up the boards. Then they set the whole thing on fire, and it burned vigorously as Harry Blomgren watched over it with a hose in case the fire got out of hand. At his side, as always, was his wife, Margareta.

At that instant, there was a sudden crash as the 1700-pound atomic bomb in a crate on wheels shot straight through the fence into the Blomgrens' former sheep pasture and didn't stop until it was in the middle of the fire.

"What on earth?" said Mrs Blomgren.

"The fence!" said Mr Blomgren.

Then they stopped talking and looked up at the group of four people who were following the trail of the cart and crate.

"Good afternoon," said Nombeko. "Would you be so kind, sir, as to spray water on that fire so that it goes out? Without delay, please."

Harry Blomgren didn't answer. He did nothing.

"Without delay, as I said," said Nombeko. "That is to say, *now!*"

But the old man kept standing where he stood, with a turned-off hose in hand. The wooden parts of the cart were starting to react to the heat. The backpack was already blazing.

Then Harry Blomgren opened his mouth after all.

"Water isn't free," he said.

Then there was a bang.

With the first explosion, Nombeko, Celestine, Holger and Holger were struck by something similar to the cardiac arrest that had ended the potter's life an hour or so earlier. But unlike him, the others recovered when they realized that it was a tyre that had blown up, not an entire region.

The second, third and fourth ones followed suit. Harry Blomgren continued to refuse to spray water on the box and the backpack. First he wanted to know who intended to compensate him for the fence. And the cost of water.

"I don't think you quite understand the gravity of the situation we find ourselves in," said Nombeko. "The crate contains . . . flammable material. If it gets too hot, things will end poorly. Frightfully poorly. Believe me!"

She had already given up hope for the backpack. The 19.6 million were no more.

"Why should I believe a total stranger and her accomplices? Tell me who will replace the fence instead!"

Nombeko realized that she wouldn't get any further with this man. So she asked Celestine to take over.

The angry young woman was happy to. To avoid prolonging the conversation more than was necessary, she said, "Put out the fire, or I'll kill you!"

Harry Blomgren thought he could see in the girl's eyes that she meant what she said, whereupon he immediately set about doing as she said.

"Good work, Celestine," said Nombeko.

"My girlfriend," said Holger One with pride.

Holger Two chose to remain silent, but he thought it was typical that when the angry young woman finally said and did something that was of use to the group, it was in the form of a death threat.

The cart was burned half away, the crate was scorched at the edges, and the backpack was gone. But the fire was out. The world as they knew it endured. Harry Blomgren cheered up.

"So can we finally discuss the question of compensation?"

Nombeko and Holger Two were the only ones who knew that the man who wanted to discuss compensation had just burned up 19.6 million kronor because he wanted to save water. From his own well.

"The question is, who ought to compensate whom," Nombeko mumbled.

When the day began, she and her Holger had a concrete vision of the future. A few hours later things were the other way around and their very existence had been threatened — twice. Now they found themselves somewhere between the two extremes. To say that life is a bed of roses, Nombeko thought, would be an exaggeration.

◆ ◆ ◆

Harry and Margareta Blomgren didn't want to let their uninvited guests go until they had made things right. But it was starting to get late, and Harry listened to the group's arguments: there was no cash to be had; there certainly had been some in the backpack that had just been burned, but now they couldn't do anything until the bank opened the next day. Then they would put their cart in order and roll on with their crate.

"Yes, the crate," said Harry Blomgren. "What's in it?"

"None of your damn business, you old bastard," said the angry young woman.

"My personal belongings," Nombeko clarified.

The group worked together to move the scorched crate from what was left of the cart it had been on to Harry and Margareta Blomgren's car trailer. Then, after a lot of nagging and a little help from Celestine, Nombeko managed to get Harry Blomgren to let the trailer replace his car in the farm's only garage. Otherwise, of course, the crate would be visible from the road, and the thought of that would keep Nombeko from a good night's sleep.

At Ekbacka there was a guesthouse that Mr and Mrs Blomgren had previously rented to German tourists until they were blacklisted by the rental agency for trying to get extra money out of their guests for practically everything. They'd even installed a coin-operated toilet.

Since then, the guesthouse had stood empty, coin-operated toilet and all (one ten-krona coin per visit). But now the intruders could be quartered there.

Holger One and Celestine took the living room, while Two and Nombeko laid claim to the bedroom. Margareta Blomgren showed them, with a certain amount of delight, how the coin-operated toilet worked and added that she wouldn't stand for any peeing in the garden.

"Could I exchange this for ten-krona coins?" said the full-bladdered Holger One, handing a one-hundred-krona note to Mrs Blomgren.

"I dare you to say 'exchange fee'," said the angry young woman.

Since Margareta Blomgren didn't dare to say "exchange fee", no exchange took place. So One did his business in a lilac bush as soon as it was too dark for anyone to notice. It was just that of *course* someone noticed, because Mr and Mrs Blomgren were sitting in their kitchen with their binoculars at that very moment.

It had clearly been negligent of the intruders to propel a cart through the couple's fence, but they had hardly done it on purpose. To then bully the couple into wasting water so that their belongings wouldn't burn was remarkable — a criminal act — but if worst came to worst it could be excused by the desperation one could imagine they had felt at the time.

But wilfully, and contrary to clear instructions, to stand by a lilac bush and urinate in the couple's garden — this was so outrageous that Harry and Margareta were beside themselves. It was theft; it was disorderly conduct; it was perhaps the worst thing that had ever happened to them.

"These hooligans will be our financial undoing," Margareta Blomgren said to her husband.

Harry Blomgren nodded.

"Yes," he said. "If we don't do something before it's too late."

Nombeko, Celestine and the Holgers went to bed. Meanwhile, the National Task Force was preparing to break into Fredsgatan 5 a mile and a half away. The woman who'd called the police was Swedish, and a Swedish-speaking man had been spotted behind a curtain on the fourth floor — the man who later jumped. A post mortem would be performed on the corpse, of course, which for now was being kept in an ambulance down the street. A preliminary examination showed the dead man to be white and in his fifties.

So there had been at least two occupiers. The police who had witnessed the incident suspected that there had been more people behind the curtains, but they weren't sure.

The operation began at 11.32p.m. on Thursday, 18 August 1994. The task force started to break in from three different directions with gas, a bulldozer and a helicopter. There was a lot of tension among the young men on the force. None of them had experienced a real-life operation before, so it was no wonder that a few shots had been fired in the muddle. At least one of them caused the pillow-storage area to catch fire, and the resulting smoke made it nearly impossible to operate in.

The next morning, in Mr and Mrs Blomgren's kitchen, the former inhabitants of Fredsgatan were able to hear how the drama ended on the news.

According to the correspondent from Sveriges Radio, there had been a bit of a struggle. At least one of the task force members had been shot in the leg; three others were poisoned by gas. The force's twelve-million-krona helicopter had crash-landed behind an abandoned pottery because it had become disoriented in the thick smoke. The bulldozer had burned, along with the building, the warehouse, four police cars and the ambulance in which the body of the man who had committed suicide was being kept while waiting for a post-mortem.

On the whole, however, the operation had been a success. All of the terrorists had been defeated. It remained to be seen how many of them there were, because their bodies had been burned.

"Good Lord," said Holger Two. "The National Task Force, at war with itself."

"Well, at least they won. That suggests a certain amount of competence," said Nombeko.

Not once during breakfast did the Blomgrens mention that they would demand payment for the same. Instead, they said nothing. They were reticent. Almost ashamed, it seemed. This put Nombeko on her guard, because she had never met two more shameless people, and that was saying something.

Her millions were gone, but Holger Two had eighty thousand kronor in the bank (in his brother's name). In addition, there was almost four hundred thousand in the business account. The next step would be to buy themselves free from these horrible people, hire a car with a trailer and move the bomb from one trailer to the other. And then leave. They had yet to figure out where to go; it just had to be far away from Gnesta and the Blomgrens.

"We saw you peeing in the garden last night," Mrs Blomgren said suddenly.

Damn you, Holger One, thought Nombeko.

"I didn't know about that," she said. "I apologize, and I suggest that we add ten kronor to the bill, which I thought we could discuss now."

"That won't be necessary," said Harry Blomgren. "Since you can't be trusted, we have already made sure to compensate ourselves."

"How so?" said Nombeko.

"'Flammable material'. Bullshit! I've worked with scrap metal my whole life. Scrap metal doesn't burn, damn it," Harry Blomgren continued.

"Did you open the crate?" said Nombeko, who was starting to fear the worst.

"I'm going to tear open their throats with my teeth," said the angry young woman, who had to be restrained by Holger Two.

The situation was far too difficult to follow for Holger One, who walked off. Besides, he needed to visit the same lilac bush as he had the night before. This he did as Harry Blomgren backed away from the angry young woman. A profoundly unpleasant person, he thought.

And then he went on saying what he had to say. The words poured forth, because he had rehearsed them during the night.

"You chose to abuse our hospitality, you withheld payment from us, you urinated in our garden; you are

311

thus untrustworthy. We had no choice but to secure the compensation you had surely been planning to evade. Consequently your bomb scrap has been forfeited."

"Forfeited?" said Holger Two, getting a mental image of a detonated atomic bomb.

"Forfeited," Harry Blomgren repeated. "We took that old bomb to a scrap dealer during the night. And we received half a krona per pound. Which was quite stingy, but still. It should just cover the costs of the damage you have caused. And that's not including the rent for staying in the guesthouse. And don't think I'm going to tell you where the scrapyard is. You've done enough as it is."

As Holger Two continued to keep the angry young woman from committing a double murder, it became clear to both him and Nombeko that the old man and woman apparently didn't realize that what they called scrap and an old bomb was actually a rather new — and fully functional — one.

Harry Blomgren said that there was a surplus from the transaction, however limited, and consequently the matters of the water, the broken fence and the urinating in the garden could be settled. Provided the guests urinated in the toilet and nowhere else from now until their imminent departure, of course. And didn't cause any more damage.

At this point, Holger Two was forced to carry the angry young woman out. In the garden, he got her to calm down a little bit. She said there must have been something about the sight of the old man and woman that she couldn't tolerate. Plus everything they did and said.

This rage was not something Harry and Margareta Blomgren had reckoned on during the previous night's trip to and from the scrapyard they had formerly owned, and which was now owned and run by their former colleague Rune Runesson. The deranged woman operated beyond the realm of logic. In short, both of them were scared. Meanwhile, Nombeko, who never became truly angry, was now truly angry. Just a few days earlier, she and Two had found a way to move forward. For the first time there was hope; there was 19.6 million kronor. All that was left now was . . . Mr and Mrs Blomgren.

"My dear Mr Blomgren," she said. "May I suggest an agreement?"

"An agreement?" said Harry Blomgren.

"Yes, my scrap is very dear to me, Mr Blomgren. Now I intend that you, Mr Blomgren, will tell me within ten seconds where you took it. If you tell me, I promise in return to keep the woman in the garden from biting you and your wife in the throat."

The pale Harry Blomgren said nothing. Nombeko went on:

"After that, if you let us borrow your car for an undetermined period of time, you have my word that we might give it back some day, and in addition we will not immediately smash your coin box and burn down your house."

Margareta Blomgren attempted to answer, but her husband stopped her.

"Quiet, Margareta, I'll handle this."

"Up to this point, my suggestions have been veiled in politeness," Nombeko continued. "Would you like us to switch to a firmer tone, Mr Blomgren?"

Harry Blomgren continued to deal with events by not answering. His Margareta made another attempt to speak. But Nombeko beat her to it.

"By the way, Mrs Blomgren, are you the one who made this tablecloth?"

Margareta was surprised by the change of topic.

"Yes?" she said.

"It's very nice," said Nombeko. "How would you like it stuffed down your throat, Mrs Blomgren?"

Holger Two and the angry young woman heard this exchange from the yard.

"My girlfriend," said Holger Two.

When things go wrong, they really go wrong. Naturally, the bomb had been taken to the only scrapyard on Mother Earth it shouldn't have been taken to — the one at Fredsgatan 9 in Gnesta. Harry Blomgren was now convinced that survival, above all else, was the most important goal. So he explained that he and his wife had gone there in the middle of the night, with the bomb in tow. They had thought that Rune Runesson would be there to receive it, but instead they were met by chaos. Two buildings only fifty yards away from the scrapyard were on fire. Parts of the road were blocked off; they couldn't get into Runesson's yard.

Runesson himself had got up and set off for the yard in order to accept the night-time delivery, but as things stood, the trailer and its scrap would have to stay on the street beyond the barricades for the time being. Runesson promised to call and tell them when they had been removed. They couldn't complete the transaction until that happened.

"Good," said Nombeko when Harry Blomgren had told her all there was to tell. "Now please go to Hell, both of you."

And then she left the Blomgrens' kitchen, gathered the group, and placed the angry young woman behind the wheel of Harry Blomgren's car, Holger One in the passenger seat, and herself and Two in the back to talk strategy.

"Let's go," said Nombeko, and the angry young woman drove away.

She went by way of the part of the Blomgrens' fence that wasn't yet in pieces.

CHAPTER
SIXTEEN

On a surprised agent and a potato-farming countess

Agent B had served the Mossad and Israel for almost three decades. He had been born in New York in the middle of the war, and had moved to Jerusalem with his parents as a child, in 1949, just after the country was formed.

When he was only twenty he was sent on his first foreign assignment: infiltrating the student left at Harvard in the United States. His task was to record and analyse anti-Israeli sentiments.

Since his parents had grown up in Germany, whence they had to flee for their lives in 1936, Agent B also spoke German fluently. This made him a good choice for operations in the DDR in the 1970s. He lived and worked as an East German for nearly seven years. Among other things, he had to pretend to be a fan of the football team FC Karl-Marx-Stadt.

However, B didn't have to pretend for more than a few months. Soon he was as inveterate a fan as the thousands of objects of surveillance around him. The fact that the city and the team changed names when capitalism finally pulled down Communism's trousers didn't affect B's love for the team. As a discreet and slightly childish homage to one of the team's obscure but promising juniors, B was now operating under the neutral but euphonious name Michael Ballack. The original was two-footed, creative and had a good eye for the game. He had a bright future ahead of him. Agent B felt an affinity for his alias in all respects.

B was temporarily stationed in Copenhagen when he received his colleague A's report about A's breakthrough in Stockholm and its environs. When A then failed to contact B again, B got the go-ahead from Tel Aviv to take off after him.

He took a morning flight on Friday, 19 August, and hired a car at Arlanda Airport. His first stop: the address his colleague A had said he was headed for the day before. B was careful to keep below the speed limit; he didn't want to drag the two-footed Ballack's name through the mud.

Once in Gnesta, he cautiously turned onto Fredsgatan and encountered — a barricade? And buildings completely burned down, tons of police, TV vans and hordes of rubberneckers.

And what was that, over there on a trailer? Was it . . .? It couldn't be. It was quite simply not possible. And yet, wasn't it . . . ?

Suddenly she was just standing there, next to B.

"Hi there, Agent," said Nombeko. "Everything all right?"

She hadn't even been surprised when she caught sight of him just outside the barricades, looking at the

317

trailer with the bomb she had come to fetch. Because why *wouldn't* the agent be standing there just then, when everything else that couldn't possibly be happening was?

Agent B released his gaze from the bomb, turned his head, and instead caught sight of — the cleaning woman! First the stolen crate on a trailer and now its thief. What was going on?

Nombeko felt remarkably calm. She realized that the agent was both at a loss and without a chance. There were at least fifty police officers in the immediate vicinity, and surely two hundred other people, including half of the Swedish media.

"Beautiful sight, isn't it?" she said, nodding at the scorched crate.

B didn't answer.

Holger Two came up beside Nombeko. "Holger," he said, extending his hand on a sudden impulse.

B looked at it but didn't take it. Instead he turned to Nombeko.

"Where is my colleague?" he said. "In the wreckage in there?"

"No. Last I heard he was on his way to Tallinn. But I don't know if he arrived."

"Tallinn?"

"If he arrived," said Nombeko, signalling to the angry young woman to back up the car.

While Holger Two hooked up the trailer to the car, Nombeko excused herself to the agent. She had some things to do, and now she had to leave with her friends. They could talk more next time they met. If they

318

should have the misfortune to run into each other again.

"Goodbye, Agent," said Nombeko, getting into the back seat next to her Two.

Agent B didn't answer, but he did think. What he thought while the car and trailer rolled away was: *Tallinn?*

◆ ◆ ◆

B stood there on Fredsgatan, thinking about what had happened, while Celestine drove north out of Gnesta, with One next to her and Two and Nombeko in continual discussions in the back. They were about to run out of petrol. The angry young woman complained that the stingy goddamn fucking bastard they'd stolen the car from hadn't even filled it up first. And then she turned off at the first service station.

After refuelling, One took Celestine's place behind the wheel; there were, after all, no more fences to break through in a rage. Nombeko had encouraged the change of driver, because it was bad enough that they were driving around with an atomic bomb on an overloaded trailer pulled by a stolen car. They might as well have a licensed driver.

Holger One continued driving north.

"Where are you going, dear?" said the angry young woman.

"I don't know," said Holger One. "I've never known."

Celestine thought. Should they maybe . . . despite all the . . . ?

"Norrtälje?" she said.

Nombeko interrupted the conversation from the back seat. She had heard something in Celestine's voice that indicated Norrtälje was something more than just one town among many.

"Why Norrtälje?"

Celestine explained that her grandmother lived there. A class traitor, difficult to tolerate. But with things the way they were ... The angry young woman could probably manage a night in her grandmother's company, if the others could. Incidentally, she grew potatoes, and the least she could do was dig up a few tubers and offer them some food.

Nombeko asked Celestine to tell her more about this lady, and she was surprised by the long and relatively clear answer.

The fact was, Celestine hadn't seen her grandmother in more than seven years. And in that time, they hadn't spoken to each other even once. But she had spent her childhood summers at her grandmother's farm, which was called Sjölida, and they'd had a ... good ... time together there (that "good" was hard to get out, because Celestine's general attitude was that nothing was good).

She went on, saying that she had become politically active in her teens. She considered herself to be living in a mercenary society where the rich just got richer, while she herself just got poorer because her father withheld her allowance as long as she refused to do what he and her mother said (such as stop calling them capitalist pigs at breakfast every morning, for instance).

At fifteen, she had joined the Marxist-Leninist Communist Party (The Revolutionaries), partly because of the bit in parentheses; she was drawn to this even if she didn't know what kind of revolution she wanted, from what to what. But she also joined because being a Marxist-Leninist was starting to be so hopelessly *out*. The Left of the 1960s had been replaced by a 1980s right wing that had gone so far as to invent their own May Day, even if those cowards had picked the fourth of October instead.

Being both out of style and a rebel was what Celestine liked best, and furthermore, it was a combination that represented the opposite of everything her father stood for. He was a bank manager, and thus a Fascist. Celestine daydreamed of how she and her friends would shove their way into her father's bank with their red flags, demanding not only Celestine's allowance but also retroactive allowances with interest, going back to when it had first been withheld.

But when she happened to suggest that MLCP(R)'s local chapter ought to go to the Gnesta branch of Handelsbanken for the aforementioned reasons, she was first booed, then harassed and finally kicked out. The party was too busy giving support to Comrade Robert Mugabe in Zimbabwe. Independence had now been won there. All that was left was to fight the one-party state. With this in mind, they were not currently interested in robbing Swedish banks of members' weekly allowances. Celestine was called a dyke by the chairperson of the local chapter and was shown the door (at the time, homosexuality was the next-worst thing there was, according to the Marxist-Leninists).

All that the kicked-out and extremely angry young Celestine could do was concentrate on graduating from school with the worst possible grades in every subject, for this was what she was actively working on in protest against her parents. For instance, she wrote her short English essay in German and claimed in a history exam that the Bronze Age began on 14 February 1972.

Right after her last day of school, she placed her final grades on her father's desk, whereupon she said farewell and moved in with her grandmother in Roslagen. Her mother and father let it happen, thinking that she would probably come back and it didn't matter if it took a month or two. After all, her absolute rock-bottom grades from school weren't enough for the more advanced lines of study at gymnasium. Or any gymnasium line at all.

Her grandmother had just turned sixty and worked hard on the potato farm she had inherited from her parents. The girl helped as much as she could; she liked the old woman as much as she had during her childhood summers. Until the old woman dropped a bombshell (if Nombeko could forgive the expression). One evening, before the fire, Grandma said that she was actually a *countess*. Celestine had had no idea. So deceitful!

"How so?" Nombeko was genuinely curious.

"Surely you don't think I sit around fraternizing with the oppressors?" Celestine said, once again in the spirit Nombeko knew so well.

322

"But she was your grandma! And still is, as far as I understand it."

Celestine replied that Nombeko just didn't understand, and that this was all she had to say on the matter. Anyway, she had packed her bags the next day and left. She had had nowhere to go and spent a few nights sleeping in a boiler room. She went to her father's bank to demonstrate. Met Holger One, a republican and the son of a junior postal clerk who had been driven by passion and died for his cause. Things couldn't have turned out better. It was love at first sight.

"And yet you're prepared to go back to your grandma?" said Nombeko.

"Well, shit, why don't you think of a better idea? We're towing a fucking bomb. I would personally much rather go to Drottningholm and set this fucker off outside the palace. At least I'd die with a little dignity."

Nombeko pointed out that they didn't need to go to the king's palace twenty-five miles away to wipe out the monarchy and everything else besides; they could do it from a distance. But she didn't recommend it. Rather, she praised Celestine for her idea about her grandmother.

"To Norrtälje," she said, returning to her conversation with Holger Two.

Two and Nombeko were trying to clean up after the group to make it hard for Agent B to find them again, although who had found whom this last time round?

One must immediately quit his job in Bromma. And he could never go back to his listed address in

323

Blackeberg. Quite simply, he would follow his brother's example and make sure to exist as little as possible.

The part about ceasing to exist ought to go for Celestine, too, but she refused. There was another parliamentary election coming up in the autumn, and a vote on EU membership after that. Without her own address, no ballots, and with no ballots she could not practise the civil duty of voting for the "Tear All This Shit Down" Party. And when it came to EU membership, she was going to vote yes. Because she was expecting the whole thing to go to hell, and in that case Sweden should be part of it.

Nombeko reflected that she had moved from a country where most of the people didn't have the right to vote to one where some people ought not to be allowed to. Their decision, in any case, was that the angry young woman would get a PO box with an address somewhere in the Stockholm area, and that she would make sure she wasn't being watched every time she opened it. This measure might have been overkill, but up to that point everything that could have gone wrong had.

With that, there wasn't much more they could do about past trails. All that was left was to contact the police in the very near future to ask for a meeting about the fact that a group of terrorists had burned down Holger & Holger's pillow company. Prevention would be better than cure when it came to that matter. But that would come later.

Nombeko closed her eyes for a moment of rest.

In Norrtälje, the group stopped to buy food with which to bribe Celestine's grandmother. Nombeko thought it was unnecessary to send their intended hostess out into the potato fields.

Then they continued their journey towards Vätö and onto a gravel road just north of Nysättra.

The grandmother lived a few hundred yards beyond the end of the road, and for many years she had been unused to having company. So when she heard and saw a strange car with a trailer drive onto her property one evening, she played it safe and grabbed her dead father's moose-hunting rifle before she went out to the porch.

Nombeko, Celestine and the Holgers stepped out of the car and were met by an old woman who notified them, with a raised rifle, that there was nothing here for thieves and bandits. Nombeko, who was already pretty tired, grew even more tired:

"If you feel that you absolutely must shoot, ma'am, shoot at the people first, not the trailer."

"Hi, Grandma!" said the angry young woman (rather happily, in fact).

When the old woman caught sight of her granddaughter, she put down her weapon and gave Celestine a big hug. Then she introduced herself as Gertrud and wondered who Celestine's friends might be.

"I don't know about 'friends'," said Celestine.

"My name is Nombeko," said Nombeko. "Things have been piling up a bit for us, and we would be grateful if you might let us offer you some food in return for allowing us to sleep here for the night."

The old woman on the stairs thought for a moment.

"Now, I don't know," she said. "But if I find out what kind of devils the lot of you are, and what kind of food you're offering, perhaps we can talk."

And then she caught sight of the two Holgers.

"Who are those two, who look so identical?"

"My name is Holger," said Holger One.

"Mine, too," said Holger Two.

"Chicken casserole," said Nombeko. "How does that sound?"

"Chicken casserole" was the password to Sjölida. Gertrud occasionally beheaded her own chickens to that very end, but to be served the casserole without all the trouble was certainly preferable.

As Nombeko went to prepare the food, the rest of them sat down around the kitchen table. Gertrud poured home-brewed beer for everyone, including the cook. This livened Nombeko up again.

Celestine began by explaining the difference between Holger and Holger. One was her wonderful boyfriend, while the other was a complete waste of time. With her back to the angry young woman, Nombeko said she was glad Celestine saw it that way, because then there would never be any reason to swap.

But things became trickier when they got to how they had ended up at Sjölida, how long they planned to

326

stay and why they were driving around with a crate on a trailer. Gertrud's tone grew sharper, and she said that if they were up to something fishy they could do it somewhere else. Celestine was always welcome, but if this were the case the others were not.

"Let's talk about it during dinner," Nombeko suggested.

Two glasses of beer later, the casserole was ready to be served. The old woman had warmed to them; even more so after she took her first bite. But now it was time for her to hear how things stood.

"Don't let the good food stop us talking," said Gertrud.

Nombeko thought about potential strategies. The easiest thing to do, of course, would be to fill the old woman with lies and then try to keep those lies alive as long as possible.

But with Holger One and the angry young woman in the way . . . how long would it take before one of their tongues slipped? A week? A day? Fifteen minutes? And the old woman, who might resemble her granddaughter in all imaginable irascible ways, what would she do then? With or without a moose-hunting rifle?

Holger Two looked nervously at his Nombeko. She wasn't planning to *tell* her, was she?

Nombeko smiled back. This would all work itself out. From a purely statistical angle, the chances of it working out were good — given everything that had happened so far, maybe they were out of the woods now. Despite the fact that they were sitting in the midst of them.

"Well?" said Gertrud.

Nombeko asked if their hostess might be open to a little business deal.

"I will tell you the whole story, from beginning to end. As a result, I'm pretty sure you'll throw us out, even if we would really like to stay for a while. But to thank me for my honesty, you let us stay overnight. What do you say? Have some more casserole, by the way. Shall I refill your glass?"

Gertrud nodded and said that she would consider agreeing to this arrangement, provided that they stuck to the truth. She didn't want to hear any lies.

"No lies," Nombeko promised. "Let's get going."

So she did.

She gave the short version of the whole story from Pelindaba on. Plus the story of how Holger and Holger had become Holger & Holger. And the atomic bomb, which had originally been meant to protect South Africa from all the world's evil Communists and had later been on its way to Jerusalem as protection against all the equally evil Arabs, and which had ended up in Sweden instead, as protection against absolutely nothing (Norwegians, Danes and Finns weren't generally considered sufficiently evil), and had gone to a warehouse in Gnesta that had unfortunately burned down.

And now, the very unfortunate fact was that the bomb was on the trailer and the group needed somewhere to stay while waiting for the country's prime minister to have enough sense to answer their calls. They were not wanted by the police, although there were reasons why they should have been. On the other hand, they'd happened to annoy a foreign nation's security service along the way.

When Nombeko was finished, everyone waited for their hostess's judgement.

"Well," she said when she had finished thinking, "you can't leave the bomb right outside the door like that. Make sure to move it to the back of the potato truck behind the house and then put the whole thing in the barn so none of us will be harmed if it should go off."

"But that probably won't help —" Holger One had time to say before Nombeko cut him off.

"You have been admirably quiet ever since we got here. Please keep it up."

Gertrud didn't know what a security service was, but it sounded safe. And since the police weren't on their heels, she thought they could stay for a while or two, in return for a chicken casserole now and again. Or a roast rabbit.

Nombeko promised Gertrud both casserole and rabbit at least once a week if she didn't make them go. Holger Two, who, unlike One, wasn't forbidden to speak, thought he should guide the conversation away from bombs and Israelis before the old woman had time to change her mind.

"What is your story, ma'am, if I may ask?" he said.

"My story?" said Gertrud. "Oh, goodness me."

♦ ♦ ♦

Gertrud started by telling them that she really was a countess, plus a grandchild of the Finnish baron, marshal and national hero Carl Gustaf Emil Mannerheim.

"Ugh," said Holger One.

"As you've been told, your most important job this evening is to keep your mouth shut," said his brother. "Please go on, Gertrud."

Well, Gustaf Mannerheim went to Russia early in his career, and there he swore eternal allegiance to the Russian tsar. This was a promise he kept for the most part, until it became irrelevant once the Bolsheviks killed the tsar and his entire family in July 1918.

"Good," said Holger One.

"I said be quiet!" said his brother. "Please go on, Gertrud."

Well, to cut a long story short, Gustaf had made himself an exceptional military career. And more besides. He rode to China and back as the tsar's spy, he felled tigers whose jaws could swallow a man whole, he met the Dalai Lama, and he became the commander of an entire regiment.

But his love life wasn't as grand as his career. Yes, he had married a beautiful Russian-Serbian woman of high birth, and they had one daughter and then another. They also had a son just before the turn of the century, but the official word was that the boy was stillborn. Then, when Gustaf's wife converted to Catholicism and left to become a nun in England, their chances of having more children together decreased dramatically.

Gustaf became depressed and got his mind off things by taking part in the Russo-Japanese war where, of course, he became a hero and was awarded the Cross of St George for extraordinary bravery on the battlefield.

But the thing was, Gertrud knew that the stillborn boy hadn't been stillborn at all. This was just something the nun-to-be had told her constantly absent husband. Instead the little boy was sent to Helsinki and placed in a Finnish foster home with a name tag around his wrist.

"Čedomir?" the baby's new father had said. "No chance. His name will be Tapio."

Tapio Mannerheim-alias-Virtanen didn't inherit much of his biological father's heroism. Instead his foster father taught him everything he knew. That is, how to counterfeit banknotes. At only seventeen, the young Tapio had nearly mastered this art form, but a few years later, after father and foster son had fooled half of Helsinki with their art, they realized that the surname Virtanen was so sullied that it was no longer functional in their chosen branch.

By that time, Tapio knew all about his noble background, and he himself was the one who came up with the idea of becoming a Mannerheim again for business purposes. Their business took off like never before until the day Gustaf Mannerheim came home from a trip to Asia where he had been hunting wild animals with the King of Nepal. One of the first things that Gustaf heard when he came back was that a fake Mannerheim had fooled the bank of which he himself was the chairman.

When all was said and done, Tapio's foster father had been seized and arrested, while Tapio managed to escape to Swedish Roslagen via Åland. In Sweden he started calling himself Virtanen again, except when it came to his work with Swedish banknotes, where Mannerheim had a better ring to it.

Tapio wedded four women in a short amount of time; the first three married a count and divorced a rascal, while the fourth knew Tapio Virtanen's true nature from the start. She was also the one who got him to quit the banknote business before things went as they had in Finland.

Mr and Mrs Virtanen bought a small farm, Sjölida, north of Norrtälje and invested their criminally procured family resources in three hectares of potato fields, two cows and forty hens. Whereupon Mrs Virtanen got pregnant and had her daughter Gertrud in 1927.

The years went by, and there was war in the world once again. As usual, Gustaf Mannerheim succeeded in all that he did (except that bit about love), becoming a national war hero once again, and eventually also the marshal of Finland and the president of the country. And a stamp in the United States. All while the son he didn't know he had pottered about a Swedish potato farm with a moderate amount of dignity.

Gertrud grew up to have about the same luck in love as her grandfather had had, in that when she was eighteen she went to a party in Norrtälje where she was courted by a petrol-pump attendant bearing vodka and Loranga orange soda. Just like that, she got pregnant behind a rhododendron bush. Their romance was over in less than two minutes.

Afterwards the attendant brushed the dirt off his knees, said he had to hurry to catch the last bus home, and departed with a "See you when I see you."

They did not, however, see each other again. But nine months later, Gertrud gave birth to an illegitimate daughter while her own mother withered away from cancer. Those left behind at Sjölida were Gertrud, her father Tapio and newborn Kristina. The former two continued to toil in their potato fields while the girl grew up. When she was about to start upper secondary school in Norrtälje, her mother took the opportunity to warn her about rotten men, whereupon Kristina met Gunnar, who seemed to be anything but rotten. They became a couple, got married, and had little Celestine. And would you believe it? Gunnar ended up as a bank manager.

"Yeah, damn him," said the angry young woman.

"You shut up, too," said Holger Two, but in a milder voice so as not to disturb Gertrud.

"I suppose life hasn't always been terribly fun," Gertrud said in summary, and she drained the last of her beer. "But at least I have Celestine. It's so wonderful that you're back, dear girl."

Nombeko, who had spent the last seven years reading her way through an entire library, knew enough about the history of Finland and Marshal Mannerheim to point out that Gertrud's story had some weak points. She didn't think it was necessarily the case that the daughter of a man who had made up the fact that he was the son of a baron would herself be a countess. So she said, "Well, good heavens! We're having dinner with a countess!"

Countess Virtanen blushed and went to the pantry to get more to drink. Holger Two saw that One was about to protest at Gertrud's story. So Two beat him to it and said that he ought to shut up right now more than ever. This wasn't a matter of genealogy but of accommodation.

◆ ◆ ◆

Gertrud's potato fields had lain fallow since her retirement a few years earlier. She had a small truck, her potato truck. Until now she had taken it to Norrtälje for provisions once a month, and it sat where it sat behind the house for the rest of the time. Now they turned it into a transitional nuclear storage facility and rolled it into the barn 150 yards away. Nombeko took command of the keys for safety's sake. The grocery shopping could be done with the help of the Toyota the Blomgrens had been so kind as to lend them for an unspecified amount of time. Gertrud no longer needed to leave Sjölida at all, and this suited her just fine.

There was plenty of room in the house. Holger One and Celestine got their own room next to Gertrud's, one floor up, while Two and Nombeko were quartered in the room next to the kitchen on the first floor.

Early on, the latter two had a serious talk with One and Celestine. No more demonstrations, no ideas about

334

moving the crate. In short, no nonsense. It would risk all of their lives, including Gertrud's.

In the end, Two got his brother to promise not to devote himself to any society-overthrowing activities and not to try to get at the bomb. But One added that Two ought to think about what he would say to their dad on the day they met again in Heaven.

"How about 'Thanks for ruining my life'?" said Holger Two.

◆ ◆ ◆

On the next Tuesday it was time to meet the police in Stockholm. Two had asked for the meeting himself. He suspected that he would be questioned about possible tenants in the condemned building, as part of the hunt for the terrorists who had never existed, much less died in a fire.

The solution was to cook up a believable story and let the angry young woman come along. There were risks involved, but Nombeko explained to her again and again the sort of trouble she would bring upon the group if she didn't stick to what they had decided. Celestine promised that she would not call the fucking pigs that during their conversation.

Holger Two introduced himself as his brother, and he also introduced Holger & Holger's sole employee, young Celestine here.

"Hello, Celestine," said the police officer, extending his hand.

Celestine took it and replied something like "Grmpf" because it's impossible to speak and bite one's tongue at the same time.

The officer began by offering his sympathies that the entire company had burned down, warehouse and all. It was a matter for the insurance companies at this point, as Mr Qvist surely understood. He was also sorry if this incident had left Miss Celestine unemployed.

The investigation was still in its infancy; they couldn't yet say, for example, who the terrorists had been. At first they had expected to find them in the charred remains of the building, but all they had found so far was a hidden tunnel through which the terrorists might have fled. It was all very unclear, because the National Task Force's helicopter had happened to crash-land right where the tunnel came out.

However, a municipal official had given a statement saying that there seemed to have been people living in the condemned building. What did Mr Qvist have to say about that?

Holger Two looked alarmed, because he decidedly was. Holger & Holger AB had had a single employee; that was, of course, Celestine here, and she took care of the warehouse, administration and other things, while Holger himself was in charge of the distribution in his free time. The rest of the time, as Mr Officer perhaps already knew, he worked at Helicopter Taxi Inc. in Bromma, although he would no longer be working there due to an unfortunate incident. Holger couldn't imagine that anyone had lived in that dilapidated shack.

336

At this point, in accordance with their plan, the angry young woman started to cry.

"Dear Celestine," said Holger. "Do you have something to say?"

Through her sniffles she managed to say that she'd had a fight with her mum and dad (which was, of course, true) so she had stayed in one of the awful apartments for a while without asking Holger for permission (also true, after a fashion).

"And now I'm going to jail." She sniffled.

Holger Two comforted the girl and said that she had done a stupid thing, and now Holger had been sitting there lying to the officer without knowing any better, but that it probably wouldn't come to prison — just steep fines. Or what did Mr Officer think?

The officer cleared his throat and said that temporarily living in an industrial area was certainly not allowed, but that it had very little — though not nothing — to do with the ongoing terrorist investigation. In short, Miss Celestine could stop crying; no one need be any the wiser about this. Here was a tissue for the young lady should she want one.

The angry young woman blew her nose, thinking that on top of everything the cop in front of her was corrupt — crimes ought to be prosecuted no matter what they were, right? But she didn't say this.

Holger Two added that the pillow company was now out of business for good, so there would be no question of any more unofficial tenants. Perhaps that brought this investigation to an end?

Yes. The police officer had no further questions. He thanked Mr Qvist and young Miss Celestine for taking the trouble to come in.

Holger thanked him back, and Celestine grmpfed once more.

◆ ◆ ◆

After murdering a newly deceased man, escaping from the police, preventing an atomic bomb from burning, and Holger One's being assaulted on Sergels Torg then jumping without a parachute from two thousand feet, the new guests at Sjölida were in need of peace and quiet. Meanwhile, Agent B, at his end, was striving for the opposite.

Several days earlier, he had allowed Nombeko and her crew to roll off with the bomb, down Fredsgatan in Gnesta. Not because he wanted to, but because he had no choice. An Israeli intelligence agent fighting over an atomic bomb on a public street in Sweden with fifty police officers as witnesses — no, that was not the best way to serve one's nation.

But that didn't mean his situation was hopeless. B now knew that the bomb and Nombeko Mayeki were still together. In Sweden. It was as clear as it was inconceivable. What had she been doing for the last seven years? Where was she now? And why?

B had checked into a hotel in Stockholm under Michael Ballack's name to analyse the situation.

On the previous Thursday, he had received an encrypted message from his colleague Agent A. It said that one Holger Qvist (as seen on TV) had been located and was about to take him to Nombeko Mayeki, the blasted cleaning woman who had fooled them not once but twice.

He had not heard from A since. And now A wasn't responding to B's messages. He had no choice but to assume A was dead. Before his death, however, A had left an impressive number of trails for B to follow. Such as the geographical coordinates of the place where the cleaning woman and the bomb supposedly were. And the address of Holger Qvist's presumed apartment in something called Blackeberg. And his workplace in Bromma. Nothing seemed to be a secret in the Swedish system, and this was a dream for any secret agent.

B had started by looking up Fredsgatan 5, which no longer existed. It had burned to the ground the night before.

Apparently someone had rescued the bomb from the flames just in time, because it was sitting on a trailer just beyond the barricades, its crate scorched. It was a surreal sight. It became even more surreal when the cleaning woman slid up beside the agent, greeted him cheerfully, took the bomb and left.

Agent B soon did the same. He bought and stumbled his way through several Swedish newspapers. A person who knows German and English can understand a word of Swedish here and there, and guess at the occasional situation. In addition, there were a number of articles available in English at the Royal Library.

Apparently the fire had broken out during a terrorist incident. But the chief terrorist, Nombeko, had just stood there calmly outside the barricades. Why didn't they arrest her? Surely the Swedish police couldn't be so incompetent as to pull a 1700-pound crate out of the flames and then forget to see what was in it before they let people roll it away. Right?

And his colleague A? Left behind in the flames at Fredsgatan 5, of course. There was no other explanation. If he wasn't in Tallinn. What would he be doing there, anyway? And what did the cleaning woman know about it? The man next to her had introduced himself as Holger. That is, the man whom A had had under control just the day before. Had Holger managed to overpower B's colleague? Had he sent him to Tallinn?

No, A was dead; he must be. The cleaning woman had fooled them three times now. It was too bad that she could die only once in return.

Agent B had a lot to go on. Some were the clues that A had given him, and some were his own, like the licence plate number of the trailer the bomb had rolled away on. It belonged to a Harry Blomgren, not far from Gnesta. The agent decided to pay a visit.

Harry and Margareta Blomgren were very bad at English and hardly better at German. But as far as the agent could understand, they were trying to get him to compensate them for a fence someone had driven through, plus a stolen car and trailer. They thought he represented the cleaning woman somehow.

In the end, the agent had been forced to take out his pistol to get control of the interrogation.

Apparently the cleaning woman and her crew had driven right through the fence and forced the Blomgrens to provide overnight lodging. The agent couldn't work out what had happened after that. The couple's linguistic proficiency was so poor that it sounded like someone had tried to bite them in the throat.

Anyway, there was nothing to suggest that the Blomgrens were guilty of anything except getting in the way of the cleaning woman. The main reason for shooting them both in the forehead anyway was that he didn't like them. But B had never taken joy in killing on such flimsy grounds. So instead he shot Mrs Blomgren's two porcelain pigs on the hearth and explained to the couple that the same thing would happen to them if they didn't immediately forget that he had ever been there. The pigs had cost forty kronor apiece; it was painful for the couple to see them go to pieces. But the thought of dying and therefore being permanently separated from the nearly three million kronor they had managed to save up over the years was even worse. So they nodded and made an honest promise never, ever to speak of this experience.

The agent kept working. Holger Qvist turned out to be the sole proprietor of a Holger & Holger Inc., which was listed at Fredsgatan 5. A company that had burned to the ground. Terrorists? Nah. It was clearly that blasted cleaning woman, who had hoodwinked not only the Mossad but also the National Task Force. An exceedingly irritating woman. And a worthy opponent.

Furthermore, Qvist was listed as living at an address in Blackeberg. The agent settled down to observe the apartment for three whole days. No lights were turned on or off. Through the letterbox he could see an undisturbed pile of advertising flyers. Qvist wasn't there; he hadn't been there since the day something had happened.

Despite the risk that he might kick up some dust, B made his way to Helicopter Taxi Inc., introduced himself as Michael Ballack, a journalist from the German magazine *Stern*, and asked if Mr Holger Qvist was available for an interview.

No, Qvist had quit as a result of having been rather badly assaulted a few days earlier. Surely Mr Ballack had heard of the incident?

Where was he now? Well, it was impossible to say. Perhaps he was in the Gnesta area — he did own a pillow-import company; he wasn't in active employ-ment there, but as far as the owner of Helicopter Taxi Inc. knew he still went down there regularly on business. And incidentally, didn't his girlfriend still live there, too?

"Girlfriend? Do you know what her name is, Mr Manager?"

No, the manager couldn't say. Celestine, maybe? It was something unusual, anyway.

There turned out to be twenty-four Celestines registered in Sweden. But only one, Celestine Hedlund, had been listed at Fredsgatan 5 in Gnesta until a few days earlier.

I wonder if you were recently out driving a red Toyota Corolla with a trailer, Celestine, the agent said to himself. With Nombeko Mayeki and Holger Qvist in the back seat. And a man I don't know by your side.

The Celestine trail soon split in four directions. She was now listed at a PO box in Stockholm. Before that, on Fredsgatan. Before that, at the home of a Gertrud Virtanen outside Norrtälje. Before that, at what was presumably her parents' home in Gnesta. It was reasonable to assume that she would end up at one of these four addresses sooner or later.

The least interesting from a surveillance perspective was, of course, the one that had been turned into a pile of ashes. The most interesting was the PO box. And then, in descending order: her parents' home and Gertrud Virtanen.

◆ ◆ ◆

On questioning Celestine, Nombeko had learned that the girl had been listed as living at Sjölida for a short time. This was distressing. On the other hand, it was unlikely that the agent chasing them knew of her existence.

The South African unofficial refugee had thus far not been excessively lucky in life, from the day she was run over by a drunken engineer in Johannesburg and on.

And she would never know about the lucky hand she was about to be dealt.

Because what happened was that Agent B started by watching the PO box in Stockholm for a week, and then he staked out Celestine's parents' house for the same amount of time. Neither was of any use.

But just as he was about to take on the least likely place, the one outside Norrtälje, the agent's boss in Tel Aviv grew weary. His boss said it seemed to him that this had turned into a personal vendetta, and that the Mossad must have other, more intellectually motivated, criteria for their activities. Surely a professional atomic-bomb thief wouldn't sit around in a Swedish forest, lying low with the bomb and everything. The agent must come home. Now. No, not very soon. Now.

PART FIVE

If the person you are talking to doesn't appear to be listening, be patient. It may simply be that he has a small piece of fluff in his ear.

Winnie-the-Pooh

CHAPTER
SEVENTEEN

On the dangers of having an exact copy of oneself

It so happened that in South Africa a man who had been deemed a terrorist was set free after twenty-seven years, awarded the Nobel Peace Prize, and elected president of the country.

At around the same time, much less was going on at Sjölida.

Days became weeks, which became months. Summer became autumn, which became winter and spring.

No ill-tempered agents from intelligence agencies in foreign countries showed up (one was in the Baltic Sea, at a depth of 650 feet; the other was sitting all by himself behind a desk in Tel Aviv).

Nombeko and Holger Two let themselves forget the bomb and other miseries for a while. Walks in the forest, mushroom picking, fishing in Gertrud's rowing-boat in the bay — all of these had a restful effect.

Furthermore when warmth returned to the earth, they received permission from the old woman to revive the potato fields.

The tractor and the machinery were old-fashioned, but Nombeko had done some calculations and arrived at the conclusion that their efforts still ought to bring in a profit of 225,623 kronor per year, while at the same time making sure that One and Celestine had something to do (other than acts of stupidity). A little bit of revenue to complement the quiet life in the countryside couldn't hurt, now that both the pillow operation and the 19.6 million had gone up in flames.

It wasn't until the first snowfall in November 1995 that Nombeko once again brought up the eternal issue of their future with her Two.

"We have it pretty good here, don't you think?" she said during their slow Sunday walk together.

"We do have it good here." Two nodded.

"It's just too bad we don't really exist," Nombeko continued.

"And that the bomb in the barn still does," said Two.

So they discussed the chances of permanently changing both of these situations for so long that their discussion ended up revolving instead around how many times they had discussed it before.

No matter how they looked at it, they came to the same conclusion time after time: they really couldn't hand the bomb over to just any old Norrtälje municipal commissioner. They *had* to make direct contact at the top level of government.

"Should I call the prime minister again?" said Holger Two.

"What would be the point?" said Nombeko.

348

They had, after all, already tried three times with two different assistants and twice with one and the same marshal of the court — and they had received the same answer each time. The prime minister and the king would receive neither man nor beast. Although it was possible that the former would receive them, provided that their errand was first described in detail in a letter, something that Nombeko and Holger Two could not imagine doing.

Nombeko revived the old idea of Holger going to college in his brother's name in order subsequently to get a job close to the prime minister.

This time, their alternative was not to stay in a condemned building until it collapsed on its own because, of course, that building no longer existed. Instead they would have to farm potatoes at Sjölida. And no matter how pleasant that was, it didn't make a very good life goal.

"But you can't finish a degree just like that," said Holger. "At least I can't. Maybe you could. It will take a few years. Are you prepared to wait?"

No problem. Years had already gone by, and Nombeko was used to waiting. Even henceforth she could pass the time somehow. She was nowhere near finished reading the books in Norrtälje library, for example. And besides, keeping track of the scatterbrains and the old woman was a part-time job in itself. Plus, of course, there was the potato farm, which could be demanding.

"So economics or political science," said Holger Two.

"Or both," said Nombeko, "while you're at it. I'm happy to help. I'm pretty good with numbers."

♦ ♦ ♦

Two finally took his entrance exams the following spring. The combination of brains and enthusiasm brought him high marks, and by the next autumn he was enrolled in both the economic and political sciences programmes at Stockholm University. His lectures occasionally coincided with one another, but then Nombeko would sneak in and take Holger's economics spot in order to reproduce the day's lecture that evening, nearly verbatim, with a comment here and there about how Professor Bergman or Associate Professor Järegård had got the wrong end of the stick.

Holger One and Celestine helped with the potatoes and regularly went to Stockholm to attend meetings of the Stockholm Anarchists' Union. This was something Two and Nombeko had agreed to, as long as they promised not to take part in any public events. Moreover, the Anarchists' Union was anarchical enough not to have a list of members. One and Celestine could be just as anonymous as the situation warranted.

Both of them enjoyed socializing with like-minded people; the Stockholm anarchists disapproved of everything.

Capitalism must be crushed, along with most of the other -isms. Socialism. And Marxism, to the extent they could find it. Fascism and Darwinism, of course (they were considered to be the same thing). Cubism, on the other hand, could be allowed to remain, as long as it wasn't fenced in by any rules.

Furthermore, the king must also go. Some members of the group suggested that anyone who wanted to could be king, but this brought protest, not least from Holger. Wasn't one king bad enough?

And would you believe it? When Holger spoke, the group listened. Just as they did when Celestine told them that she had been faithful to the self-invented "Tear All This Shit Down" Party for her entire adult life.

Holger and Celestine had found their way home.

◆　◆　◆

Nombeko thought that as long as she was going to be a potato farmer, she might as well do it right. She and Gertrud got on well. Even though the old woman grumbled about the name of the business, she really had nothing against Nombeko's choice to register Countess Virtanen Inc. in her name.

Together they set about buying up the land surrounding their potato fields to increase their planting. Gertrud knew exactly which former farmer was oldest and most worn-out. She biked over to see him with an apple cake and a Thermos of coffee, and the farmer's field changed hands even before their second cup. At this, Nombeko requested an assessment of the newly purchased land, and then she drew in an imaginary house and added two zeroes on the appraisal form.

Thus Countess Virtanen Inc. was able to borrow nearly 10 million kronor against a field valued at 130 thousand. Nombeko and Gertrud used the borrowed money to purchase more land with the help of more apple cakes and Thermoses of coffee. After two years, Gertrud was the biggest producer of potatoes in the area by acreage, but her debts exceeded current sales by at least five times.

They still had to get under way with the actual harvest. Thanks to Nombeko's loan design, the business had no monetary problems; there were problems, however, with the machinery, which was both small and outdated.

In order to deal with this, she put Gertrud behind the wheel for a trip to the city of Västerås and Pontus Widén Machinery Inc. She let the old woman do the talking with the seller.

"Hello there, I'm Gertrud Virtanen from Norrtälje, and I have a potato patch to potter around in. I pick and sell them as best I can."

"I see," said the salesman, wondering what he could possibly have to do with this old lady Virtanen's potato patch. None of his machines cost less than 800,000 kronor.

"It seems that you sell potato machinery of all sorts here. Is that right?" said Gertrud.

The salesman felt that this might turn into an unnecessarily long conversation; it was best to nip it in the bud as soon as possible.

"Yes, I have de-stoners; four-, six- and eight-row planters; four-row mounders; and one- and two-row harvesters. You would receive a special price if you were to purchase all of them for your potato patch, ma'am."

"A special price? How nice. How much would that be?"

"Four point nine million," the salesman said nastily.

Gertrud counted on her fingers as the salesman lost patience.

"Now listen here, Mrs Virtanen, I really don't have time to —"

"I'll take two of each," said Gertrud. "When can they be delivered?"

♦ ♦ ♦

Both a lot and not much at all happened during the following six years. Out in the world, Pakistan joined the exclusive club of nuclear nations, because it needed protection from neighbouring India, which had joined the club twenty-four years earlier as protection against Pakistan. The relationship between the two countries was just what one would expect.

Things were calmer in the nuclear nation of Sweden.

One and Celestine were satisfied with being dissatisfied. Every week they put in great effort for the proper cause. No demonstrations, but plenty of things in secret. They sprayed anarchist slogans on as many public-toilet doors as they could; they surreptitiously put up flyers at institutions and museums. Their main political message was that politics were shit, but Holger also made sure that the king got his share.

Along with their political anti-involvement, Holger and Celestine carried out their chores on the potato farm with a certain amount of competence. Thus they drew a limited income, and they did need money. Markers, spray bottles and flyers were not free.

Nombeko tried to keep an eye on the two loons, but she was careful not to worry Two. Even without her help, he was a clever, industrious and happy student. Seeing Holger so content made her feel the same way.

It was also interesting to watch Gertrud liven up after what one could say had essentially been a life lost. She had, after all, got pregnant at eighteen, thanks to her first and last encounter with a pig and his lukewarm spiked Loranga. A single mother, even more solitary after her own mother died of cancer and after her father, Tapio, got his fingers caught in Norrtälje's first cashpoint one winter night in 1971 and wasn't found until the next day, long after he had frozen to death.

Potato farmer, mother and grandmother. She had seen absolutely nothing of the world. But she had allowed herself to dream of how things might have been, if only her own grandmother, the noble Anastasia Arapova, hadn't been so unchristian as to send Tapio to Helsinki so that she could devote her life to God.

But that was all gone. Nombeko understood why Gertrud was careful not to look too closely into her father's history. The risk was, of course, that there would be nothing left. Except for the potato farm.

354

In any case, the return of her grandchild and the presence of Nombeko had awakened something in the old woman. She was sometimes radiant during their dinners together, which she made herself for the most part. She would cut a chicken's head off and make herself a casserole. Or she would set out nets to make baked pike with horseradish. Once she even shot a pheasant in the garden with her father Tapio's moose-hunting rifle, and was surprised when the rifle worked. And that she hit the target. It worked so well, in fact, that all that was left of the pheasant was a few stray feathers.

The world went on revolving around its sun at the constant speed and with the inconstant temper it always had. Nombeko read about big things and small, small things and big. And she felt a certain amount of intellectual stimulation as she delivered the news every evening at dinner. Among the events that occurred over the years was that Boris Yeltsin announced his retirement. In Sweden, the Russian president had become most famous for the state visit on which he was so blotto that he demanded that the country, which had no coal power plants, must close all its coal power plants.

An exciting follow-up to this event was the many ups and downs when the most developed country in the world made such a mess of its own presidential election that it took several weeks for the Supreme Court to decide 5–4 that the candidate with the most votes had lost. With this, George W. Bush became the president of the United States, while Al Gore was reduced to an environmental agitator to whom not even the anarchists in Stockholm paid much attention. Incidentally, Bush later invaded Iraq in order to eliminate all the weapons Saddam Hussein didn't have.

Among the more marginal news items was the one about how a former bodybuilder from Austria became the governor of California. Nombeko felt a twinge in her heart when she saw a picture of him in the paper, standing there with his wife and four children, smiling into the camera with white teeth. She thought that it must be an unjust world when certain people received an excess of certain things, while others got nothing. And she didn't even know, then, that the governor in question had managed to procure a fifth child in collaboration with his own housekeeper.

All in all, it was still a hopeful and relatively happy time at Sjölida, while the rest of the world behaved as it always had.

And while the bomb sat where it was.

♦ ♦ ♦

In the spring of 2004, life looked brighter than it had at perhaps any time before. Holger had almost attained his goal in political science, while at the same time he was about to complete a doctorate in economics. What had soon turned into an entire dissertation had started out as self-therapy in Two's head. It was hard to bear the thought that, with the bomb, every single day he risked being partly responsible for the destruction of half a region and an entire nation. To deal with this, he had started to look at another side of the issue, and had realized that, from a strictly economic perspective, Sweden and the world would rise from the ashes. Thus the dissertation *The Atom Bomb as Growth Factor: Dynamic Benefits of a Nuclear Catastrophe*.

The obvious disadvantages had kept Holger Two awake at night; they, too, had been researched to death several times over. Even a nuclear squabble limited to India and Pakistan would, according to the experts, kill twenty million people, before the total number of kilotons even surpassed what Two and Nombeko happened to have on hand. Computer models showed that, within a few weeks, so much smoke would have risen into the stratosphere that it would take ten years before the sun managed to penetrate it fully again. Not only above the two squabbling countries, but all over the world.

But this — according to Holger Two — was where market forces would triumph. Thanks to the 200,000 per cent increase in the incidence of thyroid cancer, unemployment would go down. Massive population shifts from sunny vacation paradises (which of course would no longer have any sun to offer) to large cities around the world would create increased wealth distribution. A large number of mature markets would become immature in a single blow, which would make markets dynamic. It was clear, for example, that the de facto Chinese monopoly on solar cells would become irrelevant.

Furthermore, by mutual effort, India and Pakistan could eliminate the entire runaway greenhouse effect. Deforestation and the use of fossil fuels could continue, with the benefit of neutralizing the two- or three-degree decrease in the Earth's temperature that the nuclear war between the countries would otherwise have caused.

These thoughts kept Holger's head above water. At the same time, Nombeko and Gertrud had made good headway on the potato business. They'd had good luck along the way — indeed — because the Russian crops had failed for several years in a row. And because one of Sweden's most discussed (and, for that matter, most meaningless) celebrities had a new, slim figure thanks to the OP diet (Only Potatoes).

The response was immediate. The Swedes were eating potatoes like never before.

Countess Virtanen Inc., previously swimming in debt, was now nearly debt-free. Meanwhile, Holger Two was just a few weeks from a double degree and, thanks to his excellent achievements as a student, was ready to start his journey towards a private meeting with the Swedish prime minister. Incidentally, there was a new one since last time. His name was Göran Persson now. He was just as unwilling as the others to answer the telephone.

In short: the eight-year plan was nearing completion. So far, everything had gone as it should. All signs indicated that it would continue to do so. The feeling that nothing could go wrong was very similar to what

Ingmar Qvist had felt in his day, just before he went to Nice.

Only to be assaulted by Gustaf V.

♦ ♦ ♦

On Thursday, 6 May 2004, the latest batch of five hundred flyers was ready to be picked up at the printer's in Solna. Holger and Celestine thought they'd really done something special this time. The flyers had a picture of the king, and next to him was a picture of a wolf. The text underneath drew parallels between the Swedish wolf population and the various royal families of Europe. The inbreeding problems were said to be the same.

The solution in the first case might be to introduce Russian wolves. In the second case, thinning the herd was considered one alternative. Or across-the-board deportation to Russia. The authors went so far as to suggest an exchange: one Russian wolf per deported royal.

Celestine wanted to take One and fetch the flyers as soon as they received word from the printer in Solna, so that they could paper as many institutions as possible that very day. Holger One didn't want to wait, either, but he said that Two had booked the car for this Thursday. This was an objection that Celestine waved away.

"He doesn't own the car any more than we do, does he? Come on, my love. We have a world to change."

★ ★ ★

It so happened that Thursday, 6 May 2004, was also supposed to be the biggest day in Two's life so far. His dissertation defence was scheduled for eleven o'clock.

When Holger, in suit and tie, went to get into the Blomgrens' old Toyota just after nine in the morning — it was gone.

Two realized that his disaster of a brother had been up to mischief, surely under the guidance of Celestine. Since there was no mobile-phone coverage at Sjölida, he couldn't immediately call them and order them to come back. Nor could he call a taxi, for that matter. It was at least a third of a mile to the country road where there was intermittent mobile-phone coverage, depending on its mood. There was no question of running there; he couldn't arrive at his defence sweating through his suit. So he took the tractor.

At 9.25 he finally got hold of them. It was Celestine who answered.

"Yes, hello?"

"Did you take the car?"

"Why? Is this Holger?"

"Answer the damn question! I need it now! I have an important meeting in town at eleven."

"Oh, I see. So your meetings are more important than ours?"

"That's not what I said. But I had booked the car. Turn round right now, damn it. I'm in a hurry."

"God. Stop swearing so much."

Two gathered his thoughts and tried a new tactic.

360

"Dear, sweet Celestine. When we get a chance, let's sit down and discuss the car issue. And who had booked it for today. But I beg you, turn round right now and pick me up. My meeting is truly impo —"

At that point Celestine hung up. And turned off the phone.

"What did he say?" wondered Holger One, who was behind the wheel.

"He said, 'Dear, sweet Celestine, let's sit down and discuss the car issue.' In short."

One didn't think that sounded so bad. He had been worried about how his brother would react.

Desperate, Holger Two stood on the country road in his suit for more than ten minutes, hoping to hitch a ride with a passerby. But in order for that to happen, there would have to be passing cars in the first place, which there weren't. By the time Two realized that he ought to have called a taxi a long time ago, it dawned on him that his coat and wallet were still hanging on a hook in the hall. With 120 kronor in his breast pocket, he made the decision to drive the tractor to Norrtälje and take the bus from there. It would probably have been faster to turn round, get his wallet, go back again, and then call a taxi. Or even better: call the taxi first, and while it was on its way, make the trip to the house and back on the tractor.

But Two, as gifted as he was, had a stress-tolerance level that wasn't much better than the potter's, may God bless him. He was about to miss his own dissertation defence. After years of preparation. It was awful.

And yet it was only the beginning.

The first and last tiny piece of luck Holger Two had that day involved the transfer from tractor to bus in Norrtälje. At the next-to-last possible second, he managed to block the bus's way so he could catch it. The driver stepped down to give the tractor driver in question a mouthful, but he stopped short when the yokel farmer he had expected was a well-groomed man in a suit, tie and patent leather shoes.

Once on board, Holger got hold of the dean of the university, Professor Berner, and he apologized and said that some extraordinarily unfortunate circumstances would cause him to be half an hour late.

The professor replied acidly that delays of dissertation defences were not in line with university traditions, but by all means. He promised to try to hold the opponents and the audience.

◆ ◆ ◆

Holger One and Celestine had arrived in Stockholm and had already signed for their flyers. Celestine, who was the better strategist of the two, decided that their first target should be the Museum of Natural History. It had a whole section on Charles Darwin and his theory of evolution. Darwin had stolen the concept of "survival of the fittest" from a colleague, and he used it to claim that the way of nature was such that the strong survived while the weak did not. Thus Darwin was a Fascist and now he would be punished for it, 120 years after his death. Celestine and Holger did not reflect upon the fact that there were some considerably Fascistic elements to their flyers as well. Time to put up posters on the sly. All over the museum. In the holy name of anarchy.

This is indeed what happened, and it went off without a hitch. Holger One and Celestine were able to work undisturbed. Swedish museums are far from crowded.

Their next stop was Stockholm University, a stone's throw away. Celestine tackled the Ladies and left the Gents to Holger. It happened as One stepped through the first door and met a certain someone.

"Oh, are you here already after all?" said Professor Berner.

Then he dragged the surprised Holger One down the hall and into Room 4 while Celestine was still busy doing her thing in the Ladies.

Without understanding what was going on, One found himself standing at a lectern in front of an audience of at least fifty people.

Professor Berner made some preliminary remarks in English, and he made use of words both plentiful and complicated; Holger had a hard time following. Apparently he was expected to say something about the benefits of detonating a nuclear weapon. Why? one might wonder.

But he was happy to do it, even if his English wasn't so great. And anyway, wasn't the most important thing not what one *said*, but what one *meant*?

He had had quite a bit of time to daydream as he picked potatoes, and he had come to the conclusion that the best thing to do would be to transport the Swedish royal family to the wilderness of Lapland and set the bomb off there, if they wouldn't all abdicate voluntarily. Hardly any innocent people would bite the dust in such a manoeuvre, and in general the damage would be minimal. Furthermore, any increase in temperature that might result from the detonation would be beneficial, since it was terribly cold up there in the north.

It was perhaps bad enough to have these sorts of thoughts in the first place. But now Holger One was expressing them from his lectern.

His first opponent was a Professor Lindkvist from Linnaeus University in Växjö. He began paging through his notes in time with Holger's speech. Lindkvist, too, chose to speak in English and he began by asking if what he had just heard was some sort of introduction to what would come next.

An introduction? Yes, one might call it that. A republic would be born and grow out of the demise of the royal family. Was that what the gentleman meant?

What Professor Lindkvist meant was that he didn't understand what was going on, but what he said was that it struck him as immoral to take the lives of an entire royal family. Not to mention the method Mr Qvist had just described.

But now Holger felt insulted. Why, he was no murderer! His basic argument was that the king and his lot should resign. Nuclear-weapons-related consequences ought to come into play only if they refused, and in that case as a direct result of the royal family's own choice, and no one else's.

When One was subsequently met by silence from Professor Lindkvist (the cause being tongue-tiedness), he decided to add another dimension to his argument: an alternative to no king at all might be that anyone who wanted to be king could do so.

"This isn't something I would argue for personally, but it's an interesting thought nonetheless," said Holger One.

It was possible that Professor Lindkvist didn't agree, because he shot a beseeching look at his colleague Berner, who in turn tried to remember if he had ever felt as unhappy as at this moment. This defence was meant to be a showpiece for the benefit of the audience's two guests of honour, namely the Swedish minister for higher education and research, Lars Leijonborg, and his newly appointed French counterpart Valérie Pécresse. The two of them had long been working to establish a joint educational programme, with the possibility in the future of bi-national diplomas. Leijonborg had personally contacted Professor Berner to ask for suggestions for a good defence that he and his minister colleague might attend. The professor had immediately thought of model student Holger Qvist.

And now this.

Berner decided to interrupt the spectacle. It was clear that he had misjudged the candidate, and it was best that said candidate leave the podium now. And after that, the room. And the university, as such. Preferably also the country.

But because he said what he did in English, One didn't quite catch it.

"Shall I start my argument again from the beginning?"

"No, you shall not," said Professor Berner. "I have aged ten years in the past twenty minutes, and I was quite old to begin with, so that will do. Please just leave."

And One did. On the way out, it occurred to him that he had just spoken in public, and that was something he'd promised his brother he wouldn't do. Would Two be angry with him now? Maybe he didn't need to know.

One caught sight of Celestine in the hall. He put his arm around her and said it was best that they work somewhere else. He promised to try to explain on the way.

Five minutes later, Holger Two came running through the doors of the same university. Professor Berner had just had to apologize to the Swedish minister for higher education, who in turn did the same before his French counterpart, who replied that, based upon what she'd just seen, she thought it would be better for Sweden to turn to Burkina Faso in its search for a partner of equal standing in educational matters.

And then the professor caught sight of that bastard Holger Qvist in the hall. Did Qvist think all he had to do was change from jeans to a suit and everything would be forgotten?

"I truly must apologize —" began the well-dressed and out-of-breath Holger Two.

Professor Berner interrupted him and said that it wasn't a matter of apologizing but of going away. As permanently as possible.

"The defence is over, Qvist. Go home. And sit down and think about the economic risks of your own existence."

♦ ♦ ♦

Holger Two did not pass the defence. But it took him an entire day to work out what had happened, and another day to understand the extent of his misfortune. He couldn't call the professor to tell him the truth: that for all these years he had been studying in someone else's name and that this other person had happened to take over on the very day of his defence. This would lead to nothing but even greater misery.

What Two wanted most of all was to strangle his brother. But this didn't come to pass, because One was at the Anarchists' Union's Saturday meeting when Two had his lightbulb moment. And by the time One and Celestine were back that afternoon, Two's condition had already turned into depression.

CHAPTER
EIGHTEEN

On a temporarily successful newspaper and a prime minister who suddenly wanted a meeting

No matter how wretched everything was, Holger Two realized after a week that he couldn't just keep lying there in bed. Nombeko and Gertrud needed help with the harvest. One and Celestine also helped with that to a certain extent, so from a purely economic perspective there was no reason to strangle both of them.

Life at Sjölida went back to normal, including the dinners together several nights a week. But the atmosphere around the table was tense, even if Nombeko did her best to create distractions. She continued her reports on what had happened and was still happening in the world. Among other things, she informed them one evening that Prince Harry of Great Britain had gone to a party dressed in a Nazi uniform (which was nearly as big a scandal as the one that would happen a few years later when he partied wearing nothing at all).

"But can't you all see how embarrassing the monarchy is?" Holger One said, apropos the uniform.

"Well, yes," said Nombeko. "At least the democratically elected Nazis in South Africa left their uniforms at home."

Holger Two didn't say anything. He didn't even tell his brother to go to Hell.

Nombeko realized that something had to change. What they needed more than anything was a new idea. What they got, for starters, was a potential buyer for the potato business.

The fact was, Countess Virtanen Inc. now consisted of two hundred hectares of potato fields; it had modern machinery, good sales, nice profits and almost no debt. This had all come to the attention of the biggest producer in central Sweden, who added it all up and put in an offer of sixty million kronor for the whole lot.

Nombeko suspected that the Swedish potato boom was nearing its end. The celebrity who had gone on the potato diet had got fat again, and according to the news bureau ITARTASS, the Russian potato harvests were about to go right instead of wrong for once.

So, even aside from the fact that Gertrud's potato farm was probably not the meaning of life, it might be time to make a deal.

Nombeko brought up the matter with Countess Virtanen Inc.'s formal owner, who said that she would be happy to change profession. She was starting to get fed up with potatoes.

"Isn't there something called 'spaghetti' nowadays?" she mused.

Nombeko nodded: yes. Spaghetti had been around for a while. Since about the twelfth century. But it wasn't so easy to grow. Nombeko thought they should do something else with their money.

And she suddenly realized what.

"What would you say if we started a magazine, Gertrud?"

"A magazine? Super! What things will it say?"

♦ ♦ ♦

Holger Qvist's reputation was ruined: he had been more or less kicked out of Stockholm University. But he did possess extensive knowledge of both economics and political science. And Nombeko wasn't exactly a dimwit herself. So the two of them could work behind the scenes.

Nombeko explained her reasoning to Two, and so far he was with her. But what scenes was Nombeko thinking they would be behind? And what would be the point of all of this?

"The point, my dear Holger, is that we are going to get rid of the bomb."

The journal *Swedish Politics* put out its first issue in April 2007. The lavish monthly magazine was distributed free to fifteen thousand of the country's most powerful people. It had sixty-four crammed pages and not a single advertisement. It would be difficult to get a return on this investment, but then again, that wasn't the point.

The venture received attention in both *Svenska Dagbladet* and *Dagens Nyheter*. Apparently the person behind the magazine was an eccentric former potato farmer, the eighty-year-old Gertrud Virtanen. Virtanen refused to grant interviews, but she had her own column on page two, where she explained the merits of the fact that, on principle, all articles and analyses in the magazine were unsigned. Each text should be judged on its content and nothing else.

Besides the part about Mrs Virtanen, the most interesting thing about the magazine was that it was so . . . interesting. The first issue received praise in the editorials of a number of Swedish newspapers. Among the lead articles was an in-depth analysis of the Sweden Democrats, who in the 2006 election had gone from 1.5 per cent of the votes to double that. The analysis was written from an international perspective and it was very well informed, making connections as far as to historical currents of Nazism in Africa. Perhaps the conclusion was a bit dramatic: it was hard to believe that a party whose supporters performed Hitler salutes at their party leader could make it all the way to Parliament, but still.

Another article described the human, political and financial consequences of a Swedish nuclear accident in great detail. At the very least, the calculations in the article would give any reader the chills. Thirty-two thousand job opportunities would be created in a period of twenty-five years, should the reactor in Oskarshamn need to be rebuilt thirty-eight miles north of where it had once been.

In addition to the articles, which practically wrote themselves, Nombeko and Two included a few items that were intended to put the new conservative prime minister in a good mood. One example was a historical retrospective of the European Union on the occasion of the fiftieth anniversary of the signing of the Treaty of Rome, which the prime minister in question happened to attend. And there was an in-depth analysis of social democracy in crisis. The party had just had its worst election results since 1914, and now it had a new party leader in Mona Sahlin. The conclusion of the article was that Sahlin could either stand alone, along with the Environmental Party, distancing herself from the Left . . . and lose the next election. Or she could include the Left — the former Communists — and build a three-party alliance . . . and lose it anyway (in fact, she tried both things — whereupon she lost her job to boot).

The magazine's headquarters were in a building in Kista outside Stockholm. At Two's request, Holger One and Celestine were forbidden to have any editorial involvement whatsoever. In addition, Two had drawn a chalk circle with a six-foot radius on the floor around his desk and ordered One never to step inside it, the only exception being when it was time to empty the waste-paper basket.

He really would have preferred not to have his brother in the building at all, but for one thing Gertrud refused to be involved with the project if her beloved Celestine wasn't allowed to help, and for another, the

372

two walking disasters needed new distractions now that there weren't any potatoes to pick.

Incidentally, Gertrud, who was the formal financier behind all of this, had her own editorial office where she sat and enjoyed the sign on the door that said PUBLISHER. That was pretty much all she did.

After the first issue, Nombeko and Two had planned another for May 2007 and a third for right after the summer holiday months. After that — they thought — the prime minister would be receptive. *Swedish Politics* would ask for an interview. And he would say yes. If not sooner, then later, if only they kept taking the correct steps.

But for once, things went better, instead of worse, than Holger and Nombeko expected. Because the prime minister was asked a question about the new magazine *Swedish Politics* during a press conference that was actually about his upcoming visit to Washington and the White House. And he replied that he had read the paper with interest, that he essentially agreed with its analysis of Europe, and that he was looking forward to the next issue.

This was the best they could have hoped for. Nombeko suggested that Holger Two contact the government offices right away. Why wait? What did they have to lose?

Two said that his brother and his girlfriend seemed to have an otherworldly ability to ruin everything and that he refused to have too much hope as long as the two of them weren't locked up somewhere. But by all means. What did they have to lose?

Thus Holger Two called, for the umpteenth time, the current prime minister's assistant, but on a different matter this time, and — Christ on a bike! — the assistant replied that she would check with the press secretary. Who called back the next day to say that the prime minister would see them at ten o'clock on 28 May for a forty-five-minute interview.

This meant that the interview would take place five days after the second issue of the magazine had come out. They wouldn't need any more issues after that.

"Or maybe you'll keep on with it?" said Nombeko. "I've never seen you so happy."

No, the first issue had cost four million kronor and the others weren't looking like they'd be any cheaper. They needed the potato money for the life they were, with any luck, on their way to making for themselves. A life where both of them existed, with residence permits and everything.

Holger and Nombeko realized that there was still a lot to do, even after they had managed to bring the atomic bomb to the attention of the man who was in charge of the country they found themselves in. It was not, for example, likely that the prime minister would be happy. And it wasn't a given that he would be sympathetic towards the situation that had arisen. Or even that he would appreciate Holger's and Nombeko's efforts to maintain twenty years of discretion.

But there was a chance. Which there wouldn't be, if they did nothing.

The second issue was a survey of international matters. Among other things, there was an analysis of the current political situation in the United States, apropos of the prime minister's meeting with George W. Bush in the White House. And there was a historical retrospective on the genocide in Rwanda, where a million Tutsis were slaughtered because they happened not to be Hutus. The difference between the two groups was said to be that, in general, the Tutsis might have been a bit taller than the Hutus.

Beyond that, there was a flirtation with the prime minister with regard to the impending repeal of the Swedish pharmacy monopoly.

Holger Two and Nombeko went through each and every letter. They couldn't afford any mistakes. The magazine must still have substance, must still be interesting — but without stepping on the prime minister's toes.

They couldn't afford any mistakes. So how could Two have suggested to his dear Nombeko that they should celebrate the completion and distribution of the second issue by going out to a restaurant? Afterwards, he cursed himself to such an extent that he forgot to kill his brother.

For left behind at the editorial offices was Gertrud, who was sleeping in her director's chair, and Holger and Celestine, who had been assigned the task of taking inventory of the stock of tape, pens and other things. Meanwhile, the finished magazine glowed at them from Two's computer.

"They're out having a good time at a fancy restaurant while we're sitting here counting paperclips," said Celestine.

"And there's not a single fucking word about the damn monarchy in this issue, either," said Holger One.

"Or anarchy, for that matter," said Celestine.

Apparently Nombeko was of the opinion that she was the sole owner of the money from Gertrud's potato farm. Who did she think she was? And now she and Two were spending all those millions on kissing the conservative, king-loving prime minister's arse.

"Come on, my dear," said Holger One, stepping into the forbidden zone around Two's desk.

He sat down in his brother's chair and clicked his way to Gertrud's column on page two. It was some rubbish about the incompetence of the opposition. Written by Two, of course. Holger One couldn't even stand to read that shit before he deleted it.

As he wrote down what was in his heart at that moment instead, he muttered that, for now, Two could be in charge of sixty-three of the sixty-four pages. But the sixty-fourth page had been coopted.

When he was done, he sent the new version to the printer with a comment to the lead typesetter that an important error in the proof had been corrected.

◆ ◆ ◆

On the following Monday, the second issue of *Swedish Politics* was printed and distributed to the same fifteen

376

thousand powerful people as the first issue. The publisher declared, on page two:

It is time for the king — that pig — to abdicate. He must also take with him the queen — that pig. And the crown princess — that pig. As well as the prince and princess — those pigs. And that old hag Lilian.

Monarchy is a form of government only fitting for pigs (and the occasional hag). Sweden must become a republic NOW.

That was all Holger One could think of to write, but since there were still six inches of the two-column space left, he used some software he hadn't quite mastered to draw a man hanging from a gallows with the word *king* on his chest. He added a speech bubble that came from the man's mouth. The hanged man didn't seem to be so hanged that he couldn't speak. And what he was saying, according to the speech bubble, was . . .

"Oink."

As if this weren't enough and then some, Celestine got in a line at the very bottom:

For more information: contact the Stockholm Anarchists' Union.

Fifteen minutes after the second issue of *Swedish Politics* was delivered to the government offices, the prime minister's assistant called with the message that the scheduled interview had been cancelled.

"Why?" said Holger Two, who hadn't yet got his hands on the newly printed magazine.

"Well, why the hell do you think?" said the assistant.

♦ ♦ ♦

Prime Minister Fredrik Reinfeldt refused to meet the representative of the magazine *Swedish Politics*. And yet he would soon do just that. Plus be saddled with an atomic bomb.

The boy who would eventually become prime minister was the oldest son of three in a family characterized by love, rules and order. Everything in its place; everyone picked up after himself.

This had such an effect on young Fredrik that, as an adult, he had to admit that the most entertaining thing he knew was not politics, but vacuuming. And yet he became a prime minister, not a cleaner. In any case, he had talent for both things. And more.

Among other things, he was elected to chairman of the student council at the young age of eleven. A few years later, he graduated first in his class when he did his military service as a ranger in the Lapland regiment. If the Russians came, they would encounter someone who also knew how to do battle at fifty-four below zero.

But the Russians didn't come. However, Fredrik came to Stockholm University, where he devoted himself to studying economics, student comedy and keeping his student apartment in military order. Soon he had a bachelor's degree in economics.

378

His interest in politics had begun in the home, too. His father was a municipal politician. Fredrik followed in his father's footsteps. He entered Parliament. He became the chairman of the Young Moderates.

His party was victorious in the 1991 parliamentary election. Young Fredrik wasn't yet playing a central role; even less so, since he had criticized party leader Bildt for being dictatorial. Bildt was humble enough to prove Reinfeldt right on that count by placing him in the party's cold-storage room, where he ended up sitting for nearly ten years while Bildt himself travelled to the former Yugoslavia to mediate peace. He thought it was more fun to save the whole world than to fail in saving Sweden.

His successor, Bo Lundgren, was nearly as good at counting as Nombeko was, but because the Swedish people didn't want to hear numbers alone but also the occasional hopeful word, things went just as badly for him.

With that, it was time for something new in the Moderate Coalition Party. The door to the cold-storage room where Fredrik Reinfeldt sat shivering was opened. He was thawed out and unanimously chosen as the party chairman on 25 October 2003. Less than three years later, he, his party and his non-socialist alliance mopped the floor with Social Democracy. Fredrik Reinfeldt was the prime minister, and he single-handedly cleaned up all the footprints his predecessor Persson had left in the government office. He mainly used green soap to do so, because it creates a dirt-repelling film on the treated surface. When he was done, he washed his hands and ushered in a new era of Swedish politics.

Reinfeldt was proud of what he had achieved. And he was content. For a little while longer.

◆ ◆ ◆

Nombeko, Celestine, One, Two and Gertrud were all back at Sjölida. If the atmosphere surrounding the group had been tense before their adventure with *Swedish Politics*, by now it was downright unhealthy. Holger Two refused to speak to his brother, or even to sit at the same table with him. For his part, One felt misunderstood and shoved aside. What's more, he and Celestine had had a falling-out with the anarchists after that reference to them in the magazine editorial. For most of the political reporters in the nation had obeyed the exhortation, streaming to the anarchists' headquarters to hear the reasoning behind comparing the royal family to a pigsty.

So now Holger One spent his days sitting in the hayloft, looking down at Gertrud's potato truck. It still contained a three-megaton atomic bomb. Which would convince the king, one way or another, to abdicate. And which Holger One had promised not to touch.

Just think — he had kept his promise all these years, and yet his brother was angry with him beyond reason. It felt so unfair.

Celestine, in turn, was angry with Two because he was angry with One. She said that Two's problem was that one couldn't study one's way to moral courage —

it was something one either had or hadn't. Two's brother had it!

Holger Two told Celestine to trip over something and injure herself as badly as possible. He himself was going for a walk.

He took the path down to the lake, sat on the bench on the dock and looked out at the water. He was filled with a feeling of . . . No, he wasn't filled with anything. He was completely empty.

He had Nombeko, and he was grateful for that. But otherwise: no children, no life, no future. Two thought that he would never, ever get to meet the prime minister: not this one, not the next one and not one of those who would follow. There were still 26,180 years left of the 26,200 it would take for the bomb to lose its efficacy. Plus or minus three months. Maybe it was just as well to stay on the bench on the dock, sitting the time away.

In short, everything was as abysmally terrible as it could be. Thirty minutes before it would get even worse.

CHAPTER
NINETEEN

On a gala banquet at the palace and contact with the other side

President Hu Jintao began his three-day state visit to Sweden by greeting the replica of the East Indiaman ship *Götheborg*, which had returned that very day to Gothenburg, the city it was named for, after a journey to China and back.

The original had made the same journey 250 years earlier. That time, its adventure had gone well despite storms, pirate waters, illness and starvation. But with half a mile left to go to the home harbour, the ship ran aground in absolutely beautiful weather and eventually sank.

Annoying, to say the least. But revenge was had on Saturday, 9 June 2007. The replica managed to do everything the original had, plus the last half mile. *Götheborg* was greeted by thousands of cheering onlookers, among them the president of China, who took the opportunity to visit the Volvo factory in Torslanda as he was in the area. He himself had insisted on this, and he had his rhymes and reasons.

The fact was, Volvo had been sulking about the Swedish government and its machinery for quite some time, since the state persisted in buying BMWs every time it needed an extra-secure vehicle. Volvo's upper management was nearly killing itself in exasperation that the Swedish royal family and ministers in the Swedish government would climb out of German cars at each official event. They had even built an armed model and demonstrated it for the security police, but it was no use. It was actually one of the engineers who had come up with the brilliant idea of offering the specially built, cream-coloured prototype of a brand-new Volvo S89 with four-wheel drive and a 315-horsepower, V8 engine to the president of the People's Republic of China. Worthy of a president any day.

Thought the engineer.

And the Volvo executives.

And — as it turned out — the president in question.

The matter was arranged ahead of time via discreet channels. The car was proudly presented to the president at the factory in Torslanda on Saturday morning, and it would be formally handed over at Arlanda Airport the next day, just prior to the president's journey home.

In the meantime, he was invited to a gala banquet at the royal palace.

◆ ◆ ◆

Nombeko had been sitting in the reading room at the Norrtälje library, going through newspaper after newspaper. She started with *Aftonbladet*, which devoted four pages to the conflict between . . . not Israel and Palestine, but a contestant in a singing contest on TV and a mean judge who had said that the artist in question couldn't sing.

"He can go fly a kite," retorted the artist, who for one thing really couldn't sing and for another didn't really know why kite flying was to be ridiculed.

Newspaper number two for Nombeko was *Dagens Nyheter*, which insisted on writing about important things and whose sales were therefore worse than ever. It was typical for *DN* to lead on its front page with a state visit instead of a fight in a TV studio.

Accordingly, the current issue had reports on President Hu Jintao, on *Götheborg*'s return to port — and on the fact that the president would be coming to Stockholm for a gala banquet with the king and the prime minister, among others, at the palace.

This information probably wouldn't have been worth much if it hadn't been for Nombeko's immediate reaction when she saw the picture of President Hu.

She looked at it and then looked at it once more. And then she said to herself, out loud, "Wow, Mr Chinese Official went and became the president!"

So both the Swedish prime minister and the president of China would be marching into the palace that evening. If Nombeko stood among all the curious onlookers and shouted at the prime minister as he passed, the best-case scenario was that she would be carried off, and the worst-case scenario was that she would be arrested and, by extension, deported.

However, if she were to shout at the president of China in Wu Chinese, the result would be different. If Hu Jintao's memory wasn't too short, he would recognize her. And if, in addition, he had even a modicum of curiosity, he would approach her to find out how on earth it happened that the South African interpreter from his past was standing here in the courtyard of the Swedish palace.

And with that, Nombeko and Holger Two had only one tiny person between themselves and the prime minister, or the king, for that matter. President Hu had all the necessary qualifications to act as a bridge between the involuntary owners of an atomic bomb on the one hand and the people they had been failing to get hold of for twenty years on the other.

Where all of this would lead them remained to be seen, but it was unlikely that the prime minister would just wave them away, bomb and all. Rather, he would probably summon the police and have them locked up. Or something in between; the only thing that was certain was that Nombeko and Holger Two had to give it a shot.

But there wasn't much time. It was already eleven in the morning. Nombeko had to bike back to Sjölida, involve Holger Two in the plan but, for God's sake, not the two crazies, or for that matter Gertrud, start the truck and make it all the way to the castle well before six, when the president would make his entrance.

◆ ◆ ◆

Things went wrong right away. Holger Two and Nombeko had sneaked into the barn and started to unscrew the far-too-authentic licence plates in order to replace them with the ones they had stolen many years ago. But, as he so often did, One was sitting in the hayloft above them, and the activity around the truck woke him from his mental slumber. His reaction was to jump silently through the trapdoor in the loft in order to get Celestine. Before Holger Two and Nombeko had finished with the licence plates, One and his girlfriend had forced their way into the barn and were sitting in the cab of the potato truck.

"Oh, so you were planning to sneak off without us, with the bomb and all," said Celestine.

"Oh, so you were planning that!" said Holger One.

But then his brother snapped.

"That is enough!" he roared. "Get out of that cab right now, you damned parasites! There is not a chance in the world that I am going to let you ruin this opportunity, too. Not a chance in the world!"

Whereupon Celestine pulled out a pair of handcuffs and shackled herself to the glove compartment. Once a demonstrator, always a demonstrator.

Holger One got to drive. Celestine sat beside him, in an unnatural position thanks to being handcuffed to the truck. Nombeko was next to her, and Two was farthest to the right, at an adequate distance from his brother.

As the potato truck rolled past the house, Gertrud came out onto the steps.

"Buy some food while you're out — we have nothing to eat!"

386

One and Celestine were informed by Nombeko that the point of this trip was to get rid of the bomb, since it so happened that circumstances were right to make direct contact with Prime Minister Reinfeldt.

Holger Two added that he would put both his brother and his horrid girlfriend through the eight-row potato-planter if they did anything besides sit where they now sat during the trip. Holding their tongues.

"We sold the eight-row planter," Holger One attempted.

"Then I will buy a new one," said his brother.

The gala banquet at the royal palace was to begin at 6p.m. The guests would be welcomed in the Inner Guards' Hall, after which the company would repair to the banquet itself in the White Sea Hall.

It wasn't easy for Nombeko to get into position in the inner courtyard, so that she would be sure to catch President Hu Jintao's attention. Curious onlookers among the general public were being gently pushed back along the sides of the courtyard, never less than fifty yards from where the guests would make their entrances. Would she even recognize him at that distance? He would surely recognize her, at least. How many black Africans spoke Wu Chinese?

As it turned out, recognition was no problem at any distance. There was an obvious hubbub among the security police as President Hu of the People's Republic of China and his wife, Liu Yongqing, arrived. Nombeko took a breath and shouted in the president's dialect:

"Hello there, Mr Chinese Official! It's been a long time since we were on safari in Africa together!"

Within four seconds, Nombeko was surrounded by two security police in civilian clothes. Within another four seconds, they had calmed down a bit, because the black woman didn't look like a threat: her hands were fully visible and she wasn't about to throw herself at the presidential couple. However, she would, of course, immediately be escorted from the area.

Except . . .

What was going on?

The president stopped short as he was entering the castle; he had left the red carpet and his wife behind him, and now he was on his way up to the black woman. And . . . and . . . *he was smiling at her!*

Some days were more difficult than others, when one belonged to the security police. Now the president was saying something to the demonstrator . . . she was a demonstrator, right? And the demonstrator answered.

Nombeko noticed the security officers' confusion. So she said in Swedish, "You gentlemen needn't look so frightened. The president and I are old friends and we're just going to exchange a few words."

Then she turned to President Hu again and said, "I think we'll have to save the reminiscing for some other time, Mr Chinese Official. Or Mr President, as it has so quickly and amusingly become."

"Yes, it has." Hu Jintao smiled. "And maybe not entirely without your assistance, Miss South Africa."

"You're far too kind, Mr President. But now the fact is — if I may get straight to the point — I'm sure you remember the crazy engineer from my old homeland, the one who invited you on safari and to dinner? Right. Things didn't go particularly well for him after that, and that's just as well, but he did succeed in scraping up a few atomic bombs, with the help of myself and others."

"Yes, right, six of them, if I remember correctly," said Hu Jintao.

"Seven," said Nombeko. "On top of everything else, he was bad at counting. He locked the seventh in a secret room, and then you could say it ended up lost. Or . . . actually, it was in my luggage . . . when I came to Sweden."

"Sweden has nuclear weapons?" Hu Jintao said in surprise.

"No, Sweden doesn't. But I do. And I'm *in* Sweden. So to speak."

Hu Jintao was silent for a second or two. Then he said, "Miss South Africa, what do you want me . . . what's your name, by the way?"

"Nombeko," said Nombeko.

"Miss Nombeko, what do you want me to do with this information?"

"Well, if you would be so kind as to pass it on to the king with whom you are about to shake hands, and if he would be so kind as to pass it on to the prime minister, perhaps he could come out and tell me what we should do with the aforementioned bomb. It's not the kind of thing you can just take to the recycling centre, after all."

President Hu Jintao didn't know what a recycling centre was (China's climate goals weren't quite on that level), but he understood the situation. And he realized that circumstances dictated that he immediately end his conversation with Miss Nombeko.

"I promise you, miss, that I will convey the matter to both the king and the prime minister, and I am pretty sure I can guarantee that you can expect an immediate reaction."

With that, President Hu returned to his startled wife and the red carpet, which led into the Inner Guards' Hall where Their Majesties were waiting.

All the guests had arrived; there was nothing more to see. Tourists and other onlookers dispersed in different directions with different goals for the rest of the beautiful June evening in Stockholm in the year 2007. Nombeko remained there, alone, waiting for something — but she didn't know what.

After twenty minutes, a woman approached. She shook Nombeko's hand as she introduced herself in a low voice; she was the prime minister's assistant and she had been asked to bring the woman to a more discreet corner of the castle.

Nombeko thought this was a good idea, but she added that she wanted to bring along the truck that was parked outside the courtyard. The assistant said that this was fine; it was on the way.

Holger One was still behind the wheel, with Celestine next to him (she had hidden the handcuffs in her handbag). The assistant got into the cab, too, whereupon it became a bit crowded in there. Nombeko and Holger Two climbed into the back.

It was a short trip. First up Källargränd and then down Slottsbacken. Then a left turn into the car park and all the way back up. Perhaps it was best for the driver to back up the last bit? Stop! That's good.

The assistant jumped out, knocked on an unassuming door, slipped in when it opened and disappeared. Then, one after another, the prime minister came out, followed by the king and President Hu Jintao, with his interpreter. The Chinese president really did seem to have vouched for Nombeko and her gang, because all the security personnel remained in the doorway.

Nombeko recognized the Chinese interpreter, even though twenty years had gone by.

"So, you didn't die after all," she said.

"Well, it's still not too late," the interpreter replied sourly. "Considering what you're apparently driving around with."

Holger Two and Nombeko invited the prime minister, the king and the president up into the back of the potato truck. The prime minister didn't hesitate. He wanted to find out if the appalling claim was true. And the king followed him. The president of China, however, considered the whole thing to be a matter of domestic politics, and backed his way into the palace, unlike his curious interpreter, who very much wanted to get a glimpse of the nuclear weapon in question. The bodyguards in the doorway were fidgety. What were the king and the prime minister doing in the back of a potato truck? It didn't feel right.

Ironically enough, at that very moment a lost group of Chinese tourists and their guide approached, so the door to the back of the truck had to be shut in a hurry. At this point, the Chinese interpreter, who had got in the way, found his fingers shut in the door. Nombeko and the others could hear his "Help, I'm dying!" outside, while Holger Two knocked on the window to the cab and asked One, behind the wheel, to turn on the lights in the back.

Holger One obediently turned on the lights, turned round — and saw the king! And the prime minister!

But above all, the king. Good God!

"It's the king, Dad," Holger One whispered to Ingmar Qvist in heaven.

And his father Ingmar replied:

"Drive, my son! Drive!"

And Holger drove.

PART SIX

I have never once in my life seen a fanatic
with a sense of humour.

Amos Oz

CHAPTER
TWENTY

On what kings do and do not do

The potato truck had no sooner started rolling than Nombeko was at the window, telling Holger One that he must stop immediately if he wanted to survive the day.

But One, who wasn't sure that he wanted to survive, asked Celestine to shut the window to block out the racket from the back.

She was happy to, and she also drew the curtain so that she wouldn't have to see His Majesty in his dark blue uniform jacket, white waistcoat, dark blue trousers with gold stripes, white dress shirt and black bow tie.

She was so proud of her rebel.

"We're going back to Grandma's, right?" she said. "Or do you have a better idea?"

"You know very well that I don't, darling," said Holger One.

The king mostly looked surprised at the situation they found themselves in, while the prime minister was upset.

"What on earth is going on?" he said. "Are you kidnapping your king and prime minister? Along with an atomic bomb! An atomic bomb in my Sweden. Who gave you permission for such a thing?"

"Well, the Kingdom of Sweden is rather more mine," said the king, sitting down on the nearest potato box. "But as for the rest, I share the prime minister's indignation."

Nombeko said that it might not matter too much who the country belonged to if it was going to be blown to kingdom come, but she immediately regretted saying this because now the prime minister wanted to know more about the damn bomb.

"How powerful is it? Tell me!" he said sternly.

But Nombeko thought they were in low enough spirits as it was; she didn't want to lower them even more. How could she have been so stupid as to bring it up? She tried to guide the conversation in a different direction:

"I am truly sorry about what has happened. It's not at all the case that this gentleman and the majesty next to him have been kidnapped — not by my boyfriend and me, at any rate. As soon as the truck stops, I promise to — at the very least — twist the nose of the man behind the wheel and make everything right."

And then, in order to defuse the situation, she added, "It's extra annoying to be locked in the back of the truck when the weather is so beautiful."

This last bit reminded the nature-loving king of the white-tailed eagle he had seen above the Stockholm Sound that afternoon.

"In the middle of the city!" Nombeko said, hoping for a second that her distraction had worked.

396

But when that second passed, the prime minister broke in and said that the group should stop discussing the weather and ornithology.

"Instead, tell me what kind of damage the bomb can do. How bad is it?"

Nombeko answered hesitantly. They were just talking about a few or perhaps several megatons.

"How many?"

"Two or three. No more."

"And what does that mean?"

He was a stubborn rascal, that prime minister.

"Three megatons is about 12,552 petajoules. Is the king sure that it was a white-tailed eagle?"

Fredrik Reinfeldt gave his head of state such a look that the latter refrained from answering. Then the former pondered whether he knew how much a petajoule was, and how bad twelve thousand of them might be, before he decided that the woman in front of him was being evasive.

"Tell me exactly what that means!" he said. "In a comprehensible manner."

So Nombeko did. She told him what it meant: that the bomb would take everything within a thirty-eight-mile radius with it, and that in the worst-case scenario, bad weather with a lot of wind could double the damage.

"Then it's lucky that the sun is shining," the king mused.

Nombeko nodded in appreciation of his positive attitude, but the prime minister called attention to the fact that Sweden was facing what might be its greatest crisis since the nation's birth. The heads of state and government found themselves roving through Sweden with a ruthless weapon of mass destruction, and they didn't know the motives of the man behind the wheel.

"Given these circumstances, mightn't the king find it more fitting to think of the survival of our nation rather than white-tailed eagles and the fact that at least we've been lucky with the weather?" said the prime minister.

But the king had been around for a while; he had seen prime ministers come and go, while he himself had endured. There wasn't really anything the matter with this new one, if he would just calm down a bit.

"There, there," he said. "Just have a seat on one of the potato boxes like the rest of us, and we'll ask Mr and Mrs Kidnapper for an explanation."

◆ ◆ ◆

In truth, he would have liked to have become a farmer. Or a steam-shovel operator. Or anything at all, as long as it had something to do with cars or nature. Preferably both.

And then he had become king.

This didn't really come as a surprise to him. In an early interview he described his life as a straight line from birth onwards. Predetermined as soon as the forty-two cannon shots rang out over Skeppsholmen on 30 April 1946.

He was named Carl Gustaf: Carl after his maternal grandfather Charles Edward, Duke of Saxe-Coburg and Gotha (who was an exciting combination of Nazi and Brit at the same time), and Gustaf after his father, paternal grandfather and great-grandfather.

Things started off terribly for the little prince. When he was only nine months old he lost his father in a plane crash. A dramatic hitch in the order of succession ensued. His grandfather, the future Gustaf VI Adolf, would have to stay alive until he was ninety-nine years old, otherwise there would be a vacancy that risked putting wind in the sails of the republicans in Parliament.

There was general agreement among the advisers that the hereditary prince should be kept within the yard-thick walls of the palace until the order of succession was secure, but his loving mother, Sibylla, refused. Without friends, her son would at worst become crazy, at best impossible to deal with.

So the prince was allowed to attend an ordinary school, and in his free time he was able to develop his interest in engines and be involved in the Scouts, where he learned to tie square knots, sheet bends and half hitches faster and better than anyone else.

However, at the Sigtuna Allmänna Läroverk boarding school he failed maths and barely passed everything else. The reason was that letters and numbers were one big mess; the crown prince had dyslexia. The fact that he was the best in the class at the mouth-organ didn't win him any extra marks, except with the girls.

Thanks to his mother Sibylla's care, he still had a number of friends out there in the real world, even if none of them happened to belong to the radical Left that almost everyone else professed to be an adherent of in 1960s Sweden. Letting one's hair grow, living in collectives and enjoying free love was not for the future king, even if he himself didn't think the last of those sounded so bad.

His grandfather, Gustav Adolf, had "duty above all" as his motto. Perhaps that was why he kept himself alive until he was ninety. He didn't pass away until September 1973, when the royal house was saved; his grandson was old enough to take over.

Since square knots and all-synchromesh gearboxes are not the first topics that come to mind when conversing with the Queen of England, the young Carl Gustaf didn't always feel at home in the smartest drawing rooms. But things got better as the years went by, mostly because he dared more and more to be himself. After more than three decades on the throne, a gala banquet at the palace in honour of Hu Jintao was a bore he could both handle and tolerate. But he would have preferred to dispense with it.

The current alternative, being kidnapped in a potato truck, wasn't exactly worth his time either, but the king thought it would probably work out somehow.

If only the prime minister would chill out a little.

And listen to what the kidnappers had to say.

♦ ♦ ♦

Prime Minister Reinfeldt had no intention of sitting down on any of the dirty potato boxes. Furthermore,

400

there was dust everywhere. And dirt on the floor. But he could listen, all the same.

"By all means," he said, turning to Holger Two. "Would you be so kind as to tell us what's going on?"

His words were polite, his tone commanding, his irritation with the king intact.

Two had rehearsed his conversation with the prime minister for nearly twenty years. He had prepared an almost infinite number of scenarios. None of them included the possibility that he and the prime minister might find themselves locked in a potato truck. Along with the bomb. And the king. With Two's king-hating brother behind the wheel. On their way to destinations unknown.

While Holger Two was at a loss for words and thoughts, his brother was in the cab, thinking aloud about what would happen next. His father had clearly said, "Drive, my son, drive," but that was it. But wasn't the simplest thing to let the king decide — either climb down from his throne and make sure that no one climbed up in his place, or climb up on the bomb so One and Celestine could blow king, parts of the kingdom and themselves sky-high?

"My brave, brave darling," Celestine said in response to Holger's ponderings.

This was the mother of all protests. Plus, it was a nice day to die, should it prove necessary.

In the back of the truck, Holger Two finally found his tongue again.

"I think we should start at the beginning of the story," he said.

So he told them about his father, Ingmar, about himself and his brother, about how one of them had decided to continue fighting their father's battle, while the other was now, unfortunately, sitting where he was sitting and saying what he was saying.

When he had finished and Nombeko had added her own life story, including the explanation of how the bomb that didn't really exist had ended up on the loose, the prime minister thought that this could not possibly be happening, but that to be on the safe side it was best to act according to the frightening prospect that it was happening despite that. Meanwhile the king, for his part, was thinking that he was starting to get hungry.

♦ ♦ ♦

Fredrik Reinfeldt tried to take in the scene. To assess it. He thought about the alarm that would be sounded at any minute, if it hadn't been already, and about how there would be a nationwide panic with the National Task Force and helicopters in the air, surrounding both potato truck and bomb. Nervous youths with automatic weapons would be hanging out of the helicopters, and they might accidentally fire shots that went through the sides of the truck and on through the layers of protective metal around all the megatons and petajoules. Alternatively they might just provoke the nut behind the wheel into doing something rash. Like driving off the road, for example.

This was all on one side of the balance.

On the other were the stories the man and the woman before him had just told. And President Hu, who had vouched for the latter.

Given the circumstances, shouldn't he and the king now do everything they could to make sure that things didn't run completely amok, so that the catastrophe they were threatened with would not be self-fulfilling?

Fredrik Reinfeldt had finished pondering, and he said to his king, "I have been thinking."

"Great," said the king. "That's the sort of thing we have prime ministers for, if you ask me."

Reinfeldt rhetorically asked His Majesty if they really wanted the National Task Force fluttering around above them. Didn't a three-megaton nuclear weapon demand more respect than that?

The king commended the prime minister for having chosen the description "three megatons" over "twelve thousand petajoules". But as the king understood it, the damage would still be considerable. Furthermore, he was old enough to remember the reports from the last time — it was in Gnesta, if the king remembered correctly — the National Task Force's first and thus far only task. Why, they had burned down a number of buildings while the suspected terrorists walked away.

Nombeko said that she had read something about that, too.

That settled it. The prime minister took out his phone and called the on-duty head of security to say that a matter of national interest had come up, that both he and the king were doing well, that the banquet dinner should be held as planned, and that this matter was to be blamed for the heads of both state and government having become indisposed. Beyond that, the head of security was to do nothing except await further orders.

The head of security on duty was sweating with anxiety. Fortunately his boss, the director of Säpo, the security service, was also invited to the banquet and was currently standing beside his subordinate, ready to take over. He was just as nervous, as it happened.

Maybe that was why the director of Säpo led off with a check question he himself didn't know the answer to. His muddled reasoning was that there was a risk that the prime minister had said what he said under threat.

"What is the name of the prime minister's dog?" he began.

The prime minister replied that he didn't have a dog, but that he promised to get a big one with sharp teeth and set it on the director of Säpo if he didn't have the good sense to listen carefully.

The situation was exactly as the prime minister had just said. The director of Säpo could check with President Hu if he had any doubts; they were with the president's friend, after all. Alternatively, he could try ignoring the prime minister's instructions, ask for the name of his pet fish (for he did have one of those), declare them missing, turn the country upside down — and look for a new job starting tomorrow.

The director of Säpo liked his job. The title was nice, and so was the salary. And he was getting close to retirement. In short, he really didn't want to search for a new job. Instead he decided that the prime minister's pet fish could be called whatever it liked.

Furthermore, Her Majesty the Queen was now standing next to him, and she wanted to say something.

Fredrik Reinfeldt handed the phone to his king.

"Hi, darling. No, darling, I'm not out partying . . ."

The threat of a task force attack from above had been averted. As the journey continued, Holger Two explained their problems in greater detail. The fact was, his twin brother behind the wheel had — just like their long-dead father — got it into his head that Sweden ought to be a republic, not a monarchy. The woman on his right was his angry and equally confused girlfriend. Unfortunately she shared his brother's views when it came to forms of government.

"For the sake of order, I would like to state that I am of a differing opinion," said the king.

The potato truck drove on. The group in the back of the truck had jointly decided to wait and see. Mostly they were waiting, of course: they couldn't see anything at all from where they sat, since Celestine had drawn the curtains of the window between them and the cab.

Suddenly their journey seemed to be over. The potato truck stopped; the engine was turned off.

Nombeko asked Two which of them should kill his brother first, but Two's thoughts lay more along the lines of where they might be. For his part, the king said that he hoped there would be food. Meanwhile, the prime minister started examining the doors. They should be able to be opened from the inside, too, right? It wouldn't have been a good idea to try this while the truck was still moving, but now Fredrik Reinfeldt couldn't see any reason to stay in this dirty place. He was the only one who had chosen to remain standing the whole time.

While this was going on, Holger One had run into the barn at Sjölida and up to the hayloft, where he lifted up a bucket, under which Agent A's pistol had lain hidden for nearly thirteen years. One was back before the prime minister succeeded in figuring out how the door mechanism worked from the inside.

"Now don't do anything stupid," he said. "Just climb down, nice and slowly."

The king's many medals jangled as he took a leap from the truck to the ground. The sound and the image of the baubles gave One renewed strength. He raised his weapon to show who was in control.

"You have a *pistol*?" said Nombeko, deciding to put off both killing him and twisting his nose.

"What is going on over there?"

It was Gertrud, who had seen through the window that the group had grown larger, and she was coming out to greet them with — as always when she wasn't sure of the situation — her father Tapio's moose-hunting rifle in hand.

"This just keeps getting better and better," said Nombeko.

Gertrud was not happy that Celestine and the others had dragged a politician home, because she didn't like such people. The king, however, was fine. And how! Since the 1970s, Gertrud had kept a picture of him and the queen in the outhouse, and they had been good company with warming smiles as she sat there in zero-degree temperatures to do her business. At first it hadn't felt quite right to wipe one's backside in front of one's king, but the pros had won, and after a while she had grown used to it. To be honest, ever since Sjölida had acquired an indoor toilet in 1993, she had missed those times spent with Their Majesties.

"Nice to see you again," she said, shaking her king's hand. "Is all as it should be with the queen?"

"The pleasure is all mine," said the king, adding that the queen was well, while he wondered to himself where he might have met this lady before.

Holger One herded everyone into Gertrud's kitchen, with the intention of holding an interrogation with His Majesty and giving him an ultimatum. Gertrud asked if they'd remembered to buy food, especially now that they had guests. And the king, besides. And that other man.

"I am Prime Minister Fredrik Reinfeldt," said Prime Minister Fredrik Reinfeldt, extending his hand. "Pleasure."

"Answer the question," said Gertrud. "Did you buy any food?"

"No, Gertrud," said Nombeko. "Other things got in the way."

"Then we'll all just have to starve."

"Couldn't we call for a pizza?" the king wondered, thinking that at the gala banquet they had probably left the sauteed scallops with lemon balm pesto behind and were up to the poached halibut with pine nuts and asparagus.

"Phones don't work out here. It's the politicians' fault. I don't like politicians," Gertrud said again.

Fredrik Reinfeldt thought for the second time that this wasn't happening. He had just heard his king suggest takeaway pizza for himself and his kidnappers.

"If you kill some of the chickens, I can scrape up a casserole," Gertrud realized. "Unfortunately I sold off my five hundred acres of potato fields, but farmer Engström probably won't notice if we swipe fifteen of his fifteen million potatoes."

Amid all this, Holger One was standing there with pistol in hand. Takeaway pizza? Chicken casserole? What was going on? The king was supposed to be abdicating or else going up in atoms.

One whispered to Celestine that it was time for them to put their feet down. She nodded and decided to start by explaining the situation to her grandmother. And so she did, very briefly. The fact was, the king had been kidnapped, and the prime minister was part of the bargain. And now she and Holger were going to force him to abdicate.

"The prime minister?"

"No, the king."

"That's a pity," said Gertrud, adding that no one should have to abdicate on an empty stomach. Were they going to make chicken casserole, or what?

The king thought homemade chicken casserole sounded both hearty and good. And if he was ever going to get anything in his stomach, it was clear that he himself would have to get moving.

He'd been on a few pheasant hunts over the years, and from the start, when the king was just a crown prince, people hadn't lined up to dress his haul for him. The young man had had to be toughened up, and now he thought that if he had been able to shoot and pluck a pheasant thirty-five years earlier, he should be able to behead and pluck a hen today.

"If the prime minister will get the potatoes, I can deal with the chickens," he said.

Since by that point Fredrik Reinfeldt was almost certain that what was happening really wasn't, he walked out to the potato field, pitchfork in hand, dressed in patent-leather shoes and an Italian tailcoat from Corneliani. In any case, it was better than the alternative — getting chicken blood on his shirt and God only knew where else.

The king was quick on his feet for a man of his age. Within five minutes he had caught three young cocks, and with the help of the axe managed to separate heads from bodies. Before doing so he had hung his uniform jacket on the outer wall of the henhouse, where the Order of the Seraphim, Gustaf V's Royal Jubilee medal, Gustav VI Adolf's memorial medal, the Order of the Sword and the Order of the Polar Star glittered in the

409

evening sunlight. The Order of the Vasa, on a chain, was hanging on a nearby rusty pitchfork.

Just as the prime minister had suspected, the white dress shirt was soon dotted with red.

"I have another one at home," the king said to Nombeko, who was helping with the plucking.

"I thought you might," said Nombeko.

When she stepped into the kitchen a moment later, with three plucked chickens in her hands, Gertrud clucked happily that it was casserole time! Holger One and Celestine sat at the kitchen table, more confused than usual. Even more so when the prime minister came in, with muddy feet and a bucket of potatoes. And then the king, in a dress shirt covered in chicken blood. He had forgotten his uniform jacket and the Order of the Vasa on its chain back at the henhouse and on the pitchfork.

Gertrud took the potatoes without a word and then commended the king on his skill with an axe.

Holger One was displeased that Gertrud was fraternizing with His damned Majesty. The same went for Celestine. If she had been seventeen, she would have left immediately, but now they had a task to accomplish, and she didn't want to have to be separated from her grandmother out of anger once again. Unless they were forced to blow both people and chickens sky-high, but that was another matter.

One still had his pistol in hand, and it bothered him that no one seemed to care. Nombeko thought that what he deserved more than anything was a twisted nose (she was no longer angry enough to be able to kill him), but she also wanted to enjoy Gertrud's chicken casserole before, in the worst case, life on earth was over for all of them. And after all, the biggest threat to that wasn't the bomb, but that scatterbrain waving the weapon.

So she decided to help her boyfriend's brother with some logic. She explained that the pistol was unnecessary if the king didn't run away, and if the king *did* run away, Holger still had thirty-eight miles to set off the bomb instead. Not even a king could run that far in under three hours, even if he had taken off all those heavy medals.

All Holger had to do was hide the key to the potato truck. Once that was done, he would have created a balance of terror at Sjölida. No one would need to keep their eyes on anyone else. Instead, they could eat their food in peace and quiet.

One nodded thoughtfully. What Nombeko had said sounded reasonable. Plus, he had already stuffed the key to the potato truck in one sock without realizing how clever this was. After another few seconds' worth of thinking, he put the pistol in the inner pocket of his jacket.

Without putting the safety on first.

While Nombeko was talking reason into One, Celestine had received orders from her grandmother to help cut up the chicken into casserole-size chunks. Meanwhile, Holger Two was instructed to mix drinks *exactly* according to her instructions: a splash of Gordon's gin, two splashes of Noilly Prat, and the rest equal amounts of schnapps and Skåne akvavit. Two didn't really know what she meant by a "splash", but once he'd decided on an amount he thought that two splashes was probably double as much. He sneaked a taste of the finished concoction and was so happy with the results that he tasted it once again.

At last, everyone was sitting at the table except for Gertrud, who was putting the finishing touches to the casserole. The king looked at the two Holgers and was struck by how similar they were.

"How can anyone tell you apart, if you also have the same name?"

"One suggestion is to call the one with a pistol 'the idiot'," said Holger Two, feeling a certain amount of satisfaction at having said it out loud.

"Holger and the Idiot . . . yes, that might work," said the king.

"No one calls my Holger an idiot!" said Celestine.

"Why not?" said Nombeko.

The prime minister felt that it was in no one's best interests for a fight to break out, so he hurried to praise Holger for having put away the weapon, which led Nombeko to elucidate the prevailing balance of power for everyone.

"If we catch Holger, the one we don't call an idiot when his girlfriend is listening but are welcome to otherwise, and tie him to a tree — then the risk is that his girlfriend will set off the bomb instead. And if we tie her to a tree next to the first one, who knows what the girl's grandmother will think to do with her moose-hunting rifle."

"Gertrud," the king said approvingly.

"I'll have you know that if you touch my little Celestine, bullets will fly in every direction!" said Gertrud.

"Well, there you go," said Nombeko. "We don't need the pistol. I even got the idiot to realize that a while ago."

"Dinner's ready," said Gertrud.

On the menu was chicken casserole, home-brewed beer and the hostess's own special blend of schnapps. People could help themselves to casserole and beer, but Gertrud would handle the schnapps. Everyone got his own glass, including the feebly protesting prime minister. Gertrud filled them to the rim and the king rubbed his hands:

"A little bird told me that the chicken will be delicious. But now let's see about the rest of it."

"Cheers, King," said Gertrud.

"What about the rest of us?" said Celestine.

"Cheers to the rest of you, too, of course."

And she drained her glass. The king and Holger Two followed her example. The others sipped theirs more tentatively, except for Holger One, who couldn't bring himself to drink to the king, and the prime minister, who poured his schnapps into a geranium when no one was looking.

"Why, it's Marshal Mannerheim!" the king said approvingly.

No one but Gertrud knew what he was talking about.

"Splendid, King!" she said. "Might one tempt the king with another? After all, a person can't stand on one leg."

Holger One and Celestine felt increasingly troubled by Gertrud's delight in the man who was meant to abdicate. And who was, moreover, sitting there in a bloody dress shirt with rolled-up sleeves instead of a uniform jacket. One didn't like not catching on, even though he was quite used to it.

"What's going on?" he said.

"What just happened was that your friend the king recognized the world's most excellent drink," said Gertrud.

"He's not my friend," said Holger One.

♦ ♦ ♦

Gustaf Mannerheim was no bluff of a man. After all, he had served in the tsar's army for several decades, travelling around Europe and Asia by horse.

So when Communism and Lenin took over Russia, he went back home to Finland, which was free, and became a commissioned officer and eventually president. He was designated Finland's greatest soldier of all time, receiving orders and distinctions from all over the world — and on him was conferred the unique title of Marshal of Finland.

Marskens sup, or "the Marshal's shot", came into being during the Second World War. It was one part aquavit, one part vodka, a splash of gin and two splashes of vermouth. The drink became a classic.

The first time the Swedish king had enjoyed it was on a state visit to Finland more than thirty years earlier, when he had been king for just over a year.

Twenty-eight years old, nervous and with trembling knees, he had been received by the experienced Finnish president Kekkonen, himself a bit older than seventy. With the prerogative of age, Kekkonen had immediately decided that the king needed to get something inside his chest, which was already so heavy with medals, and after that the rest of the visit went swimmingly. A Finnish president doesn't serve any old drink; it had to be *marskens* and thus was born a lifelong love between king and schnapps, while the king and Kekkonen became hunting pals.

The king emptied his second schnapps, smacked his lips, and said, "I see that the prime minister's glass is empty. Shouldn't he have a refill, too? By the way, hang up your jacket. Your shoes are covered in mud anyway. And it goes halfway up your legs, I see."

The prime minister apologized for his appearance. In the light of what he now knew, of course, he ought to have arrived at the palace for the gala banquet in overalls and rubber boots. And he added that he preferred to refrain from drinking; anyway, it seemed that the king was drinking for them both.

Fredrik Reinfeldt didn't know how he should tackle his carefree king. On the one hand, the head of state probably ought to take this exceedingly complicated situation seriously and shouldn't just sit there drinking buckets of alcohol (in the prime minister's moderate eyes, two glasses was about as much as a bucket).

On the other hand, the king seemed to be creating confusion among the revolutionary republican ranks around the table. The prime minister had registered the whispering between the man with the pistol and his girlfriend. Clearly, something was bothering them. The king, of course. But not in the same way that he was bothering the prime minister. And not, as it seemed, in that simple, down-with-the-monarchy way that had probably been the start of it all.

Something was up, anyway. And maybe if he just left the king alone, they would find out what it was. It would be impossible to stop him anyway.

He was the king, after all!

♦ ♦ ♦

Nombeko was the first to empty her plate. She had been twenty-five before she'd eaten until she was full for the first time, at the expense of President Botha, and since then she had taken advantage of every chance she got to do so.

"Is it possible to have seconds?"

It was. Gertrud was pleased that Nombeko was pleased with the food. Gertrud was pleased in general, it seemed. It was as if the king had touched her soul. With something.

Himself.

Marshal Mannerheim.

Or his shot.

416

Or a bit of everything.

Whatever it was, it might be a good thing. Because if the king and Gertrud together managed to confuse the coup-makers, the latter's idea of what must happen next would become muddy.

A spanner in the works, as it was called.

Nombeko would very much have liked to talk strategy with the king, the topic of which would be that he should continue digging around in the Mannerheim regions, but she couldn't reach him: he was absorbed in their hostess, and vice versa.

His Majesty had an ability that the prime minister lacked: he could take pleasure in the present moment, quite regardless of external threats. The king enjoyed Gertrud's company, and he was sincerely curious about the old woman.

"Gertrud, what is your relationship with the marshal and Finland, if you'll excuse my curiosity?" he said.

This was the exact question that Nombeko had wanted to hear answered but had been unable to ask.

Good, King! Are you that clever? Or did we just get lucky?

"My relationship to the marshal and Finland? Oh, the king doesn't want to know that," said Gertrud.

Of course you do, King!

"Of course I do," said the king.

"It's a long story," said Gertrud.

We have plenty of time!

"We have plenty of time," said the king.

"Do we?" said the prime minister, and received an angry look from Nombeko.

This doesn't involve you!

"It begins in 1867," said Gertrud.

"The year the marshal was born." The king nodded.

You're a genius, King!

"Oh, the king is so clever!" said Gertrud. "The year the marshal was born, that's exactly right."

Nombeko thought that the description of Gertrud's family tree was as great a botanical contradiction as the first time she'd heard it. But her story had not lessened the king's good humour in the least. He had, after all, once failed maths at Sigtuna Allmänna Läroverk. Perhaps that was because he hadn't managed to calculate that barons, false or not, do not generate countesses.

"So she's a countess!" he said appreciatively.

"She is?" said the prime minister, who was better at calculating, and who received yet another angry look from Nombeko.

There was certainly something about the king that was weighing on Holger One and Celestine. It was just a bit hard to put a finger on it. Was it his bloody shirt? The rolled-up sleeves? The gold cuff links the king had placed in an empty shot glass on the kitchen table for the time being? His disgustingly medal-covered uniform jacket hanging on a hook on the henhouse wall?

418

Or merely that the king had just chopped the heads off three chickens?

Kings don't chop the heads off chickens!

For that matter, prime ministers don't pick potatoes (at least not in a tailcoat) but, above all, kings don't chop the heads off chickens.

While One and Celestine worked through this appalling contradiction, the king managed to make things even worse. He and Gertrud walked into the potato field, and then to the old tractor, which of course the group no longer needed, and that was good, because it didn't work anyway. Gertrud described the problem to her king, who replied that the MF35 was a little peach, and one had to pamper it to get it to work. And then he suggested cleaning the diesel filter and the spraying nozzle. If there was just some juice left in the battery, it would probably rumble to life after that.

Diesel filter and spraying nozzle? Kings don't fix tractors.

Dinner was over. After coffee and a private walk to take a look at the MF35, the king and Gertrud returned for one last Mannerheim together.

Meanwhile, Prime Minister Reinfeldt cleared the table and cleaned up the kitchen. In order to avoid dirtying his tailcoat more than was necessary, he put on the countess's apron.

Holger One and Celestine sat whispering in a corner, while his brother and Nombeko did the same in another corner. They talked about how the situation looked and what their next strategic move ought to be.

That was when the door flew open. In came an older man with a pistol. He bellowed in English that everyone should stay where they were, and not make any sudden moves.

"What's happening?" said Fredrik Reinfeldt, dish-scrubbing brush in hand.

Nombeko answered the prime minister in English. She told the truth: the Israeli Mossad had just barged into the house with the aim of commandeering the atomic bomb in the potato truck.

CHAPTER
TWENTY-ONE

On a lost composure and a twin who shoots his brother

Thirteen years is a long time to spend behind a desk without anything sensible to do. But at any rate, Agent B had finished the last day of his career. He was sixty-five years and nine days old. Nine days earlier, he had been sent off with almond cake and speeches. Since the speech from his boss was lovely but insincere, the almond cake tasted bitter.

After one week of retirement, he had made up his mind. He packed his bags to go to Europe. To Sweden.

He had always been bothered by the case of the cleaning woman who had disappeared with the bomb that had been honestly stolen by Israel, and the feeling seemed to have followed him into old age.

Who *was* she? Beyond her thievery, she had probably killed his friend A. Former Agent B didn't know what was spurring him on. But if something is bothersome, that's it.

He ought to have had more patience at that PO box in Stockholm. And he ought to have checked Celestine Hedlund's grandmother. If only he had been allowed to.

That was a long time ago now. And the clue hadn't been much of a clue to start with. But still. Former Agent B's first plan was to travel to the forest north of Norrtälje. If that didn't result in anything, he would stake out that post office for at least three weeks.

After that, perhaps he could retire for real. He would still wonder, and never find out. But at least he would feel that he had done all he could. Losing to a superior opponent was bearable. But giving up before the final whistle had been blown wasn't. Michael Ballack never would have done that. Incidentally, the two-footed star of FC Karl-Marx-Stadt had made it all the way to the national team, and become captain.

B landed at Arlanda Airport. There he hired a car and drove straight to Celestine Hedlund's grandmother's house. He had thought the house would probably be empty, boarded up — or maybe that was what he was hoping to find. After all, the main goal of this trip was to bring the agent peace of mind, not to find a bomb that wouldn't let itself be found anyway.

At any rate, there was a potato truck in the road just outside the grandmother's house — and all the lights were on! Why was it there? What could it contain?

The agent climbed out, sneaked up to the truck, looked into the back of it, and — it was as if time stood still. The crate with the bomb was in there! Just as scorched at the corners as last time.

Since the world appeared to have gone crazy, he checked to see if the keys were in the ignition. But he wasn't that lucky. He would have to confront them inside the house after all, whoever they might be. An eighty-year-old woman, certainly. Her grandchild. The grandchild's boyfriend. And the goddamn fucking cleaning woman. Anyone else? Well, maybe the unknown man who had been spotted in the Blomgrens' car that time outside the burned-down buildings on Fredsgatan in Gnesta.

Agent B picked up the service weapon he just happened to have packed with his things on the day he retired, and cautiously tested the doorknob. It was unlocked. He just had to step in.

♦ ♦ ♦

Fredrik Reinfeldt (with dish-scrubbing brush in hand) had blurted out his question about what was happening. Nombeko answered him in English and told the truth: that the Israeli Mossad had just barged into the house with the aim of commandeering the atomic bomb in the potato truck. And maybe, while he was at it, killing one or two of the people in the room. In that regard, she believed that she herself was of immediate interest.

"The Israeli Mossad?" said the prime minister (also in English). "What right does the Israeli Mossad have to wave weapons around in my Sweden?"

"My Sweden," the king corrected him.

"Your Sweden?" Agent B heard himself say, looking back and forth between the man with the apron and the dish-scrubbing brush and the man on the sofa with the bloody shirt and empty schnapps glass in hand.

423

"I am Prime Minister Fredrik Reinfeldt," said the prime minister.

"And I am King Carl XVI Gustaf," said the king. "The prime minister's boss, one might say. And this is Countess Virtanen, the hostess of this gathering."

"Why, I'm much obliged," the countess said with pride.

Fredrik Reinfeldt was almost as upset as he had been a few hours earlier in the potato truck when he realized that he had been kidnapped.

"Put down your weapon at once. Otherwise I will call Prime Minister Olmert and ask what is going on. I presume you are acting on his orders?"

Agent B stood where he was, struck by something that could be compared to a brain fart. He didn't know which was worst: that the man with the apron and the dish-scrubbing brush claimed to be the prime minister, that the man with the bloody shirt and the schnapps glass claimed to be the king, or the fact that Agent B thought they both looked familiar. They were the prime minister and the king. In a house in the middle of the forest, beyond the end of the road in Swedish Roslagen.

An agent of the Israeli Mossad never loses his composure. But Agent B was in the process of doing just that. He lost his composure. He lowered his weapon. He put it back in the holster inside his jacket. And he said:

"May I have something to drink?"

424

"Such luck that we haven't put the bottle away yet," said Gertrud.

Agent B took a seat next to the king and was immediately served the marshal's shot. He drained his glass, gave a shudder and gratefully accepted another round.

Before Prime Minister Reinfeldt had time to commence the shower of questions he had for the intruder, Nombeko turned to Agent B and suggested that the two of them should tell boss Reinfeldt and his boss the king exactly what had happened. From Pelindaba on. Agent B nodded numbly.

"You start," he said, showing Countess Virtanen that the glass in his hand was empty again.

So Nombeko started. The king and the prime minister had already heard the short version while they were locked up in the back of the truck with the bomb. This time she went into greater detail. The prime minister listened intently as he wiped the kitchen table and the counter. The king listened, too, from his spot on the kitchen sofa next to the very delightful countess, with the less-delightful agent on his other side.

Nombeko started in Soweto, then moved on to Thabo's diamonds and how she got run over in Johannesburg. The trial. The verdict. The engineer and his passion for Klipdrift. Pelindaba and all its electric fences. The South African nuclear weapons programme. The Israeli involvement.

"I cannot confirm that," said Agent B.

"Watch it," said Nombeko.

Agent B considered. It was all over for him anyway. Either by way of life in a Swedish prison or by way of the prime minister making a call to Ehud Olmert. The agent preferred life in prison.

"I have changed my mind," he said. "I can confirm that."

As the story went on, he had to confirm more than that. The interest in the seventh bomb, the one that didn't exist. The agreement with Nombeko. The idea of using the diplomatic post. Agent A's initial hunt when the mix-up was discovered.

"What happened to him, by the way?" said Agent B.

"He landed in the Baltic Sea in a helicopter," said Holger One. "Rather hard, I'm afraid."

Nombeko went on. About Holger & Holger. Fredsgatan. The Chinese girls. The potter. The tunnel. The National Task Force's intervention. How the force waged several hours' worth of war with itself.

"Everyone who's surprised, raise your hand," the prime minister mumbled.

Nombeko went on. About Mr and Mrs Blomgren. About the diamond money that had gone up in flames. About the meeting with B outside the condemned building. About all the fruitless phone calls to the prime minister's assistant throughout the years.

"She was just doing her job," said Fredrik Reinfeldt. "Gertrud, do you happen to have a broom? All that's left is the floor."

" 'Countess', please," said the king.

426

Nombeko went on. About the potato farm. Two's studies. The idiot's interference in the dissertation defence.

"The idiot?" said B.

"That's probably me," said Holger One, feeling like there might possibly be something to that name.

Nombeko went on. About the magazine *Swedish Politics*.

"That was a good magazine," said the prime minister. "For one issue. Which of you wrote the editorial in the second issue? No, wait, don't tell me. Let me guess."

By now, Nombeko had nearly finished. By way of conclusion, she explained her connection with Hu Jintao. Her plan to attract his attention outside the palace. And how Holger One — the original idiot — then kidnapped them all.

Agent B drained his third schnapps and felt that he was sufficiently anaesthetized for the time being. Then he added his own story, from his birth onwards. After his retirement, this matter had continued to bother him. So he had travelled here. Not at all on Prime Minister Olmert's orders. Completely on his own initiative. And boy, did he regret it now.

"What a mess!" said the king with a laugh.

The prime minister had to admit that His Majesty had summed things up quite well.

◆　◆　◆

Around midnight, the director of Säpo was on the verge of not being able to take it much longer.

The king and the prime minister were still missing. According to the president of the People's Republic of China, they were in good hands, but wasn't that what he thought about the people of Tibet?

Of more significance, of course, was that the prime minister had called and said that everything was fine, and that everyone should lie low. But that had been several hours ago. Now he wasn't answering his phone, and it was impossible to search for the phone's signal. Furthermore, the king didn't have a phone.

The gala banquet was long since over, and rumours were spreading. Journalists were calling to ask why the hosts hadn't been there. The court's and the government's press staffs had replied that the king and the prime minister had unfortunately and independently become indisposed, but that there was no danger to either of them.

Unfortunately it is not in journalists' genetic makeup to believe this sort of coincidence. The director of Säpo could sense that they were all champing at the bit. Unlike the director of Säpo himself, who was just sitting around, twiddling his thumbs. Because what on earth was he supposed to do?

He had made a few discreet overtures, such as speaking to the director of the National Task Force. The director of Säpo didn't say why he was calling; he just said there might be a delicate situation brewing and that there might be cause for a break-in-and-rescue type of action. Like the one in Gnesta a decade earlier. Sweden was a peaceful country. One task force action every ten or fifteen years was about what one could expect.

The director of the National Task Force had proudly stated that Gnesta had been his first and thus far only job and that he and his group were at the ready, as always.

The director of Säpo hadn't been around back when parts of Gnesta had burned down. And he hadn't read the reports about it. He had confidence in the National Task Force. Although it was concerning that the most basic prerequisite for a successful rescue of the king and the prime minister was not at hand.

Namely, the knowledge of where the hell they were.

♦ ♦ ♦

B asked for a fourth schnapps. And a fifth. The agent didn't know much about Swedish prisons, but he was pretty sure that free drink wasn't part of the package. Might as well help himself while he still could.

The king expressed approval of the pace the agent was setting.

"Why, you caught up with and surpassed me in forty minutes," he said.

The prime minister looked up from the floor he was in the process of cleaning. You didn't just sit around joking with a foreign nation's intelligence service like that.

Countess Virtanen was radiant in the king's company. The fact that he was a king was a good start, plus he chopped chickens' heads off like a real man, he knew who Mannerheim was, he recognized the marshal's shot, and he had hunted moose with Urho Kekkonen. *And* he called her "the countess". It was as if someone was finally noticing her, as if she had become a Finnish Mannerheim again after having been a potato-farming Virtanen for her entire adult life.

No matter what happened when the Mannerheim schnapps left her body and the king had gone — Gertrud made up her mind then and there on the sofa with His Majesty and the infinitely weary agent: from now on, she would be a countess. To the fullest!

Holger One had completely lost his footing. He realized that what had kept his convictions about a republic alive all these years was his mental image of Gustaf V with his dress uniform, medals, monocle and silver cane. This was also the picture that he, his brother and his father had thrown darts at when the boys were little. And it was the image he had sold to his beloved Celestine. And she had accepted it.

Were they really going to blow up Gustaf V's great-grandson, as well as themselves, the brother of one and the grandmother of the other because of it?

Oh, if only he hadn't cut the heads off those chickens. And hung up his uniform jacket. And rolled up the sleeves of his bloody shirt. And instructed Gertrud in how to fix a tractor. And tossed back shot after shot without batting an eyelid.

It didn't help that the prime minister was, at this very moment, on his hands and knees to scrub a spot off the floor, having cleared the table and washed and dried the dishes. But still, this was nothing compared to the truth that had been dashed to pieces before their very eyes.

The one about how kings don't cut the heads off chickens.

What Holger needed now, more than anything else, was confirmation that the true faith still held water. If he could just have that, he would get Celestine on his side.

The monarch of all monarchs in his father's story had, of course, been Gustaf V; he was the one sent by the devil to poison Mother Earth above all others. Holger realized now that what he needed to hear was the current king's reverence for this devil spawn. So he approached the king where he sat cooing away with the eighty-year-old woman. And then he said:

"Listen, King."

The king interrupted himself in the middle of a sentence, looked up, and said, "Yes, that's me."

"I want to ask you something," Holger One said, making sure to use the informal "you" with His Majesty.

The king didn't answer; he politely waited for Holger to continue.

"It's about Gustaf the Fifth."

"My great-grandfather," said the king.

"That's right, you all get passed down that way," said Holger, without really understanding what he meant. "What I want to know is what His Majesty — I mean you — think of him?"

* * *

Nombeko had discreetly come closer to hear how the conversation between king and idiot would proceed. She whispered to herself, You've been perfect so far, King, now give the right answer!

"Gustaf the Fifth?" said the king, suspecting a trap.

◆ ◆ ◆

The king let his thoughts run through the generations for a moment.

Being head of state wasn't always as easy as a commoner might think. He was thinking not least of Erik XIV, who was first called insane (though that was on a partly sound basis) and then locked up by his brother and eventually served poison-spiked soup.

Or Gustav III, who went to a masquerade ball to have a little fun — and was shot. That was certainly amusing. What's more, the shooter's aim was so bad that the poor king lived for another two weeks before he died.

And above all, Gustaf V, whom Holger the republican seemed to have become hung up on. His great-grandfather had been a delicate child; he seemed to drag his feet, and for that reason he was treated with the new invention of electricity. People thought a few volts through the body would get the feet moving.

Whether it was those volts or something else was impossible to say, but Gustaf V later guided the neutral Sweden through two world wars in a very upright manner. All while he had a queen from Germany on

432

one side, and on the other a son and crown prince who had stubbornly married British not once but twice.

Gustaf V may have gone a bit too far just before the First World War, when he demanded a stronger military so loudly that Prime Minister Staaff resigned in a rage. Staaff thought it was more important to introduce universal suffrage than to build an armoured boat or two. The fact that his great-grandfather had made this demand just before the shot in Sarajevo and had thus been right was something no one cared about: kings were expected to keep quiet. The current king himself had experienced this personally the time he happened to opine that the sultan of Brunei was a dependable fellow.

Ah, well. His great-grandfather ruled for almost forty-three years and skilfully fended off all the political upheavals of the time. Consider the fact that the monarchy didn't actually go under, even though every Tom, Dick and Harry suddenly got the right to vote and did it so badly that social democracy came to power. Instead of the revolution that was expected, it happened that Prime Minister Hansson sneaked up to the palace now and then to play bridge in the evenings, no matter how republican he was.

So the truth was, his great-grandfather had been above all a saviour of the monarchy. But right now the important thing was handling a situation in the very spirit of his great-grandfather, with just enough determination and respect for reality thrown into the mix.

The king understood that there was something important behind the question from the man he wasn't allowed to call "the idiot". But since the idiot in question could hardly have been born before the king's great-grandfather died in 1950, they couldn't have had anything to do with one another. This whole thing must go further back in time than that. To be quite honest, the king hadn't been listening very closely when Nombeko gave her lecture; he had been far too busy with the countess. But back in the potato truck, the other Holger had said something about the twins' father having been the one who had established the concept of republicanism in the family, once upon a time.

To quite an extent, apparently.

Had the twin brothers' father had some conflict with Gustaf V somehow?

Hmm.

The king was taken by a forbidden thought.

The fact was, back when Great-grandfather and Great-grandmother had said, "I do," in September 1881, the idea of marrying for love had not been invented in royal circles. Nevertheless, Great-grandfather had been hurt when his queen travelled to the warmth of Egypt to improve her health and to devote herself to adventures of the kinkier sort in a Bedouin tent with a simple baron from the court. And a Dane, besides.

From that day on, it was said that the king was no longer interested in women. It was less clear how he felt about men. There had been rumours throughout the years, not to mention that extortion incident, when a charlatan demanded money from the king at a time when homosexuality was illegal and could threaten the monarchy. The court did everything it could to keep the charlatan happy and — above all — silent.

He was given money and a little more money and a little more on top of that. He received help operating both a restaurant and a hotel. But once a charlatan, always a charlatan — the money always went down the drain and he always came back wanting more.

Once he was stuffed full of banknotes and shipped across the Atlantic to the United States, but it is unclear whether he even made it there before he was back and making more demands. Another time — as the war was raging — he was sent to Nazi Germany with the promise of a lifelong monthly allowance from Sweden. But that devil groped little boys there, and otherwise behaved like the exact opposite of Hitler's ideal Aryan male in all ways. He was thus immediately sent back to Sweden after having irritated the Gestapo to such an extent that he was very close to ending up in a concentration camp (which, one couldn't deny, would have been rather advantageous for the Swedish court).

Back in Stockholm, the charlatan wrote a book about his life. The whole world would know what had happened! No, it absolutely would not, thought the chief of police in Stockholm; he bought the entire run of books and locked them in a cell at the police station.

Eventually it was no longer possible to hush up the unpleasant story (things probably would have been different in Brunei). Then society came to the king's aid and sentenced the charlatan to eight years in prison for this and that. At that point, Gustaf V was already dead and the charlatan made sure he was, too, at his own hand, once he was released again.

A sad story, that. But, of course, it's not impossible that the charlatan was something more than just a charlatan. At least when it came to the story of his relationship with Gustaf V. And it was impossible to rule out that the king had been close to him and other boys and men in that . . . at the time . . . unlawful manner.

What if . . .

What if the Holgers' dad had been abused? What if that was why he had started his crusade against the monarchy in general and Gustaf V in particular?

What if . . .

Because *something* had happened.

With that, the king had finished thinking. He hadn't thought correctly in every respect, but he had thought cleverly.

"What do I think about my great-grandfather Gustaf the Fifth?" the king said again.

"Come on, give me an answer!" said Holger One.

"Between you and me?" said the king (while Countess Virtanen, Celestine, Holger Two, Nombeko, the prime minister and a now-sleeping Israeli former agent were right next to them).

"By all means," said Holger One.

436

The king asked his blessed great-grandfather in Heaven to forgive him. And then he said:

"He was a real bastard."

Up to that point, it might have just been the case that the king was a child of nature and it was a happy accident that he and Gertrud had found one another. But when he besmirched the good name of Gustaf V, Nombeko knew that the king, too, had realized what a situation they truly found themselves in. The king had robbed his great-grandfather of honour and glory, simply because it was probably the best thing for the common good.

One's reaction remained to be seen.

"Come on, Celestine," said Holger One. "Let's take a walk to the dock. We need to talk."

One and Celestine sat down on the bench on the dock on Vätösund. It was slightly past midnight; the short Swedish summer night was dark but not particularly cold. Celestine took Holger's hands in her own, looked him in the eye, and started by asking him if he could forgive her for being almost noble.

Holger mumbled that he could; as far as he knew, it wasn't her fault that her grandmother Gertrud's father had been a baron alongside his more honourable work as a counterfeiter of banknotes. But it did hurt a bit, of course. If it was even true — the story seemed a bit wobbly in places. And, of course, there was a mitigating factor in that Grandfather Gustaf Mannerheim had thought the better of things in his later years and become president. Furthermore, he'd been a noble-man, faithful to the tsar, but then he had taken over a republic. Ugh, everything was such a mess.

Celestine agreed. She had felt like a failure throughout her whole upbringing. Until the day when Holger stood there and turned out to be whom and what she was looking for. And who later jumped from a helicopter and fell two thousand feet to save her life. And then they had kidnapped the King of Sweden to get him to abdicate, or else be blown to pieces along with all his medals, and themselves, too.

For a moment, Celestine's life had seemed to be both comprehensible and meaningful.

But then came the chopping off of the chickens' heads. And the king had made himself useful fixing her grandmother's tractor after coffee. Now he had not only blood on his shirt but motor oil, too.

All this while Celestine had seen her grandmother come to life again. She found herself feeling ashamed at the way she had once just left, without even saying goodbye — all because Grandma happened to have the wrong grandpa.

Shame? That was a new feeling.

Holger said he understood that Celestine had been influenced by her grandmother's evening, and he said that he was at a loss. It wasn't just the king and his monarchy that must be eradicated, it was everything the monarchy represented. So it couldn't just start to represent something different right before their eyes. The king had even sworn once. God only knows, maybe he'd even gone out to sneak a smoke with Gertrud.

438

No, Celestine didn't think he had. They had gone out together for a while, that was true, but it was probably just for the tractor.

Holger One sighed. If only the king hadn't turned his back on Gustaf V the way he'd just done.

Celestine asked if they should fetch him and try to find a compromise, and she realized she'd never used that word before.

"You mean set off the bomb just a little bit?" said Holger One. "Or that the king should abdicate part-time?"

But bringing him to the dock and talking through the situation in a peaceful, orderly manner couldn't hurt. Just the king, Holger One and Celestine. Not Two, not Gertrud, not the prime minister, and absolutely not that venomous snake Nombeko or, for that matter, the sleeping agent from Israel.

Holger didn't know exactly where the conversation should begin and where it was meant to go, and Celestine had even less of an idea. But if they chose their words carefully, maybe there was still a chance.

The king wasn't happy to leave his countess, but of course he would agree to a night-time conversation with Miss Celestine and the man whom he wasn't allowed to call "the idiot" if they wished to have one and if it might lead things in the right direction.

Holger One began the conversation on the dock by saying that the king ought to be ashamed that he couldn't behave like a king.

"We all have our shortcomings," said the king.

One continued, admitting that his beloved Celestine had allowed herself to be happy about the . . . lively relationship the king had established with Gertrud.

"The countess," the king corrected him.

Well, no matter what she was called in various camps, she was one reason why it was no longer obvious that they must blow up the king and parts of the country, even if His Majesty were to refrain from abdicating.

"That's great then," said the king. "I guess I'll choose that."

"Abdicating?"

"No, refraining from abdicating, since it will no longer have the dramatic consequences you had previously indicated."

Holger One cursed himself. He had started at the wrong end: he'd begun by discarding the only trump card he had in his hand — the threat of the bomb. Why did everything always have to go wrong — no matter what he tried to do? It was becoming more and more clear to him that he was what people called him.

The king could see that Holger One was suffering from inner turmoil and added that Mr Idiot shouldn't be too upset about the way things had turned out. After all, history shows us that it's not enough to chase a king away from the throne. It's not even enough when an entire royal line ends.

"It's not?" said Holger One.

◆ ◆ ◆

As it began to grow light in Roslagen, the king told the cautionary tale of Gustav IV Adolf, for whom things had not gone especially well, and what this had led to.

It all started when his father was shot at the Royal Opera House. The king's son had two weeks to get used to his new role while his dad lay there dying. This turned out to be far too little time. In addition, his father had succeeded in hammering into the boy that the Swedish king was given his post by the grace of God and that the king and God worked as a team.

A person who feels the Lord watching over him finds it to be a minor thing to go to war in order to defeat both the Emperor Napoleon and Tsar Alexander — all at once. Unfortunately, the emperor and the tsar also claimed to have divine protection and acted accordingly. Assuming they were all correct, God had promised a little too much in too many directions at the same time. All the Lord could do about that was to let their true relative strengths settle the matter.

Perhaps that was why Sweden took a pasting twice over, ended up with Pomerania occupied, and lost all of Finland. Gustav himself was chased off the throne by enraged counts and bitter generals. A *coup d'état*, to put it simply.

"Well, fancy that," said Holger One.

"I'm not finished yet," said the king.

The former Gustaf IV Adolf became depressed and took to the bottle. What else could he do? Since he was no longer allowed to be named what he no longer was, he started calling himself Colonel Gustavsson instead, and wandered around Europe until he died alone, alcoholic and penniless at a Swiss boarding-house.

"Well, that's excellent," said Holger One.

"If you didn't keep interrupting me, you would already have realized that there's a different point to my story," said the king. "For instance, the fact that another king was put on the throne to replace him."

"I know," said Holger One. "That's why you have to get rid of the whole family at once."

"But not even that can help," said the king, continuing his story:

"Like father, like son", as they say, and this wasn't a risk the coup-makers wanted to take. So they declared that the exile of the incompetent Gustav IV Adolf went not only for the king himself but also for his entire family, including the ten-year-old crown prince. They were all declared to have forfeited the right to the Swedish crown for all time.

The man placed on the throne instead was the brother of the murdered father of Gustav IV.

"This is starting to get out of hand," said Holger One.

"Not much longer until I make my point," said the king.

"That's good."

Anyway, the new king was called Karl XIII, and everything would have been fine and dandy if not for his only son, who lived for just one week. And no new sons seemed to be forthcoming (or perhaps they did come forth, but not from the right woman). The royal line was about to die out.

"But of course he had a solution to that, right?" said Holger.

"Oh, yes, first he adopted a princely relative, who also had the poor taste to die."

"And the solution to that?"

"To adopt a Danish prince, who also died right away of a seizure."

Holger said that if he didn't know better, he would say that the king's story was shaping up to end well.

Instead of answering, the king continued: after the fiasco with the Danish prince, they turned to France, where it turned out that Emperor Napoleon had an extra marshal. When all was said and done, *Jean Baptiste Bernadotte* was the crown prince of Sweden.

"And?"

"And he became the first member of the new dynasty. I'm a Bernadotte, too. Jean Baptiste was the great-grandfather of my great-grandfather Gustaf the Fifth, you know."

"Ugh, yes."

"It's pointless to try to kill off royal dynasties, Holger," the king said politely. "As long as people want a monarchy, you can't get rid of it. But I respect your views — after all, we do live in a democracy. Why don't you join the largest political party, the Social Democrats, and try to influence them from within? Or become a member of the Republican Association and shape public opinion?"

"Or build a statue of you and let it fall on top of me so I can be spared everything," Holger One mumbled.

"Pardon?" said the king.

♦ ♦ ♦

The sun came up before anyone in Sjölida had been even close to going to bed, except for Agent B, who was having a restless sleep while sitting on the sofa.

Nombeko and Holger Two replaced the king on the dock on Vätösund. This was the first time Holger and Holger had had a chance to exchange a few words with each other since the kidnapping.

"You promised you wouldn't touch the bomb," Holger Two said angrily.

"I know," said Holger One. "And I kept that promise all these years, didn't I? Until it ended up in the back of the truck along with the king while I was at the wheel. Then I couldn't keep it any more."

"But what were you thinking? And what are you thinking now?"

"I wasn't thinking. I seldom do — you know that. Dad was the one who told me to drive."

"Dad? But he's been dead for almost twenty years!"

"Yes — it's strange, isn't it?"

Holger Two sighed.

"I think the strangest thing of all is that we're brothers," he said.

"Don't be mean to my darling!" said Celestine.

"Shut up," said Holger Two.

Nombeko could see that One and Celestine's conviction that the best thing for the country was to obliterate themselves and an entire region was starting to waver.

444

"What are you thinking about doing now?" she asked.

"All this damn talk about thinking," said Holger One.

"I don't think we can kill someone who makes my grandma laugh," said Celestine. "She hasn't ever laughed in her life."

"And what would you be thinking, Idiot, if you were to try after all?"

"I told you not to be mean to my darling," said Celestine.

"I haven't started yet," said Nombeko.

Holger One was silent for a few seconds; then he said:

"To the extent that I think, I think it would have been easier with Gustaf the Fifth. He had a silver cane and a monocle, not chicken blood on his shirt."

"And motor oil," said Celestine.

"So you want to get out of this in the best possible way. Have I understood correctly?" said Nombeko.

"Yes," Holger One said quietly without daring to look her in the eye.

"Then start by handing over the pistol and the keys to the truck."

Holger gave her the keys first, but then he managed to drop the pistol on the dock, whereupon a shot was fired.

"Ow, damn it," Holger Two said, and collapsed.

CHAPTER
TWENTY-TWO

On a final clean-up and breaking camp

It was nearly three in the morning when the prime minister returned to Sjölida after a trip to the country road on Countess Virtanen's moped. His mobile phone had enough coverage out there for the prime minister to make a few short calls to inform the king's staff and his own, as well as the world's most relieved director of security police, that the situation was under control, that he was counting on being at the government offices some time in the morning, and that he would like his assistant to have a suit and clean shoes waiting for him.

The most acute phase of the drama seemed to be over, and no one seemed to have been hurt, except for Holger Two, who had been accidentally shot in the arm by his brother and who was now swearing in his bedroom next to the countess's kitchen. It was a substantial flesh wound, but with the help of Marshal Mannerheim's schnapps (as a combination of disinfectant and anaesthetic) and a bandage, there was reason to believe that Two would be as good as new in a few weeks. Nombeko noted lovingly that Holger Two hadn't milked his injury one bit. In fact, he was lying in bed and using a pillow to practise the art of strangling someone with just one hand.

The victim he had in mind, however, was keeping a safe distance. He and Celestine had lain down to sleep under a blanket on the dock. Meanwhile Agent B, who had been so threatening for a minute or two, was still partaking of the same activity in the kitchen. To be on the safe side, Nombeko had worked his pistol out of its holster inside his jacket. Without any further mishaps.

The king, Countess Virtanen, Nombeko and the prime minister gathered in the kitchen with the sleeping agent. The king wondered happily what was next on the agenda. The prime minister was too tired to become more irritated with the king than he already was. Instead he turned to Nombeko and requested a private conversation.

"Shall we go and sit in the cab of the potato truck?" she said.

The prime minister nodded.

The head of the Swedish government turned out to be as bright as he was good at drying dishes. He first confessed that what he wanted to do most of all was report everyone at Sjölida to the police — including the king for his general lack of concern.

But upon closer consideration, the prime minister had looked at things more pragmatically. For one thing, kings can't be prosecuted. And perhaps it wouldn't be quite fair to try to get Holger Two and Nombeko locked up; if anything, they had done their best to bring order to the chaos. Nor was the countess really guilty of any crime either, the prime minister reasoned. Especially if one refrained from checking to see if she had a valid licence for that moose-hunting rifle she had waved around earlier.

That left the agent from a foreign nation's intelligence agency. And the idiot and his girlfriend, of course. The latter two probably deserved a few hundred years each in as secure a facility as possible, but it might be both easiest and best if the country dispensed with this tempting vendetta. After all, any legal action would require a prosecutor to ask questions, and in this case the answers risked causing lifelong trauma to tens of thousands of citizens, no matter how such answers were formulated. An atomic bomb on the loose. Right in the middle of Sweden. For twenty years.

The prime minister shuddered; then he continued his argument. The fact was, he had found yet another reason to refrain from legal action. When he was out on the country road with the moped, he had first called the director of Säpo to calm him down; then he called his assistant with a practical question.

But he hadn't raised the alarm.

An overzealous prosecutor, egged on by the opposition, might very well try to claim that the prime minister himself had prolonged the drama and contributed to something unlawful.

"Hmm," Nombeko said thoughtfully. "Such as 'causing danger to others', according to the third chapter, ninth paragraph of the criminal code."

"Two years?" asked the prime minister, who was starting to suspect that Nombeko knew absolutely everything.

"Yes," said Nombeko. "Considering the potential for devastation, one probably shouldn't hope for a single day less than that. Not to mention driving a moped without a helmet. If I know Sweden, that might be another fifteen years."

The prime minister thought about the future. He was hoping to take over as president of the Council of the European Union in the summer of 2009. Sitting in prison until then would not be the best way to prepare for that. Not to mention the part where he would be fired as prime minister and party leader.

So he asked the clever Nombeko for her opinion on how they could all get out of this, given that their goal was to send as much as possible of as many of the last twenty-four hours' events as possible into eternal oblivion.

Nombeko said that she didn't know anyone who could clean up as well as the prime minister. The kitchen was sparkling clean after the chicken casserole, beer, schnapps, coffee and everything. All that was left was . . . to clean up the sleeping agent, wasn't it?

The prime minister frowned.

Along the same lines, Nombeko thought that the most pressing matter was to separate the idiot and his girlfriend from the bomb. And then to lock it up in some bunker somewhere.

The prime minister was tired; it was so late that it would be more accurate to say it was early. He confessed that he was having trouble formulating his thoughts and words. But he'd had time to think about that bunker part himself while his brain was still working. About having the bomb disarmed there, or at least walling it in and suppressing the memory of its existence.

Now, the fact is that time is no kinder to prime ministers than it is to anyone else. Sometimes, in fact, it's the opposite. The next thing on Fredrik Reinfeldt's official agenda was a meeting with President Hu at the government offices; it was to begin at ten o'clock, and it would be followed by lunch at the prime minister's residence, the Sager House. Before then, he wanted to have a shower so he didn't smell like a potato field and to change into clothes and shoes that weren't covered with mud.

If the group managed to get going soon, it might work. But it was going to be hard to find time to locate a deep and remote bunker to hide and forget the atomic bomb in along the way. That would have to wait until the afternoon — no matter how important it was.

The prime minister was ordinarily a man who listened, seldom speaking very much. Now he was surprised at how frank he was being with Nombeko Mayeki. Although maybe it wasn't that surprising after all. We all need someone to share our innermost thoughts with, and with whom could he discuss the three-megaton problem that was weighing on them if not with the South African woman and perhaps her boyfriend?

The prime minister realized he needed to increase the number of people who knew about this greatest of secrets. He planned to start with the supreme commander of the armed forces, who had the ultimate responsibility for that bunker, wherever it might be. Since the SC probably couldn't disarm the bomb or wall up the bunker entrance behind himself all on his own, another person or two would need to be involved. That meant that the following people, at the least, would know what they ought not to: (1) the supreme commander, (2) disarmer A, (3) bricklayer B, (4) the illegal immigrant Nombeko Mayeki, (5) the nonexistent Holger Qvist, (6) his far-too-existent brother, (7) the brother's irascible girlfriend, (8) a former potato farmer and current countess, (9) His Unconcerned Majesty the King, as well as (10) a retired Mossad agent.

"There is no way this can end well," said Prime Minister Reinfeldt.

"Yes it can," said Nombeko. "Most of the people you just listed have every reason in the world to keep quiet about what they know. Plus, some of them are so confused that no one would believe them if they did tell."

"Are you thinking of the king?" said the prime minister.

The prime minister and Hu Jintao were to enjoy lunch at the Sager House in the company of some of Sweden's most important industry leaders. Afterwards, President Hu would go straight to Arlanda Airport, where his very own Boeing 767 was waiting to transport him to Beijing. Only then would the supreme commander be summoned to the government offices.

"In this case, do I dare trust Miss Nombeko with the bomb while I'm with Hu and for the time it will take to bring the SC in on the matter?"

"Well, Prime Minister, I'm sure you know best what you do and do not dare to do. But I've been jointly responsible for that thing for twenty years already, and it hasn't blown up yet. I'm sure I can manage a few more hours."

At that very moment, Nombeko saw the king and the countess leaving the kitchen and making their way down to the dock. It was possible that they were up to something. Nombeko thought fast.

"Dear Mr Prime Minister. Go to the kitchen and deal with the Mossad agent in accordance with the intelligence I know you possess. Meanwhile, I'll go down to the dock and make sure that the king and his countess don't get up to anything stupid."

Fredrik Reinfeldt understood what Nombeko was getting at. His entire being told him that one couldn't do something like that.

Then he sighed — and went in to do something like that.

"Wake up!"

The prime minister shook Agent B until he opened his eyes and remembered, with great horror, where he was.

When Fredrik Reinfeldt saw that the agent was responsive, he looked him in the eye and said:

452

"I see that your car is sitting outside. I suggest — for the sake of the good relationship between the people of Sweden and Israel — that you immediately get into it, drive away from here and leave the country at once. I further suggest that you were never here and that you never come back."

The honest prime minister felt physically ill at the thought that within a few hours he had not only committed potato thievery but was also now about to send an intoxicated man out in traffic. Plus everything else.

"But Prime Minister Olmert?" said Agent B.

"I have nothing to discuss with him, because you were never here. Right?"

Agent B was certainly not sober. Moreover, he was half asleep. But he realized that he had just got his life back.

And that he had to hurry, before the head of the Swedish government changed his mind.

Fredrik Reinfeldt was one of Sweden's most honest people, the sort of person who had paid his television licence fee ever since he had lived in his very first student apartment. The sort who, even as a child, had offered a receipt when he sold a bunch of leeks to his neighbour for twenty-five öre.

No wonder, then, that he now felt the way he did as he let Agent B go. And as he made up his mind that all the rest of it should be hushed up. Buried. The bomb, too. In a bunker. If only it would work.

Nombeko returned with an oar under one arm and said that she had just stopped the countess and the king from rowing out to poach fish. When the prime minister didn't answer, and since Nombeko could see the tail-lights of Mossad Agent B's hire car as it left Sjölida, she added:

"Sometimes it's impossible to do the right thing, Prime Minister. Just more or less wrong. The final clean-up of the countess's kitchen was in the best interests of the country. You mustn't have a guilty conscience over that."

The prime minister was silent for a few more seconds. Then he said, "Thank you, Miss Nombeko."

Nombeko and the prime minister went down to the dock to have a serious talk with Holger One and his Celestine. Both had fallen asleep under their blanket, and next to them, in a row and partaking of the same activity, lay the king and the countess.

"Get up now, Idiot, or I'll kick you into the water," said Nombeko, nudging him with her foot (she was carrying around an inner frustration that could not be relieved in any other way than by twisting his nose — at the very least).

The two former kidnappers sat up on the dock while the rest of the knocked-out gang woke up. The prime minister began by saying that he was planning to refrain from turning the kidnapping, the threats and everything else into a police matter, as long as Holger and Celestine cooperated to the fullest from now on.

Both nodded.

454

"What happens now, Nombeko?" said Holger One. "We don't have anywhere to live. My studio in Blackeberg won't work, because Celestine wants to bring her grandma along if Grandma wants to come."

"Weren't we going to poach fish?" said the newly awakened countess.

"No, first and foremost we're going to survive the night," said the prime minister.

"A good ambition," said the king. "A bit defensive, but good."

And then he added that it might be just as well that he and the countess had never set out in that rowing-boat. KING SEIZED FOR POACHING FISH was probably a headline that malevolent journalists could not have resisted.

The prime minister thought that no journalist on earth, malevolent or not, would voluntarily resist that headline as long as it had earning capacity. Instead he said that he would appreciate it if His Majesty dismissed all thoughts of criminal action from his mind, for the number of crimes already committed on this night could fill an entire district court.

The king thought he could poach fish as much as he wanted, given who he was, but he had enough sense, and by a decent margin, not to say this to the prime minister.

Thus Fredrik Reinfeldt could continue the all-round salvaging of situation and nation. He turned to Countess Virtanen and entreated her to give a short and plain answer to the question of whether she wanted to leave Sjölida with her granddaughter and her boyfriend.

Well, the countess had noticed that her zest for life had returned. This was probably because she had got to be with her beloved Celestine for so long, and because of the king, who had turned out to be so knowledgeable about Finnish-Swedish history and its traditions. And, of course, the potato field had already been sold, and, to be honest, being the publisher of a magazine had been pretty boring for the short time it had lasted.

"And besides, I'm sick of being single. Might the king know some second-hand baron to introduce me to? He doesn't have to be handsome."

The king said that barons were in short supply, but this was as far as he got before the prime minister interrupted him, saying that this wasn't the time to discuss the existence of second-hand barons, ugly or otherwise, because it was time for all of them to leave. So the countess was planning on coming along?

Yes, she was. But where would they live? Old ladies could be lodged in any old cottage, but countesses had their reputations to think of.

Nombeko thought things were getting out of control. But there was quite a bit of money left from the potato farm, enough for housing worthy of the countess and her court. And more besides.

"Pending an available castle, I suppose we'll have to check you into a respectable establishment. A suite at the Grand Hôtel in Stockholm — would that do?"

"Yes, for a transitional period," said the countess, while the former MLCP(R) rebel Celestine squeezed her grimacing boyfriend's hand hard.

◆ ◆ ◆

It was six in the morning before the potato truck with the atomic bomb was once again on the road. Behind the wheel was the prime minister, the only one of them who was both a licensed driver and sober enough to drive. Nombeko was on the right, and Holger Two, his arm in a sling, was in the middle.

In the back of the truck, the king and Countess Virtanen were still going strong. The king had a number of tips regarding her future housing. The classical palace of Pöckstein near Strasbourg in Austria was for sale and might possibly be worthy of the countess. It was just an awfully long way from Drottningholm, for afternoon tea. So Södertuna Castle would be better; it actually wasn't too far from Gnesta. From medieval times. But maybe it would be too simple for the countess?

The countess couldn't say for certain. They would have to view each available lodging and get a sense of what was simple and what wasn't.

The king wondered if he and the queen could come on some of the planned viewings. Not least the queen could be of service with advice on what attributes any palace garden worth its name must have.

Yes, by all means, that would be nice, if they wished. It might be nice to meet the queen in a different environment from when one was doing one's business in an outhouse.

The king was dropped off first, at 7.30 a.m. outside Drottningholm Palace. He rang the bell and had to argue for a while that he was who he said he was before he was finally let in by an embarrassed guard commander. Who noticed as the king passed that he had dark red spots on his shirt.

"Is His Majesty hurt?" the guard called after his king.

"No, it's chicken blood," said the king. "And a little motor oil."

The next stop was the Grand Hôtel. But here the logistics became thorny. Holger Two had a fever from being accidentally shot by his brother. Two ought to be put to bed and given painkillers, because the bottle of Mannerheim's schnapps was empty.

"So you think I'm going to check into a hotel and let myself be looked after by the fool who just nearly killed me?" said Holger Two. "I'd rather lie down on a park bench and bleed out."

But Nombeko cajoled him, promising that he would get to strangle his brother, or at least twist his nose (if she didn't get there first), but that this couldn't happen until his arm had healed. Wouldn't it be extraordinarily ironic if he were to lie down and bleed to death on the very day they were about to get rid of the bomb?

Holger Two was too tired to contradict her.

By about twenty to nine, Two had been put to bed and served double Treo tablets for his fever and pain.

He drained the glass and fell asleep in fifteen seconds. Holger One lay down on the sofa in the suite's sitting room to do the same, while Countess Virtanen set about investigating the minibar in the bedroom.

"You all go on. I can take care of myself."

The prime minister, Nombeko and Celestine were standing outside the entrance of the hotel in order to work out the details of what they had to do during the next few hours.

Reinfeldt would leave to meet Hu Jintao. Nombeko and Celestine were supposed to spend that time driving around central Stockholm with the bomb, as carefully as possible.

Celestine would be behind the wheel; there was no other chauffeur available. Holger Two, of course, had been shot and put to bed, and the prime minister himself couldn't continue to drive around with the horrible weapon while also meeting the president of China.

That left the unpredictable, formerly young, possibly just as angry woman. Under Nombeko's supervision, but still.

While the trio was still standing outside the entrance to the hotel, the prime minister's assistant called to tell him that his suit and clean shoes awaited him at the government offices. But they had also had a call from the Chinese president's staff, raising a concern. The president's interpreter had been badly injured the evening before, and had just been operated on at Karolinska Hospital for four broken fingers and one crushed thumb. The president had asked his co-workers to suggest that the prime minister might have a convenient solution to the interpreter problem for the morning's meeting and the following lunch. The assistant suspected that he was referring to the black woman she had met briefly outside the palace. Might that be the case? And if it was, did the prime minister know where she could be found?

Yes, the prime minister did know. He asked his assistant to hold on for a second and turned to Nombeko.

"Might you consider attending the morning meeting between me and the president of the People's Republic of China, Miss Nombeko? The president's interpreter is in the hospital."

"And complaining that he's about to die?" said Nombeko.

Before the prime minister had time to ask what she meant by that, she added, "Absolutely. Of course I can do that. But what will we do with the truck, the bomb and Celestine in the meantime?"

Letting Celestine be alone with the truck and the bomb for several hours felt . . . not good. Nombeko's first idea for a solution had been to handcuff her to the steering wheel. But her next idea was better. She returned to the suite and was soon back.

"Your boyfriend is now chained to the sofa he is snoring so beautifully on. If you do anything stupid with the truck and the bomb while the prime minister and I meet the president of China, I promise I will throw the key to the handcuffs into Nybroviken."

Celestine snorted in reply.

Prime Minister Reinfeldt rang two of his bodyguards and asked them to come to the Grand to pick up Nombeko and himself in a car with maximally tinted windows. Celestine's orders were to stay in the first car park she saw until he or Nombeko called her. It would just be a few hours, the prime minister promised, longing so hard to reach the end of the yesterday that was still going on that he was about to burst.

CHAPTER
TWENTY-THREE

On an angry supreme commander and a beautifully singing woman

Fredrik Reinfeldt sat down in one of the easy chairs in his office with a sandwich and a triple espresso. He had just undergone a renovation in the form of a shower, fresh clothes and mud-free shoes. Already sitting in the other easy chair was his South African Chinese interpreter with a cup of Swedish tea in hand. In the same clothes as the day before. On the other hand, she hadn't been digging in any potato fields.

"Ah, so that's what you looked like before you got dirty," said Nombeko.

"What time is it?" said the prime minister.

It was twenty minutes to ten. There was time to prepare the interpreter.

The prime minister said that he was planning to invite Hu Jintao to the climate change summit in Copenhagen in 2009, which would take place at the same time as he himself would become the president of the EU Council.

"There will probably be some talk about the environment and various efforts in that field," he said.

"I want China to be a part of the upcoming climate treaty."

"Well, how about that," said Nombeko.

One controversial matter was that the prime minister also planned to discuss Sweden's views on democracy and human rights. At those points, it was extra important for Nombeko to interpret word for word, rather than in her own words.

"Anything else?" said Nombeko.

Well, they would also be discussing business, of course. Imports and exports. China was on its way to being increasingly important to Sweden as an exporter as well.

"We export twenty-two billion kronor's worth of Swedish goods on a yearly basis," said the prime minister.

"Twenty point eight," said Nombeko.

The prime minister emptied his espresso and inwardly confirmed that he was experiencing the most bizarre twenty-four hours of his life by a nearly infinite margin.

"What else does the interpreter have to add?" he said.

He said this without sarcasm.

Nombeko thought it was good that the meeting would be about democracy and human rights, because then, afterwards, the prime minister could say that the meeting had been about democracy and human rights.

She's a cynic, too, in all her brilliance, thought Fredrik Reinfeldt.

♦ ♦ ♦

"Prime Minister. It's an honour to meet you, now that circumstances are more orderly." President Hu smiled, extending his hand. "And you, Miss Nombeko — our paths cross again and again. Most agreeable, I must say."

Nombeko said that she felt the same, but that they would have to wait a bit longer to talk safari memories, because otherwise the prime minister would probably become impatient.

"By the way, he's planning to come out of the gate with a few things about democracy and human rights, which he thinks you aren't very good at. And he's probably completely on the wrong track there. But don't worry, Mr President, I think he'll mince along pretty carefully. Let's get on with it — are you ready?"

Hu Jintao made a face at what was coming, but he didn't lose his temper. The South African woman was far too charming for that. Besides, this was the first time he'd worked with an interpreter who translated what had been said even before it had been said. Or the second time. The same thing had happened once in South Africa, many years earlier.

Sure enough, the prime minister moved forward cautiously. He described the Swedish view of democracy, emphasized Swedish values regarding free speech, offered his friends in the People's Republic support in developing similar traditions. And then, in a low voice, he demanded the release of the country's political prisoners.

464

Nombeko interpreted, but before Hu Jintao had time to answer, she added, on her own authority, that what the prime minister was really trying to say was that they couldn't lock up authors and journalists just because they wrote objectionable things. Or displace people, censure the Internet . . .

"What are you saying now?" said the prime minister.

He had noticed that her translation was twice as long as might reasonably be expected.

"I was just passing on what you said, Prime Minister, and then I explained what you meant by it to help the conversation move along a little faster. Both of us are a bit too tired to sit here all day, aren't we?"

"Explained what I meant? Did I not make myself clear enough earlier? This is top-level diplomacy — the interpreter can't just sit there making things up!"

By all means. Nombeko promised to try to make things up as little as possible from now on, and she turned to President Hu to say that the prime minister wasn't happy with what she'd added to the conversation.

"That's understandable," said Hu Jintao. "But interpret this: say I've absorbed the prime minister's and Miss Nombeko's words and that I possess the good political sense to tell them apart."

At this, Hu Jintao began a lengthy reply, which brought up Guantánamo in Cuba, where prisoners had been sitting for five years while waiting to find out what they were charged with. Unfortunately the president, too, was fully aware of the regrettable incident in 2002 when Sweden had obediently done what the CIA told them to do and deported two Egyptians to prison and torture, whereupon it turned out that at least one of them happened to be innocent.

The president and prime minister continued to exchange words and sentences for another few rounds of this before Fredrik Reinfeldt thought they'd done enough. And so he turned to the environment. This part of the conversation flowed more smoothly.

A little while later, they were served tea and cake — the interpreter, too. In the informal atmosphere that a coffee circle often brings, the president took the opportunity discreetly to deliver a comment in which he expressed hope that yesterday's drama had by now been resolved for the better.

Yes, thanks, the prime minister said that it had, without sounding completely convincing. Nombeko could tell that Hu Jintao wanted to know more, and out of sheer politeness, she added — over Reinfeldt's head — that the bomb had been locked into a bunker and that the entrance had been walled over for good. Then she thought that perhaps she shouldn't have said what she'd just said, but that at least it hadn't been completely made up.

When he was younger, Hu Jintao had done a bit of work with nuclear weapons-related issues (it had started with his trip to South Africa), and he was curious about the bomb in question on behalf of his country. Of course, it was a few decades old, and China didn't need a bomb; the Chinese military had plenty of megatons already. But if all the intelligence reports were correct, the bomb in disassembled form could give China a unique look into South African — that is, Israeli — nuclear weapons technology. And that, in turn, could become an important piece of the puzzle in the analysis of the relationship and relative strengths between Israel and Iran. As it happened, the Iranians were good friends to the Chinese. Or halfway good. Oil and natural gas flowed east from Iran, while at the same time China had never had more trying allies than those in Tehran (with the exception of Pyongyang). Among other things, they were hopelessly difficult to read. Were they in the process of building their own nuclear weapons? Or were they just making a lot of noise with rhetoric and the conventional weapons they already had?

Nombeko interrupted Hu Jintao's thoughts:

"I think I can tell that you're speculating about the bomb, Mr President. Shall I ask the prime minister if he's prepared to give it to you? As a gift to cement peace and friendship between your countries?"

While President Hu thought that there might be better gifts of peace than a three-megaton atom bomb, Nombeko continued to speak, arguing that China already had so many bombs of that sort that one more or less could hardly do any harm. In any case, she was sure that Reinfeldt would be very happy to see the bomb disappear to the other side of the Earth. Or even farther, if it were possible.

Hu Jintao replied that it certainly was in the nature of atomic bombs to do harm, undesirable as that may be. But even if Miss Nombeko was correct in guessing that he was interested in the Swedish bomb, he could

467

hardly ask the prime minister for that sort of favour. So he asked Nombeko to go back to her interpreting before the prime minister had reason to become irritated once again.

But it was too late:

"What are you talking about, for God's sake?" the prime minister said angrily. "You were supposed to interpret. Nothing more!"

"Yes, I'm sorry, Mr Prime Minister. I'm just trying to solve a problem for him," said Nombeko. "But it didn't go well. You two go ahead and keep talking. Environment and human rights and such."

The prime minister's recurring feeling about the past twenty-four hours came back again. The thing that could not possibly be happening this time was that his own interpreter had gone from kidnapping people to kidnapping conversations with the head of state of another country.

During lunch Nombeko earned the fee she had neither asked for nor been offered. She kept up a lively conversation between President Hu, the prime minister, and the CEOs of Volvo, Electrolux and Ericsson — and she hardly inserted herself at all. There were just a few instances when her tongue happened to slip a bit. Such as when President Hu thanked the CEO of Volvo a second time for the fantastic gift the other day and added that the Chinese themselves couldn't build such nice cars, and instead of saying the same thing once again, Nombeko suggested that he and his country might as well purchase all of Volvo so they didn't have to be jealous any more.

Or when the CEO of Electrolux was discussing the way the company's various products were performing in China, and Nombeko sold Hu the idea that, in his capacity as secretary of China's Communist Party, he might consider a little Electrolux-encouragement for all the loyal members of the party.

Hu thought this was such a lovely idea that he asked the CEO of Electrolux, right there at the table, what kind of rebate he might be offered if he put in an order for 68,742,000 electric kettles.

"How many?" said the CEO of Electrolux.

♦ ♦ ♦

The supreme commander was on holiday in Liguria when he was summoned by the prime minister, via his assistant. He quite simply had to come home — it wasn't formulated as a request from the government offices, but as an order. It was a matter of national security. The SC must be prepared to present "the current status with regard to military bunkers" in Sweden.

The SC confirmed that he had received the order, and then he spent ten minutes pondering what the prime minister could possibly want before he gave up and requested a JAS 39 Gripen for a flight home at the speed the prime minister had indirectly decreed (that is, twice the speed of sound).

But the Swedish Air Force can't land and take off at just any old airfield in northern Italy; rather, it was directed to Christopher Columbus Airport in Genoa, which was a two-hour trip for the SC, given the traffic that always and without exception prevailed on the A10 and along the Italian Riviera. He would not make it to the government offices before four thirty, no matter how many sound barriers he broke along the way.

♦   ♦   ♦

The lunch at the Sager House was over. There were still several hours left before the meeting with the SC. The prime minister felt that he ought to be with the bomb, but he decided to trust Nombeko and the untrustworthy Celestine for a little while longer. The fact was, he was totally, terribly exhausted after having been involved in absolutely everything without any sleep for more than thirty hours. He decided to take a nap in his office.

Nombeko and Celestine followed his lead, but in the cab of the truck in a parking spot in Tallkrogen.

♦   ♦   ♦

Meanwhile it was time for the Chinese president and his entourage to journey homewards. Hu Jintao was pleased with his visit, but not even half as pleased as his first lady, Liu Yongqing, was. While her husband had devoted his Sunday to politics and boiled cod with butter sauce, she and a few women in the delegation had had time for two fabulous field trips. The first was

470

to the farmers' market in Västerås; after that they had gone to a stud farm in Knivsta.

In Västerås, the first lady had rejoiced over exciting, genuine Swedish handicrafts before she came to a stand with a variety of imported knickknacks. And in the middle of it all — the first lady didn't believe her eyes! — an authentic Han dynasty pottery goose. When Liu Yongqing asked three times, in her limited English, whether the seller was really asking the price he quoted, he thought she was haggling and became angry:

"Yes, that's what I said! I *will* have twenty kronor for the piece and not one öre less!"

The goose had once been included in a few boxes of junk he bought from an estate sale in Sörmland (the now-dead man had, in turn, bought the goose from a strange American at Malma Market for thirty-nine kronor, but of course the current seller didn't know that). He was actually tired of the piece, but the foreign woman's manners had been so gauche, and she had clucked with her friends in a language that no one could understand. So now the price he'd set was a matter of principle. Twenty kronor or no deal. It was as simple as that.

In the end, the old woman had paid up after all — five dollars! So she couldn't count, either.

The seller was satisfied; the first lady was happy. And she would become even more so when she fell madly in love with the three-year-old black Caspian stallion Morpheus at the stud farm in Knivsta. The horse had all the attributes of a full-grown, normal-size horse — but he was no more than three feet tall at the withers and, like Caspian horses in general, would never get any taller.

"Must have!" said Liu Yongqing, who had developed a unique ability to get her way since becoming the first lady.

But because of everything the entourage wanted to bring back to Beijing, Cargo City at Arlanda Airport demanded a ridiculous amount of paperwork. There they had not only every practical tool for loading and unloading, but also full knowledge of what stamps were needed in which circumstances. The valuable Han dynasty goose slipped past. But things didn't go as smoothly with the horse.

The president was already sitting in his presidential chair on his presidential plane, asking his secretary why their departure was being delayed. In reply he was told that the small problem was that the shipment with the president's Volvo from Torslanda still had about fifteen miles to go before it arrived, but that things weren't going quite as well with the horse the first lady had bought. They were so strange at this airport: they seemed to act as though rules were there to be followed, and it didn't matter that it was the Chinese president's plane they were talking about.

His secretary admitted that these conversations had been a bit tough to conduct, since the interpreter was still in hospital and wouldn't be well enough to leave with them. The secretary had no intention of burdening the president with all the details, but the short version was that the delegation would very much like to call

472

upon that South African woman one last time, if the president thought it was advisable. Thus they wondered if they could have permission from the president to ask her.

This is how it came to be that Nombeko and Celestine were awakened by a phone call as they lay head to foot in the cab in the parking space, and they took off for Cargo City at Arlanda with potato truck, bomb and all to help the president of China and his delegation with their various Customs declarations.

◆ ◆ ◆

If you don't think you have enough problems, you should acquire a mammal in Sweden just hours before you're about to fly home to the other side of the world, and then insist that the animal must travel in your luggage.

One of the things that Nombeko was supposed to help with was getting the Board of Agriculture to issue a valid certificate of export for the Caspian horse that had looked deep into the eyes of First Lady Liu Yongqing a few hours earlier.

The horse must also have proof of vaccination to show to the correct representative of the authorities at the airport. Since Morpheus was Caspian and the destination of the journey was Beijing, the general regulations from the Chinese Board of Agriculture required a Coggins test in order to make sure that the horse, which had been born and raised in Knivsta, six hundred miles south of the Arctic Circle, wasn't suffering from swamp fever.

Furthermore there must be sedatives on the plane — syringes to inject the horse with should it panic while airborne. Plus a slaughtering mask in the event that things and the horse got completely out of control.

Last but not least, the district veterinarian from the Board of Agriculture had to examine the animal and be there to identify it at the airport. When it turned out that the director of the district veterinary office for Stockholm County was on a business trip in Reykjavik, Nombeko gave up.

"I have become aware that this problem demands an alternative solution," she said.

"What are you thinking?" said Celestine.

Once Nombeko had solved the horse problem for Hu Jintao's wife, she had reason to hurry back to the government offices to give a report. It was important that she get there before the supreme commander did, so she chose to hop into a taxi after having given Celestine a strict admonition not to call attention to herself or the potato truck while in traffic. Celestine promised not to, and she would surely have kept her promise if only the radio hadn't happened to play Billy Idol.

What happened about twenty miles north of Stockholm was that a traffic jam formed as the result of an accident. Nombeko and the taxi made it through, but Celestine and the potato truck got caught in the rapidly growing lines of cars. According to the account she gave later, it is physically impossible to sit in a stationary vehicle while the radio is playing "Dancing with Myself". Thus she chose to keep going forward, in the bus lane.

This is how it came to be that a head-banging woman in a potato truck with stolen licence plates passed an unmarked police car in the line of waiting cars north of Rotebro on the wrong side — and was immediately stopped for a talking-to as a result.

While the police inspector checked the licence number and learned that it belonged to a Fiat Ritmo whose plates had been reported stolen many years ago, his trainee colleague went up to Celestine, who rolled down the window.

"You can't drive in the bus lane, accident or no," said the trainee. "May I see your licence, please?"

"No, you can't, you pig bastard," said Celestine.

A few tumultuous minutes later, she had been stashed in the back seat of the police car, in handcuffs not unlike her own. All while the people in the non-moving cars around them took pictures like mad.

The police inspector had many long years of service behind him, and he explained in a calm voice to the young lady that she might as well tell them who she was, who owned the truck, and why she was driving around with stolen licence plates. Meanwhile the trainee investigated the back of the truck. There was a large crate in it, and if one were to bend it just right at one corner, one could probably get it . . . yes, there it went.

"What on earth?" said the trainee, and he immediately called his inspector over to show him.

Soon the police officers were back with the handcuffed Celestine to ask more questions, this time about the contents of the crate. But by now she had caught up with herself.

"What was it you said, you wanted to know my name?" she said.

"Very much so," said the still-calm inspector.

"Édith Piaf," said Celestine.

And then she began to sing the long-cherished words of "*Non, je ne regrette rien*": No, no regrets . . . no regrets — none at all . . .

Still singing, she was taken to the Stockholm police station by the inspector. During the trip, the inspector thought that you could say what you wanted about working as a police officer, but it was always interesting.

The trainee was assigned the task of cautiously bringing the truck to the same place.

♦ ♦ ♦

At four thirty on Sunday, 10 June 2007, the Chinese national plane took off from Stockholm Arlanda, destination Beijing.

At about the same time, Nombeko got back to the government offices. She managed to talk her way into the most holy of places by getting hold of the prime minister's assistant and explaining that she had important President Hu-related information for her boss.

Nombeko was let into the prime minister's office a few minutes before it was time for the supreme commander to make his entrance. Fredrik Reinfeldt looked much more alert now: he had slept for almost an hour and a half while Nombeko was out at Arlanda doing magic with papers, horses and other things. Now he wondered what she had on her chest. He had imagined that they wouldn't speak again until after the SC had been brought in and it was time for . . . as it were . . . terminal storage.

Well, the prime minister needed to know that circumstances had just rendered the meeting with the supreme commander unnecessary. However, it would probably be a good idea to give President Hu a call as soon as possible.

Nombeko went on, telling him about the pony-size Caspian horse and the nearly infinite amount of bureaucracy that was required if the animal were not to remain on the ground, which the first lady and her husband would find generally irritating. Instead, Nombeko had thought of an unconventional solution: to let the horse share space with the already properly declared Volvo that the president had received from Volvo at Torslanda on Friday.

"Do I really want to know this?" the prime minister interrupted her.

"I'm afraid that it's best you do know," said Nombeko. "Because the fact is, the horse didn't fit in that crate with the Volvo. But if one were to tie up the animal and shut it into the crate with the atomic bomb and move all the documentation from one crate to the other, Sweden would get rid of both Caspian horse and bomb in a single trip."

"Do you mean to say —" said the prime minister, stopping in the middle of his sentence.

"I am sure that President Hu will be delighted to take the bomb home: it will supply his technicians with all sorts of details. And after all, China is already full of medium- and long-range missiles — surely one three-megaton bomb more or less won't make any difference. And just think how happy the president's wife will be to have the horse! It's just a pity that the Volvo ended up staying in Sweden. We have it in the back of the potato truck. Perhaps you could assign someone to ship it over to China as quickly as possible, Prime Minister? What do you think?"

Fredrik Reinfeldt did not faint as a result of the information he had just received, because he didn't have time to. His assistant was knocking on the door to inform him that the supreme commander had arrived and was waiting outside.

♦   ♦   ♦

Just a few hours earlier, the SC had been sitting there eating a late breakfast with his wife and their three children by the harbour in lovely San Remo. After the alert from the government offices, he had hurried into a taxi to go all the way to Genoa, where he was picked up by a textbook example of the pride of the Swedish Air Force, the JAS 39 Gripen, which took him to Sweden, to the military airfield Uppsala-Ärna, at twice the speed of sound and a cost of 320,000 kronor. From there he was taken by car and was delayed by a few minutes because there had been an accident on the E4. While the traffic stood still, the SC witnessed a bit of everyday drama on the side of the road. The police had stopped the female driver of a truck before the very eyes of the SC. The woman had been handcuffed, and then she started singing something in French. A strange incident.

And after that, his meeting with the prime minister was even stranger. The SC had been worried that they were on the brink of war, given the emphasis with which the head of state had summoned him home. Now the prime minister was just sitting there, asking for reassurance that the Swedish bunkers were in working order and serving their purposes.

The SC replied that, as far as he knew, they were all fulfilling their functions, and there were certainly a few empty spots here and there, depending on what the prime minister wanted to put in storage, of course . . .?

"Great," said the prime minister. "Then I won't trouble you any longer, Supreme Commander. After all, I hear you're on holiday."

When the SC had finished mulling over what had happened and decided that it was impossible to understand, his confusion turned into irritation. Why couldn't he take a holiday in peace? Finally he called the pilot of the JAS 39 Gripen training plane that had picked him up earlier that day, which was still at the military airfield north of Uppsala.

"Hi, the SC here. Listen, could you be a pal and fly me down to Italy again?"

There went another 320,000 kronor. Plus another eight thousand, since the SC decided to engage a helicopter taxi for the trip to the airport. Incidentally, he made the trip in a thirteen-year-old Sikorsky S-76, which had once been purchased with the insurance money from a stolen machine of the same type.

The SC made it to San Remo for the evening's shellfish dinner with his family with fifteen minutes to spare.

"How was your meeting with the prime minister, darling?" said his wife.

"I'm thinking of changing parties for the next election," the supreme commander replied.

◆ ◆ ◆

President Hu took the call from the Swedish prime minister while he was still airborne. He really never used his limited English for international political conversations, but he made an exception this time. He was far too curious about what Prime Minister Reinfeldt might want. And they hadn't got very many seconds into the conversation before he burst out laughing. Miss Nombeko was truly something special, didn't the prime minister agree?

The Volvo had certainly been nice, but what the president had been given instead was absolutely a cut above. Plus, his beloved wife was so pleased that the horse had come too.

"I'll make sure the car is shipped to you as soon as possible, Mr President," Fredrik Reinfeldt promised, wiping his forehead.

"Yes, or my interpreter could drive it home," Hu Jintao mused. "If he ever gets better. No, wait! Give it to Miss Nombeko. I think she deserves it."

In return, President Hu promised not to use the bomb in its current condition. Rather, it would immediately be taken apart into small pieces and would thus cease to exist. Perhaps Prime Minister Reinfeldt would like to hear about whatever the president's nuclear technicians learned along the way?

No, Prime Minster Reinfeldt would not like that. This was knowledge that his country (or the king's) could do without.

Said Fredrik Reinfeldt, thanking President Hu once again for his visit.

◆ ◆ ◆

Nombeko returned to the suite at the Grand Hôtel and unlocked the handcuffs on the still-sleeping Holger One. After that, she kissed the equally asleep Holger Two on the forehead and put a blanket over the countess, who had fallen asleep on the carpeted floor next to the minibar in the bedroom. Then she went back to her Two, lay down beside him, closed her eyes — and actually had time to wonder what had become of Celestine before she dozed off herself.

She woke up at quarter past twelve the next afternoon to One, Two and the countess announcing

481

that lunch was served. Gertrud had slept the most uncomfortably, on the floor beside the minibar, so she was the first to get back on her feet. For lack of anything better to do, she had started to page through the hotel's information booklet — and discovered something fantastic. The hotel had arranged things so that first you worked out what you wanted and then you picked up the phone and told the person on the other end what you wanted, and that person in turn thanked you for calling and then, without delay, delivered what you had asked for.

Apparently it had an English name: "room service". Countess Virtanen didn't care what it was called, or which language it was called it in — could it really work in practice?

She had started by ordering a bottle of Marshal Mannerheim's schnapps as a test — and it had arrived, even if it took an hour for the hotel to get it there. Then she ordered clothes for herself and the others, giving her best guess on the sizes. That time it took two hours. And now a three-course meal for everyone, except little Celestine. She wasn't there. Did Nombeko know where she might be?

The newly awakened Nombeko didn't know. But it was clear that something had happened.

"Did she disappear with the bomb?" said Holger Two, feeling his fever rising at the very thought.

"No, we've got rid of the bomb once and for all, my love," said Nombeko. "This is the first day of the rest of our lives. I'll explain later, but let's eat now. Then I think I'd like to shower and change my clothes for the

482

first time in a few days before we look for Celestine. Very good initiative on the clothes, Countess!"

Lunch would have tasted wonderful if it weren't for the fact that Holger One sat there moaning about his missing girlfriend. What if she had set the bomb off without him?

Nombeko said, between bites, that if Celestine had done what he'd just guessed, Holger probably would have been involved whether he liked it or not, but that it clearly hadn't happened because they were sitting there eating truffle pasta together instead of being dead. Furthermore, the thing that had plagued them for a few decades was now on another continent.

"Celestine is on another continent?" said Holger One.

"Eat your food," said Nombeko.

After lunch she took a shower, put on her new clothes, and went down to the reception desk to arrange for a few restrictions concerning future orders from Countess Virtanen. She seemed to have acquired too much of a taste for her new, noble life, and it was only a matter of time before she started calling for jet planes and private performances by Harry Belafonte.

Down in the foyer, the evening papers stared her in the face. The headline in *Expressen*, with a picture of Celestine quarreling with two police officers, said: SINGING WOMAN ARRESTED.

An early-middle-aged woman had been arrested the day before along the E4, north of Stockholm, for a traffic offence. Instead of showing identification, she had claimed to be Édith Piaf and refused to do anything but sing "*Non, je ne regrette rien*". And she had kept singing until she fell asleep in her cell.

The police didn't want to release a picture, but *Expressen* did; it purchased a number of splendid photographs taken by private citizens. Did anyone recognize the woman? She was apparently Swedish. According to several of the photographing witnesses, she had insulted the police in Swedish before she turned to singing.

"I think I can guess what the insults were," Nombeko mumbled. She forgot to talk to the reception staff about the room-service restrictions and returned to the suite with a copy of the paper.

The closest neighbours of the sorely tested Gunnar and Kristina Hedlund in Gnesta were the ones to spot the picture of the Hedlunds' daughter on the front page of *Expressen*. Two hours later, Celestine was reunited with her mother and father in her cell at the police station in central Stockholm. Celestine realized she was no longer angry with them, and she said she wanted to get out of this goddamned jail so she could introduce them to her boyfriend.

The police wanted nothing more than to get rid of the bothersome woman, but there were a few things that needed to be taken care of first. The potato truck had fraudulent licence plates, but — as it turned out — the truck itself wasn't stolen. The owner was Celestine Hedlund's grandmother, a slightly crazy eighty-year-old woman. She called herself a countess and claimed that this meant she ought to be above any sort of suspicion. She couldn't explain how the fraudulent plates had ended up on the truck, but she thought it might have happened sometime in the 1990s, when she'd lent the truck to potato-picking youths from Norrtälje on several occasions. The countess had known since the summer of 1945 that the youth of Norrtälje were not to be trusted.

Now that Celestine Hedlund had been identified, there was no longer any reason to keep her in custody. She could expect to be fined for unlawful driving, but that was all. It was, of course, a crime to steal someone else's licence plates, but no matter who the thief had been, the crime had happened twenty years before and was thus beyond the statute of limitations. Beyond that, it was a crime to drive around with fraudulent plates, but the police commander was so tired of listening to "*Non, je ne regrette rien*" that he chose to see it as something she had done without malicious intent. It also happened that the commander had a cabin just outside Norrtälje, and the hammock in his garden had been stolen the summer before. So the countess might have a point about the morals of Norrtälje youth.

The question of the brand-new Volvo in the back of the potato truck remained. A preliminary call to the factory in Torslanda had brought the totally sensational news that the car belonged to Hu Jintao, the president of China. But once the executives at Volvo had contacted the president's staff in Beijing, they called back to say that it turned out the president had given the car to a woman whom he didn't want to name.

Celestine Hedlund, one could surmise. Suddenly the bizarre matter had become one of top-level international politics. The commander in charge said to himself that he didn't want to know any more. And the prosecutor in charge agreed. So Celestine Hedlund was released: she and her parents drove off in the Volvo.

The police commander made very sure to check which of them was behind the wheel.

PART SEVEN

Nothing is permanent in this wicked world
— not even our troubles.

Charlie Chaplin

CHAPTER
TWENTY-FOUR

On existing for real and on a twisted nose

Holger One, Celestine and Countess Virtanen, who had decided to change her name to Mannerheim, soon learned to like living in their suite at the Grand Hôtel. Thus there was no rush to find a suitable castle to move into.

One of the best things was this completely fantastic "room service". Gertrud even got One and Celestine to try it out. After a few days they were quite attached.

Every Saturday, the countess threw a party in the sitting room, with Gunnar and Kristina Hedlund as guests of honour. Now and then, the king and queen turned up as well.

Nombeko let them have their way. On the one hand, the bill from the hotel was colossal, but on the other hand, there was still a considerable amount of the potato money left.

She herself had found a place for her and Two, at a safe distance from the countess and her two fans. Nombeko had been born and raised in a tin shack; Holger had grown up in a draughty cottage. Then the two of them had shared a life in a condemned building, followed by thirteen years in a room next to a rural kitchen in a house beyond the end of the road in Roslagen.

After that, a one-and-a-half-bedroom apartment in Östermalm in Stockholm seemed no less luxurious than the countess's potential future castle.

But in order to buy the apartment, Holger Two and Nombeko first had to deal with the fact that neither of them really existed.

For Nombeko's part, it took only an afternoon. The prime minister called the minister for migration policy, who called the director of the Migration Board, who called his best worker, who found a record of Nombeko Mayeki from 1987, decided that Miss Mayeki had been in Sweden since then, and immediately promoted her to a citizen of the Kingdom of Sweden.

Holger Two, for his part, stepped into the Tax Agency offices in Södermalm in Stockholm and stated that he did not exist, but that he would very much like to do so. After a great deal of running around the hallways and being directed from one door to the next, he was sent to the Tax Agency offices in Karlstad, to a Per-Henrik Persson, the country's leading expert on complicated questions of national registration.

Per-Henrik Persson might have been a bureaucrat, but he was a pragmatic sort. When Holger had finished his story, the bureaucrat reached out his hand and squeezed Holger's arm. Then he said that it was clear to him that Holger did actually exist, and that anyone who claimed otherwise would be wrong on that count. Furthermore, said Per-Henrik Persson, there were at least two things to suggest that Holger was Swedish and nothing else. One was the story he had just given. In Per-Henrik Persson's extensive experience, such a story would be impossible to make up (and that was *despite* Holger having skipped all the parts that included the bomb).

The other was not the fact that Holger both looked Swedish and sounded Swedish when he spoke, but the fact that he had asked if he should take off his shoes when he stepped into Per-Henrik Persson's carpeted office.

For the sake of formality, though, Persson asked Holger to come up with a witness or two, a few citizens of integrity who could vouch for him and the story of his life, so to speak.

"A witness or two?" said Holger Two. "Yes, I think I can find a few. Would the prime minister and the king do?"

Per-Henrik Persson said that one of them should be enough.

◆ ◆ ◆

While Countess Mannerheim and her two assistants decided to build a new home instead of looking for an old castle that would be impossible to find anyway, Holger Two and Nombeko set about living life. Two celebrated his newly won existence by explaining enough of his story to Professor Berner at Stockholm

University for the professor to decide to give him another chance to defend his dissertation. Meanwhile, Nombeko amused herself by completing three years' worth of mathematics courses in twelve weeks, while also working full-time as an expert on China in the government offices.

In the evenings and at weekends, Holger and Nombeko went to interesting lectures or to the theatre, to the Royal Opera sometimes, and to restaurants to spend time with new friends. They exclusively did things that, viewed objectively, could be considered normal. At home in their apartment, they were delighted every time a bill came through the letterbox. For only a person who truly exists can be sent bills.

Holger and Nombeko also started a ritual at home: just before bedtime each evening, Holger would pour a glass of port for each of them, whereupon they drank to yet another day without Holger One, Celestine and the bomb.

◆ ◆ ◆

In May 2008, the twelve-room, Västmanland-style manor house was finished. It was surrounded by 120 acres of forest. In addition, Holger One had exceeded Nombeko's budget by purchasing a nearby lake, on the grounds that the countess still needed somewhere to fish for pike now and then. For practical reasons, there was also a helipad complete with a helicopter, which Holger illegally flew to and from Drottningholm each time the countess went to tea or dinner with her best friends, the king and queen. Sometimes Holger and Celestine would be invited, too, especially since they had started the non-profit Preserve the Monarchy and donated two million kronor to it.

"Two million to preserve the monarchy?" said Holger Two as he and Nombeko stood outside the new manor house with housewarming flowers in hand.

Nombeko didn't say anything.

"You think it seems I've changed my mind about certain things?" said Holger One as he invited his brother and his brother's girlfriend to step inside.

"That's the least one could say," said Holger Two as Nombeko remained quiet.

No, Holger One didn't really agree with that. His father's battle had been sparked by a different monarch in a different time. Since then, society had evolved in all ways, and different times call for different solutions, don't they?

Holger Two said that Holger One was currently talking more nonsense than ever before, and that his brother probably couldn't even grasp that this was saying a lot.

"But please go on. I'm curious about the rest of it."

Well, things in the 2000s went so terribly fast: cars, planes, the Internet — everything! So people needed something stable, constant and secure.

"Like a king?"

Yes, like a king, Holger One said. After all, the monarchy was a thousand-year-old tradition, while broadband had only existed for less than a decade.

"What does broadband have to do with it?" Holger Two wondered, but he didn't receive an answer.

Holger One continued, saying that every country would be wise to gather around its own symbols in these times of globalization. But, he said, the republicans wanted to do the opposite — sell out our country, exchange our identity for the euro, and spit on the Swedish flag.

It was at around this point that Nombeko couldn't help herself any longer. She went up to Holger One, took his nose between her index and middle fingers — and twisted.

"Ow!" yelled Holger One.

"God, that felt good," said Nombeko.

Celestine was in the 860-square-foot kitchen, which was the next room. She heard Holger's cry and came to his rescue.

"What are you doing to my darling?" she yelled.

"Bring your nose over here and I'll show you," said Nombeko.

But Celestine wasn't that stupid. Instead she took over where Holger had been interrupted.

"Swedish traditions are under serious threat. We can't just sit on our fat arses and watch it happening. Given the circumstances, two million kronor is *nothing* — the worth of what's at stake is enormous, don't you get it?"

Said Celestine.

Nombeko looked intently at her nose. But Holger Two got there first. He put his arm around his girlfriend, thanked them and left.

494

♦ ♦ ♦

The former Agent B was sitting on a bench in Gethsemane, searching for the peace of mind this biblical garden always brought him.

But this time it wasn't working. The agent realized there was something he had to do. Just one thing. After that, he could leave his former life behind him.

He went home to his apartment, sat down at his computer, logged in via a server in Gibraltar — and sent an anonymous, unencrypted message straight to the Israeli government offices.

The message read, *Ask Prime Minister Reinfeldt about the antelope meat.*

That was all.

Prime Minister Olmert would have his suspicions about where the message had come from. But he would never be able to trace it. Besides, he would never bother to try. B hadn't been much in anyone's good graces during the last few years of his career. But his loyalty to the country had never been in question.

♦ ♦ ♦

During the big conference on Iraq in Stockholm on 29 May 2008, Israeli Minister of Foreign Affairs Tzipi Livni took Swedish Prime Minister Reinfeldt aside and spent a few seconds looking for the right words, before she said:

"You know how it is, in positions like ours, Prime Minister. Sometimes you know things you shouldn't, and sometimes it's the other way round."

The prime minister nodded. He thought he knew what the minister of foreign affairs might be getting at.

"The question I'm about to ask might seem odd. In fact, it's almost certain that it will, but after much deliberation Prime Minister Olmert and I have decided to ask it anyway."

"Please say hello to the prime minister for me. And ask away," said Prime Minister Reinfeldt. "I'll answer to the best of my abilities."

Minister of Foreign Affairs Livni hesitated for a few more seconds, and then she said, "Is it possible that the prime minister is aware of twenty pounds of antelope meat that is of interest to the nation of Israel? Once again, I apologize if you find this question odd."

Prime Minister Reinfeldt gave a forced smile. And then he said that he was well aware of the antelope meat, that it had not tasted good — antelope meat wasn't one of the prime minister's favourites — and that it had been dealt with in such a way that no one else would be able to have a taste of it henceforth.

"If you have any further questions, Mrs Minister, I'm afraid I'll have to owe you the answers," Prime Minister Reinfeldt concluded.

No, Minister of Foreign Affairs Livni didn't need to ask any more questions. She didn't share the prime minister's aversion to antelope meat (vegetarian though she might be) but, then, the important thing for Israel was knowing that the meat hadn't ended up with the sort of people who lacked respect for international rules pertaining to the import and export of animal products.

"It's nice to hear that the good relationship between our nations seems to endure," said Prime Minister Reinfeldt.

"It does," said Minister of Foreign Affairs Livni.

♦ ♦ ♦

If God does exist, he must have a good sense of humour.

Nombeko had longed to have a baby with Holger Two for twenty years; she had given up hope five years earlier, and she had made it to forty-seven years of age when she realized in July 2008 that she really was pregnant (on the same day that George W. Bush in Washington decided that Nobel Peace Prize winner and ex-president Nelson Mandela could probably be taken off the US list of terrorists).

But the comedy doesn't end there. Because it soon came to light that the same went for the somewhat younger Celestine.

Holger Two said to Nombeko that the world had done nothing to deserve offspring from Celestine and his brother, no matter what one thought of the world. Nombeko agreed on principle, but she insisted that they continue to focus on themselves and their own happiness as they had been doing, and let the idiots and the one idiot's grandmother worry about themselves.

And so they did.

* * *

Holger Two and Nombeko's baby came first: they had a daughter in April 2009; she weighed six pounds and five ounces and was utterly beautiful. Nombeko insisted on naming her Henrietta after her paternal grandmother.

Two days later, Celestine gave birth to twins via a planned Caesarean section at a private clinic in Lausanne.

Two nearly identical little babies.

Two boys: Carl and Gustaf.

♦ ♦ ♦

After Henrietta was born, Nombeko left her job as an expert on China. She had liked her job, but she felt that there was nothing more to do in that area. The president of the People's Republic of China could not, for example, be any more satisfied with the Kingdom of Sweden than he already was. He didn't regret having given Nombeko the lovely Volvo for a second, but because he had liked the car so much, he called his good friend Li Shufu at Zhejiang Geely Holding Group and suggested that Geely buy the whole company. It had actually been Nombeko's idea from the beginning, when the president thought about it.

"I'll see what I can do, Mr President," said Li Shufu.

"And then if you could get a good price on an armoured car for your president, I would be more than grateful," said Hu Jintao.

"I'll see what I can do, Mr President," said Li Shufu.

The prime minister was up in the maternity ward to congratulate Nombeko and Holger with a bouquet of flowers. And to thank the former for her extraordinary efforts in her role as expert on China. Just think: she had got President Hu to allow Sweden to finance a professorship in human rights at Beijing University. How she had managed that was beyond the prime minister. And for that matter, the chairman of the EU Commission, José Manuel Barroso, had called Reinfeldt to ask, "How the hell did you do that?"

"Good luck with little Henrietta," said the prime minister. "And give me a call when you want to start working again. I'm certain we'll find something for you. Absolutely certain."

"I promise I will," said Nombeko. "I'll probably be calling soon, because I have the world's best economist, political scientist and stay-at-home dad by my side. But now it's time for you to toddle along, Prime Minister. It's time for Henrietta to eat."

◆ ◆ ◆

On 6 February 2010, Hu Jintao, the president of the People's Republic of China, landed at Oliver Tambo International outside Johannesburg for a state visit.

He was greeted by Minister of International Relations Nkoana-Mashabane and a number of other potentates. President Hu chose to say a few official words at the airport. He spoke about the common future of China and South Africa, about his confidence in looking forward to strengthened bonds between the two countries, about peace and development in the world, and about a few other things that one could believe if one so chose.

When this was done, an extensive two-day programme awaited the president before he would travel on to Mozambique, the next country on his tour of Africa.

The thing that differentiated his visit to South Africa from those to Cameroon, Liberia, Sudan, Zambia and Namibia in the previous days was that the president insisted upon spending his evening in Pretoria in complete privacy.

Clearly, the host country couldn't say no to this. So the state visit was paused just before seven o'clock in the evening and resumed at breakfast the next day.

At the stroke of seven, the president was picked up outside his hotel by a black limousine, which took him to Hartfield and the Swedish embassy.

The ambassador herself greeted him at the door, along with her husband and baby.

"Welcome, Mr President," said Nombeko.

"Thank you, dear Mrs Ambassador," said President Hu. "It's about time we got to talk safari memories together."

"And a little human rights," said Nombeko.

"Ugh," said Hu Jintao, and he kissed Mrs Ambassador's hand.

Epilogue

Things weren't as much fun as they had once been at the sanitation department of the City of Johannesburg. For many years, there had been quotas of *blacks* in the organization, and everyone knows what *that* did to the jargon on the job. The illiterates of Soweto, for example, could no longer be called what they were, whether they were that or not.

That terrorist Mandela had finally been released from his prison, and that was bad enough. But then the blacks elected him president, at which point Mandela set about destroying the country with his damned equality for all.

In his thirty years with the department, Piet du Toit had managed to climb all the way up the ladder to the post of deputy director.

But now a new life awaited him. His despotic father had died and left his life's work to his only son (his mother had been dead for many years). His father was an art collector, and that would probably have been fine if only he hadn't been so darned conservative. And if he hadn't consistently refused to listen to his son. There were Renoirs, Rembrandts and the occasional Picasso.

There were Monets and Manets. There were Dalís and Leonardo da Vincis.

There were other things, too — and what it all had in common was a minimal increase in value. At least compared to what it would have been if his father hadn't been so stubborn. Moreover, the old man had acted downright unprofessionally by keeping all that crap hanging on his walls at home instead of in an air-conditioned vault.

Piet du Toit had to wait for ages before he could take over and put it all right, because his father not only didn't listen, he also refused to die. Not until his ninetieth birthday, when a slice of apple got stuck in his throat, was it finally his son's turn.

The heir waited until the funeral, but no longer, before he rapidly sold off all his father's paintings. Since a few minutes ago, the capital had been reinvested in a manner that would have made his father proud if only he'd had any sense. The son was at the Julius Bär bank on Bahnhofstrasse in Zürich, and he had just received confirmation that his entire family fortune, amounting to 8,256,000 Swiss francs, had been transferred to the private account of a Mr Cheng Tao in Shanghai.

What the son was investing in was the future. Because given the rapid development in China, the creation of a middle class and an ever-larger upper class, the value of traditional Chinese art was certain to increase many times over in just a few years.

Via the fantastic Internet, Piet du Toit had found what he was looking for, whereupon he made his way to

502

the Swiss city of Basel and entered into an agreement with Cheng Tao and his three nieces to buy their exclusive stock of Han dynasty pottery. They had certificates of authenticity; Piet du Toit had gone through them with a magnifying glass, and everything was in order. The stupid Chinese didn't even realize what a goldmine they were sitting on. Why, they were all going to move home to China, along with the nieces' mother. Move home to China? Instead of enjoying life in Switzerland? This was where Piet du Toit himself felt he belonged, where he didn't have to be surrounded by illiterate natives day in and day out. Where he could be with like-minded people of the correct race, education and class. Not like that stooping Chink Cheng and his crew. It was a good thing they were going back to that godforsaken corner of the world where they came from. In fact, they'd already left, and that was probably for the best. That way they wouldn't realize how they'd been fooled.

Piet du Toit had had one of the hundreds of pieces sent to Sotheby's in London to be valued. This was a requirement of the Swiss insurance company: they weren't satisfied with the certificates of authenticity alone. The Swiss did sometimes show their bureaucratic side, but when in Rome . . . Anyway, Piet du Toit knew what he knew. He had used his wealth of experience to make sure of the authenticity of the pieces. And then he had made his move without letting in any competitors who would just drive up the price. That was how to do business.

The phone rang. It was the valuer from Sotheby's. The call had come just when he'd expected it to, down to the second. People with class kept their appointments.

"Yes, this is Piet du Toit, although I prefer *art dealer* du Toit. What's that? Am I sitting down? Why the hell does it matter?"

Acknowledgements

Many, many thanks to my agent Carina, publisher Sofia, and editor Anna for being so good at your jobs.

Just as many thanks to bonus readers Maria, Maud and Uncle Hans. And to Rixon, of course.

Thanks, too, to Professors Lindkvist and Carlsson, as well as Police Inspector Loeffel in Växjö for giving me facts that I later misrepresented in my own way. And to my friend and Africa correspondent Selander, for the same reason.

Hultman in Zürich can very well have thanks, too. And Brissman, even though he's a Djurgården fan.

Last but not least I want to thank Mum, Dad, Östers IF and Gotland, just for existing.

Jonas Jonasson

Also available in ISIS Large Print:

Saving CeeCee Honeycutt

Beth Hoffman

When Camille Sugarbaker Honeycutt, the pretty but crazy 1951 Vidalia Onion Queen, dies suddenly, her twelve-year-old daughter CeeCee has barely a hope left in the world. To her rescue arrives Great Aunt Tootie in the most magnificent car CeeCee has ever seen, and she is whisked away to the storybook city of Savannah.

Some of the flowers Aunt Tootie holds are born to bloom only south of the Mason-Dixon Line and soon, among the sweet scent of magnolias and the loving warmth of Tootie and her colourful collection of friends, it looks as though CeeCee has arrived in paradise. But when a darker side to the Southern dream threatens this delicate, newfound happiness, Aunt Tootie and her friends must rally to CeeCee's aid.

ISBN 978-0-7531-9014-2 (hb)
ISBN 978-0-7531-9015-9 (pb)

The Rosie Project

Graeme Simsion

Don Tillman is getting married. He just doesn't know who to yet.

But he has designed "The Wife Project", using a 16-page questionnaire to help him find the perfect partner. She will most definitely not be a barmaid, a smoker, a drinker, or a late-arriver.

Rosie Jarman is all these things. She is also fiery and intelligent and beautiful. And on a quest of her own to find her biological father — a search that Don, a genetics professor, might just be able to help her with.

The Wife Project teaches Don some unexpected things. Why earlobe length is an inadequate predictor of sexual attraction. Why ice-cream tastes different in New York. Why he's never been on a second date. And why, despite your best scientific efforts, you don't find love: love finds you . . .

ISBN 978-0-7531-9246-7 (hb)
ISBN 978-0-7531-9247-4 (pb)

How It All Began

Penelope Lively

When . . .

Charlotte is mugged and breaks her hip, her daughter Rose cannot accompany her employer Lord Peters to Manchester, which means his niece Marion has to go instead, which means she sends a text to her lover which is intercepted by his wife, which is . . . just the beginning in the ensuing chain of life-altering events.

In this engaging, utterly absorbing and brilliantly told novel, Penelope Lively shows us how one random event can cause marriages to fracture and heal themselves, opportunities to appear and disappear, lovers who might never have met to find each other and entire lives to become irrevocably changed.

Funny, humane, touching, sly and sympathetic, *How It All Began* is a brilliant sleight of hand from an author at the top of her game.

ISBN 978-0-7531-9046-3 (hb)
ISBN 978-0-7531-9047-0 (pb)

The Van

Roddy Doyle

The third book in the Barrytown Trilogy

Jimmy Rabbitte is unemployed and rapidly running out of money. His best friend Bimbo has been made redundant from the company where he has worked for many years. The two old friends are out of luck and out of options. That is, until Bimbo finds a dilapidated "chipper van" and the pair decide to go into business . . .

By the bestselling author of *The Commitments* and *The Snapper*, *The Van* is a tender tale of male friendship, swimming in grease and stained with ketchup.

ISBN 978-0-7531-9262-7 (hb)
ISBN 978-0-7531-9263-4 (pb)

NW

Zadie Smith

This is the story of a city. The north-west corner of a city. Here you'll find guests and hosts, those with power and those without it, people who live somewhere special and others who live nowhere at all. And many people in between. There are the rare times when a stranger crosses a threshold without permission or warning, causing a disruption in the whole system. Like the April afternoon a woman came to Leah Hanwell's door, seeking help, disturbing the peace, forcing Leah out of her isolation . . .

Following four Londoners as they try to make adult lives outside of the council estate of their childhood. Their London is a complicated place, as beautiful as it is brutal, where the thoroughfares hide the back alleys and taking the high road can sometimes lead you to a dead end.

ISBN 978-0-7531-9214-6 (hb)
ISBN 978-0-7531-9215-3 (pb)

ISIS publish a wide range of books in large print, from fiction to biography. Any suggestions for books you would like to see in large print or audio are always welcome. Please send to the Editorial Department at:

ISIS Publishing Limited
7 Centremead
Osney Mead
Oxford OX2 0ES

A full list of titles is available free of charge from:

Ulverscroft Large Print Books Limited

(UK)
The Green
Bradgate Road, Anstey
Leicester LE7 7FU
Tel: (0116) 236 4325

(Australia)
P.O. Box 314
St Leonards
NSW 1590
Tel: (02) 9436 2622

(USA)
P.O. Box 1230
West Seneca
N.Y. 14224-1230
Tel: (716) 674 4270

(Canada)
P.O. Box 80038
Burlington
Ontario L7L 6B1
Tel: (905) 637 8734

(New Zealand)
P.O. Box 456
Feilding
Tel: (06) 323 6828

Details of **ISIS** complete and unabridged audio books are also available from these offices. Alternatively, contact your local library for details of their collection of **ISIS** large print and unabridged audio books.

B